ACCUSATION

"Let's talk cases," Matt Rafferty said. "A certain party was screwing a colored girl who used to work in the Comets' front office. I knew it all along, maybe you did too. But he was screwing her and she happened to be mistress and maybe whore to Brown, who kept her in a dishy pad uptown like a regular black Princess Grace. So he finds out she's two-timing him and—since we're not talking about a well-mannered, law-abiding citizen—he decides to waste the other guy. Only it backfires on him. Now, you know damn well who that other party was and you're keeping your mouth shut because he's an old buddy of yours. And if word ever got out it would blow his ambitions sky-high, might put him behind bars for ninety-nine—"

Mo Silver stood up, his wide shoulders hunched and anger flaring in his smoky eyes. "Get out of this office!"

The reporter jumped to his feet and glared at the attorney. "All right, Silver. I'm going. But remember what I said. I got enough info now to sink your old pal and maybe you too for conspiring to obstruct justice."

We will send you a free catalog on request. Any titles not in your local book store can be purchased by mail. Send the price of the book plus 50¢ shipping charge to Tower Books, P.O. Box 270, Norwalk, Connecticut 06852.

Titles currently in print are available for industrial and sales promotion at reduced rates. Address inquiries to Tower Publications, Inc., Two Park Avenue, New York, New York 10016, Attention: Premium Sales Department.

SEASON OF POWER

**Sam Tanenhaus
and
Gregory Tobin**

TOWER BOOKS NEW YORK CITY

To Roe Richmond

A TOWER BOOK

Published by

Tower Publications, Inc.
Two Park Avenue
New York, N.Y. 10016

Copyright © 1981 by Sam Tanenhaus and Gregory Tobin

All rights reserved
Printed in the United States

This is a work of fiction and all characters, with the exception of public figures, are the product of the authors' imaginations. Any similarity between these characters and real persons living or dead is purely coincidental.

"There is one question I should like to ask you. It is this. If, as you say, there is only the bad to start with, and the good must be made from the bad, then how do you ever know what the good is? How do you even recognize the good? Assuming you have made it from the bad. Answer me that."

"Easy, Doc, easy," the Boss said.

"Well, answer it."

"You just make it up as you go along."

—Robert Penn Warren,
All the King's Men

Part 1

The All-American

1

"Listen, Mike," said the recruiter, a thin nervous man with olive skin and a tic. "Right from the top I said I'd be honest with you, strictly on the up and up. So here goes. Last season we finished third in the Missouri Valley. Seventeen and nine and dropped four of those nine outside the conference 'cause we play a tough schedule. The toughest, in my book. I happen to think that's the only way to play it, but that's a question of philosophy and we don't have to go into that now. But let me tell you something in the strictest confidence."

The recruiter paused and gathered his breath and his pale eyes darted from Mike Merritt, who was barely listening, to his mother, who hung on every word. "Coach Butcher and me were going over our squad not too long ago and he says to me, 'Howard, in your opinion what do we need? 'Cause let's say we got some alums who could be made very happy.' And I say to him—'cause first thing you gotta know, Mike, is I say what's on my mind—I say, 'Just what do you mean by happy?' And Coach looks me right in the eye—you'll respect him for that, all the men do—Coach looks me in the eye and he says, 'Howard, we just might get ourselves a fine new coliseum. Not arena or fieldhouse but *coliseum*. Pack in fourteen grand and put Illinois Western on the basketball map. A showcase.' This makes me think a bit. Finally I say, 'Coach, you know as well as me what we need is a shooter. Not a gunner who'll pop every time he touches the ball but a pure shooter, kind that turns games around.' So Coach smiles real slow and real ironic and he says, 'Sure that's what we need. Another Maravich. Maybe while we're at it we'll snatch up Hayes too. They're all a dime a dozen, right?' I tell him, 'Coach, I know where there's such a kid, better'n Maravich if you ask me 'cause even if he's smaller he's a lot stronger and still growing.' I can tell by those hands and feet. What size are you, Mike, twelve and a half?''

"What?" Mike was staring out the window at the empty street. The oak leaves shone like spangles against the clear sky.

"Thirteen," said Evelyn Merritt. "Order 'em special from Springfield."

" 'Yep,' I say, 'the kid's got a jumpshot like blown glass. Smooth and clean and pure. Took a little school nobody ever heard of all the way to the B final. Hit for twenty-four in the second half and he was the quickest man on the court. Jumps center, owns the boards, and I mean *owns*, and shoots like a dream. And you know where he is?' " The recruiter paused dramatically, then tapped Mike on the knee. " 'Right in our own backyard!' And Coach, well he's skeptical. He says, 'How come nobody else is after this boy, Howard?' And I said, 'They are, Coach, that's just the point. They're *all* after him, in the Midwest anyway. Drake, Marquette, DePaul, I said. I know for a fact they're after this fella.' "

"You'll have another cup of coffee, won't you, Mr. Smiley?" said Evelyn Merritt. She was an erect handsome woman with gaunt cheeks and a long delicate nose.

"Just one more, ma'am. It's one fine cup of coffee too. Tell you, spend as much time on the road as I do and you get to appreciate a good cup of homemade coffee. Forget the instant stuff you see on TV."

Evelyn returned with the steaming cup. "You know Mike is a good student too," she said.

Howard Smiley brought a hand to his tie and his eyes

took in the small living room. "Well, of course, I can tell by this home. You gotta fine respectable home here. This is the kind of home produces champions. The good old-fashioned values. Some folks are ashamed of the old values, can you believe it? I wouldn't have guessed it myself. Maybe on the coasts where they're not real stable, but not out here in God's country. But you spend as much time on the road as me and you get a nose for picking up on the way folks live. Mrs. Merritt, may I be so bold as to inquire if you are a churchgoing woman?"

"Yes, indeed. Williamsburg Methodist. Mike too and his Dad before he died."

"I'm sorry, ma'am. I didn't know—"

"Listen, the Lord takes as well as gives and it's best to face that fact. God's wisdom is hard for us to understand sometimes. In our ignorance."

Howard Smiley set down his cup and fastened his pale gaze on Evelyn Merritt. "Ma'am, without a doubt those are the finest words I've heard in a long time. They're inspirational. And it may interest you to know that Illinois Western is a Methodist school. That's right, founded by Methodists over eighty years back and the tradition is still going strong." He drained his cup in one huge swallow and patted Mike on the knee. "Well, son, got to be on my way. We'd sure like to get a commitment since it's near June and time's awasting. A letter of intent would be much appreciated. Ease our minds a bit."

Mike shook his head. "Sorry, Mr. Smiley, but I'm still not sure. If I decide on Western I'll let you know."

The recruiter ran a hand through his thinning hair and his mouth tugged down at the corners. "You know what we've got to offer and we think it's as good as anywhere in the Midwest. It's getting awful late to keep everybody hanging."

Mike felt the man's eyes travel the length of his six-three frame as he got to his feet. "Thanks a lot for taking the trouble to come and talk to me, Mr. Smiley."

He showed the recruiter to the door and watched him

drive away.

Evelyn said, "You could have given that man a single encouraging word. He came all the way out here and on Saturday too. Why, you didn't even look at him."

"Spend as much time on the road as he does and you get used to people not looking at you. Besides it was easier said than done the way his eyes kept slipping around."

"And what was wrong with what he had to say, I'd like to know?"

Mike shrugged. "Nothing I guess. I'm just not interested in going to college fifty miles from home."

"I have never seen a boy so all of a sudden anxious to leave the place he's spent his entire life. You didn't used to hate it so."

"I don't hate Williamsburg, Mom, or Illinois. Yale's the school I want, is all."

"You'd be wise to put Yale out of your head. We can't afford their fancy loans. A loan is a debt and we have debts enough, thank you."

"You're right. Forget the loan."

"Michael, that College Fund is just a wish and nothing more. You heard what Mr. Smiley said, time's awasting. And the last fella said the same. Other boys aren't so high and mighty and they'll jump at the chance. You're not the only basketball player in the state of Illinois."

"I know, Mom. If the Fund doesn't come through I promise I'll sign on with another college."

Evelyn touched a graying curl. "Well. It's getting near lunchtime."

"I'm not real hungry."

His mother peered up at him through narrowed eyes. "You are acting mighty strange, mister. Never practicing when used to be I had to drag you in off the driveway and then from the table 'cause you ate like a horse, but lately you've been like a bride before the wedding. What's more, yesterday Maybelle Hawkins told me she saw you twice on Cemetery Hill, last

Saturday and the Saturday before that. First I didn't think anything of it, of course, because of Diane. But then I saw that poor sweet girl at Gibson's the other day and she looked about to cry. Said you hadn't called her in six weeks."

"It's the Fund. It's got me jumpy."

"Too jumpy for you to talk to the prettiest girl I ever laid eyes on? Too jumpy to eat? Why, night before the district final you ate a whole chicken and I worried you'd get sick right on the court. In front of strangers and all those reporters, too. And who are you to turn a deaf ear to that poor man who was only doing his job and came all the way out here to help you? I was ashamed, a witness to my own son acting rude and superior in his own living room."

"Mom, I'm sorry, I really am. But there's so much on my mind these days I just don't know what I'm doing."

"Is something going on?"

"No."

"What do you do up there on the hill?"

"Nothing. Just walk."

"Do you go to the cemetery? Is that what you do, go to your father's grave?"

"Mom, why can't he be here?"

"I know it's hard. I'm only your mother but I can tell you it's not good keeping things to yourself. You can't hide your troubles forever. Someday they'll explode. I know it. Same thing happened to your dad. Always keeping his troubles locked up inside."

Mike wrapped his big arms around her. "Don't worry, Mom. I'll straighten out soon, I promise. And if the Fund doesn't come through you can pick my school. If I don't make Yale it doesn't matter where I go. I'll even go to Western."

"Well that's not the way I like to hear you say it, but I sure would feel better with you close by instead of a thousand miles away. I'll be so lonely after you go."

Mike kissed her tired cheek with a loud smack and she pushed him away with a little laugh. Mike headed to the door.

"Where are you off to now?"

"To the track to run out some of this craziness."

"All right. But be back by six, 'cause I'm defrosting a chicken and I expect you to eat it."

It was an ordinary Saturday in Williamsburg. The domelike sky, for these were the rolling plains of Illinois, hung enormous and blue. Somewhere an engine coughed, ripping the still afternoon. The backyards Mike traversed were alive with kids. They piped his name and crowded around, waist-high, eyes wide and brimming with love. He flashed a winning smile and waved a big hand, sparking his magic at them without breaking stride. He emerged on Broad Street and followed it past the gas station and the Maid-Rite. Always there were the grinning faces, the flapping hands, the "Hey Mikes" boomed from gleaming pickups and front porches. How did you give the blur of faces what they wanted once they tumbled from the bleachers and into the very space all around you? How did you elude a townful of searching eyes?

Striped arms and a red light marked the railroad crossing although the Rock Island line no longer rattled through town. He walked south along the tracks, slicing through the golf course. Once you could jump a boxcar from here to Kansas City or even farther. In the Thirties one summer when jobs were scarce his father rode to Houston to work on the oil rigs. Now the sunken ties were rotten and overgrown with goldenrod and prickly weeds. The worn rails attenuated like arrows into the distance. A golf ball arced lazily, diamond-bright against the sky.

Soon he came upon the foot of the hill, thick with oaks. He hugged the gravel lip of Union Road, snaking upward past the cemetery. He did not pause before his father's tombstone which still was white and unweathered after eight months. A path wound up through hedges and a tangled field. By the time he reached the summit he had worked up a mild sweat. A few big houses hid behind the trees. He looked at the golf course below and the grid of streets and the patchwork of houses where he lived. Beyond the truckstop at the edge of town the farmland rolled into the horizon. By midsummer waves of corn would bristle in the sweltering heat and dust would powder the cardboard sidewalks.

He circled a white house. Mrs. Davidson opened the screen door.

"It's after two," she said. "I've been going crazy."

"This recruiter came by and wouldn't leave. Mom kept pumping him full of coffee."

This drew a smile. At twenty-eight she sometimes looked no older than her stepdaughter Diane. "I suppose I've got to wait my turn like everybody else. Come upstairs, there's a breeze."

In the bedroom the billowing curtains unveiled the rectangled sky. Mike collapsed on the bed and Mrs. Davidson faced him primly, hands folded in her lap. Her red dress had thin straps which met behind her neck in a bow.

"Just two more weeks of waiting," said Mike.

"Yes. We have only one day after this."

"Mm-hm."

"Aren't you sorry?"

"Sure. But it'll be a relief too. No more sneaking around like a thief."

"You know," said Mrs. Davidson, "you haven't once mentioned wanting to see me—after."

It had never occurred to him. He sat up. "We couldn't do that."

"Like we can't now?"

"But this is different. Now there's a reason, what with the scholarship and Mr. Davidson being on the committee, practically running it—"

Her blue eyes flashed like brittle shards of the sky. "If only you knew how mercenary you sound. What about what *we* have—doesn't that mean anything to you?"

14

Suddenly she was perched on his lap, dangling legs pale in the dazzling light. She stirred and he was hot and nuzzling the soft curve of her neck, inhaling scented powder from her bare shoulders. It stung his nose like dust. The first time he held her it was evening. They stood downstairs in the dusky foyer. That was back in April, when he was working parttime at Mr. Davidson's law firm. One night he brought his boss home drunk and helped Nancy Davidson hoist him upstairs and into this very bedroom. She fed him dinner, then offered him a ride home. In the closet she fingered her coat then turned to him swiftly, taking his hand. "I can help you," she murmured. "I can get you what you want." As if nothing were more obvious than what Mike Merritt wanted. He stood rocklike and mute, blood pulsing in his head as her clothes whispered onto the floor. Naked, she was beautiful and pale as the moon or a licked bone. Oh God, he thought, oh Jesus. Her eyes cut the murk like gimlets. From upstairs came snores, hemming them in. He thought of Diane, whom he loved. He thought of his mother padding about the kitchen, splashing milk on his corn flakes, frying an egg. Then he thought of Yale. He thought of mullioned windows and black spires piercing the sky and the pounding blood became a drumbeat of names. Commons and Harkness and Jonathan Edwards. What could he do? Who knew what guises destiny chose?

"Don't you care for me, Michael?" she was saying now, breathing into his ear.

"Sure."

Mrs. Davidson ruffled his curly hair and blew on his forehead. "Is it wrong to care for me?"

"No."

"To make me happy with your beautiful body?"

"No."

"Tell me you love me."

Words he had never spoken to anyone else, not even Diane, after their single clumsy attempt at sex, when he thought he really did love her. It had been like work, two fumbling virgins tangled in her pink sheets in the bedroom down the hall. Nothing hurt more than telling her it was over but her stepmother had insisted. Not to protect Diane but to make her suffer. Mrs. Davidson could be downright scary. Also shrewd, as when she told him to quit the job at the law firm. "Conflict of interest," she called it.

"I love you," he croaked.

She was on top of him now, pushing him onto his back, playful as a monkey. Her nimble fingers unstrung his sweatpants then slipped his T-shirt over his heat. An arm bent winglike behind her back, tugging at the bow, unzipping the dress. Underneath she wore nothing and gave off an odor of salt. Her breasts loomed then crushed into his chest and her tongue bloomed sweetly in his mouth. His hands skimmed along her taut back then palmed the smooth downy buttocks. Her thighs parted like cream and she impaled herself, wriggling.

"Deeper."

He kissed her neck and her throat and nibbled her breasts. Then he plunged to the hilt and their flesh slapped together. Her hands bore into his chest with astonishing strength. She locked her elbows and rode him, tiny and weightless, narrow shoulders bunched.

"Slower. I want it to last." Her head tossed like a flower on its stem.

He thought of the final in Carbondale in March. They lost by one.

"Oooh!" Her cries soared and dipped and soared again, wild, unanswerable, and sad. Her hands slithered around his waist. "Faster, damn you. Faster. Lover, oh lover! Oh yes!"

He rocked into her, gripping the backs of her thighs. He thought of diving into a cool glassy lake. "Oh, Mrs. Davidson." He shook with pleasure then burst and their cries mingled in the tangy air.

Moments later she was drawing little circles on his chest. "Next week I want you to come Sunday. Papa Bear and Goldilocks are going to St. Louis at dawn. So you come early. It's our last time and I want you to myself all day."

"But that means missing church. Mom'll kill me."

"No she won't," said Mrs. Davidson. "She'll pray for you."

The next week was his last at Whitman High and it dragged on interminably. There were fun times, skipping school with the gang for a drive into the country, sipping beer for the first time, diving from the sheer walls of the old quarry outside town. But he passed up the prom and evenings he practiced in the driveway, jumpshooting for hours, his ankles manacled by weights, while kids from the neighborhood watched in awe.

"Come on, Mike, let's see you dunk it. Gee, now do one backwards, both hands."

Howard Smiley and the scores of other recruiters were not mistaken about the way Mike Merritt handled a basketball. The newspapers and the local aficionados, all season long, had stretched to find comparisons. Not simply because he owned every record in western Illinois, or because he took a nowhere team to the state finals. There was something else about the way he played, a dream-like intensity, as if he toted in his head a platonic vision of the game and wouldn't rest until he made it come true on the court. Mike himself just shrugged. He'd heard such talk for four years now. He wasn't born jamming balls into rims, or firing jumpshots from the key. It was work, hard and painful, though not joyless. Nature had blessed him with wide sloping shoulders and sturdy legs and huge hands. But the rest was work.

When he practiced he thought about Yale and his father and Mrs. Davidson, and especially Mom. His edginess had worn off on her. At times she monitored his every move with hawklike tenacity, wondering aloud about his appetite and the hours he spent alone, urging him to call Diane. But other times she seemed unaware of his presence, and floated about the house in a cloud of abstraction, grappling with demons of her own. There were moments when he feared she had found out him out but he couldn't imagine her keeping such suspicions to herself. Her shifting moods were baffling —but hell, he had it coming, scheming to leave her in the small house with only memories for company.

He also thought about the future and where he belonged in it. It was a question that had plagued him since his father's death. Words like ambition and achievement and accomplishment roamed his mind like shadows. He knew they added up to something, the thing that was expected of him, though he wasn't exactly sure what that thing was. For if people in Williamsburg were divided about everything else they were firmly agreed on Mike Merritt's future. There was a star in the firmament emblazoned with his name. "The kid's going places," they said. "He can't miss."

His father's death a summer ago had brought into sharper focus a truth not wholly new to him: a lifetime in the heartlands might amount to no more than an excruciating march toward diminishment and failure, the glittering promise of youth swallowed by the sea of farmland, bleached by the killing sun. Dad had thrown away a career in baseball. He was a great catcher and he tore up the Double-A league, but Mom didn't like the uncertainty of the minor league ballplayer's life and dragged him home to the town where they had both grown up.

So Mike was determined to leave Williamsburg. There was nothing for him there any more. And Mrs. Davidson, on their last day together, did nothing to change his mind.

They were sitting in the living room. With Ralph and Diane gone for the day Mrs. Davidson grew bold. The curtains were pulled back from the glass doors. Outside was the pool, empty but for the leaves mashed in the drain. Her garden was a tapestry of bobbing colors, daffodils and tulips and primroses and lilacs reeling in the breeze that combed the hill.

"Stay and talk to me," Nancy Davidson said as Mike stood up to leave. "Or don't talk at all and just make love to me again."

"I can't. I already missed church and I'll have to lie to Mom about it. She fixes a big Sunday dinner at three. If I miss that I'm sunk. I don't really know how to thank you. I guess I'll know for sure on Friday if things—worked out."

She stared at him then broke into brittle laughter. Both hands were wrapped around a tall glass filmed with the sugary mix she stirred into her gin. "My God, listen to you! 'Gee, Mrs. Da-ay-vidson, I ju-u-st don't know—' "

"You don't have to do that," Mike said. It was insulting as hell, and just who did she think she was anyway? She had nothing to be proud of. "Don't tell me I'm the first, 'cause I've heard about others. The guys say all kinds of things. Last year Tank Morrison—"

She cackled. "Tank Morrison! That bull thought I was some kind of tackling dummy. I will not stand for that town whore line. It's—it's medieval. Though I can assure you plenty of men in this town wish it was true. Those leering friends of Ralph's, stinking of alcohol, with their Bibles." Then she started to cry. If only he knew what it was like to be herself, a woman still young, not yet thirty, imprisoned in this hateful town. Her family were strangers. Diane hated her. He ought to hear the names, the accusations that came out of his little cheerleader's mouth! And Ralph, foul and gross. Always drunk or snoring, usually both. What did they all expect of her? At nineteen married to a man she hardly knew. What did she know about being a wife or a mother, especially to another woman's child? She had ears, she knew the filth that was spoken on the streets of pious Williamsburg. Some of them even had the nerve to claim she had lured Ralph Davidson into marriage! Why, he had begged her, yes on his knees, when he was in Chicago after his blessed angel died. She should never have consented. He had tricked her with promises of summers in Europe and trips to New York. A hundred times she had thought about leaving, but where could she go?

Mike Merritt needn't worry about his stupid scholarship. "You'll be on your merry way to fame and fortune or whatever it is Mr. All-Americas with their big grins look for. You'll get it because I know things. I know things about this terrible place and the terrible people in it. Don't ask me what. You're better off not knowing. Sometimes I wish I didn't know. You know too much and things are never the same for you, never. Oh, don't you see what *we* have is holy? Why it's much finer and more exalted and *real*. Nothing in this awful sleepy town is real. Nothing ever happens. I wish I could go away with you to Yale! I'd keep your apartment for you. Maybe I could take classes too. We'd live in one of those boxy little apartments students live in nowadays. I was in one once when I visited my sister at Northwestern. There was no bed, just an enormous mattress and all these spider plants in the window."

Her eyes were dry now and creased at the corners. "Wouldn't you like me to go away with you? Wouldn't that be a good idea?"

She wasn't talking just to him now. She was apostrophizing every lover she had had (how many had there been?) and her voice was distant and thin.

Her face fell into her hands. And then Mike left. He mustn't be late for dinner, not on Sunday.

Graduation Day it poured and Mike took the wheel of the ancient Ford, maneuvering cautiously on the slick streets. Cars were streaming in the direction of the high school. The sky sagged mauve over the little town and you couldn't see beyond Main for the fog.

"Such a shame," said Evelyn Merritt. "It's so pretty on the lawn."

"Smaller crowd, too, indoors. Gym'll only hold eight

hundred."

"I was just thinking about when Dad and I graduated back in '40. When the high school was still up on the hill. That same night he proposed. At the Grad Dance, which is what we had instead of the prom, well, out*side* the dance, under one of those beautiful cottonwoods. It was a lovely night, warm, and you could hear the music inside only faintly, like a hum."

"What was Dad like then?"

"Oh, he was very serious and confident too. All he could talk about was baseball."

A single photograph was preserved from this time. It was piled with others in a shoebox Mike stumbled upon recently cleaning the basement. Everything in the picture looked brown. The patch of lawn where they stood, slightly off center, the old school in the background, the corner of sky. Brown too was the eerily mature couple, gaunt-jawed children of the Depression, slightly resentful of the camera.

They turned onto Main and fell into the procession leading up to the school, creeping at a funereal pace marked by the squishing wipers. A booth stood before the lot and a guard checked admission tickets. The dull brick of the building was glazed scarlet by the rain and the playing fields were mottled with muddy ponds. They found a place in back then scuttled through the downpour. Inside Mike accepted his mother's hug. She was off to the gym and he joined the throng moving toward the cafeteria.

For him this was the hour of reckoning but the faces in the cafeteria were festive and laughter rang above the clattering rain. He felt with horror the gulf separating him from his classmates. Even the other guys in the running for the scholarship seemed relaxed compared to himself.

Tables had been folded and pushed out of sight in the big room except for two stacked with caps and gowns. He got in line and stared over bobbing heads.

"Hey, Mike, hey buddy boy!"

"Glad you could make it, stud!"

"Gonna take home that Yale bacon?"

"They got one big enough for you?"

"Can't wait to see how cute that boy looks in one of those tassles."

He smiled at his friends' jokes but his mind wandered and his stomach knotted. This was worse than the night before the final when he dreamed about Delaney, the rawboned St. Mary's forward everyone said was the toughest rebounder in the state, a bruiser under the boards. In his dream every time Mike reached his favorite spot at the key the ball stuck to his hands like glue and his feet took root in the floor. Then a mountain of flesh loomed and clapped a meaty ham over the ball. He was spooked clear through the warmup weave before the game. Delaney turned out to have a snarl rendered comical by his gapped teeth. His reddish skin glowed. Two minutes into the game he shot Mike a stinging elbow. So the next time up the court he planted his foot on Delaney's instep and returned the elbow for good measure. Thus they jousted all game. It was fun, like the roughhouse clowning he and Dad indulged in on the driveway after Mike got too good for them to play it straight.

Mike received his cap and gown from Diane Davidson. She was chairman of the graduation committee. For an instant her cornflower eyes held his then flashed away into the matrix of faces. If only he could apologize or explain. "Hi, Diane."

"Hello."

"Well—"

"Well what?"

"Well, it looks like we made it."

"Made what?"

"To—to the end."

She shook yellow locks off her shoulder. Even in her cap and gown it was the blonde vigor you noticed, just as you did when she gamboled along the sidelines like nobody else, as fresh as spring in Whitman's green and white. She had beautiful strong legs.

"Maybe for you it's the end," said Diane. "But for me it's just the beginning."

This brought a blush to Mike's cheek. Not for himself, strangely, but for her. He rooted for her to humiliate him properly. She was finished with him, however, and had already turned to the next in line.

The shrill sounds of the band clanged and the graduating class straggled into line, marching solemnly into the gym, filing singly past Principal Elmo Jefferson to receive their diplomas. They mounted the bleachers, two hundred dazed seniors facing an audience of expectant families and relatives.

Mike spied his mother near the back, twisting a handkerchief. Closer to the fore Mr. Davidson speared a cigarette into his flushed face. Mike tried vainly to read something in the heavy features. Beside him his wife barely reached his shoulder. She looked as cool as on her best days although the gym was hot and rank and smoked fogged the rafters like steam. On the fan-shaped backboards, tilted up and away toward the ceiling, the rims were still bare from when he had snipped the nets after Whitman's victory in the sectionals.

Awards were handed out for every achievement under the sun. One by one the valedictorian and the class president and the editor of the paper received plaques to thunderous applause. Mike got a trophy for basketball.

Then Elmo Jefferson delivered his commencement address, lecturing his captive audience until boredom shadowed their faces like the hand of death itself. He reminded them that this year of 1968 was troubled indeed. All over the country young people were turning their backs on the traditions of their parents and their parents before them. Universities had become battlegrounds instead of hallowed places of learning. Overseas too was a war, an unpleasant war, but like all wars one that had to be fought. And the bespectacled administrator wished to pay a special tribute to those boys who had already enlisted in the service of their country.

At last he eased into his introduction to the College Fund, outlining its history and purpose and citing "those essential, inestimable qualities—leadership, discipline, seriousness of purpose—which governed the committee in its choice." He reviewed the achievements of past winners. Two doctors, a lawyer, a research chemist, even a high school educator like himself.

Mike was going crazy, sweating like a dog. Damn Elmo Jefferson and damn Mrs. Davidson! She wouldn't meet his eyes. Had she lied to him all along? Maybe she had promised the scholarship to others, perhaps to all seven finalists, seducing them all in the white bedroom or the foyer or on the claret-colored carpet in the living room. Had he not been properly respectful or grateful or anxious enough to please? He shouldn't have left while she was still crying on Sunday. But, damn, he had to. With Mom waiting—

"Michael Albright Merritt!"

He nearly toppled off his plank. He was pounded, hugged, kissed, and punched. Thank you, Mrs. Davidson. Thank you, Mr. Davidson. Thank you, God.

Afterwards his mother cried on his shoulder. He left her accepting congratulations from a clutch of churchwomen and elbowed his way through the hilarious crowd. Ralph Davidson stood in a group swilling liquor from a thermos.

"Congratulations, son."

"I just wanted to thank you and the other members of the committee. I hope I live up to the honor."

"Wish I could take credit for it, kid, but you'd better thank these guys instead. They wouldn't let me vote, the bastards. Conflict of interest 'cause you worked for me back in April. Can you beat that? Bunch of hardline bastards, aren't you boys?"

"Quit talking, Ralph, and pass along that flask."

Mike found the door and pushed the metal bar and he was outside. The rain still slanted down heavily, pelting the roofs in the asphalt lot. Rising green out of the grape sky was the hill where Hugh Merritt was buried and where Mike Merritt had killed his innocence as calmly as you squash a mosquito. Beyond the fields, planing into the fog, soaking up enrichment for the summer bounty of crops, stretched the endless farmland. And somewhere beyond was Yale.

It would be a long summer. Thankfully there were things to do. The house needed another coat before he left and he ought to lend his grandfather a hand on the farm. He couldn't work for Mr. Davidson anymore. He was finished with that family. Diane was the only one who had cared and he had failed her miserably.

Patience was required now and it was a virtue he lacked. Only patience would carry him through the summer and beyond the plains to greet his shining future.

2

The train from Chicago to New Haven took almost two days and Mike Merritt spent his time reading the university class bulletin, eating sandwiches and pies his mother had fixed, and resisting the advances of a fat pimply girl. The land whipped past his window and he saw the train stations, but not much else, in Cleveland, Pittsburgh, Philadelphia, and New York. And he slept a lot of the way. He dreamed of one day returning to those cities with money in his pocket and a beautiful woman on his arm. A woman like Mrs. Davidson.

The station in New Haven was a scene of utter confusion. It seemed thousands of people were there, most of them students with trunks and crates and duffle bags and backpacks—and tans. Mike didn't have a deep tan like those he saw all around him, but he did have a mammoth foot locker in one hand and a large clothes bag slung over his shoulder. That identified him as a student. His wide-eyed hesitant stumbling toward the information window identified him as a freshman.

"Yeah?" was the nasal statement from the bald man behind the glass.

"How do you get to Vanderbilt Hall on the—"

"Any of those cabs out front, sonny. They'll take you there. Just speak up." He looked past Mike. "Next. Yeah?"

Mike hoisted his locker up on his other shoulder and headed for the exit. Although it was early afternoon the sky was nearly black. A heavy warm rain sheeted down from the dense clouds. Well-prepared students were armed with umbrellas, while newcomers like Mike, who had never in his life entertained the idea of owning an umbrella, stood drenched and bewildered.

Taxi cabs filled quickly with three or four passengers and sped off. Just as quickly a new fleet appeared then in jumped more students and off they flew. The trick, Mike figured, was to get in a group. But nobody seemed to know anybody else and most were as confused as he was. Whom should he ask?

Before he took a step toward a likely partner someone tapped him on the shoulder and said: "You want to share a cab?"

He turned around and looked down at a slender boy with thick sandy hair and pale blue eyes. He wore a camel's hair sport jacket, an open-necked white shirt, and a pair of blue trousers. Water beaded harmlessly on his polished brown shoes. He was carrying two small suitcases and a big black umbrella with a gleaming handle.

Mike said, "Sure."

The well-dressed boy signaled a cab. The driver pulled up and relieved them of their luggage, stowing their bags in the trunk and Mike's foot locker on the floor behind the front seat.

"Should we get someone else to share the ride?" Mike asked. He only had a hundred dollars to his name and he knew most of that would go for books. "How much does it cost?"

The boy smiled and said, "I don't think there'd be enough room for anyone else with those long legs and that railroad-car of a trunk of yours. Hurry up, get in."

Mike bent his tall lean body into the back seat. The other boy folded his umbrella and stepped in behind him. "Where are you going?" he asked Mike.

"Vanderbilt Hall on the—"

"Good. So'm I." He turned to the driver. "Vanderbilt Hall. Chapel Street side." To Mike he said, "I hope they have the big gate open. With all this baggage. By the way, I'm Kent Crosby. Call me Bee." He held out a delicate hand with tapered fingers.

"Mike Merritt. I'm—"

"You're my roommate is who you are!" Bee laughed. "What a coincidence! Vanderbilt 5C right?"

"Right," replied Mike. "How did you know?"

"My brother works in the Yale College Dean's office and he tells me all sorts of things. Look," Bee said conspiratorially, "anything you ever want to know— you ask me. My brother knows all the dirt and if I can get him drunk enough he'll spill his guts. For example, do you know whose daughter the chairman of the English department married in a bid to become Master of Branford, our college?"

"I plan to major in history myself," Mike offered.

"And you play basketball."

"How did you know?"

"Besides the lanky six-three frame, you mean?"

Mike was puzzled. How could this guy know so much? Who was he anyhow? My roommate did he say? All these questions.

"Didn't you know you made the New Haven papers? Not *The New York Times*, mind you, but good press nonetheless. I'm not a fan, really, but I read the sports section so I have something to talk about with my brother. I have one brother and three sisters. Now I've got three roommates, including a virtual giant from the Land of Lincoln. And probably square. Are you square?"

Square? Mike wondered. Well, I've been laid a few times. I've been drunk, slightly, once on beer. Never smoke marijuana. Hate cigarettes and pills and crowded parties. Go—that is, went—to church on Sunday with Mom. Probably square.

"I don't know," Mike said lamely.

"Well, if you don't know, brother, then you're square." Bee let loose with a high-pitched laugh. He put a reassuring hand on Mike's shoulder. "I'm sorry," he said. "I shouldn't make you uncomfortable on what is apparently your first day in New Haven. And I *have* been a talkative bore. Maybe it's in my genes."

"On the contrary," Mike said, attempting to sound casual, masking profound embarrassment and a sense of inadequacy in the presence of this worldly contemporary. He smiled valiantly.

"We're here," Bee announced.

The cab pulled up beside a huge building of dark stone with a forbidding wrought-iron gate opening onto a stone-paved courtyard dotted with black puddles. The rain continued relentlessly. Bee paid the driver, refusing an offer from Mike to split the fare. They retrieved their luggage; Mike took his locker and Bee managed the rest, and the umbrella. They jogged into the courtyard. Bee turned sharply to the left, nudging Mike to follow. They stepped into an arched doorway.

"I've already got my keys," Bee said. "Let's go on up and I'll take you over to the freshman counselor for yours."

Five steep flights up. They both were panting as Bee unlocked the door.

The outer room was spacious, with a large fireplace and three tall windows. Mike went to the windows and gazed out. Chapel Street was almost invisible in the dark rain. Already there were a small couch and two comfortable-looking chairs in the room. There was a stereo on the mantel, flanked by two speakers. On the floor stretched a not-quite-wall-to-wall blue carpet, and a shaggy throw rug lay in front of the fireplace.

"Somebody else must already be here," Mike said.

"No."

"Then whose stuff is all this?"

"Mine. And you're welcome to make use of it."

"I thought you came in on the train today."

"Both bedrooms are pretty small," Bee said, leading his tall roommate to the room on the courtyard side. "I've already set up shop in this one. I don't want to be on the street side. Do you?"

The door was sufficiently low to offer Mike a

problem. The ceiling was barely six inches from his head. "Tight squeeze," he laughed. A bunk bed and two desks and two chairs, one of them with three legs, were crammed into the tiny room.

"The other room's no bigger—and it's a lot noisier. How 'bout you and me taking this room? I have a feeling you're no slob and I certainly don't want to room with a slob. We can make the place livable. So what do you think?"

"Sounds all right to me," Mike said, flattered at Bee's eagerness to make him feel at home. "Just one thing," he added. "Can I have the lower bunk? My—"

"Your legs will hang over the edge of the bed. And you want to be able to put a chair there. Right?"

He's a mindreader, Mike thought.

"I'm not a mindreader," Bee said, "if that's what you're thinking. It's just that I've read that some professional ballplayers do it when they sleep in those small beds in cheap hotels in cities like Cleveland and Buffalo."

Later in the day their other two roommates arrived. First there was Frank Carlotti, a burly football player from North Haven who looked to Mike like a good-natured guy; and then Kevin James, a pale, mousy, horn-rimmed boy who claimed he wanted to be a doctor and wanted to be left alone—he had work to do, he said.

The next few days were balmy as Mike tried to get his bearings. He found his way around campus with a map he looked at furtively then stuffed into his back pocket. Manicured grass courtyards and tall trees broke up the blocks of massive stone structures which served as residence halls and libraries and faculty offices. Upperclassmen returned and populated the sidewalks and streets and dining halls. After several hours of sight-seeing Mike ate a solitary meal in Commons, the marble facilities built to commemorate the men who had given their lives for God, for country, and for Yale in the

Great War. Freshmen ate here five days a week. Only on weekends could they dine in their colleges with the upperclassmen.

At registration, again in Commons, Mike wore out three pencils filling in dozens of forms for the Registrar and the Bursar and the Food Service and the Branford Dean and the Yale College Dean and the Health Office and the Athletic Department. American Civilization. Composition. Intro to Psych. French. Biology. Requirements. Alternate choices. Major? Social Security number. In case of emergency. The College Fund. Campus jobs. Dining Plan A. Home address. Father. Deceased. Mother. Housewife. Why Yale? In case of emergency. No allergies. Check-up. Basketball program. Game schedule. In case of emergency. ROTC? No.

There were meetings with his Dean and the Master of Branford. Freshmen get-togethers, barbecues, and pick-up softball games. Hot days. Breezy nights. Laughter and song floated through Mike's window as he lay in bed unable to sleep.

While good soldier Mike immersed himself in freshman activities that first week Bee worked at making himself scarce. Late at night he climbed into the upper bunk, taking pains not to disturb Mike, and every morning he disappeared. One day after breakfasting alone at Commons Mike caught Bee before he left. He shook his roommate awake and reminded him that course books were now available at the Co-op. Bee, barely awake, mumbled something about having enough books of his own and drifted back into slumber. Three hours later he returned with a shopping bag full of texts and notebooks only to find Bee still asleep, his head buried beneath a pillow. Mike secretly wondered at his roommate's strange habits then hurried off to join a tour of Science Hill.

A week into the semester Mike was on his way to Sterling Library with an armload of books when he encountered Bee. The slender boy called to his friend across High Street. "Mr. Lincoln!" he cried. "How are you, sir?"

Mike smiled. Already he had missed Bee's effervescent company. "Fine," he said. "How are *you*? Where have you been? Don't you know classes have started?"

"You're concerned about me! Why, that's sweet." Bee put a hand upon Mike's shoulder as they strolled toward the library. "Classrooms give me boils," he confided. "All over my body. Bad for my health, you see. But don't you worry, Mr. Lincoln, I'll get by. I always do."

Then Bee waved a friendly farewell and left Mike standing, puzzled, at the gloomy ivied doorway.

Mike doggedly took notes at every lecture, attended every discussion group, and took every exam on time. He spent several hours each evening in Sterling poring over obscure books or in the lab bungling experiments. Bee made a habit of negligence. He stayed in Vanderbilt and read all day, and at night he brought home a sixpack of beer which he consumed as he read some more. On a few occasions he convinced Mike to knock off at ten for a beer or a pizza or a movie. Most often though academic warrior Mike Merritt was at his books until the early morning hours, skirmishing with difficult words and ideas, feeling unprepared for the long lonely siege ahead.

"So what's doin' tonight?" Bee asked one evening. He stood at the doorway of their tiny room with a bottle of Schaefer in his pale hand.

Mike was hunched over his small desk. His dark hair was rumpled, his eyes dulled. "I've got a history paper due tomorrow. My first paper. I've started it five times. It stinks. I don't know how to write."

"What class?"

"American Civilization."

"Hey, I'm taking that class too. You mean we have a paper due tomorrow?" Never having been to a lecture nor glanced at a syllabus, Bee counted on chance revelations like this to keep him afloat academically. "How many pages?"

"Five," Mike said.

"On what?"

"Anything pre-1800. A book or a battle or a painting or a person. I picked Ben Franklin's autobiography and I read it, but what the hell do you say about it? Everything I put down on paper sounds like a seventh-grade book report. Plot, setting, characters. Only this book's weird. I never knew Franklin was such a strange guy."

"Most guys are strange in one way or another," Bee said. "Even the best of us. Franklin couldn't get enough sex, that was his problem. All those guys, the Founding Fathers, were like that—some sexual hang-up or other. They relieve their frustrations in a public way, creative or destructive or a little bit of both. Roosevelt, Napoleon, Lincoln, maybe even our guy Mike Merritt. Who knows . . ."

Mike laughed. "You've got sex on the brain. I can't write about that in a paper."

"Why not? If you don't I will. What more appropriate topic? Sex in history. You take Franklin and I'll take some Puritan—Jonathan Edwards. He must have had a bizarre sex life, sweating under those black robes and stiff collars and wigs all day, screwing his congregation by night. Probably liked little boys."

"You write about whatever you want. I'll stick to Franklin and the Indians."

"Just trying to help." Bee put a finger to his chin. "What time is it?"

"Eight," Mike said.

"We can work together! Five pages is nothing. We can help each other. I'll be right back."

Bee was out the door. Fifteen minutes later he reappeared with a sack of doughnuts and two big cups of coffee. "For the boys," he said. "They're going to work hard tonight."

And they did. Mike wrote slowly, methodically,

consulting notes and rereading passages in his book. He wrote in a clear hand on a yellow legal pad. Bee sat down at his typewriter, a new electric marvel, a gift from his parents, and rapidly filled five pages with neatly typed sentences. He titled it, "The Puritan Affair: Libido vs. the Law in Seventeenth Century America." Mike read it and was astonished by the wit and intelligence it displayed. He could never write like this—never.

"This is really good, Bee," Mike said, throwing down his pencil and rising to stretch his long legs. He towered over his friend who sat with a smug grin, his elbows on the typewriter. "It's beyond me, though." He yawned. It was nearly midnight. "I'll never finish this."

"I'll type it for you," Bee volunteered. "I can even correct your atrocious spelling and grammar if you'd like."

"Great." Then Mike paused. "But don't put in any sex. Just what I wrote."

"You don't trust me?" Bee asked with a foxy wink and a curious tilt to his well-groomed head.

"Not completely," Mike said with a smile.

"Write, write," Bee replied. "Let's get this over with."

Mike continued to write. Bee went for another round of coffee. By two o'clock Mike had enough for Bee to begin typing. By three he was halfway there. They were finished at six.

Mike read the final product. "This looks good," he said. "Thanks a lot, Bee."

"What say we climb up on the roof and get a load of the glorious sunrise at this the turning point in our college careers. I feel a positively energizing second wind."

Mike agreed. There was a door to the roof a half-flight up the stairs out in the hallway. It was locked, however, forcing them to exit through a tiny window. **Mike barely fit.**

The roof itself was steep and they crawled to a

relatively safe spot by a brick chimney. There they sat silently gazing at the fitful morning sky. To the east and north the spires and towers of the university rose darkly against the pink and blue horizon. To the west and south the city stirred, trucks rumbling through the streets and early risers marching to work. The air had a fresh bite to it and both boys breathed in the new day. Mike stood, hugging the chimney, attempting to absorb as much of the scene as he could.

A sense of excitement welled inside him as he thought of how many days and how many miles he had put between himself and the lazy, seemingly long-ago town of his boyhood. What was his mother doing now? She probably was awake, sitting at the kitchen table with a steaming cup of coffee, a curler hanging crazily from her graying hair. And Mrs. Davidson? Lying half-asleep beside her snoring husband, her breasts rising and falling softly, her fantasies receding with the light of day. And Dad? Resting on the hill. And here I am, he thought, his eyes ranging across the glowing sky. There is so much to do, to see, to experience—so much to pack into the next four years.

"So what great thoughts lie behind those big, brown Midwestern eyes of yours? Worlds to conquer and all that?"

"You know, Bee, there's really no reason for me to speak to you at all. You always seem to know what I'm thinking, and you say it better than I ever could."

Bee's eyes fell. "I'm sorry, Mike. Maybe I kid too much."

"Wait a minute," Mike said, holding up a big hand. "All I'm saying is that you're a smart guy. I don't mean to criticize. I get a kick out of talking with you. I learn a lot. You can say and write things that would never cross my mind. Sometimes it's annoying—I mean, you can be—that is—it's just that you're never serious, always so sarcastic about everything and some things are sacred, I think."

"For instance?" Bee pointed to the rosy sky in the

east. "The sun? I can buy that. The sun is sacred. God and country? That's a different story. Maybe I know too much, but to me it stinks—religion and politics. School? Everyone in my family's been to Yale, for three generations. So it's no big deal. It's expected. What's left?" He considered for a moment. "Friendship," he said. "That's probably the only thing sacred in this world. Good friends can help each other through life. I helped you with your paper last night, but one day you'll help me with something."

"Like what?" Mike shook his head. "You want to learn to shoot freethrows?"

"Why not?" said Bee, putting a hand on Mike's knee. "In case I get fouled."

Mike stiffened as he felt Bee's grip on his knee. What's he really thinking? he wondered. He can be a pretty strange guy sometimes.

"Have you ever been in love, Mike?"

Mike turned to his friend who was looking out over the city. "Sure. I had a girl in Williamsburg—"

"No names, please," Bee said. He stared up at the whispering clouds. "Did you make love to her?" Before Mike could answer Bee continued, "Sure you did. She probably tore you pants off."

"Not quite. We just did it once. It was great, but—well, she didn't want to do it anymore." He wondered if he should tell Bee about Mrs. Davidson. He probably wouldn't believe it. When Mike looked back on it, he could hardly believe it himself.

"Stupid girl," Bee spat, shaking his head. "Women. They don't realize what we go through. They don't appreciate men. I'd rather have a good friend like you than some ungrateful little cunt any day of the week."

"Damn it, Bee. There you go again. Diane wasn't that bad. She—"

"I said no names. Please." He looked directly at Mike. "I'm sorry. I see what you mean. Cynical, spoiled rich kid dumps on women. I guess they're not all that bad. But even the good ones—are they worth the trouble?"

"I don't know." Mike recalled the relationships between his mother and his father, Nancy and Ralph Davidson, Diane and himself. All of them were far from perfect. But still—men and women: that's what it's all about, isn't it?

"We're friends, right?"

"Of course," said Mike.

"Yeah, I guess we've established that. What I mean to say is, well, I like you a lot, Mike. You're different."

"How? Different from what you know, maybe. But then you're different from anybody I've ever met."

"For someone who always has a wise comment, I'm finding it hard to say what I want to say." Bee's crystal blue eyes were cracked with pain. "You wouldn't stop liking me if I told you something, would you?"

Mike was puzzled. Bee was always making wisecracks and bursting bubbles. Mike had never seen him so uncertain, almost embarrassed. He slugged his friend on the arm. "I'll tell you what—if I don't like what you say I'll toss you off the roof. Splat. End of argument."

Bee smiled sadly. "You probably will."

"For God's sake, Bee, what is it? You look like somebody has broken your heart."

"That's just it. I don't want to have it broken."

"Ha! B. Kent Crosby is in love! Who is she? Where is she? Some rich New York girl? An older woman? Let me tell you, older women are best. Not that I've had all that much experience, but—"

"Shut up, Mike!" Bee cried. "It's not a girl. I—" He summoned all his nerve to say it. "I love you, Mike. It's real. I know you'll hate me, but Jesus you shouldn't." Then, seductively, "I could please you. I could make you feel good like you never believed possible. I know what a big guy like you needs. Girls don't—"

"No, Bee! Stop it!" For a brief second Mike was tempted to fulfill his threat to hurl the boy from the roof.

"I knew it, I knew it," Bee moaned. "Stupid. God

I'm stupid. Mike—"

But Mike crawled away toward the window. He slipped back into the building. Bee sat slumped against the chimney crying.

Basketball practice began in November. For Mike it was an opportunity to put everything else out of his mind for two or three hours a day. For a week after his rooftop conversation with Bee, the two of them avoided each other as best they could. But as the strain between them continued Mike felt badly—and partly to blame. After all, Bee could prove to be a valuable friend and it shouldn't matter what kind of sexual problems he had. He was different, that was all, and Mike would have to get used to it.

Mike initiated the reconciliation by having dinner with Bee one night in Commons. The two began to talk and by December they were friends again. Neither of them mentioned the incident; it was forgotten. They studied for finals together, Bee consenting to open a school book for the first time all term.

Meanwhile, on the court, Mike was busy impressing Coach Jock Ryan and his teammates. He moved with a confidence and grace that Yale basketball hands had never before seen in one of their own. He easily won a starting spot on the freshman squad. The season didn't start until January, however, and Mike had two weeks off for Christmas. He would spend his vacation at home with his mother.

The day before his train left he and Bee were the only two occupants of 5C still in residence. The other two boys had already gone.

When Mike came back from practice Bee was on the telephone.

"I don't know if I could stomach another Christmas bash," Bee said. "Tell Steven thanks but no thanks. . . . What? . . . No, I doubt if I'll change my mind. . . . A date? Are you kidding? I haven't spoken to a female in six months. . . . No. I doubt it. . . . Same to you. Good-bye."

Bee hung up. "My brother," he told Mike. "There's a party tonight for second- and third-generation Yalies over at the Yale Club. There's nothing I'd rather not do than sit around and drink punch with a bunch of phony blue-bloods like myself. What's the point? Who cares whose old man was once a fucked-up freshman like we are?"

"I don't know," Mike said. "I haven't been to a party all term. Been studying and practicing too much. I wouldn't mind seeing how the other half lives."

"You've *got* to be kidding," said an exasperated Bee.

"No, I'm not. After all, you're the one who has tried to convince me to have new experiences, to try different things."

Bee's finely wrought features tinged pink. "And you're the one who has refused my advice all term," he said quietly.

"C'mon, Bee," Mike replied. "We've both made mistakes. I'd like to go to a party tonight. It could be fun—you and me. I don't know, I feel like getting a little drunk maybe."

"If you insist. But I warn you, you'll be bored stiff."

Bee called his brother and made arrangements to go to the party. After dinner he and Mike dressed. Mike wore his only sport jacket and a tie that had been his father's. Bee, in a dark blue blazer and blue tie, looked even more elegant than usual.

It was a cold night. The Yale Club of New Haven was in a small white frame house on Elm Street across from the Green. Bee, having been there a few times, acted as Mike's guide. "Don't let it get to you, Mike," he advised. "Don't take them too seriously. Tell them your father is a banker if it makes you feel any better."

Although he didn't let on to Bee, Mike was delirious with excitement. The party would be his first taste of the Yale of tradition and wealth. This, he thought, is the reason I'm here. As he and Bee entered the club he felt the way he had before the final against Delaney and St.

Mary's.

A doorman took their coats. Bee led Mike into a simply furnished, spacious room where two dozen young men lounged with drinks in their hands, chatting animatedly among themselves. A few acknowledged Bee with nods and stared at Mike as the two made their way to the punch bowl. Bee served Mike a cupful then drained one himself and took an immediate refill.

"Decent punch," Bee said with a nod. "It'll do the trick anyhow."

Mike sampled his and agreed. "I haven't had a drink for months but this stuff might get me hooked." They both laughed.

Mike looked at the paintings and prints on the walls. He had never seen artwork outside of a museum, up close where he could touch it. If only Mrs. Davidson could see the hillbilly now. His eyes traveled around the room. There were a few older men, in their thirties, a couple of girls with their hair pulled severely back, but mostly it was a male undergraduate crowd. All were dressed similarly: white button-down shirts and ties, blue jackets and blue or gray slacks, brown loafers. Their hair was short and slicked down, an occasional uncontrollable curl or insistent cowlick marring the studied uniformity of the Old Blue look.

Bee brought one of the older men over to Mike. The athlete knew immediately that it was Bee's older brother. They shared the same clear eyes and sandy hair and slight build.

"Mike, I'd like you to meet my brother, Anthony Crosby. Anthony, Mike Merritt, my roommate."

"Nice to meet you, Merritt. Bee talks of nothing but you—when he talks to me at all. He seems to have lost interest in the college gossip. Used to be he never got enough."

Mike took Anthony's soft hand and shook it firmly. "Glad to meet you too, sir."

Bee howled. "Sir! Oh, I love it! Didn't I tell you, Anthony. He's a down-home Midwesterner. The real

McCoy."

"Have you been drinking, Bee?" Anthony asked.

Bee winked at Mike. "We dropped some acid before we came over. Mike's a real drug head too."

Anthony looked earnestly at Mike who could smell liquor on his breath as the elder Crosby spoke. "I hope you've learned to take my brother with a grain of salt."

Mike nodded. "That I have."

"Enough of this," Bee insisted, grabbing Mike's arm and steering him away. "Let's have some more punch."

Mike gulped the remainder of his drink and handed his cup to Bee who poured him a generous helping of the rich scarlet liquid. He felt a pleasant buzz in his head. His arms and legs grew light and seemed to move of their own accord as Bee led him to a sofa.

During the next hour Bee introduced Mike to a group of party guests. Taylor and Tyler and Bennett and Bertrand and William and Wesley—or something like that. Mike was having trouble remembering names and faces and whose father was who and why. He smiled a lot and ran a hand through his hair, which he was sure was a mess, and found himself bragging about his exploits in the state final against St. Mary's. "We came that close!" he announced loudly, his thumb and index finger a fraction of an inch apart. Tears welled in his eyes and he slumped back on the sofa. The conversation continued without him.

Periodically Bee, who apparently retained most of his senses, made a trip to the punch bowl. Soon he and Mike were talking privately.

"So you've survived your first brush with wealth and power."

"Wealth and power 're where 't's at. An' 'at's where I wanna be, Bee. Heehee." He giggled and put a hand on his friend's knee and whispered confidentially, "How's yer ol' man make hiss money, ol' boy? Thass the trick, huh?"

Bee showed his fine teeth in a big smile. He shook his head. "We'd better get you sober before you take on

Wall Street, kid."

Mike jumped up. "Who's sober?" he demanded.

The party limped to a conclusion. The blazer-clad and loafer-clad Tylers and Bennetts and Wesleys wobbled toward the door, ties askew and cowlicks shamelessly poking up from their crowns.

Mike stood there swaying, challenging Bee to walk a straight line. "Gotta do it 'n case we get picked up by cops if they think we're drunk and I don' wanna spend a night in jail. Hell—I gotta train ta catch in the mornin'."

"Maybe we better go," said Bee. He retrieved their coats, struggling to get the tall boy into his. It took Mike several tries to get his arms into the proper sleeves and to button the right buttons.

They stumbled out into the bitter night, their arms locked for mutual support. Mike swallowed the cold air greedily. It was a short walk back to the Old Campus but it took them twenty minutes because Mike insisted on practicing his pivot and his jumpshot. "Look," he told Bee. "You guard me. There's the basket. Merritt takes the pass, fakes, jumps, shoots, scores!" he called, his shouts reverberating off the dark stone walls.

Finally they made it to Vanderbilt and climbed the stairs to their room.

Mike collapsed on a chair in the living room. He wrestled his way out of his coat and tossed it on the floor. "God i's hot in here," he intoned. "Le's open a window, Bee ol' boy."

"You better get to bed, kid. You've got to catch a train tomorrow—remember. Back to the Great Plains and Mom and the Girl You Left Behind."

"Shit," said Mike vehemently. "That little bitch. She's probably screwed every guy in town by now. Her stepmom, though: there's a real woman. Old Man Davidson. Doesn't know what he's amissin'. Wonder if he knows . . ." His head fell onto his chest.

Bee took Mike by the shoulders and shook him. "C'mon, Big Boy, time for bed." He pulled at Mike who rose clumsily to his feet, dropping his arms onto Bee's shoulders. Bee held his friend at the waist. They danced awkwardly into their room where Mike fell onto the bed.

"Thanks, Bee. Good frien'. Real pal. Fun party. God, I made a fool 'f myself."

"No you didn't. Those guys all drink like fish themselves but they're too uptight to really let loose and have any fun. Don't worry. I'm just glad we went—together."

"We'll always be frien's, Bee. Always. Right?"

"Right, Mike. Friends." Bee stood over the tall boy who lay with his eyes closed and his mouth open, drifting quickly into slumber.

"Mike?" Bee said quietly. Mike began to snore. "Mike?" Bee repeated. He shook him gently. "You need to get out of your clothes."

Mike's hand found Bee's face. "Thanks, frien' Great time. Bes' frien'. Owe you one."

"Let me help you. Let's get your shirt off. Okay?"

"Thanks, Bee. Yer a good guy. I jus' can' un'erstan' . . ."

"What, Mike? What can't you understand?" Bee unbuttoned Mike's shirt. He pulled it open, exposing a broad hairy chest upon which he placed his hand. Mike groaned softly. "What can't you understand?" Bee asked.

"A guy like you," said Mike in a distant voice. "Why you wanna be queer."

Bee lifted his hand. He pulled Mike's shirt away, then his shoes and socks. "And I can't understand why a guy like you should hurt his best friend." He sat down on the bed. His hand rested again on Mike's chest. "Huh? Mike?"

Mike opened his eyes. "I dunno, Bee. Sometimes I think . . ." He closed his eyes. His breathing was rapid. Bee's hand moved softly across his friend's shoulders and chest and stomach. "Stop it, Bee," Mike said weakly.

"You're so handsome, Mike. Why can't you enjoy

it?"

"It's just not right," the athlete said. He didn't protest however as Bee unbuckled his belt and unzipped his pants. Bee tugged at the pants and Mike lifted his hips so that they slid to his ankles. Bee pulled them off and tossed them onto a chair. His hands continued to explore Mike's long handsome body. Mike said nothing.

Bee stood up and quickly shed all his clothes except his shorts. He climbed onto Mike's bunk. He lay down beside his friend. "Mike," he whispered. "Mike, let me love you." Mike said nothing. Bee kissed him. "Mike?" Mike's eyes remained closed. He did not move.

Bee's tongue licked at the hair on Mike's chest, grazing his nipples which stood at attention. The smaller boy's hand found its objective inside Mike's briefs and gently began pumping.

Without a word Bee bent over Mike and lovingly took his friend into his mouth and began sucking. Mike let out a whimper and his hands instinctively went to Bee's head, holding it in place. His long muscular legs twitched as Bee's busy fingers inched their way beneath him, squeezing his buttocks. The athlete arched his back and moaned. "Jesus, Bee . . ."

Then Bee removed his mouth and took Mike's penis between two fingers and slowly worked them the length of the shaft.

"No, no," Mike pleaded. "Suck me, Bee. Please."

"I just wanted you to say it," replied Bee. He took Mike into his mouth once again and rapidly drew him to the brink of climax.

"Thank you, thank you, thank you," Mike gave out gutturally. His eyes welded shut as he released a long low groan. Bee took his friend's hot emission, swallowing most of it with difficulty, the rest dripping from his mouth.

Then he sat up. He stared at Mike's limp body for several minutes. Mike plummeted into a deep sleep. Bee lay down beside him again, his arm over Mike's chest, and soon he too fell asleep.

3

In late October of Mike Merritt's sophomore year, the Yale varsity held an informal scrimmage. Bee Crosby, sporting a blue-and-white carnation and sipping brandy from a thermos, decided that if anyone was more conspicuous than himself among the handful of spectators it must be the stocky, curly-haired young man who took a seat in the row below. During the warmup he munched on a bag of french fries, wiping his fingers on his cut-off shorts. He drew the last noisy dops of Coke through a straw when the whistle blew to start the game.

The opening minutes of the scrimmage resembled a practice session more than a contest. Coach Jock Ryan, nearly as feeble an institution as Yale basketball itself, whistled plays dead then walked his impatient charges through them step by step. Finally, throwing up his hands, he gave up and let them play.

As the first half drew to a close the fellow in front of Bee delicately unwrapped a meatball grinder and bit off a huge chunk, his eyes fixed all the while on Mike Merritt, who faked a jumpshot from deep in the corner and swept into the basket for a reverse layup. In his excitement the stocky spectator leapt to his feet. Two sauce-drenched meatballs slithered onto his leg. He wiped it with his sweatshirt until Bee's handkerchief dangled over his shoulder.

"Thanks," he said gruffly and mopped a heavy, hairy leg.

"He's marvelous, isn't he?" said Bee, who moved down a row. He offered the thermos. "Have a swig. It's brandy."

The stranger swallowed and scowled. "Yes, he's good. Almost too good."

"How so?" Bee stuffed his soiled handkerchief into his pocket.

"Nobody out there can play with him."

"You think he's that good?"

"Haven't you been watching? See now. He's waiting for something to open up but nobody's moving. There! Look at that pass."

"But it bounced off the other guy's hands."

"Should have been ready for it."

They watched the remainder of the half in silence, trading the jug of brandy.

"I'm afraid that aside from the heroics of my roommate I'm completely ignorant of basketball," Bee confessed during the brief intermission. "My roommate is the fellow we were discussing."

"Mike Merritt? I saw him play on the freshman team. What's he doing at Yale?"

"Perhaps basketball isn't his only concern."

"For his sake I hope so."

"I'm Bee Crosby."

"Mo Silver."

Bee smiled in recognition. "Law student and politician. And devotee of basketball."

"Activist," corrected Mo Silver, "not politician."

"Listen to this," said Bee the following Wednesday. He was reading the *Daily News*. Mike was stretched on the couch gazing out the window of their third-story suite in Branford.

"Come on, Bee. You've already convinced me that those guys can't write. What do you have to read another one of those idiotic articles for?"

"This is actually quite good. It's the work of an admirer of yours."

Mike averted his gaze from the darkening sky. "What are you talking about? Let me see."

Bee held the paper clear of his roommate's lunging arm. "Take it easy, Adonis, your name doesn't appear. It's a polemical essay and therefore deserves to be read aloud."

Mike groaned as Bee began to read in a clear voice.

" 'It is our belief that radicalism is inevitable at Yale. Why? Because Yalies will one day look hard into their textbooks and see only meaningless words, because they will one day peer into their own hearts and minds and find mere emptiness. Yale students will rebel against the very institutions that shelter them and for no other reason than boredom.' " Bee smiled. "I like that." He read on: " 'And what will be the cause of this boredom? What will lead to the tears of anguish that not even their monogrammed handkerchiefs will dry—' "

Mike sat up and applauded. "It's not me he's talking about. It's you. Read on."

Bee threw the paper at Mike. "Read it yourself."

Mike skimmed the article. "I don't know any Morris Silver. I don't think I know anyone in the Law School. Why would he be an admirer of mine?"

"He told me you're sure to be the terror of Ivy League basketball."

"That guy? The one you sat next to at the scrimmage?"

"I let him use the only silk handkerchief to my name! The schmo defiled it after plunking a meatball on his leg."

"That's what happens to rich guys who get chummy with radicals."

"I let him drink my brandy too."

"Old Morris sounds like quite an organizer. He says there's going to be a demonstration on the anniversary of Nixon's election. Was he behind that big to-do last year?"

"Apparently so."

"There's a meeting this Friday. Let's go. We can quietly slip in and out. Innocent observers."

"So he can wag an accusing grinder at me, another hapless aristocrat? That kind of treatment this boy doesn't need. I'm not even faintly curious."

"Don't be so damn touchy. You seemed to like him all right a week ago. Besides it's your turn again to try something new."

Friday evening at eight o'clock the roommates stepped out of Branford into a brisk night. Bee shivered.

"You should have worn a warmer jacket, Bee. Those sport coats of yours are snazzy enough when it's warm, but winter isn't too far off."

Bee walked quickly to match Mike's long strides. "When the cold gets unbearable I stay in warm well-heated rooms."

"Don't you like to get outside more and look around? I like the way this place looks when it's damp like this and foggy. Like the Old Campus over there. All those lighted windows."

"Reflecting the labors of terrified little freshmen."

"And freshwomen, don't forget."

"Please. Let me forget."

It was disappointing to Bee that Mike didn't want him as a lover. He'd been clear about that, the morning after the Christmas party. No hard feelings, you understand, no harm done, but no more sex. Bee was a helluva guy, a great friend, a charmer, and wise, but Mike stood firm. Bee let out a sigh. At least they were still friends, and for that he was grateful. No baiting remarks from Mike, no hurtful accusations, no ugly pummeling fists. There was more to this basketball wizard than met the eye. He consistently foiled your expectations. He was interested in things, hungry for knowledge, eager for adventure. And there was the sense Mike had of his own destiny. He knew he was going places, and in the wide winning smile Bee read an invitation to come along, just for the ride, for the fun and the wonder of it.

"For once I've got to agree," Mike admitted. They swung onto Wall Street and entered the Law School and followed a scribbled arrow pointing down a dark corridor. "Here it is," Mike said.

"Let's go back to the sanctity of our elitist room."

"Nothing doing. This could be interesting."

Mike pushed open the door. The roomful of activists, most of them lounging on desks or sprawled on the floor, fell silent. "CIA," pronounced a bearded student. This was greeted with laughter. "I'm not joking," he insisted. "I don't like the looks of these guys."

"Cut it out, Robert." Mo Silver, sitting on the floor below the blackboard, pad and pencil on his lap and a can of Coke by his knee, beckoned Mike and Bee into the room.

"Have a seat. These meetings are open to everyone, including the CIA." He addressed Robert: "As it happens, I know these guys."

Mike and Bee found two seats in an obscure corner. After a fidgety minute Mike struggled out from behind the writing table—the damn thing bent him up like a pretzel—and sat cross-legged on the floor.

"Now," said Mo Silver, "the question remains—where to hold it? I still say the Green. So what if it brings out the local cops? If we're afraid of the enemy we may as well not protest at all."

Robert disagreed. "Our purpose isn't to incite. Last year Woodbridge worked out fine. We made our point. We got the coverage we wanted and some sympathy."

"The problem with that, Robert, is that it labels us again as angry little Yalies. We can't afford to ignore the city around us. Alicia says she's got over two thousand signatures from local people. It's their demonstration too. Or it ought to be. Hell, they're the ones who have the most to complain about."

"Hear, hear," called two activists bent over a huge water pipe.

Mike saw Mo's point; the demonstration had to be carried off dramatically. Even if you didn't want an actual confrontation you couldn't look like you were afraid of one. When the matter came up for a vote, he didn't dare raise his hand, but he was glad when Mo prevailed.

"Okay," Mo continued, presiding from the floor. "Now there's the matter of our statement. I think we should subject it to general revision, but here's what Al and Randy came up with."

Al looked up from the pipe. Randy struck another match.

After a few sentences Bee snorted. Mo stopped reading. "Problem with that, Bee?"

"It's not English. You don't resolve a problem. As for constantly using the passive voice—" This was met with catcalls and groans.

Mo said, "What would you say there instead?"

"Come off it, Mo," someone protested. "This isn't a fucking grammar lesson."

"Go ahead, Bee," Mo urged.

"Let me hear more of it first so I can get the sense."

Mo read and Bee listened, cupping his ear. He looked thoughtful for a second after Mo finished the sentence.

"How's this: 'Like all of Yale's secret societies the Corporation derives its power from the veil of mystery that protects its unconscionable actions. And since no simple cry for honesty will penetrate that veil we must gradually tear it away, until, at last, we have cornered the cowering beast that lurks behind.'"

"Oh, Christ," said Robert.

Mo nodded tentatively. "What do you say—Randy, Al?"

Randy held up a thumb and exhaled a huge cloud of smoke. "Sure," called Al. He didn't look up from the little mound of pot he was cleaning for the next bowl. "Why don't we have Bee go over the entire statement?"

"A good suggestion," Mo answered. "We'll arrange a time later."

The meeting broke up shortly. Mo Silver approached the roommates. "How about going to Naples for a pizza?"

"I'm afraid I only have one monogrammed handkerchief and pizza can be pretty messy," Bee replied coldly.

"You're not mad about that, are you? I thought you'd know it wasn't personal."

"What was it then?"

"Rhetorical. Look, I'm buying."

"We'll come," Mike decided.

A strong breeze gusted over the flat Cross Campus

lawn. Mo zipped his windbreaker and said, "I hope Robert didn't frighten you with his accusation. It's not as unreasonable as you might think. We *have* been spied upon. We know that for a fact."

"By the CIA?"

"By someone. You won't believe it but there are government agents here at this very minute."

Mike looked around uneasily at the silent buildings. "Who? Where?"

"I wish I knew."

"Sounds like paranoia to me," Bee commented skeptically.

"No, it's not paranoia. I know there are agents around. I've seen at least one. Coming out of my apartment as a matter of fact. I didn't see him leave the apartment itself but the building. He must have spotted me coming from my window. When I got there the door was unlocked and a lot of my stuff was tossed all over the place. This was a week after the big protest last year. Were either of you there?"

"Just in passing," Mike said.

"Well this guy was there with a camera."

"Have you seen him since?" Bee asked.

"Not since the time I saw him come out of my apartment. They got him out of there fast after he blew his cover."

"I just can't believe it," Mike said. "It doesn't seem possible."

"Nobody can prove it, but rumor has it that the FBI has special orders to investigate campus activities. Subversives." Mo spat out this last word.

"But why? What do they have to gain?"

Mo dropped into a whisper. "Don't you know? There are communists around."

"That's absurd," Bee scoffed. "That's finished, all the Cold War stuff—spying and witchhunts and the rest."

"Yes. And Vietnam."

In the crowded restaurant the threesome drew stares. Mike, almost six-four—"The boy won't stop growing,"

Bee complained—towered over his two companions, the one slender and fair, the other stocky and dark.

Mo did most of the eating, as well as the talking. "What do you know about Vietnam?" he asked Mike.

"Not a hell of a lot. I guess I just think of it as the place where all the losers in my high school went."

"A good place to begin. Why didn't you enlist?"

"I guess it never occurred to me."

"Do you know what Vietnam looks like? What it s population is, or its crops or its customs? Of course not. It's just a pawn in a power game. War is great for the economy, keeps the big bankers and industrialists happy. Something to invest in, a chance to grease up the machinery and grind out tanks and missiles. It allows the Pentagon boys to flex their muscles. Ever hear a general complain because there was a war going on? Or a politician—with few exceptions? Nothing suits a politician better. Inflame the voters with a lot of wild talk about communists pounding on the door and you'll coast right into Washington."

"Sounds awfully cynical," Mike said.

"You bet it is. It's what keeps the capitalist ship afloat."

Bee perked up. "Carlyle. Captains of industry. Take the helm, we're off to war."

"Exactly. And wave some flags and start a parade. Everybody loves a parade."

"Wait a minute," Mike objected. "What about the other side, the Russians? What makes them so great? We can't let them just move in and take over."

"Take over what? Don't you see, there's nothing there. Let Vietnam decided its own fate. The Russians aren't sending troops in—we are."

"They give them money. And weapons."

"To defend themselves against American aggression. Stop by the center sometime and pick up some of our literature."

Bee frowned. "There's got to be a less painful way."

"Then read Bernard Fall. Or Gibbon, if that's more your style. Find out what happens to imperialist powers when they overextend themselves."

After they exhausted the subject of Vietnam, Mo talked a bit about his past and Brooklyn, where he grew up and went to college. "My father owns a grocery store. 'I want my son should be a lawyer,' he told me. Every day of my life. From the first time I got an A in spelling. 'Take your father's advice, Morris. You got a good head on your shoulders. You should be using it to make money.' " Mo stopped to inhale the final slice of mushroom pizza. "Little did he know his son would turn out to be a subversive. In a way I feel badly. Everything he wanted and couldn't get is tossed in my lap and I'm just not interested. I guess these days not too many of us are."

"Some of us are," Mike pointed out.

Mo looked at him appraisingly. "Where does a guy like you fit into all of this? You're the archetypal Yale hero. What's your interest in activism?"

"Frank Stover here is interested in all aspects of Yale's diverse activities," his roommate answered for him. "From the classroom to the basketball court to pot-filled dens of iniquity."

"While Bee on the other hand," said Mike, "isn't interested in anything about Yale."

"Now that's funny," mused Mo. "Bee, you strike me as the sort of guy whose father came here and his father before that."

"All the more reason to take a detached view of the place."

"Sure you don't mean apathetic?"

"Absolutely sure. There are all kinds of causes. Who knows—I may have one or two up my sleeve."

Mo apologized. "It seems I'm always accusing you of something."

"Happens all the time."

"Well," Mo said after he had picked at the last pieces of cheese that adhered to the metal platter. "I guess it's time to head home. Where do you guys live?"

"Branford."

"Good. They have a soda machine."

"This looks like a party," Bee commented as he and Mike approached the New Haven Green at six o'clock on the first Tuesday in November. "I'm glad we're prepared." He patted the thermos hidden inside his quilt. Mike had a sleeping bag under his arm.

A large elevated platform stood in the center of the Green. On all sides spread waves of students. Bottles flashed in the spotlights and joints glowed red. In the distance a few policeman moved idly through the crowd, smacking billy clubs against their palms, advising one group or another to put out whatever it was they were smoking.

Mike and Bee gathered leaves for padding and unfolded their blankets beneath a tree. Bee opened the thermos with a flourish and took a long swallow. "Hits the spot, it does," he said, shivering slightly and passing the brandy to Mike.

Mike gulped and pointed to the platform. Mo Silver stood at the microphone. To cheers and shouts he held up a hand. Then he glanced at a clipboard.

"I don't think I've ever seen him without food before," Bee remarked. "He looks naked. Like me without my booze."

Mo's voice rang out clearly. "Okay. The thing is to keep this going. We estimate twenty-five hundred now and we're scouring the dorms and libraries for more." Applause, whistles. "Robert Goff is presently meeting with the first faculty coalition to oppose the war—" More applause. "And we hope they will also make their way to our demonstration tonight." Cheering.

Mo stepped away from the mike to confer with some other organizers.

"Let's move closer," Mike suggested.

"No. This is fine. Once the music starts you'll be glad you're not closer."

"Don't tell me the Whiffs are going to sing."

Bee pointed. "You see those speakers on the platform?"

Mike peered. "Yes, I do now."

Ten minutes later a band took the stage and tuned

54

their instruments. Someone next to Bee tapped his shoulder and offered him a burning joint. Bee accepted it eagerly and then offered it to Mike who shook his head. "No thanks."

"How can you turn down grass at a time like this? Refusing a toke is like a vote for Nixon."

"Maybe later."

"I'll hold you to that, Jack Armstrong."

The brandy and the band and the crowd and the last days of autumn made Mike dizzy. He stretched out on the blanket, folding his arms behind his head, and stared overhead into the latticed branches.

"Last chance before it's laid to rest," said Bee. He held a red-hot roach.

Mike lunged for it, burning his fingertips. "Ow!" He dropped the roach on the quilt. Shaking his head, Bee flicked it away.

"Try again," a voice said. Mike looked up at a girl offering a fresh smooth joint.

Mike hesitated. "Thank you very much," said Bee, grabbing the reefer. "It's yours, fella, go to it. Here, I'll give you a head start." Bee lit the cigarette, inhaled deeply and passed it on. After the third toke, with Bee badgering him to "keep that green grass in your pink lungs," Mike coughed like a consumptive.

The music caught his attention now. How clear and true it sounded! The wash of guitars and the deep rippling bass, the sharp martial clatter of the drums. This is my music. This is *our* music, he thought. But who are we?

"These cats aren't bad," said Bee.

"What else is going to happen, do you figure?"

"Some more speeches, I expect, and some more music."

"That's it?"

"Yes, I suppose. What did you imagine it would be?"

Mike struggled for words. "I don't know exactly. Something—I don't know—some kind of focus, some explosion. I guess I wonder what makes twenty-five hundred of us here anything more than a crowd."

55

"Nothing. It's just a question of how you view crowds. You've never been in crowds. You're always surrounded by them. Welcome to the crowd crowd."

"Sometimes I wish you weren't so damn clever, Bee. You seem to know me better than I know myself."

"Not on your life. You're so predictable at times that you're inscrutable."

"I don't get it."

"You're always conforming to conflicting standards. At first I thought you were just the local-yokel-cum-stud-cum-jock. But you're not that really. Then I thought, maybe a super-straight arrow, a bootstrapper. But you're too curious about things to be that."

"So what am I?"

"A menace. You're too good to be true."

"It's just not so. I wonder when you'll believe me."

"Hey, it's cold out here," Bee announced. "We're also out of booze." He tipped the thermos. A single drop trickled onto the quilt. "What do you say I run back to the room and get us some more brandy and a couple of blankets?"

"Sure, if you don't mind making the trip."

"No sweat." Bee scrambled to his feet. "See ya soon."

Mike felt restless. He swayed as he got to his feet. He wandered toward a bonfire which illumined a large patch of the Green. A dozen similar fires burned, each one encircled by students tossing in garbage and bottles and leaves. The flames leapt higher and higher. Then two small fires hissed and shrank into darkness. Fireman appeared, wielding long hoses. Police supervised the activity, roughly pushing students aside. Two protestors were spirited off into a police van on the far side of the Green.

Suddenly Mike was shoved forward violently. He stumbled over a pair of legs. Three policemen were breaking up the crowd, waving their clubs.

"Put out that goddamn fire now," a cop yelled.

"Fuck you," came the reply.

"All right, smart ass."

A club cracked the student's shoulder. He cried and fell to the ground. A second policeman hauled him away, dragging him over the Green.

"You fucking pig!" a girl screamed. The first cop grabbed her, lifted her off the ground, and carted her off kicking and scratching. When a third moved in Mike entered the fray. He dived at a pair of blue-clad legs. The cop came up swinging and Mike rolled free only to be pinned to the cold ground.

"Take it easy, boy. You're coming with us."

The jail was a forbidding lime-colored cavern. A hefty sergeant behind a metal desk booked Mike and a cop tossed him into a cell. He noted glumly the stained concrete walls, the mattress on a plank, where a man lay sleeping, and the cracked and foul commode tipped against the dank wall. He touched the bars. Cold.

A voice spoke from the corner. "Look who I've got for company. Mr. Yale himself." It was Robert, who had accused him and Bee of being spies.

"Yeah," said Mike. "I penetrated the ranks. They took away my device, the fools, so I can't bug this cell."

Robert Goff grinned through his beard. "Guess I was a little rough on you guys."

"Not as rough as those bastards." Mike jerked a big thumb toward the bars.

"Yeah, the pigs can be mean."

Mike dropped onto the floor across from Robert, who handed him a burning spliff. A deep toke sent him spinning. "You mind if I ask a stupid question?"

"Shoot."

"Do you think what happened to us is really political, or are we just a bunch of kids who got out of hand?"

Robert stroked his beard. He was a skinny guy and wore his shiner like a badge. "What do you mean?"

Mike took another toke. The sweet smoke clouded his throat. "There's something missing. I found myself wondering about that on the Green. Why isn't something final about to happen? How come I'm not afraid? What makes me so sure everything'll be the same? It was like a—a—"

"It was like a party," Robert finished.

"That's what Bee said. It doesn't seem as if anybody cares. Anybody in the administration. They just ignore it, so you start to think there's nothing there."

Robert took three rapid tokes. "That's their strategy," he gasped. "That's how they keep us down, by refusing to take us seriously. But just remember what we're fighting for. War has got to stop. It's not just tripped-out acid heads saying it—it's an entire generation. It's fucking common sense and nobody in power wants to hear it. They think they're fucking heroes! Bombing the shit out of whole towns, sacrificing a nation and a people just to prove how big and tough *we* are and that *we* own the world. Talk to people. A jock like yourself must know a lot of uptight squares. Talk to them about the war. Tell them what I've been telling you and see what kind of reaction you get. All of a sudden this rage comes over them and they sputter and just won't listen. That's the worst part, once they start mouthing the bullshit they just won't listen. There's an ugly streak in Americans. We got a dose of it tonight."

Mike turned over in his mind this bit of intelligence. He sucked on the roach.

"And it's not just the war that's rotten, Mike. It's our entire social and economic system. The blacks are in revolt, even some at Yale, though most of them buy the old rap. They want to get ahead on the white man's terms, win a place in the white man's world. It's frustrating as hell. That's why Mo got together this coalition. To involve everyone. All the disenfranchised. Ever strike you as weird that Yale is in the middle of a fucking slum? The University ignores the people they trampled on to build their ivory towers. Who cleans your bathrooms and serves your institutional pie? The blacks, the slaves on the Yale plantation."

"Keep talkin', brother." A leathery face with bloodshot eyes peered up from the plank. "My boy works at Yale. On the maintenance crew. Tried to start a union and they almos' fired him. I said, Oscar, you keep your unions to yourself or they bust yo' ass right outa there."

"Oscar Hayman?" asked Robert.

The black face broke into a wide grin. "You got it, brother. I'm Ernie."

They shook hands all around.

"I met Oscar last year," Robert added. "I worked on the union drive with him."

"Ain't no justice in this country fo' a black man," Ernie Hayman said. "This a white man's country. Always was, always will be."

"But it doesn't have to be that way," Robert objected. "What about Watts and Newark and Detroit?"

"Niggers gettin' killed. That's what that bullshit be. Niggers gettin' they ass shot off by the man. Happen befo', happen again. This a white man's country."

"How come they arrested you, Mr. Hayman?" Mike asked.

Ernie Hayman laughed. "Shit, man, I got in a fight over to the Swingin' Do'. You know the Swingin' Do'?"

"The Swinging Door? On Chapel Street?"

"You said it, brother. Nigger owed me cash and wouldn't pay up and I know he gots the money 'cause I seen him outside with a hoe. That nigger be tellin' me he ain't gots bread then he be fuckin' some hoe." Ernie Hayman shook his head. "Can't trust nobody. Only a damn fool be givin' money to that nigger."

Robert looked stricken. "But, Mr. Hayman, don't you see who the real enemy is? It's not your brother. It's the racist system that's keeping you both down. If you were able to live a decent, respectable life—"

"Who you sayin' ain't respectable, white boy?"

Mike intervened. "I don't think my friend meant to say you weren't respectable, Mr. Hayman. He's on your side."

"Ain't no white man on Ernie Hayman's side. 'Specially some Yale Jewboy."

A cop came by and opened the cell. "All right, Hayman. We gotta move you next door. Make room for more of these demonstrators."

"It's about time. They bullshit be givin' me a headache."

"All right. Quit complaining. Out you go."

Ernie Hayman stalked proudly out of the cell. He stopped to point a threatening finger at the students. "You keep away from my boy Oscar. He makin' good money and he don't need some Jew bastard gettin' him fired."

Robert shook his head.

Then a handful of Yalies were herded into the cell. Mike recognized Al and Randy, the pair from the meeting. "Took all our grass," mourned Al—or was it Randy?

"Fucking quarter ounce. Pure gold. It's a sin, a crime against nature."

"We just smoked my last joint," Robert said. "Looks like you guys'll have to go cold turkey tonight."

"Think we'll be here all night?" said Mike. "I've got practice tomorrow."

"We'll be here until somebody posts a bond. There are a couple of big shots from the ACLU at the Law School. Mo'll talk to them. Don't sweat it. We'll be out in the morning."

"I guess we'll be out of here before Mr. Hayman," said Mike.

After his release the next morning Mike headed straight for his room in Branford. He hadn't slept a wink all night and he tried desperately to catch up. His alarm clock abetted him and he got to Payne-Whitney half an hour late for afternoon practice.

Jock Ryan was running the team through some plays but when he spied Mike he blew his whistle and marched over to his sophomore star.

"Glad you could make it."

Mike apologized. "I was in a jail cell last night."

"You think I don't know where you were? You think everybody on this goddamn campus doesn't know? If you weren't so goddamn good I'd throw you off this team and you'd never play basketball again."

Mike was too surprised to reply. His teammates eyed him. He searched their faces for a sympathetic glimmer but found none. So this is how it's going to be. "If you don't want me on the team—"

"We thought about it," said Ryan. "In fact we put it to a vote. You made it, but not by much. Take my advice and confine your heroics to the court. Maybe you're ignorant about Yale athletics, but we rely on alumni for support. And the last thing they want to hear about is some guy clowning around with good-for-nothing radicals. We were doing fine before you graced us with your presence so why don't you take laps around the track for the duration of practice? The rest of us have work to do."

The bastard. "All right, Coach."

He limbered up and trotted, following the line that rimmed the courts.

"Speed it up, Merritt," called Wally Chambers, a belligerent guard and the team captain.

Mike ignored him.

"I said speed it up."

"Fuck you."

A basketball whizzed by his head and another bounced off his leg. His teammates scrambled all over the court, digging up balls to hurl at him as he ran his laps. Wild shouts about cop-baiters and dirty commie fags echoed in the hot gym. Turn the other cheek, he told himself. You've had enough scrapes for the time being. At last the balls stopped pelting him and he continued loping around the court, running out his anger.

All right, Merritt, now you know where you stand.

4

By his junior year Mike Merritt's basketball—and political—accomplishments brought him to the brink of national celebrity. At six-five and still growing, with his charcoal hair curling over his ears and his face becoming more and more darkly handsome, he resembled an outsized Heathcliff who had come from nowhere to capture the attention of the campus and the community at large. He drew standing-room-only crowds to Payne-Whitney: tweedy faculty members, rabid New Havenites, and rumpled sportswriters, with a healthy smattering of student radicals who took time off from planning marches and rallies to cheer on one of their own. As the leader of a young Yale team, Mike was a consensus All-American and one of the country's leading scorers—the kid with the movie-star face and the magical jumpshot and a political conscience to boot: a rare bird indeed.

And then there were girls. The previous year the University began to admit women. Mike was excited. Bee was displeased: "What do we need a bunch of smelly cunts running around here for?"

The two friends shared a first-floor corner suite in Branford College—two bedrooms and a spacious living room with, of course, a big stone fireplace. The phone rang constantly, much to Bee's consternation since he spent most of his time in the room reading and writing. Usually the calls were for Mike—who was never there—and nine times out of ten the caller was female. Bee would be polite but discouraging: "Mr. Merritt will be in Providence for the weekend. May I have your name and number?" He never recorded any of the messages.

It was just as well. After the initial elation over women on campus, Mike discovered that few if any met his expectations. Most of them, in the words of his fellow jocks, were "ugly" and "brainy bitches." He looked for feminine companionship on occasional road trips to Vassar and Holyoke and Smith, as generations of Yale men before him had. But ultimately he came home dissatisfied.

Bee, who by this time had had a few liaisons himself—with a graduate student, a music professor, a townie or two—shook his head: "Is it worth all the trouble to try to melt these ice princesses, Mike, when you could have all the hot loving you can handle right here at home?"

"I reserve my love for basketball," Mike said.

"The hell you do," Bee replied acidly. "You just like to take showers with all the other boys. I know you."

Mike laughed. "Clean body and a clean mind—that's me."

"God help me," his friend moaned. "I'm the only man alive who knows the whole truth!"

Spring came early to New Haven, and Mike faced the conclusion of his second varsity season and a shot at the Ivy League crown. Friday afternoon, before the Saturday-night championship game against Penn, he rested in his room, writing a note to his mother.

It looked as if he would spend another summer in Williamsburg shooting baskets in the driveway and finding a job that might—just might—net him a hundred bucks a week. But his mother cherished his summers at home. He was a man in the house, someone to talk to, a shoulder to cry on. Mike knew he belonged there but he felt cheated somehow. Bee spent his summers at the Crosby home in Westchester and on the beaches of Long Island. Mo, who would graduate in two months, had a job in New York City after he passed the bar. Other friends vacationed in Europe or traveled cross-country. You'd think Mom would understand, he told himself. He filled the letter with assurances that he was eager to get home to see her. I can't disappoint her, he told himself. After all she has been through. After all she's done for me.

He put his feet up on the desk, his pen in his mouth, and looked onto the sun-splashed macadam walkway outside his window. Passersby, with books under their arms, strolled along the shimmering slate sidewalk or paused to lie on the grass and bask in the warm clear day. How have I survived? he asked himself. If it wasn't for basketball, and for Bee, I'd be nowhere.

"Oh, Mr. Lincoln!" He heard Bee's lilting cry and saw the familiar face in his doorway. "Why, what are you doing in these parts? We thought you done gone and forgot about us poor folk, you shameless fame-seeker, you."

Mike laughed. "Speak of the devil. I was just thinking about you."

"How very condescending of you, sir." Bee stepped into the room and dropped onto Mike's bed. "Pray tell, when you do find the time for fond thoughts of old friends? They *are* fond thoughts?"

"The fondest."

"Well now, that's quite a coincidence. I was just thinking fondly of you. Hoping against hope that I might see you before the big game tomorrow. To wish you luck, of course."

"Thank you. We're going to need it."

Bee threw his hands into the air. "Such modesty! I can't decide if it's a great honor or a big bore to know such an outstanding citizen-athlete. If I didn't know better, I'd say that you practice that sad hound-dog look in the mirror."

"Get off my case, Bee. I've got a lot on my mind."

"Of course you do. Of course you do. Far be it from me . . ." Bee stood and bowed and backed out of the room. "A thousand pardons . . ."

"Get back in here, you jerk!" Mike yelled. Bee returned and sat back down on the bed with a big smile. "What's up?" Mike asked.

"Nothing much. I just finished a column for the *News*—another brilliant polemic against that man Nixon and his boy Agnew—*and*—" He paused significantly and brought a long white cigarette from his shirt pocket. "I scored some good grass. Wanna smoke it, Big Boy?"

Mike frowned. "C'mon, you know I can't during the season. I can't jeopardize our chances tomorrow night."

"Jesus! He talks like I'm pushing smack." Bee tossed his head in mock exasperation. "One joint is going to destroy Our Man Merritt's career and cost Yale a championship? Let's be reasonable, kid."

"Since when are you reasonable?"

"You're right. Not since that fateful night on the roof when I lost my head over a big hunk of athletic boyhood. Well, I suppose I'll have to cultivate my vices alone, in private, without the approval of my peers." He looked at Mike with mischief in his eyes. "You're sure you don't want to enjoy a little buzz on this most glorious afternoon? Spring has sprung, man!"

The sun hovered at the western edge of the sky, sending a warm soft light into Mike's room. He gazed out the window at the shadowy maroon walls of Jonathan Edwards College. He mumbled, "If it'll get you off my back—"

"Oh goody!" Bee exclaimed. "Excuse me for a moment. I'll get a light." He bounded out of the room. Mike heard drawers opening and closing next door. Then Bee returned brandishing a gold-plated cigarette lighter with his initials carved on it. He had taken up cigarettes recently, after he decided he was a writer. "This is a special occasion," he declared, applying the flame to the tip of the joint.

Bee inhaled long and luxuriantly. He passed the reefer to Mike who took two short tokes, held in the smoke for half a minute, and exhaled. Bee shook his head. "Destroying those fine pink lungs. That's what you're doing." Then he let out a long loud wail: "Oh, God! To think I had a hand in the corruption of this model youth."

"Shut up and smoke."

"That's more like it."

They smoked in silence. A breeze insinuated itself into Mike's room. The blue smoke curled languidly and spilled out the window into the afternoon sunshine. They shared the initial thrill of the drug with grins on their faces. The white joint burned to an ember in Bee's fingers as he eagerly took the last of the pungent smoke through his nose. "Ouch!" He tossed the glowing remains onto Mike's floor and stomped on it. "The bitch."

Mike put his feet back on top of the desk. "What now? You've got me high."

Bee smiled impishly. "Well, there are any number of things two healthy young animals like us could do."

Mike clasped his hands behind his head and looked to the ceiling. "Yeah, we need some girls."

Bee pouted. "Spoilsport."

"You know, though," Mike continued, "of all the girls I've dated—"

"Ha! 'Dated,' he says."

Mike looked at his friend. "All I'm saying—if you'd give me the chance—is that I do find our friendship more, uh, whatever, than—I mean these girls don't have their heads screwed on right."

"You're screwing their heads *on*, then? When I had assumed the opposite."

"Like I've always said, Bee. You're never serious. I wonder about your involvement in the movement. Even your writing. Sometimes I wonder if you're serious about that." Mike shook his head. "I don't know."

"What's not to know?" Bee said. "I'll tell you anything you want to know, kid. Seriously. Not that it'll do you any good. I'm a worse guru than I am a fag."

"Don't sell yourself short on either count," Mike said. "It's just that when they started admitting girls I thought, Great, now I can find a woman right here. Probably a smart one. A pretty one—"

"And a rich one."

"Maybe. But not necessarily. Just a decent one. But hell, these sad sacks they let in. They're no better than the Holyoke or Sarah Lawrence chicks. Or even Albertus Mattress." He shrugged. "It makes you think. Is there a chance in the world to find the right one?"

"Things don't work that way," Bee said. "You should know that by now."

"Okay, let's drop it."

"You brought it up." Then he added, "I'm going to get drunk."

"Where?"

"Happy hour in Trumbull. Twenty-five cents a drink—if you can tolerate the music of the Whiffs."

"Jesus. There's a war on and you drink and the Whiffenpoofs sing and I bounce a basketball around. Maybe you and I should enlist and get it over with."

Bee grabbed Mike's arm. "Buck up, boy. It can't be that bad. Always darkest and a silver lining and all that. I don't know what it is, but it's sure got you in a funk."

Mike rose. "Sorry, Bee. So many things lately. Game tomorrow night. I'm behind in all my classes. Mo's always dragging me to some meeting or other. No girl. I don't know what I want."

Bee stood beside his friend. "Let's you and me go to Trumbull and hoist one and have dinner and I'll make sure you're tucked in early. What say?"

"Sure. Only no alcohol. And no tucking in."

"Definitely a spoilsport."

In the Trumbull common room forty students were drinking and listening to the University's famous singing group. It was a small paneled room and the singers stood in front of stained-glass mullioned windows open to the deep green courtyard behind the college. Bee hovered near the bar for quick refills and

Mike leaned against one wall looking at faces in the crowd. Mostly boys. Four or five women. Only one of them worth looking at. A tall blonde. Long hair, long neck. Small breasts accented by a pale blue sweater. Long legs beneath a plaid skirt. He had never seen her before.

"The Whiffenpoof Song" ended the performance. There was a smattering of applause followed by a general dash to the bar. Bee came over to Mike. "A madhouse!" he scoffed, nodding toward the gaggle of thirsty undergraduates. "This is civilization?"

Mike stared at the girl who remained seated, sipping her drink. Why have I never seen her before? What year is she? Does she have a boyfriend? A group of male students sat around her gulping their drinks, trying to make conversation.

"She *is* pretty," Bee said.

Mike muttered his agreement.

"What would you say if I told you I knew her name and address and phone number?"

"Do you really?"

"Her father and my father are like that," Bee said, holding his crossed fingers up to Mike's face. "Old Blue. Sickening."

Mike scowled. "Save the snide remarks. What's her name?"

"What's it worth to you?"

"For God's sake, Bee!"

"All right. You're no fun. I'll go you one better. Want me to introduce you to her?"

Mike most emphatically did. Bee led him to the other side of the room where, like a reluctant queen bee, she sat surrounded by her drones. Bee abruptly interrupted the desultory conversation with a disdainful glance at the drones.

"Patty, may I speak to you?"

She brightened. "Hello, Bee. Certainly. Excuse me." She acknowledged her admirers and gratefully latched onto Bee. "Thank you," she whispered.

Bee took her hand and said confidentially, but loud enough for Mike to hear, "Don't thank me yet. I'm about to introduce you to a most unsavory character. You may wish you were locked in a room with a dozen of those fleas after you meet this guy."

"He couldn't be that bad," she said with a glance at Mike's reddening face.

"Patricia Leslie Holmes," Bee intoned, "meet Michael Albright Merritt, my roommate."

"How do you do?"

"How do you do?" She extended her hand. Mike took it and pumped it awkwardly, smiling shyly.

"I'm sure you two have a lot to talk about," said Bee. "I'm going to join the mob at the bar for another drink." He wobbled away, his head held high, an unlit cigarette dangling from his wan lips.

"Of course I've seen your picture in the paper," she said after a long silence. "But you must be tired of people saying that."

"Oh no." Then he reconsidered. "I mean, yes I am, but it's always nice to know that someone is interested enough . . ." He shrugged. "I guess I'm used to it."

"Are you going to the concert tonight at Woolsey Hall?" she asked.

What concert? She goes to concerts. "I have to get to bed early," he said. "Game tomorrow."

"That's right. A championship of some sort. Bee mentioned it. He's always going to games these days. He never used to be the least bit interested in sports."

"Do you know Bee very well, Patricia?"

"Patty," she said. "Yes. We've been friends since we were children. Our families summer together in the Hamptons. We're old friends."

Mike looked down at the carpet and then directly at Patty. "Could I ask you a question?"

"Why not."

"Are you a Yalie? I mean, I haven't seen you—"

She smiled. "Why is everyone so reluctant to talk about women at Yale? It's not as if we're threatening the institution. I want the best education I can get. Just as you do."

"Sure," Mike said reassuringly. "I'm all for women at Yale. It's just that there aren't too many, uh, who, uh, like to get out and enjoy themselves. It seems like they're always studying." He took a drink of his ginger ale, cursing himself. What an ass, he thought. Stupid. Say something interesting.

Patty sighed. Her blue eyes caught his. "You men can be cruel sometimes. Not you in particular maybe. But there are lots of women who'd go out if you'd ask them. My roommate for instance. She's always complaining about the same thing. Only she says that it's the men who are always studying. Or doing something which I won't repeat."

"I bet you don't have any trouble getting a date." Stupid. A stupid, obvious thing to say.

"That's flattering, but I don't get out much really."

What does that mean? God, not another ice queen. She's so pretty. Sounds intelligent. Bee, where are you? What do I say?

"I know what you're thinking," she said. "That I'm contradicting myself. But I think of it this way: I've only got four years here. There will be plenty of time after that to worry about who's going to take you out to dinner."

"I see your point," he said.

She looked toward the bar. "Want another drink?" Mike asked.

"No. Just wondering where Bee went. We're supposed to go to that concert together."

"I wish I could go too, but I have to turn in early."

"He'll probably be drunk, poor boy. Now *he* needs a girlfriend. I could never understand why—"

"I think Bee keeps his affairs to himself," Mike said quickly. "I know he's had one or two."

"Men are so secretive. That's why I gave up long ago."

Mike agonizingly picked his brains for something to

say. Something to get her in his corner. Some way to ask her out. Just come right out and say it. "Patty—"

"There's Bee," she said. "Excuse me, Mike." She called to Bee who came toward the pair smiling widely, a plastic cup in hand, punch spilling onto his white sleeve.

"Hail, hail, the gang's all here," he said.

Patty frowned. "Bee, are you going to be able to make it to Woolsey?"

Bee squeezed her elbow. "Now, young lady. A gentleman can always hold his liquor."

"That's the trouble," she said with a wink at Mike. "I've never known you to be a gentleman."

"Foul!" cried Bee. He lifted his arms and nearly spilled the rest of his drink on Mike.

"You need some food in your stomach," Patty suggested. "Let's go to Silliman for dinner."

"Is that your college?" Mike asked.

"Yes," she said.

"And no she won't mind if you call her sometime," Bee said with a laugh. "And yes if I can suffer through this string quartet tonight I'll drag her to the game tomorrow. I haven't been able to unload my extra ticket. Surprisingly enough."

"Well, I've got to eat too and get to bed," Mike said. "You two have a good time. Nice to meet you, Patty."

"You too, Mike."

"Thanks, Bee."

"Don't mention it, kid."

Payne-Whitney Gymnasium was already filled to near-capacity forty-five minutes before the game when Bee and Patty arrived. She held his arm as he steered her toward the seats which Mo had saved for them. She wore a white turtleneck sweater and a pair of brown slacks; her golden hair was pulled back with combs and two tiny gold earrings dangled from her pale ears. Bee, in a corduroy jacket and dark velvet pants strode self-confidently along the sidelines with his ward, looking for the familiar figure of Mo Silver among the noisy crowd.

"I don't see our radical friend," he said in her ear. "I hope we're not too late to squeeze in."

"I'm sure he's here," she said. "He sounds dependable."

"No question about that. From what I've seen you can depend on him to eat at least as much as a horse every day—and probably two horses on Sunday."

"Bee," she chastened, "you can be so mean."

"Not mean. Just frank. Oh!" He pointed toward a spot near halfcourt. "There he is."

They stepped carefully among the bodies in the bleachers until they reached their destination. Mo was there with a hot dog stuck in his mouth and a huge Coke between his legs, waving to Bee. The couple squeezed past him and took their seats.

"Hello there, Bee," Mo said, his mouth full of steaming frankfurter and bun.

"Hello, Mr. Silver. I hope we didn't interrupt your dinner."

"Oh no," said Mo, applying a napkin to his mustard-marked mouth. "I've already eaten. Just having a snack."

"I'd like you to meet Patricia Holmes, an old friend of mine," Bee said. "Patty, Morris Silver, future practitioner of radical law and architect of a better society."

Patty and Mo shook hands after he wiped his on his pants leg. "I want you to know Bee speaks very highly of you—in private." She smiled.

"I should hope so," Mo said. "I can't imagine him railing against someone as harmless as me *all* the time. But it's just as well. I wouldn't know how to handle a compliment from him."

"Almost as modest as our guy Mike Merritt," said Bee to Patty with a gentle nudge. "Almost."

Patty laughed. "I think this is going to be a fun game."

They turned their attention to the court where both teams were warming up. Bee pointed to the burly Penn team which was executing a layup drill like clockwork. "Looks like the All-Soviet squad," he said to Patty.

"They're going to give us a rough time," said Mo. "Penn is a good team. Second best in the league."

"But they don't have Mike Merritt," Bee chimed in. "And we do."

"It's a five-man game, Bee."

"You're saying our boy Merritt isn't worth six of them?"

Mo slurped his Coke. "Mike controls the action better than anyone. But he's got to work with four others, though he does that pretty well too. Do you know how many assists he has this year?"

"God, I'm sorry I said anything," Bee moaned, his hand on his forehead in playful exasperation. "How many assists?"

"One hundred and seven. That's more than five per game. And he averages fourteen rebounds, which is just short of phenomenal. Those stats tell you more about him than just how many points he scores—and no one in the country scores more than Mike."

Patty, sitting between these two Mike Merritt fans, looked from Mo to Bee and back again. Mo attacked a second hot dog. Bee tapped her on the shoulder and pointed to the Elis' end of the court.

There Mike was going through his own shooting drill. A teammate fed him the ball from under the basket as he stood twenty feet away and poured in five shots at a time from selected points around the floor. The scattered applause crescendoed as he dropped in shot after shot without a miss. Patty watched as he jumped gracefully, hung in the air, and tossed perfectly arched shots into the goal. He moved "around the world," from one side of the basket to the other, and then stepped back a few feet and repeated the performance. Again, he didn't miss a single shot.

Patty watched the tall rangy figure with increasing

admiration. He was good. For all the talk about him he was better than she thought. She didn't know much about the game but it was apparent that Mike was a real star. And he had great-looking legs.

As the game got under way Mo and Bee talked less and watched more. It would have been difficult to communicate anyway because the crowd screamed and clapped at every play. And as it turned out there wasn't too much of a contest.

Mike shot from the corner unmolested for the first few minutes, hitting four out of five. Then, when Penn double-teamed him, he drove to the hoop and passed off to the open man. If his teammate missed, he was there to battle for the rebound. He scored several baskets underneath—leaping above the arms and elbows thrown in his direction.

"How many points does he have now?" Patty asked absently as the game neared its conclusion. She had not taken her eyes off Mike, but had sat silently watching him. Neither the frenzied din in the gymnasium nor occasional exchanges between Bee and Mo penetrated her consciousness. There was only this graceful handsome athlete, this friend of Bee's whom she had met last night.

"What did you say?" She turned to Bee.

"Mo says thirty points," he repeated.

"That's good, isn't it?"

"Exceptional," said Mo. "Care for an M&M?"

"No thank you."

The crowd roared again. On the court, Mike grabbed a rebound, sparked a fastbreak, converted the layup, and was fouled. He was on the freethrow line now with a chance for a three-point play.

He wiped his brow, bounced the ball the prescribed three times, and sent a high arching shot through the net. The buzzer sounded. Mike was taken out of the game. The gym exploded. He turned and waved to the fans. Coach Ryan gave him a grudging pat on the posterior and handed him a towel. Mike sat down for the remaining two minutes of the game.

Patty watched him as he joked with his teammates and put the towel over his head. He still seemed a lot like a little boy and she wondered what sort of man he would become.

In April the Alumni Association threw a dinner party for the Ivy League champions at the opulent Yale Club of New York. Jock Ryan herded his boys onto the train in New Haven and off again at Grand Central, then two blocks to the Club, up the elevator to the top floor, and out into the ballroom where over one hundred blue-suited alumni were gathered, already enjoying cocktails.

Mike's collar choked him. He tugged at his tie as he stepped out of the elevator with his teammates. The production was mainly in his honor: Yale's All-American, the country's leading scorer, everyone's dream kid. The fact that his neck itched and his pants were too short and he needed a haircut—and some sleep —did not lessen his excitement. He stepped into the throng milling beneath two magnificent crystal chandeliers and felt a strange tug at his soul, a stirring of pride, an awareness of new ambition.

Coach Ryan led the team to the bar and announced that he was going to try the non-alcoholic punch. It was implicit that he expected the boys to follow suit. Most did. Mike and two others went for the hard stuff, happy that the season was over and the coach's rules about drinking no longer held.

Sipping his scotch and soda, Mike looked around the high-vaulted room. He wished Patty Holmes were with him to share the thrill, to see him honored by his peers and elders.

Before he finished a second scotch, dinner began: a sumptuous formal meal, six courses and five wines. Mike watched the host operate to learn which fork to use when and how much to dish onto his plate when the waiter brought a platter of food. Then there were speeches from the Alumni Association chairman, the president of Yale, the athletic director, Coach Ryan, and—when the party spontaneously called for a speech after he received the most-valuable-player award—Mike Merritt.

He held the plaque to his chest and flashed his famous smile. "Thank you all very much," he began. "I am honored and very happy to receive this award which I will always cherish." It's what I'm supposed to say, he told himself, no matter how silly it sounds. What the hell else? He found himself speaking almost automatically, but with conviction, with authority. He was surprised that these words came from his own lips: "My only wish is that my father could be here tonight to share this with me. He would be proud to see me win an athletic award like this one—that's for sure. He was a good ballplayer himself. But more than that he would be proud that I attend school with, and play basketball with, Yale men. He always impressed upon me the necessity to associate with the best and to try my hardest so that one day I may become the best at whatever I choose to do." Bee and Mo would shit in their pants, he thought. "I would like to thank my fellow players and Coach Ryan, because they have made me their most valuable player by being invaluable themselves. They're great guys. Thanks."

The coach and Mike's teammates rushed to the lectern at the head table where Mike stood holding the plaque above his head. They cheered him and slapped his back. The alumni stood and applauded. Mike was halfway between tears and anger. He remembered the humiliation of that practice session last year. Now the same guys who had wanted to kick him off the team were Ivy League champs—thanks to Mike Merritt. The alumni didn't know any better, of course, but his teammates and Coach Ryan . . . hell, maybe they didn't know any better, either, he decided: they all had their own concerns.

A full hour later, as the party wound down and Mike

had recovered from his emotional moment in the limelight, he sat alone in one corner of the great room staring out of the tall latticed windows into the dark spring night. What is Patty doing? he wondered.

A quiet but resonant voice interrupted his thoughts. "Mr. Merritt." Mike turned and saw a slight, white-haired man with dark eyes standing stiffly in a finely tailored gray suit. He wore a dashing silver tie with what looked like a diamond tiepin in it. Mike stood and put out his hand. The man shook it firmly. He smiled slightly. "I'm Mortimer D. Wright, Class of '33."

"Nice to meet you, Mr. Wright." Hadn't he heard that name before? Was this man somebody famous?

"Sit down. I'd like to speak with you for a moment. If you don't have to go immediately."

"Well." He looked at his watch. It had belonged to his father and he had only recently begun to wear it regularly. It seemed to make time more abundant—or at least it did in his inebriated state. "It's ten now. We leave on the late train. It's right across the street . . ."

"I take it then that you do have time," the man insisted.

Mike looked up sheepishly from his watch into Wright's dark definite eyes. "Yes, sure. I guess I do." He sat down on one of the high-backed velvet-covered chairs close to the windows. Wright took the one next to him.

"Let me get right to the point," Wright began. "I want to talk about you. Frankly, I've never been as impressed with an after-dinner speaker as I was with you tonight. Have you studied speech or debate?"

Mike had to laugh. "No, sir. But thank you. That's quite a compliment. I meant what I said tonight. I do wish my father was here."

"I'm sure you did and I'm sure you do. Tell me about your father. He must have been a remarkable man."

"In his own way he was. And so is my mom. I've been pretty lucky, I guess."

"It sounds as if you have indeed."

Mike noticed a gleaming diamond ring on one of the man's fingers. A rich sonofabitch, he laughed to himself. I wonder what he does for a living? And what does he want from me? Patience, he reminded himself.

"Tell me, Mr. Merritt, how have you become such an accomplished athlete? Did your father insist that you play basketball?"

"Oh no, sir. I've wanted to play ball ever since I was little. Dad and I put up the basket over the garage and we'd play together once in a while. But he never pushed me. He always encouraged me, but he never forced me to practice or anything like that. I suppose he knew that I wanted to play and to be good—and he let me do it myself. He and Mom came to all my games—until he got sick." He stopped talking and looked at the blue carpet, clutching the arms of his chair as the room began to spin.

Wright changed the subject. "So what are your career plans? I'm sure you realize that your Yale education will be a fine foundation for whatever you choose to pursue."

Mike nodded and sipped at his scotch. "I'm thinking of law school. That's what my friend Mo Silver recommends. And I think my mother would like it. When the time comes I'll decide. Until then . . ." He waved a hand significantly.

"Yes, you're young yet." Wright paused, sizing up this attractive undergraduate athlete with a stern eye. "And what are your plans this summer?"

Mike sighed. "Back to Williamsburg, I guess. No place else to go really. Mom expects me home. I wish—well, there's no reason to waste time hoping for the impossible."

"I'm curious, my boy," Wright said. "What does a young man on top of the world consider impossible?"

"Well, there's this girl—" He laughed. The older man did not. "Anyway, this girl I'd like to spend some time with. She's a class behind me at Yale."

"Mm-hn," Wright offered; his brow creased at the mention of the unpleasant fact.

"She lives in New York City and I—well, I sure would like to see her this summer, but, as I said, I'll be painting houses in Williamsburg or something. Got to earn some money for next year."

"Would you consider a position in New York if one were offered to you?"

"I don't know, Mr. Wright. I sorta promised my mother—"

"Is she in any financial trouble?"

"No—but almost. Some of the money I earn summers goes to her. She buys a lot of groceries when I'm around."

Wright crossed his legs. Dark blue eyes flashed from his pink mask. "Allow me to make a proposition, Mr. Merritt, which you are free to accept or reject. All I ask is that you consider it."

"Fair enough."

"My bank is associated with—actually I am on the board of directors of—Future Leaders, Inc., a nonprofit organization dedicated to developing leadership in public and private secondary schools around the country and to preserving the free enterprise system through education. We are a new and growing organization and we are looking for fresh young blood. After all, a bunch of old businessmen are likely to be somewhat out of touch with the new generation." He paused. Mike nodded silently, more than a little confused.

"This summer we are taking on two interns," Wright continued, "two college students to help run our New York office and to organize a series of seminars for young people from the area and the state at large. I think you are precisely the person we are looking for, Mr. Merritt."

"Thank you, sir," Mike said. The room spun more violently as Wright's offer pierced the alcoholic fog of Mike's mind. New York! Is this really happening to me?

"A job here in the city?" he blurted.

"That's right. Future Leaders is located in a suite in the Pan Am building, just across the street from here." He pointed out the tall windows to the east. "I'd like to show it to you and to discuss the matter at some length. The way I see it, I think we both can do each other some good. What do you say?"

"Well, our train leaves at—" He consulted his watch once again. "In a half hour."

Wright leaned toward him and, with serious eyes, said, "I have a feeling Jock Ryan won't mind if you spend the night here at the Club—as my guest, of course. That would give us tomorrow to talk further."

"I don't know what my mother would think," Mike began. He polished off his drink. "I'll have to think about it."

"We can talk about your mother too, my boy. There's no reason she shouldn't receive some consideration if we're going to take her son from her for a summer. We can work something out, I'm sure."

Mike spent the night in a big bed in a big room on the tenth floor. He quickly fell into a deep sleep and dreamed of Patty—and New York—and Bee—and his mother—and his father. All of them, in New York, the sun shining brightly—lying beneath a tree in the park as the sun cuts hotly through the branches and shines on Patty's face. . . .

The next morning he breakfasted with Wright and toured the offices of Future Leaders, Inc. and discussed sending some money to his mother—a hundred dollars a week off the top of his substantial salary—and decided to take the job.

5

Not all of New York was like the Yale Club.

First there was his "furnished apartment," so described by Future Leaders, Inc., which sublet the airless chamber from a vacationing Columbia student. "Furnished" translated into a narrow soiled mattress—six inches shorter than Mike—an easy chair with a crippled leg, and a forest of spider plants which swallowed greedily the sliver of light that kissed the grimy window. This viewless aperture characterized his first few weeks as Mike groped like a blind man through the teeming, labyrinthine city. A morning on Wall Street, that afternoon in a museum. Greenwich Village, the Cloisters, the Statue of Liberty. In discouraging succession the monuments flashed by Mike and his associate, a bright but, alas, plain young woman from upstate New York. Together they charged from sight to sight in accordance with the manic orientation program of Future Leaders. At seminars Mike doggedly took notes and at night he studied the subway map. Fortunately, the first batch of imported high-schoolers was not scheduled to appear until July.

But he was not entirely cowed. For one accustomed to celebrity, anonymity came as an unexpected relief. He didn't even draw stares. What All-American stood tall enough to rival buildings that obliterated the sky? And in rare moments of repose, when a tour was cancelled and the day was his own, he responded to the challenge of New York: the city of cities. Filth and strange smells and bleating horns flourishing alongside fame and wealth and beautiful women. The sidewalks glittered with mica by day and at night Manhattan seemed a vast carnival stitched together by winking lights.

His chief disappointment was that he rarely saw Patty Holmes. She was not an easy girl to get close to. New York was her home and a daunting array of activities monopolized her time. When she wasn't cataloguing or assessing paintings at the 57th Street gallery where she worked fulltime, she flitted between openings, closings, receptions, and lectures, with an energy belied by her quiet demeanor. Thus Mike settled for twice-a-week lunches and an occasional movie. She sweetly but firmly declined all invitations to his apartment and concluded their dates with a frustrating peck on the lips. This was romance?

"Face it fella," said Bee one evening over the phone. "You're pussy whipped."

So much for encouragement from his friends. Mo might have lent a more sympathetic ear but he was incommunicado, gearing up for the bar exam in Brooklyn. They agreed to see a ballgame together after the test but until then Mo insisted he be left to his solitary lucubrations.

One Saturday when Mike was feeling particularly restless he decided to explore his own neighborhood. He left his apartment on 112th Street and proceeded down Broadway, encountering fewer white faces with each block. He abandoned the avenue for 106th Street, a boulevard lined with charred buildings and studded with potholes.

He joined a throng crowded around a fenced-in basketball court. The exultant shouts and the pounding feet excited his eagerness to pick up a basketball again. And this game looked like fun, although it scarcely resembled the disciplined sport he had been taught first at Whitman High and then at Yale. He recognized it as street ball, New York City basketball. Not much defense to speak of but these guys could jump and they attacked the hoop with glee, batting the ball after missed shots, slapping the backboard, rattling the netless rim. For all its freewheeling abandon the game was supervised by a referee and someone was keeping score on a blackboard. At least two of the players had real talent. They covered the small court effortlessly and without a wasted movement.

Someone tugged at his sleeve. Mike looked down at a small boy, no older than six.

"You pick me up?"

"Sure," Mike replied. "Here you go." He hoisted the boy onto his shoulders.

A man standing next to Mike chuckled genially. "That little dude picked the right man, all right." he said. "You play ball, my man?"

"As a matter of fact, I do."

"Think you can play with them?"

"I imagine so."

A short middle-aged fellow scrutinized Mike through narrowed, creased eyes. "I seen jou play. On TV."

The little boy on Mike's shoulders bent down his round face. "You on TV?"

"A couple of our games have been televised, I guess."

The short man snapped his fingers as he tried to recall something. "Don't tell me. I know who jou are. Jou play for, for—Columbia?"

Mike shook his head.

"I know. I know. Jou play for Jail! In Connecticut!"

A second man nodded. "That be the school where they live in castles."

Mike smiled. "You got it."

"Mike Merritt," an ectomorphic young man spat from beneath a huge puffy Afro. "Mr. Honky All-American."

"Stay cool, Rodney," a companion admonished. "The man's all right."

"I want to see him play with those niggers out there."

The first half of the contest was whistled to an end by

the somber balding referee. The teams gathered in opposite corners and walked off their exhaustion.

"What league is this?" Mike asked of no one in particular.

"Neighborhood league."

"These are just players from the neighborhood?"

"That's right, bro," the belligerent Rodney answered. "No fancy Ivory League honkies."

He turned again to the players milling about the court. One team's T-shirts read 10th; the other read 12th. That must be his street, 112th. The center sat on the freethrow line, rubbing his leg. A teammate bent over him, looked up, and called, "Hamstring!" Teammates huddled worriedly around their injured center. A forward, evidently the team captain, scouted the spectators for a replacement.

"That dude be gone," Rodney pronounced, wagging his Afro.

"You play, mister," urged the little boy on Mike's shoulders. "You tall."

"Jou should play. He be right."

Mike was skeptical. For one thing he was wearing street clothes. For another, well, All-Americans didn't belong in playground games. "I don't know—"

"You chickenshit?" Rodney taunted.

Mike ignored him.

"I said, you chickenshit, big man?"

"No. It's up to them." He pointed through the fence.

"Cut the bullshit, man. You want to play, you play."

The captain continued to scan the crowd for a replacement. His eyes fell on Mike.

"Take this big dude here, Bobby," said Rodney. "He dyin' to play."

"You live around here, bro?"

"Yes, on 112th Street."

"Then you in," Bobby decided.

Mike looked down at his shoes. Bobby pointed to the stricken player.

"Check that dude out. He got the Cons."

To his relief, the center's shoes were nearly his size. He performed his ritual warmup of "around the world." The basket took some adjusting to; the bolts were loose and the rim drooped inches too low. But after a bit of experimenting his shots began to fall with the automatic regularity that astonished Yale fans.

Mike played as inconspicuous a role as possible. He seldom left the unfamiliar center position, cutting off the lane, deflecting rebounds to his teammates, setting picks for his guards. An occasional jumpshot drew compliments and cheers from the crowd.

"He shoot like the 'O'!"

"He play like a nigger. That man is bad!"

Quickly 12th erased an eight-point deficit. With only a few seconds left in the game they led by eleven. After the victory, Mike shook hands all around.

"You gonna be here all summer, my man?" Captain Bobby asked. "You my number-one draft pick."

"Sure," Mike answered. "If it's not against the rules. I'm only here for the summer and I play for a college team—"

Bobby held up his hand. "Ain't in'erested in no history, man. You know Langston Hughes Gym, 99th and Amsterdam? That's where we practice."

"I'll see you there, I guess. Thanks a lot."

"You got it, man."

Mike left the court and looked for Rodney, who was nowhere to be found.

The same day he stenciled a "12" on his T-shirt word came down that Mike Merritt was ineligible to complete in the neighborhood league. He was flattered when Bobby asked him to take over as coach and twice a week he led boisterous and inspired practices at Langston Hughes Elementary School. For all the pointers he gave his team about boxing out for rebounds and running simple plays, it was Mike who did most of the listening and learning.

Here was a world of experience he knew only dimly. Three of the kids—the oldest was seventeen—had wives, and four others had children. None would graduate from high school and several, like Captain Bobby, had given up on education well before they got that far. Shouldn't these kids benefit from programs like Future Leaders? Why spend money and time on overachievers from New Rochelle and Great Neck who found reinforcement wherever they turned?

The time wasn't ripe yet, but Mike resolved to bring the matter up with Mortimer Wright. Perhaps he could make him see the light. Mo and Robert and those guys would approve—it was right up their alley—using the tools of capitalism to thwart its own corrupt purposes, applying the machinery of the rich to uplift the poor.

As rewarding as his work with the kids of 112th Street was his slow but gradual progress with Patty Holmes. Hope glimmered as she grew to realize that Mike Merritt was not just another pretty face, another jock. The job at Future Leaders impressed her as serious and worthwhile and her heart softened at the stories he related from his two evenings a week at the elementary school. In the horror she expressed, he noted a kind of titillation. He recalled a remark of Bee's: "All these puritanical types are secretly turned on by pornography." At the time of its utterance the statement seemed another of Bee's outrageous generalizations, calculated to shock, but he wondered idly if it weren't true.

In July a heat wave blistered into the city and overworked citizens fled to the beaches and the woods. He was almost sorry to see it happen since he was at last adjusting to the frenzy of urban congestion. His regret soon vanished, however, when Patty called him with the news that her parents were gone for the weekend, thus providing her with a few moments to "live it up" outside the pale of their stern watchful eyes. Had it been any other girl the message would have been clear: I am available, do with me what you will. But this was Patty Holmes and from her he had learned to expect nothing.

Friday night he rode a crosstown bus to the Upper East Side. The Holmeses inhabited a handsome townhouse with a monumental stone stoop. A uniformed maid opened the heavy black door. She was a tiny woman and fright momentarily clouded her gaze before she led him mutely into the living room. This was only his second visit. There had been an awkward dinner with her parents—burdensome silences interspersed with a tight-lipped catechism: "How marvelous. Do you have a career in mind yet?"

Tall windows overlooked the serene immaculate street and paintings selected by Patty graced the walls of the otherwise austere living room. He was too nervous to sit. What would she look like? What did she have in mind? Don't blow it, Merritt. Tonight you're a gentleman.

He heard a faint rustling. Patty, wrapped in a deep blue gown, leaned in the entranceway.

"I feel lightheaded," she said.

"Yes," he said. "This heat—"

She giggled and brought a hand to her mouth. "It's not just the heat. I've been drinking. Gin is so strong. It looks like water but—" She shook her lovely head. She danced into the room and plopped into a chair.

"You've been drinking gin?"

"That's what I said, isn't it, silly?"

"If you're not feeling well . . ."

She pouted. "You sound just like Daddy. Can't a girl enjoy herself once in a while?"

"Sure. I just thought—"

"Well, don't think. Tonight I'm having a good time. And I hope my gentleman caller isn't going to be an awful bore."

He turned red.

"Would you like a drink? Take my advice and put something in it. The gin I mean."

"It would hit the spot," he admitted.

She giggled again. "That's what Daddy always says. What a funny expression. I used to ask him, what spot?

You see I thought there was this little spot inside that was moving around, and if you hit it it would stop moving. Clarice!"

Clarice was the maid. She appeared noiselessly. "Yes, Miss Patty?"

"Please bring me and this stirring tree of manhood a gin and . . ." She crimpled her brow. "A gin and . . ."

"Tonic?" Mike suggested.

Patty beamed. "Yes, that's it! Isn't he wonderful, Clarice? He knows everything."

"Yes, miss."

Damn it, now she was making fun of him. Like Mrs. Davidson. He didn't speak like a hillbilly anymore. What was the problem this time? Overeagerness?

"I made reservations, in your name of course, at a restaurant on 61st Street. It's awfully good. I hope you'll like it."

"I'm sure I will."

Clarice returned with the drinks. Patty gulped hers like a creature dying of thirst. "This is wonderful. Like candy compared to the last one."

"Hits the spot?"

This struck her as hilarious. She shook with laughter and the few unconsumed drops in her glass spilled on her dress.

Mike leapt to his feet and pulled a handkerchief from his suitpocket.

"Oh, sit down. I'm not going to *expire*."

Obediently he dropped back into his chair.

"What are a few drops of booze on my bosom? I like that! Bo-o-o-*ze* on my bo-o-o-*zum*. Isn't that funny?"

"If you say so."

"Well, I do. So there."

Finally they made it out the door. The air was still heavy and fetid. A short walk brought them to the restaurant where the maitre 'd greeted them with a bow.

"Reservations for Mr. Michael Albright Merritt and date," boomed Patty.

The maitre 'd permitted himself a wormy smile.

"Do you remember," said Patty, "when Bee introduced us? Michael Albright Merritt meet Patricia Leslie Holmes. Bee's so funny."

Mike was staring rapturously at her golden hair. It was set aglow by a candle that shone through tinted glass. "Yes, he is."

Patty propped her oval face on her hands. "You know what I think?" she whispered dramatically.

"I haven't the slightest."

"I think Bee's—*gay*."

"What makes you say that?"

She stifled a laugh as heads turned. "You mean you're his roommate and you don't know?"

"Well, I never asked. I mean it's his business."

She shook her head mournfully. "How sad to be a man. There's no real intimacy between you. All that backslapping but no real intimacy."

The waiter appeared with a bottle swaddled in a napkin. Almost missing his cue, Mike grabbed the glass, took a gulp and favored the waiter with an exaggerated nod. Patty laughed, Mike turned red again, and the waiter smirked. When their food came the pair ate with the solemn ravenousness of coal miners, hardly exchanging a word.

After dinner they were off to Broadway. It was Mike's idea, since he had never seen a show and his mother pestered him in letters to take one in. The cab lurched through midtown and came to a violent stop outside the theater. Mike and Patty followed a noisy group—"New Jersey," announced Patty. "It's written all over their doubleknits"—into the dense and smoky lobby. Mike loosened his tie, while Patty fanned herself with a *Playbill*.

"Buy me a drink?" she asked.

"I'm sorry. I should have offered."

Ten minutes later he returned with a gin and tonic in each hand. Patty didn't see him. She was talking to a bearded man Mike vaguely remembered from Yale. A professor.

Patty finally turned to him and took his arm. "Mike, I want you to meet Mitchell Farris. Mitchell's responsible for my job with the gallery."

Mitchell? Mike unloaded Patty's drink and took the professor's strong hand. "Nice to meet you, Mr. Farris."

"The pleasure's mine. I've seen you play. You're not from the city, are you?"

"No. Just working here for the summer."

"You couldn't have a better guide than Patty. Quite a coincidence our being here at the same performance. My parents are in town from Buffalo and for them the city begins and ends on Broadway."

"Mitchell's a wonderful teacher," Patty confided after he left. "He really understands contemporary art and he knows everyone in the galleries here."

They had to leave the show after the second act, because there was a song called "Hits the Spot" which plunged Patty into riotous gales of laughter. A death scene followed but her giggles persisted, drawing baleful stares from their neighbors.

"Did I spoil it for you?" Patty said once they were back on the street. "If I did I'm really sorry, but I get that way. Something strikes me as funny and for the life of me I just can't stop giggling."

"No harm done."

"I'll make it up to you. The rest of the night is on me. Shall we go to the Village?"

"Why not?"

Traffic was heavy on Broadway. Despite the cabby's reckless efforts they crept at a snail's pace. Mike took Patty's hand when they drew to a halt on 34th Street. He contemplated Madison Square Garden. What would it be like to play there? New York fans were supposed to know basketball better than any others. Hell, if they were all like Mo it would be a privilege to play for them. Someday, if he was lucky, maybe he would. Suddenly his possibilities seemed endless. A career in pro ball. Why not? He loved the game. Coaching the kids on his block reminded him just how much. Playing for Yale was fun and rewarding but the professional game was a different story. And with a lovely aristocratic wife in the stands . . .

"What's on your mind?" Patty asked, squeezing his hand.

"Everything. A lot of things, anyway. When I think where I was three years ago. It's all so new. So much is happening so quickly."

"Such a hurry," she said. "You're in such a hurry. Maybe tonight I'm in a hurry too," she added.

She edged closer to him as the light changed. Mike put his arm around her shoulders and held her tightly. She dropped her head onto his chest, then drew back with a smile. They kissed and then her face was buried in his neck and he was stroking her soft hair.

Nursing capuccino at Le Figaro Mike tried to explain basketball to Patty. "I always thought of it as just a game, but Bee says it has all these, uh, metaphorical applications. Bee's term, not mine."

"Such as."

"Well, Bee says it's a—"

"What do *you* say?"

He grinned. "I guess to me it's just a game. But what isn't? Politics is a game and so is law. I guess I haven't given much thought to other professions."

"Are you going to do *all* those things?"

"Not at the same time."

"You have a good mind. Do you think professional basketball would satisfy it?"

"For a while. It might sound ridiculous but I've learned a lot playing basketball. And I have this craving to match myself against the best. It's all wishful thinking anyway. Ivy League competition isn't exactly the toughest."

"Don't be so modest. I've read the papers. They say you're the best player in the country. What comes next? Let's continue this fantasy."

"After pro ball? Maybe law school. I'm not sure

about that. It's really Mo's idea. He says it's the best way to prepare for a political career."

Patty smiled. "President Merritt."

She saw through him, all right. The thought had crossed his mind. He'd always been a leader and from his involvement in the anti-war movement he'd developed some ideas about democracy. With the right man in office and the right people behind him America could fulfill its great promise—to all people. You saw those kids eager for instruction on the court and their excitement touched you somewhere deep. Watch it, Merritt, he thought. You're getting ahead of yourself.

"How about Senator Merritt?" he said.

"A modest proposal."

It was midnight when they strolled through the pretty streets of the West Village. The small, big-windowed houses didn't blot the sky like the buildings uptown and the warm summer night was clear.

Patty pointed to a yellow brick house. "That's Mitchell's place for the summer."

"Oh? Have you been inside?"

"Just once. Early this summer, before he and his wife separated. They had me over for dinner. I was so surprised when he told me he and Mary Ann were through. They seemed so happy together."

"I guess I was sort of jealous of him. You seemed intimate before the show."

"How flattering." She linked her arm in his. "My head is starting to clear. I was really spinning before."

They ended up on a small dock. The Hudson flowed invisible in the darkness and across the water traceries of lights punctured the night.

"Is that New Jersey?"

"Yes. Hold me. I'm chilly." Mike settled his jacket around her shoulders. "It's so big. It practically reaches my knees."

"Ever since I was fourteen I've had to get specially tailored clothes. I'm a freak, I guess."

"Don't say that. You're perfect."

"Patty," he began.

She withdrew from his embrace and clasped the jacket tighter. "Let's go some place."

"Where?"

"I don't care. Any place but my house. Not with Clarice."

Their third cab of the night moved easily through vacant streets. What a night it had been so far! Patty rested her face against his shoulder as the city rushed by, a lovely intelligent face, marmoreal yet soft.

It twisted into a look of displeasure when they stepped into the unlit hallway of Mike's building. She shivered. "How can you stand to live in a place like this?"

"I thought it was pretty bad myself until I got a look at some of the places the kids live in. You should see Bobby's apartment. Fifteen people in four rooms and it's a miracle the bathroom ceiling hasn't collapsed."

She trooped gamely up three flights of urinous stairs. Mike switched on his light and Patty let out a muffled gasp. "Is that your bed?" She pointed at the mattress.

"It's a lot more comfortable than it looks. Here—" He moved a book off the fusty armchair. "Would you like some water or milk or something? I'm afraid I haven't done too much shopping. My job keeps me out late most evenings."

Patty shook her head and placed herself gingerly on the wounded chair.

"You'll get used to it," he assured her. "Look at all the plants. See those instructions on the wall? The guy I'm subletting from left them. There's more to it than just watering them. Some of them, in fact—"

"Please, let's not talk about plants. Come here."

She stretched her arms. Mike rushed over. In his excitement he forgot about the infirm leg which collapsed with a deafening crash as he sailed into her arms. They spilled onto the floor and Patty screamed. Then they both laughed and he kissed her, gently at first, then with passion. He led her to the mattress.

"Your tie," she whispered and fumbled with the knot. He kissed her again.

"My dress." She sat up and reached for the zipper.

"Here, let me." Mike settled behind her and gently unzipped the blue gown, slipping it over her smooth shoulders. Nibbling her neck softly, he unhooked her brassiere and cupped her small breasts. She freed herself and stepped out of the dress. Watching her fold it neatly and place it on the broken chair, he felt an inexplicable twinge of sadness.

"How about you?"

Zealously he removed his shirt, pants, watch, and socks. They stared for a moment in mutual wonder then fell onto the mattress. He covered her with kisses, lingering on her breasts, her pale thighs, her silky pubic hair.

"Oh, Mike."

He slipped his hands between her legs, which suddenly clamped together.

"What's wrong, Patty? Don't you want to?"

A painful expression transformed her lovely features. "I do but I—" She covered her face with her hands. Mike pulled them away firmly. Tears dampened her cheeks.

"Is this the first time?"

"No, but," she lifted her eyes toward the cracked ceiling, "it's never been good. I'm afraid."

Mike cradled her head. "I wouldn't hurt you."

"Why does this always happen? What's wrong with me? Other girls love it and I want to. I don't want to be some horrible old prude who's afraid of being touched by a man. It's not healthy—not in this day and age. Oh, Mike, I'm so sorry."

He placed a finger on her quivering lips. "There's nothing to be sorry about."

She threw her arms around his neck. "Thank you."

He tasted her salty tears. She relaxed and stroked him hesitantly. He lowered his face to moisten her with his lapping tongue. Her breath grew short but again she resisted when he moved to penetrate.

"Please, Mike, no."

In frustration he rolled off her and onto his back,

folding his arms behind his neck. His shoulder pressed against the cold floor. Patty pulled back onto her knees, planted them between his legs, and began to pump him, pulling down his underwear with her free hand. He grasped her head. She licked his belly then clumsily took him into her mouth. He flinched when her teeth nipped sensitive skin.

"Sorry," she muttered and began to suck, too hard at first. He regulated her bobbing head with a firm hand. Her hands rested on his thighs as she sucked without enthusiasm. He thrust against her slowly, his pleasure mounting. When he came she tried to lift her head out of the way but he resolutely kept her in place until she started to gag. He released her and felt semen dribble down his thigh.

She sprang clear. "Oh! I need a towel or something."

He staggered into the bathroom and groped for a towel, which he tossed onto the mattress. Patty had drawn the light blanket up to her face. She wiped her glistening forehead.

"I'm afraid I'm not worth a damn in bed."

He knelt beside her. "You're wonderful."

"Don't say that. It's not true. I'm a prude."

"It takes time. Don't be sad. You make me want to cry too."

"I'd better be going."

"It's so late. Why don't you stay?"

"I can't. I'd like to but I really have to go."

She clambered to her feet and grabbed her clothes and scurried into the bathroom. She emerged minutes later, looking more or less recovered. "Could you call a cab?"

"Are you sure—"

She shook her head. "Not tonight."

Ten minutes later honking sounded outside the window. He escorted her downstairs and settled her into the cab. The rumble of the worn engine was the only sound that pierced the dead night. Then it was gone, trailing a ribbon of exhaust, and Mike was alone.

Three weeks later he found himself in the quaking bowels of the IRT racketing toward Times Square. Wedged in between other straphangers he cursed New York, Mortimer Wright, and his own preposterous size. The flatulent air went nowhere but up. To keep from suffocating he stood on his toes and pushed his nose close to a fan mounted like a hubcap on the ceiling.

Three strides into the air-conditioned offices of Future Leaders, Inc., his soggy shirt stiffened into a plane of ice. At the coffeemaker he dried his sweaty face with napkins. A cup of muddy brew woke him up but stirred his insides to a boil.

At least he was seeing Mo today. The bar examination was finally over and Mike happily agreed to celebrate with his friend at a baseball game.

Inside the associate directors' office, co-associate Jane Henson mopped perspiration from her brow with a damp handkerchief. A dozen crumpled tissues sat like soggy carnations in a row on her cluttered desk.

"How long can this last?" Mike asked desperately as he collapsed into his swivel chair.

"You ain't seen the worst of it, yet, amigo." She grimaced as she tasted her coffee. "This sludge is unusually awful today."

"Goddamn it—I'm going to take this tie off." He jerked at it until it hung twisted below his collar.

"It looks like one of those ducks that hang in Chinese groceries."

"You can laugh, but this boy has secured permission to go to the ballpark today to see your beloved Mets."

"Lucky bastard. How'd you swing it?"

"I asked Mr. Wright a long time ago. And, you'll recall, I came to work one Friday when no one had to although the management *sincerely* hoped—"

He cackled gleefully at the balled-up tissue that floated softly toward his head. He snatched the missile out of the air and slam-dunked it into the wastepaper basket.

"This boy's letting a one-day pardon go to his head."

"You bet. Now to await the phone call from Mr. Mo

Silver to arrange the particulars of this historic meeting. He's been living like a hermit all summer preparing for the bar exam."

"Celebrations are nice," Jane said a touch wistfully.

At that moment the phone rang. Mike reached solemnly for the receiver. "Michael Albright Merritt, co-assoc—" He winked at Jane.

A familiar voice singed his ears and Mike's hand shot to his naked collar. "Yes, sir? Mr. Wright?"

"I hear things are getting pretty slow in your office."

"Well that's not strictly true, sir. Just the other day Jane and I—"

Wright chuckled drily. "No one's accusing you of anything, son. Just have a change of routine to offer. I want you to meet some acquaintances of mine. They've heard good things about what we're doing and they're anxious to learn more. You're my spokesman. Dinner at the Yale Club. You come along and answer some questions."

"I'm honored, Mr. Wright, but do you remember me telling you I was going to a baseball game with a friend of mine? It's something of a celebration."

"What's that? A ballgame? There's a ballgame every day in New York. I need you for this." Wright paused. "This is a real opportunity for you."

"I realize that, Mr. Wright, and I really appreciate it . . ." his voice trailed off.

"Good. Yale Club at seven."

Jane offered a commiserative smile. "That's what you get for being the fair-haired boy."

"The last thing I thought would happen. Why can't you just say no to Mr. Wright?"

"You can."

Mike looked at her in puzzlement. "How?"

"Just tell him."

"Easy for you to say."

"Sure is. I've done it. That Friday you were gloating about."

"That's not the same."

"What's different about it? Special orders from

Wright to stick around when we didn't have to. So I didn't. His word isn't God's."

"I suppose you're right."

Again the phone rang. Mike answered reluctantly and spiritlessly.

"Is this the office of Establishment Hero Mike Merritt?"

"Mo! How was the exam?"

"A waste of time like all exams. Listen to these tickets I got. Lower boxes along first base. Perfect view of Aaron in right. Game's at two. Only if we get there early we can catch batting practice. How about I come up to your office? I want to get a look at this bankers-for-the-people setup."

"I can't go." Mike forged ahead into the silence at the other end. "Just before you called Mr. Wright got ahold of me and ordered me to appear at some kind of dinner with him and some bigshots."

"Fuck the bigshots. We've planned this—"

"I tried to beg off, but he just wouldn't listen."

"Well, I guess I can find someone else."

"Jesus, Mo, you know how much I looked forward to seeing you. I got a letter from Bee. He's going to his parents' place on Long Island and he wants you and me to go out there for the weekend."

"Wants *you,* you mean. The Gatsby scene isn't for me, I'm afraid."

"We'll do something else."

"Sure. After you clear it with Wright, give me a call."

Click.

"Bummer," Jane said sadly.

"Gin and tonic, old sport?" asked Bee.

"Don't mind if I do."

"Patty?"

"Of course."

Mike grinned as Bee, clad in a skimpy striped bathing suit, sunglasses perched on his head, disappeared in the direction of the Holmeses' summer estate.

"What's so amusing?" Patty asked from beneath a sun hat.

"It's hard to believe you and Bee actually grew up like this." Patty sighed ambiguously as Mike surveyed the surroundings. Directly ahead, on the landward porch, family and guests raised their glasses and burst into laughter that skipped over the swimming pool to the lounge chairs where the couple lay. Bee re-emerged with a tray bearing a huge container and three glasses. He solemnly filled each glass to the brim and resumed his supine position, lowering his sunglasses over his eyes.

"Now that you've got a drink in your hand, Mike, tell me about your meeting with Mortimer Wright and his stuffy pain-in-the-ass friends."

"I told you before, Bee, I got so drunk I can barely remember what I said."

"You must have said something right."

"Let's see," Mike puzzled. "This guy named Carroll said—" he snapped his fingers in sudden recollection. "I know how it started. I quoted your remark about Jock Ryan. Remember you said you can fire a Yale man for any reason but incompetence?"

Bee snorted. "You told him that?"

"Carroll turned out to be a friend of old Jock's. He said Jock's opinion of yours truly wasn't any higher than my opinion of him."

"That asshole. Because of the demonstration, no doubt."

Patty frowned. "You should be more tolerant, Bee."

"My horizon of tolerance does not include total assholes. *Anyway*—"

"Anyway, Carroll—I wish I could remember his first name—said that Jock wasn't too sure I understood just what it takes to be a Yale athlete."

"Give me a break," Bee objected.

"Let him finish, Bee."

"Yez, Miz Patty. I'z sorry."

"So all this stuff came out about how I was consorting with radicals and advocating the destruction of the government. I explained that pulling a cop off a kid's back doesn't quite constitute anarchy. Then I just started rambling, about Nixon and Vietnam and the kids I coached this summer and how good they were and how something ought to be done for them—"

"And Mortimer Wright said, 'You're my boy. We'll invest a few tax-free millions into a gleaming recreation center.' "

"Not exactly. But he said he might look into it and he wants me to act as some kind of consultant."

Bee shook his head. "How sad. A corporate lackey."

Mike responded with his newly evolved line. "If I can accomplish some good what difference does it make? Politics is the art of compromise. If we want to change things we have to rely on guys like Wright. He's got the means to effect our ends. It's not as if I've given him my soul. I know what I'm doing."

"I don't deny it for a minute. Underestimating you, Mr. Lincoln, is a mistake this boy's never made. I just hope you keep me along for the ride. But now I'm going to tackle Neptune. Anyone care to join me? I didn't think so." He left his sunglasses behind but carried his drink with him.

"Let's go someplace private," Mike suggested to Patty as she took his hand.

"Anywhere in particular?"

"This is your turf. You ought to know some good places to hide."

She shook her blonde head. "I'd feel funny, with all these people wandering in and out and—"

"How long before everybody clears out?"

Patty shrugged. "Most of them have places around here so they pretty much come and go as they please. And we can do the same."

"So let's go to one of their houses."

"Such an impatient boy. Am I really that irresistible?"

Mike sprouted a hard-on as she reached a hand onto his bare thigh and kissed him langorously. "Oh my," Patty said. "Nobody's looking." Her hand crept into his trunks. Mike yelped when she fingered his balls. She puckered her lips as she dutifully massaged his cock. He seized her thigh and muttered to her quickening strokes. A few seconds later she withdrew her dripping hand and dived into the pool.

Mike stood up. "I think I'll join Bee," he announced. Patty waved as he stepped barefoot around the pool and paused on the thick grass that ran down to the ocean.

The "Summer Holmes," as Bee called it, sat almost at the center of the bay. In the distance the Crosby place, a rambling structure like Patty's, seemed to rise out of the ocean, its windows shimmering in the sun. Mike raised a hand to shield his eyes. Bathers, residents and guests of houses rimming the bay, dotted the curving beach. A dog racing freely over the wet packed sand, stopped dead in its tracks, snagging a stick in its teeth. He trotted back, panting, to a couple cavorting in the ocean spray. Bee was nowhere in sight.

Mike picked his way down a path to the beach where he waded into a modest wave. A familiar figure surfaced nearby.

"Come on in!" Bee called. "Only take your suit off."

Mike glanced around nervously.

"No one will see," Bee urged. "What's a little salt on your balls?"

Mike quickly slipped off his suit. "No funny stuff. I'm just taking this off to cleanse myself."

"It'll take a lot more than that."

Mike swam beyond the first crest of breaking waves and turned over onto his back. He closed his eyes and floated. He was concentrating on the sensation of the lapping waves when a hand tickled his balls.

"Goddamn it, Bee!" Mike swam in pursuit and practically caught up to his tormentor when a wave picked them both up and flung them near the shore.

"Let's go for another drink, handsome. But you'd better put your trunks back on. Here, I'll get them for you."

Bee skipped onto the beach and ran off, waving them

above his head.

"Come back here, you idiot!"

"Catch me!" Bee darted into the water, forgetting about Mike's considerable reach. He grabbed Bee and dunked him.

"You sneaky bastard. I thought you had your suit off too."

"Whatever gave you that idea? Princess Patty didn't play arpeggios on my neglected flute."

Mike stepped into his trunks. "You saw?"

"What's a hand job from her compared to what ol' experienced Bee can serve up?" Mike pushed him back into the water.

Patty was climbing up out of the pool when the two friends appeared. She shook the water out of her hair. "Oh, I want a drink too," she said as Bee began to pour.

"She wants." Bee leveled a finger at her. "I need."

"You sound like an alcoholic, Bee."

"He is an alcoholic," Mike said.

"Why do you drink so much?"

"I've been disappointed in youth."

"Don't be so dramatic," Patty said.

"I can't help it. I have a dramatic nature."

Patty smiled at Mike. "How do you put up with him?"

"We all have our peculiarities."

"Does that include me?"

"Of course."

"The lad knows whereof he speaks," Bee interjected. "It's one of the inalienable rights of our democracy—to be fucked up in a way all your own."

They settled back into the deck chairs. The sun was sinking slowly. Tattered islands of pink and orange scudded across the cornflower sky.

"First sunset I've seen all summer," Mike said.

Bee proposed a toast. "To Mike's and my last year as Yalies and to the right to be fucked up."

"I'll drink to that," Mike Merritt decided.

6

Mike Merritt lay on his hotel bed with the New York, New Haven, and Philadelphia newspapers scattered like dead leaves all around him. He pored over the sports pages all morning. There were dozens of stories about the NCAA Eastern regional playoffs between the Yale Bulldogs and the South Carolina Gamecocks—all with the same theme: MERRITT VS. MOORE, A CLASSIC CONFRONTATION. A QUESTION OF MERRITT. MERRITT—MORE OR LESS THAN MOORE? DREAM GAME OF THE DECADE.

After he had absorbed as much as he could stand he sipped his coffee and jumped out of bed. He walked to the window and gazed out. Philadelphia. So what? He paced the room. He was nervous and scared. He walked again to the window and looked into the dark drizzly day. His stomach was an aching knot. He played the game over and over again in his head.

Now a senior and three-time All-American, leader of the two-time Ivy League championship squad, Mike had fought his way into the national tournament almost singlehandedly. There were some tough contests along the way against a few nationally-ranked teams, but tonight's confrontation with Lincoln Moore and the Gamecocks, Atlantic Coast Conference champs, would be the toughest yet.

Lincoln Moore. At six-seven the fleet high-jumping black kid from Detroit was slightly taller than Mike Merritt and no less skillful at sending soft twenty-footers snapping through the net or snagging rebounds at both ends of the court. Nor had there been any shortage of publicity during his varsity years at South Carolina. Moore was Mike's only rival for No. 1 pick in the upcoming National Basketball Association draft.

Inevitably, the racial aspect of the match-up was on everyone's mind and the papers were full of it. But Mike was a reluctant White Hope: he was afraid that Moore was even better than the papers advertised.

A mist shrouded the old city and automobiles flew by on the streets below like wet black beetles with bright yellow eyes. Mike, still in his bathrobe, opened the window and breathed in the chilly March air. He heard the hum and splash of the streets ten stories down. A taxi pulled up and Mike watched Bee Crosby hop out and enter the hotel.

The three and a half years he had known Bee seemed almost a lifetime. He remembered their first meeting at the train station as clearly as if it had been a movie he saw just yesterday: the slight, smiling, tawny-haired boy eager to help his new rommate, contriving to meet Mike, "before anybody else got his hands on you." That was the essence of Bee Crosby: the faithful friend, amusing and sad, ever eager to please, always ready with a joke or a word of consolation. After graduation —by the skin of his pearly teeth—Bee planned a grand European tour. "To see the queens," he claimed. "I plan on getting laid every night of the week. They say the most beautiful boys in the world are in Copenhagen. I can't wait!" Bee will get on all right, Mike told himself. If only he'd cut down on his drinking.

Mike was less certain about Patty Holmes. She seemed more and more withdrawn these days. Preoccupied and unresponsive when, however infrequently, they slept together. He did his best to remain the patient solicitous lover, but he was unable to reach her. Often she was out when he called her room and her roommate seemed never to know where she was. Was she seeing someone else? Who could it be? One thing was certain:

Patty didn't like the idea of Mike playing for an NBA team. They had squabbled more than once over that issue. She wanted him to go directly to law school. He had already been accepted by five institutions, including Yale.

Bee took a neutral stance. "I trust you to make up your own mind," he told Mike. "You're a big boy." Patty remained adamant. When she and Mike were together she talked of little else. But Mike held off. He at least wanted to see who would draft him and how much money the team offered. How could he show her it was important for him to discover where he fit in, to know for sure how far he had come after all the years he had dedicated to the game? Why couldn't she understand that? And where was she now? She said she'd be in Philadelphia for the game, that she would call. But he hadn't heard from her.

Mike returned to his bed and picked up *The New York Times*. "Yale's Mike Merritt will always be remembered as one of the college game's all-time great players—whatever happens this evening at the Spectrum." Mike disagreed. The ultimate test was this game. Yale's chances for the national finals rested on his shoulders.

There was a knock on the door. "Come in," Mike called.

Bee entered the room, carrying a trench coat in one arm and an umbrella in the other, the same umbrella he had the day they met. Bee's gleaming smile was the same too.

"Good day, Merritt. Thought I'd drop by to wish you luck."

"Thanks, Bee."

Bee wagged a finger at his friend. "You should *not* leave your door unlocked, you know. Even if this is the City of Brotherly Love, some big black brother might walk in on you while you're working that big tool of yours and simply rape you. It's not unheard of. I'm tempted myself."

Mike saw the look in Bee's eyes. "How many times do I have to tell you: Mental preparation is as necessary—"

"—'for the serious athlete as physical conditioning. You cannot separate the two.' Okay, I'll only be a minute. I thought I'd drop these off." He took some newspapers from his trenchcoat. "You're big in Boston, but Cleveland likes the nigger."

"I've been reading plenty," Mike sighed. "Too much maybe."

Bee sat on the edge of the bed. "I'd be scared too if I had to face that big black shitkicker and his redneck teammates." He grinned. "But then again I'm not America's best white basketball player."

Mike was submerged in his own concerns, "Say, Bee," he asked, "do you know if Patty is here in the city?"

Another knock at the door sent Bee scurrying in that direction. When he opened it, Robert Goff stepped into the room, his chestnut hair and beard spilling wildly onto his shoulders and chest, his intense eyes hidden behind lavender-tinted rimless glasses.

"Hello, Bee." He grabbed the slight young man's hand in a fervent soul handshake. He went to Mike who stood in his long scarlet robe. Again the tight handclasp. "Hey, brother." He looked up into Mike's dark face. "You've gotten taller."

"The boy won't stop growing," interjected Bee. "Say, Samson, is this a business or social call?"

"A bit of both," Robert said. "Haven't seen you guys in a long time."

Mike returned to his bed and Bee went to the telephone. "Well," he said, looking at his watch, "it's past eleven. I think I'll have drinks sent up. Anyone else interested?"

"I could use a beer," said Robert.

Mike did not respond to the question. He turned to Robert. "So what's up? You here for the game?"

"You might say that," Robert began. "Actually, I'm

here with the Student Coalition. I'm New Haven organizer and—"

"I thought you graduated last year," said Bee, cupping his hand over the receiver.

"I did—barely—but I thought I'd stick around. There's a lot of organizing to do: on campus and in the community. After Cambodia and the Black Panther thing—well, that was a real turn-on, if you know what I mean. I thought the movement really gained momentum that summer. Now we've got to keep it alive. And as long as there's a war on—"

"You'll have something to do," said Bee.

Robert Goff bristled. "Look, Bee, I'm capable of finishing my own sentences. We're not writing some fucking manifesto here, so stay off my back, all right?"

Bee ordered a bottle of Beefeater gin and two bottles of beer.

"What *are* you going to do after the war is over?" asked Mike.

"I don't know," Robert said sadly. "I'm taking this one step at a time. Hell, I'm working for a revolution. We've got to get that asshole Nixon out of the White House and we've got to end this war. Right now the students and the blacks are carrying the burden for the rest of the country. Nobody else gives a shit. You both know that as well as I do." He regarded Mike who listened silently. "You were there in that jail cell. You remember."

"Yeah, I remember." Now it seemed so long ago: a game he had played with the other college kids. But no one would let him forget it. Sure, he hated the war—everyone with a tincture of compassion in his soul hated it. But lately, well, there were a thousand other things in his mind. Tonight would require every ounce of concentration he could muster. And it was getting more difficult by the minute to block out the distractions. "That was over two years ago," he added.

"Goddamn it, Mike! You tell me what's changed in two years. Is the war over? Has there been any progress in race relations since '68? How many women faculty members are there at Yale? How many black professors or black history courses? Nothing's fucking changed, man!"

"You still have a taste for beer. That hasn't changed," Bee offered.

"What the hell is your problem?" Robert exploded. "You and your nasty articles in the *Daily News*. You're nothing but a fucking dilettante, Crosby. You've never risked a hair on your head for anybody else. Mike and I were on the front lines when you were out getting more booze. This is more important than any of us—or all of us. Can't you see that?" He turned to Mike. "You can, can't you Mike?"

"I'm all ears, Robert," said Mike.

"Anyhow," Robert continued, addressing Mike, "we're organizing the protest this afternoon at Freedom Hall and later tonight at the game." He assumed that Mike knew what he was talking about, but the athlete's face betrayed his ignorance, so Robert pressed on. "Well, we thought—with your past involvement in the movement at Yale—that you'd be interested in being a part of the demonstration. You could generate a lot of good publicity for us." He spoke quickly and with assurance.

Mike held up his hands. "Sorry, Robert. I have a game to play tonight. That's why I'm here in the first place."

"Look," Robert went on earnestly. He pulled up a chair to the side of the bed. "This is crucial. We've put together one of the Coalition's biggest rallies ever—right here in Rizzo country with people from schools all over the East. We had to fight like hell with the fascist bastards to get a permit, but we got one. Everyone's going to be at Freedom Hall at three. We've got quite a list of speakers, including Coffin, and if you'd agree to say a word or two—"

"I'm flattered that you asked, Robert, but I haven't really been involved for a couple of years. You know as well as I do that arrest business was blown up all out of proportion. I've spent so much time at basketball that I'm sort of out of touch." He shrugged. "I have a million things to think about and I really can't—"

"Have you thought about those burning babies? About Cambodia? About the defoliation of a whole country?" Robert's furry face reflected frustrated rage. "I can't criticize your playing ball while Nixon and Kissinger and the Pentagon are greasing their war machine with boys not as lucky as you," he said, a scowl in his beard, "but I don't see why you can't take an hour out of your busy schedule to live up to your reputation as the All-American with a conscience. Just by standing up on that platform you give us the credibility we need. You can't think so little of the movement that you don't know that."

Bee lit a cigarette. "I can tell you that the rumors of Mike Merritt's radicalism are greatly exaggerated. And I can tell you that I'm getting thirstier by the harangue."

"Butt out, Bee," Mike said. He reddened. Robert Goff knew what he was doing: shaming Mike into participation. But he couldn't let Robert or anyone else distract him from the game. "If there was a way to help," he said, "I'd love to. But I've got a pregame routine that's pretty strict and I can't afford to change that now, especially today. I have my teammates and my school to think about too."

Robert leapt to his feet, his eyes flashing behind his shades. "Bullshit. If you really wanted to do something, you could."

"Believe me, Robert, if there was something that wouldn't conflict with the game I'd do it. I hate the war as much as the next guy."

The activist sat down. "After all we've been through together . . . ." He sighed. "Okay, Mike. I understand. If there were something that wouldn't interfere with the game—*then* you'd do it?"

Mike was suddenly suspicious. Goff had something

up his sleeve. Damn it, he's going to hook me into something. Goff hadn't changed a bit: he was still the hothead—act now, think later. Jesus, didn't he have anything better to do?

"Well, I suppose—unless the coach—"

"Fuck the coach."

Bee stared at Robert in surprise. "Well, Samson, that may be where your head's at."

"Bee, please shut up!" Mike turned to Robert. "What do you have in mind?"

The Student Coalition had bought nearly five hundred seats for the Yale-South Carolina game and planned to send a delegation to the arena. The students would wear black armbands and carry posters.

"You can do two things for us," Robert told him. "First, wear this." He produced a strip of black cloth from his denim jacket. "Wear it on your arm or on your uniform or whatever. It's a sign of solidarity." He handed it to Mike. "Second—I want you to sit down for *The Star-Spangled Banner*."

Bee whistled. Robert Goff glared at him.

"I don't know," Mike murmured. "I'll have to think about it."

Robert stood up. "I wouldn't have come here at all if I hadn't given it a lot of thought. I even talked to Mo—I know you two are real tight—and I asked him if he thought it would interfere with your game. He sounded pretty excited about the whole idea."

"Mo did?" Mike was mystified. Mo had counseled him throughout his senior season, preparing Mike for the professional offers that would come his way. Although he was busy as a new associate in a public-interest firm in Lower Manhattan, he attended as many games as he could, and he was in touch with Mike weekly by telephone. Just a few days ago the lawyer had called to wish Mike luck against South Carolina—and to tell him to put everything out of his mind but the game.

"Yeah. I don't think we've lost Silver yet. Everybody

says he's sold out—but I don't think so. I guess he's just sort of misguided. Hell, that's what law school does to a guy."

"He said he wanted me to do this?"

"Well, not in those exact words," Robert amended. "But he wanted me to ask you."

"All right." Mike Merritt nodded reluctantly. Why would Mo do this to me? Of all people he should know better. "I'll do what I can."

"Look, I'd better go. There's a lot to do down at Freedom Hall." Robert took Mike's hand once again. "Thanks, brother. This means a lot to all of us in the movement. I know you won't regret it."

"Sure, Robert. Thanks for coming by."

"Keep the faith."

When Robert was gone Bee shook his head. "He didn't even wait around for his beer."

"I don't want to hear it, Bee," said Mike. "You can be a real asshole sometimes."

"I guess these bleating-heart radicals bring out the worst in me."

"Yeah, and your worst is pretty damn bad. Why don't you get lost too. I've got to get some rest."

Bee retreated, crestfallen, toward the door. "What about the drinks I ordered?"

Mike fell onto the bed. "Just leave—please."

"I'm sorry, Mike." There was no response so Bee quietly let himself out.

Mike kicked the pile of newsprint onto the floor and tried unsuccessfully for a few hours to catch some sleep. At three o'clock he dialed Mo Silver's number in New York. He had to know why Mo had saddled him with this mess. After several rings the lawyer answered.

"Hello, Mo. This is Mike."

"Hi, buddy. You all rested up?"

"Well, I would be—but Robert Goff came by. Why did you do it, Mo? He said you told him to ask me. You know how much this game means to me. Why?"

"What the hell are you talking about, Mike? I

haven't spoken to Goff in over a year."

The Philadelphia Spectrum was packed that evening for the Eastern regional final between the South Carolina Gamecocks, ranked No. 9 in the nation, and the Elis, who were No. 19. It had been a long season for both teams, but especially for Yale which was accustomed to a blessedly brief Ivy League schedule punctuated by occasional meetings with a Big Ten powerhouse or a highly touted private university in the East. This year Yale had played twenty-five games, the most in its history, and had won twenty, again the most ever. The Gamecocks were 23-4 having survived a tough ACC season, including a post-season conference tournament, to win its NCAA berth.

As the teams took the court the crowd, mostly from New Haven, came alive. But Mike, during the final warmups, barely realized that fifteen thousand screaming fans were there, above him, around him, so intense and desperate was his concentration on the task at hand. He practiced his freethrows, already sweating madly. Beneath his warmup jacket he wore the black armband pinned to the left shoulder of his white uniform. He hadn't yet taken off the jacket and dreaded the moment he had to. That would be before the National Anthem—an agony he'd experience in a few minutes. He had decided to go through at least part of the protest. Damn Robert Goff. But he had promised.

God only knows why, he mused. This is the last time I'll allow myself to be talked into—

"Ladies and gentlemen," a loud voice announced, "welcome to tonight's contest between the Gamecocks of South Carolina—" There were shouts of support. "—and the Yale—" The voice was lost in the unearthly din of rabid Ivy League fans. "Tonight's starting lineups. For the Gamecocks—"

Jesus, I can't do it, Mike said to himself as the opposing team trotted out, one by one, to center court. He gripped a ball tightly in his arms, his biceps tensed, his knuckles white. It's such a small thing . . . and I didn't really promise to do anything. Mo told me to forget it.

"And for the Bulldogs—" Another roar nearly drowned out the hapless announcer.

Coach Jock Ryan, his mouth set sternly, his eyes, as always, narrow slits, patted each boy firmly on the butt as his name was called and he took his place in the center circle. The entire team was annonced—Mike Merritt last: "And the three-time All-American, Yale's all-time leading scorer and rebounder, for two years the leading scorer in the country, Mike—" Again there was a deafening storm of eager wild voices. The coach said something to him and sent him onto the court with a pat of encouragement. Mike trotted slowly toward his teammates as the entire arena stood. His teammates formed a circle around him, joined hands, performed their ritual "Go" cheer, and ran back to the bench. The starters peeled off their jackets.

"Ladies and gentlemen," came the voice over the loudspeaker, "please stand and join Yale University's world-famous Whiffenpoofs as they sing our National Anthem."

Mike eased slowly back toward the bench. He looked around and saw the Student Coalition section seated quietly in the upper balcony; he remained on his feet. The Whiffs began to sing. No one seemed to notice Mike. He put his head down and closed his eyes. Halfway through the song he looked up.

Ten feet away, to his left, a television camera was directed at him. He saw a small red light go on for a few seconds and then it was off. The camera wheeled away and *The Star-Spangled Banner* ended.

"All right, men," Ryan said as Mike moistened his sneakers on a wet towel in front of the bench, "the talking's done and it's up to you. Merritt." He turned to Mike. "I want you to jump center. If the other coach is smart he'll put Moore in there and you're the only one who can match him. We'll stick with our Blue Zone D unless and until they get a lead on us. Understood? Okay." He paused for a moment, looking each boy in the eye. "I'm proud of you and your great university is proud of you—no matter what happens. Now get out there and win this game!"

Whistles blew and sneakers squeaked as both teams took the floor for the tipoff.

Mike stepped into the center circle next to Lincoln Moore. Moore smiled. His head seemed as big as a watermelon and as black as Mike's best shoes. His powerful hand enveloped Mike's as they exchanged the customary sign of good sportsmanship. Moore's legs seemed fully six feet long and his thighs bulged tightly against his crimson trunks. He's bigger than I thought, Mike noted. Although when they stood side by side Moore was a mere inch taller, he carried more weight on his giant frame. As they crouched below the ball waiting for the referee to toss it into the air Mike noticed his opponent's long, long arms and marveled again at the size of his hands. A natural athlete. God help me, Mike prayed—for the hundredth time in the past twenty-four hours.

The little referee lofted the ball above their heads and Mike and Moore jumped. Moore beat Merritt by the length of his hand, slapping the ball toward his team's goal. But Yale's center, hugging the circle on the defensive side, blocked out his South Carolina counterpart and recovered the tip. Yale had the basketball.

The two teams broke swiftly for the Yale basket, South Carolina taking a man-to-man defensive posture, the Bulldogs falling into their offensive pattern. Matt Casey, Yale's stocky, five-nine sophomore playmaker, set up the play, dribbling to the top of the key. Mike sailed down the lane and crossed beneath the basket, trying to lose Moore on a pick. Moore stuck to him tenaciously. Mike crossed the lane again, and then again, as Casey passed the ball around, waiting for a chance to hit Mike. Finally, Mike lost Moore behind a double pick and raced to the corner, twenty feet from the basket. In a split second Casey sent him the basketball. Mike was at the top of his jump by the time Moore got to him. He sent a high, arching shot toward the goal. It snapped through the net.

Mike let his arms flop to his side as he headed for the other end of the court. Okay, he told himself, relax. I feel it. Defense. I'll play my game. Be tough. Be patient. Okay!

Three minutes into the first half the Bulldogs led 8-5. Mike had six points, Moore had two. Moore was tough under the boards, but Mike battled for every rebound, cleverly blocking the bigger man out as much as he could. Moore was fast and God could he jump, but Mike knew he could keep him off balance if he kept moving, if he played smart.

Suddenly, Ryan called a time-out. Mike saw that the coach was fuming, his neck scarlet above his starched white shirt and Yale-blue tie—and the old guy was glaring directly at him. The armband, Mike remembered. But, Jesus, he's not going to make a big deal over that—not when we're taking it to Lincoln Moore and his boys.

"What the hell do you think you're doing, Merritt?" Ryan hissed as Mike caught the towel the manager tossed him.

"What do you mean, Coach? I think we can take 'em. Maybe our zone—"

"Forget out zone and tell me what the hell you think you're doing. What is that black thing on your uniform, boy? If this is another one of your publicity stunts you might as well go take a shower right now. I'll not have this team and this school made a mockery of by some ungrateful grandstanding kid!"

"It's just something I promised to do, Coach. I swear it won't interfere with the game. If it did, I wouldn't—"

"Don't tell me it's not interfering with the game, Merritt." Ryan waved two scraps of paper under Mike's nose. "These are messages from alumni in the stands who see what you're doing and don't like it one bit. And they tell me that people are sending in telegrams wondering why the hell Yale's All-American is carrying on like some sort of hippie. Let me tell you, Merritt—"

"Coach—"

"Shut up and listen to me." The officials blew their whistles to signal the end of the time-out. Mike looked at his teammates who were staring at the floor. "Yates, get in there for this clown. Keep Moore off the boards and pass that ball. Casey, you're doing a good job. Keep it moving!" Ryan planted himself on the bench. "You, Merritt, sit down and take that goddamn black thing off your uniform. You're not setting foot on the court until you come up with some explanation for your behavior."

Mike sat on the bench, his towel draped over his shoulders, his mouth open in disbelief. "Coach," he began.

"Shut up. I've got a team to coach. And take that damned thing off your shoulder."

Mike ran the towel across his face and looked up into the thousands of faces around the arena. Some of them were looking back at him and pointing. Most, however, were watching the game, unaware of the snafu on the sidelines. He wondered if Patty was there watching him too. What would she think of this mess?

Goddamn you, Jock Ryan. Goddamn you to hell. "I'm not going to take it off," he muttered half to himself. "I promised."

Ryan was on one knee yelling at Casey: "Low post swing! Low post swing!" He returned to the bench. "Merritt, if you don't take that thing off right now I'm going to rip if off for you."

Just then a Gamecock stole the ball from Yates and sped the length of the court for a layup. Yale led by one point now. On the inbounds pass after the basket, Casey tossed the ball to his fellow guard who put it to the floor only to lose it to his quick South Carolina opponent. The other guard zipped the ball to Moore who sailed toward the hoop and dropped it in.

It was only five minutes into the game but Mike and a restless 15,000 fans were worried: with Mike Yale had a slight chance of winning; without him they had none. Jock Ryan turned and shot him a hateful look. The athlete stubbornly pulled the towel tighter around his neck and turned his attention to the game.

The Bulldogs had the ball. Casey was at the point trying to set up the offense the coach had called for. But nobody was moving. Ryan was livid. "Move! Move!" Casey drove frantically for the goal even though his teammates were clogging the lane. As he dribbled through the crowd and leapt for the basket, Lincoln Moore left his man and stepped in front of Casey. Casey's shot went up and met Moore's outstretched hand. Moore slapped the ball halfway down the court to a waiting guard. Two more points for South Carolina. Yale trailed by three.

"Merritt!" Ryan roared.

"Yes, sir." Mike scrambled to the seat next to the coach. He was prepared for anything the old man might say, no matter how unpleasant, but he was not prepared to remove the black band from his uniform.

Ryan's gray eyes were watery and angry. "Boy, you've cost this team too much tonight. I don't like myself for doing it, but I'm going to put you back in. We'll discuss the ugly business of your attitude, in the lockerroom at halftime. Until then I want you to concentrate on Yale basketball and I want you to get my team back in this game. Do you understand me?"

"Yes, sir."

"Score some points."

"Yes, sir."

The arena rocked with cheers when Mike Merritt stepped back into the game. The Gamecocks led 17-8 with twelve minutes left in the half.

The Bulldogs switched to a man-to-man fullcourt press, with Mike assigned to Lincoln Moore under the South Carolina basket. The black player was smart and knew that continuous motion is the essence of the game.

Moore never stood in one place longer than it took him to cut, pivot, or shoot. And on defense, he anticipated Mike's strategies and kept his long arms between Mike and the ball. Mike therefore had to work doubly hard just to get his hands on it. And once he got it he had to maneuver over or around Moore who, a big tree of a kid, might as well have been an entire forest of dark obstruction.

The tempo of the game picked up. Both teams unloaded their fastbreaks and as halftime approached the score was 37-33, Yale trailing South Carolina. Suddenly Yale caught fire with four baskets from Mike and two from his teammates. With thirty seconds left Yale led 45-43. Then Casey knocked the ball away from a Gamecock guard toward Mike. Mike scooped it up and headed for his basket. Moore was on Mike's tail by halfcourt and had caught up with him at the freethrow line. Both teams stood flat-footed on the other end of the court, watching Merritt and Moore one-on-one.

Mike put the ball to the floor, took a step, and jumped for the basket with his arms outstretched to lay the ball up. But there was Lincoln Moore. As Mike lifted the ball, Moore's great hand met it and the two of them went crashing to the floor. No whistle blew. The ball squirted loose and rolled away. Both men scrambled for it. The whistle shrieked. Almost in unison the arena crowd stood and booed. It was a foul on Mike. Undisturbed, the Yale star trudged down to the other end of the court where Moore made the foul shot and the bonus. They were tied at 45.

Yale got the ball with a few seconds left. At the buzzer Mike shot and missed. He saw Ryan throw down a towel in anger. Then Mike caught Moore watching him as they walked to the lockerrooms. Moore walked up to him and smiled. "Good game, man," he said.

Mike stopped and held out his hand. Moore took it. "Same to you. Good luck next half."

"Good luck to you, man—you'll need it." Moore smiled.

Mike was the last one back in the lockerroom. He took his place among the unsmiling teammates and gritted his teeth when Coach Ryan stepped up to the blackboard.

"The first item of business I'd like to dispose of, if you men will pardon me, is the question of Mr. Merritt's strange behavior. I demand he remove that ludicrous patch from his uniform or not be allowed to play second half, despite what that might cost the team. Do I hear any objections?" There were none. "Merritt?"

Mike unpinned the armband and tossed it on the floor.

"That's better," said Ryan.

Yale's strategy for the next half would be to contain South Carolina, to stay within striking distance and to feed the ball to Mike Merritt. Yale played even with the Gamecocks for the first several minutes of the half and then Mike committed three fouls in two minutes. One more and he would be out of the game. He knew he wasn't good for much longer than five minutes so he shot every chance he got, hoping to give his team a lead before he fouled out. He drove fiercely to the basket and battled for his own rebounds. On the fastbreak he'd pull up short at the freethrow line and pop a jump shot. He hit two from the corner before Moore could get out to cover him.

He fouled out with three minutes left in the game, Yale leading 87-86. He had scored thirty-five points. He sat on the end of the bench with a towel over his head oblivious to the game. The roof caved in and the Bulldogs lost 92-89.

Then Mike Merritt's days at Yale were over. Four years melted into one last gilded day beneath the hot May sun.

A wild sea of blue caps and gowns washed into the streets of New Haven and flooded the Old Campus for graduation ceremonies. The graduates were rowdy and irreverent, singing drunken songs and halfheartedly shouting anti-war slogans. Faculty members and parents grimaced and squirmed silently in their chairs. Cameras clicked and mothers waved. The dark towers of the freshmen dormitories cast an ever-shrinking shadow on the Old Campus green. When all were seated a former Secretary of State, Class of '21, served up a platterful of platitudes for his commencement address. Mike and Bee joked together and shared a spliff. For them the ritual unfolded as if in a giant open-air cathedral with the sun streaming through a stained-glass sky. The high priests of culture and education and politics prayed to their gods and patted themselves on the back.

Bee removed his blue mortarboard and fanned himself. "I never realized what a privilege it has been to be a part, however insignificant, of this great community of learning," he sighed.

"I should have thrown you off the roof when I had the chance," said Mike, between tokes.

"Then who would have opened your eyes to the finer things?"

Mike mulled the question. "It's not as if I don't have a mind of my own."

"Great raw material," said Bee, smoke streaming from his nostrils. "But, like Michelangelo's statues, you had to be freed from your marble prison."

"Well, thanks for springing me, then, old friend. And pass that thing over here."

After the speeches the graduates marched, in joyous disorder, to their residential colleges. At Branford Mike and Bee and their classmates each received a diploma from the Master and a hug from the Master's wife. Everyone then bolted for the booze. The graduates and their families and the Master, the Dean, and the Fellows and their families gathered in the inner courtyards to drink and chat beneath the sun-dappled stone walls of the old college. The bells of Harkness Tower, which rose above the golden cloistered buildings, pealed merrily.

Evelyn Merritt laughed gaily, her hazel eyes sparkling. She stood near a great oak in the gray-cobbled courtyard, wearing a plain blue dress and neat blue hat, her hands encased in a pair of white gloves she hadn't taken out of the drawer since Mike's graduation from Whitman High. "I always thought our church in Williamsburg had to be the most beautiful building in the world," she told Patty Holmes, "but I'm not so sure now." She craned her neck to take in the ornate tower.

Patty, in a bright daisy-colored summer dress, smiled. She thought Mike's mother was cute—whatever problems she had with the son. "It *is* a beautiful campus."

"How do you children get any studying done with all this—all this to look at?" The windows seemed to wink back at her as they reflected the brazen noontime sun.

"I think most of us don't even notice the surroundings," said Patty. "There are too many other distractions."

"Oh?" Evelyn Merritt queried.

Mike and Bee returned with the drinks for which they had been dispatched. Bee served Mike's mother her ginger ale. "Are you sure you don't want me to have the man spike that for you, Mrs. M.?"

"Good heavens, Bee, are you trying to get me to start drinking after all these years? Lord knows I never touch anything stronger than grape juice."

"I never touch the stuff either," confided Bee. "Except on special occasions like this." He lifted his plastic cup and drained half of it. "Moderation in all things—that's my motto," he said solemnly.

Mike shook his head in disbelief. Bee had come on strong with his mother since their first meeting last night. But Evelyn Merritt found him charming.

She laughed again. "I know you better than that, Bee," she teased. Then she was serious. "All young men go through that stage. My Hugh used to crave a beer now and then. And I knew better than to deny him."

"So, what did you think of the ceremonies, Mom?"

Mike interjected. He discreetly planted his foot on Bee's toes.

"Lovely." Then a puzzled look came to her face. "But none of the young people listened to anything those men said. I thought their speeches were beautiful."

"So did they, I'm sure," said Bee.

"What Bee means to say—" began Mike.

"What I mean to say, Mrs. M., is that I wish I could speak half as well. I suppose I spend too much time in my closet—writing and brooding." He glanced at Mike with a sly smile.

"The Bible advises praying there too," Evelyn said. "The closet, that is." She took a sip of her ginger ale and her eyebrows rose gleefully as she regarded her son and his two friends. "It's too bad your mother and father aren't here, Bee. I would love to meet them."

"I'm sure they'd love to meet you too," he told her. "My little sister would have been *so* disappointed if they hadn't been at *her* graduation. They've all been through this Yale business before."

"Well, it's too bad," Evelyn Merritt continued. "I know they must be proud of you."

"It's enough for me to have you here, Mrs. M. From all that Mike has told me, I feel as close to you as I do my own mother." Evelyn blushed.

"Anybody need another drink?" Bee asked as he finished off the last of his own. The mumbled "no thank yous" sent him on a solitary trek back to the bar.

"I think he's nice, Mike," Mrs. Merritt said. "You've chosen some fine friends." She sent a significant glance in Patty's direction. "Believe me, it's a load off my mind. I wasn't sure how you'd do way out here—so far from home and all. But you've given me reason to be real proud."

It was Mike's turn to color. He turned to Patty whose icy blue eyes revealed that she was not so proud, nor so patient. He would have to speak to her alone—soon. There would be another argument; he could feel it coming on. Or rather, it would be the same old argument, and he dreaded it.

"Don't you think he looks especially handsome today, Patty? So grown up. I wish I had a camera."

"Mom," Mike said between his gritted teeth.

"You're right, Mrs. Merritt," Patty agreed. "I think graduation agrees with him." She looked into Mike's dark eyes. "The end of one life and the beginning of another. And there are a lot of decisions to be made."

I thought you had already made up my mind for me, he told her with his eyes. You and Mom make quite a team. Why is it that these women give me so much trouble? What is it they want? "I'm just glad I have you two on my side," he countered.

"So who's taking sides?" Bee had returned. "I'm on the side of right."

"Before we start fighting any more wars, I have to go." Patty took Evelyn Merritt's white-gloved hand. "Good-bye, Mrs. Merritt. I'm very happy I had a chance to meet you."

The woman squeezed the girl's hand. "And I'm happy to have met you, dear. You come to Williamsburg sometime." She gazed up at her son. "I hope you bring her home some day, Mike."

"Sure, Mom. Patty has to catch a train back to the city."

Patty kissed Evelyn on her worn cheek. "Bye."

Bee raised his glass. "To my favorite lovebirds. Happy trails, Miss Holmes."

"I'm sure I'll see you later, Bee. Don't bore Mrs. Merritt too much. I know how you are with a captive audience."

"We'll get along just fine," Evelyn volunteered. "You have a safe trip."

Mike and Patty walked out onto the Common where they stood among a small copse of conifers. The grass glowed emerald beneath the shimmering sun beyond. But here the shadow embraced them in its cool arms. The smell of pine in summer filled Mike's nostrils, the smell of promise. He knew what was coming.

"Your mother tells me you're going to sign the contract," Patty said simply, her eyes smoldering.

Mike sent a hand through his thick curly hair. "She wants me to go to law school too."

"I know that," she said sharply. "My question is: Are you going to sign?"

"I don't know, Patty."

"I thought we had decided."

Her "we" rang in Mike's brain with a note of seriousness and danger, a note more frequently played lately in their intimate conversations. An obscure fear rose in him and he yearned to be somewhere else, to be somebody else. He didn't want to be with her now, to hash this out again for the hundredth time. She demanded too much of him.

"I've talked it over with Mo. He'll represent me. If he can get a good contract I won't rule out the possibility of playing for the Comets. I'll be in New York—"

"You could go to law school in New York." She wrapped her fingers tightly around his arm. "Mike, I don't want you to throw your life away playing a little boy's game. There's so much more to you—to life—than that."

"I can always go to law school a few years from now, or go parttime while I'm playing. Don't make me choose now. I need time."

She shook her head. "You've had all year. You can't have your cake and eat it too."

He looked down at her perfect face, her fine-spun hair blowing gently in the breeze, the yellow dress clinging to her willowy young body. "I know how you feel and you know how I feel. I haven't closed any doors yet and several have opened for me." He looked earnestly into her azure eyes. "The way I look at it, I'm the luckiest guy in the world. Five law schools to choose from. Pro basketball offers. And the most lovely and understanding woman in the world—"

She narrowed her eyes. "I know you, Mike Merritt. I

know what you're thinking. Don't play the bright-eyed innocent with me."

"Just what the hell do you mean by that?"

" 'Closing doors.' Mike, you're not telling the truth. You want to play professional basketball. You always have. I remember that night when you went on about going up against the best, Madison Square Garden, and all that. You've already made up your mind. You're just stringing us along—your mother, me, and everyone else." She relaxed her grip on his arm. "I don't like this side of you, Mike."

"What side? I haven't said or done a thing and you make it sound as if I've made some sort of pact with the devil. I just haven't made up my mind."

"I don't believe you," she said. She turned and began to walk away, into the glare of the sun.

"Come back here, goddamn it, Patty." He went after her with long angry strides. "You're not talking sense."

"No one can talk sense to you, Mike. Not when you don't listen to a damn thing they tell you. You've made up your mind. I can see it in your face."

"What do you want from me?" It was a desperate question. Yes, he *had* made up his mind. After the season the New York Comets management told him they intended to pick him first in the June college draft. He sent them to Mo who told him to play it cool. Mo was confident he could get a big six-figure contract for two or three years—if he wanted it. But Mo too hoped Mike would go to law school. As did Evelyn Merritt. As did Patty. As did everyone but Bee who stuck with his earlier dictum: "You're a big boy. Do what you want to do." And Mike Merritt wanted to play basketball in the NBA. It was his childhood dream come true. He couldn't pass up the chance. He'd be a fool. . . .

The tears welled up in Patty's eyes and spilled down her cool cheeks. "I don't know what I want from you. I never thought I'd be begging you for anything."

"Patty, there are some things—I mean, sometimes I feel as if there really is such a thing as destiny and that

I'm a part of something much larger than both of us. Basketball is a means to an end. It's not—"

"Mike, you're wasting your mind, your talents. You could be so much, do so much."

"Like what? Bee says the law is just kicking niggers' asses for white folks. I don't want any part of that."

"Bee is often quite wrong in what he says. Besides, is that what your friend Mo is doing? I thought you admired him. Is he out there just to make money?"

"No—but he's different."

"You're different too! Why can't you see that. You could make a big difference."

"Yeah, and I could also make a lot of *respectable* money." He knit his dark brow. "That's what you want. You want to marry a lawyer or banker—someone like your old man. Christ, I'd think you'd have had enough of that by now."

Hot tears streamed down her face. "Damn you, Mike Merritt," she cursed. Then she was gone, the yellow dress slicing across the lawn and disappearing into the dark porte-cochere beneath the great tower.

When Mike rejoined them, Bee and Evelyn Merritt were locked in a discussion of the Methodist Church. Mike stepped to the bar and got two drinks.

Bee dropped a cigarette and crushed it with his toe. "Your mother almost has me returning to the Christian fold," he announced.

"Now, Bee, some things shouldn't be joked about," Evelyn said.

"All right, Mrs. M. Listen, tomorrow William Sloane Coffin is preaching at Battell Chapel. We could all three get some religion there. What do you think, Mike?"

"Sure," Mike assented absently.

He nodded gravely. Was Patty right? Who was he kidding? Had he let them all down? But, hell: he was in a hurry with a long way to go. Why should they want to hold him back now?

Part 2

The Champion

7

As the 34th Street bus labored like a dinosaur through the dense streets, Mike opened the letter.

> *Dear Prince of Darkness:*
> *I miss you most so you get my first note. You'll find here no attempt to describe the beautiful ghost that haunts Old Europe. Florence is where I'm staying now and so far it's my favorite. But then so were all the others. Yesterday I found the house where Dante was born. Really a nice little bungalow and too bad they booted him out. Just this minute it has begun to rain. Sounds like a boxcar of rice being emptied on the roof of my quaint* pensione.
> *Scoured the* Trib *for Comet stats. Didn't see your name.* Perche? *How's the love life? I would have locked you in a chastity belt before I left but tempered steel is no match for a sex-crazed bimbo.* Mes affaires *have been, in a word, stupendous. A sweet middle-aged Roman called me the Blond Byron!* Mirabile Dictu. . . .

He dropped the letter in his lap. At least someone was enjoying himself.

"You're Mr. Merritt, aren't you?"

He considered answering but the voice thundered from a dozen seats away, near the rear of the bus.

"I said you're Mr. Merritt aren't you?"

"Well, yes."

As if regulated by a single switch the sea of heads turned toward him.

His accuser, an enormous woman with a face the

color of boiled ham, raised a thick finger. "This man was my son's hero until the other day. He went to see him play and waited over an hour for an autograph and he wouldn't give it to him. My boy came home in tears. These youngsters make more money in a year for doing nothing than decent hardworking people earn in a lifetime and they don't have the courtesy to answer a little boy's prayers."

He blanched under the scrutiny of pitiless faces. He remembered the brat now. He had inherited his mother's voice. "Merritt, you suck!" he shrilled from the mob outside the Garden. "Gimme your autograph!"

His accuser introduced her next piece of evidence, this morning's *New York Star*. On the back page, letters as tall as his pinky denounced THE NEWEST BUST. Mike's own copy was rolled up and stuffed in his briefcase.

"I'm glad this fella Rafferty at least tells the truth," said the woman. She departed, to Mike's relief, at Fifth Avenue. "You'll get what's coming to you," she warned. "Just wait."

The guys on the team were right. Keep away from public transportation. This was going to be a bad day. First the terrible article by Matt Rafferty, fourth in a series on Mike's failings, and now this. He suddenly wished he hadn't arranged to meet the reporter later this afternoon.

He couldn't recall a single time in his life when so much had gone so badly. Patty knew what she was talking about. It was what he deserved for playing a little boy's game instead of going about the business of becoming a man.

Where was she at this moment; what was she doing? Had she found someone else, someone brimming with the qualities he lacked—maturity, seriousness? Was he well-traveled, an art-lover? For whom did the eyes now sparkle, the pale polished cheeks glow?

At Seventh Avenue a cluster of hands yanked the

buzzer. Mike followed the crowd hiving onto the sidewalk. It flashed beneath an impeccable autumn sky. Among the decaying streets and soot-blasted buildings of Depression Manhattan Madison Square Garden squatted intrusively. Once inside the arena he followed a lime corridor to the Comets' promotion department.

On a teammate's advice Mike had carefully avoided this outpost of the Comets organization. He assumed his disappointing start justified this policy until an angry letter from a Comets vice president reminded him that "good faith cooperation with the organization top to bottom" headed the list of nebulous riders on his celebrated contract. He should have listened to Mo who wanted the riders stricken altogether.

Just inside the open door of the promotion department a young woman smiled up at him from behind the massive switchboard atop her metal desk. "I know who you are," she murmured as Mike started to give his name.

"Then tell me who you are."

Her laugh was silky and rich. "I'm all kinds of people."

"Well, give me one name to go on."

"Darlene. Simmons. That's one name extra."

He took a seat in a high-backed chair of unyielding leather. Why did he never feel whole without a woman; why had it always been that way? Did they see through him, beyond the ambition and the gifts, to the weakness, the frailty, the fears? Men you played with or against. You faced them in battle and either won or lost. But women wanted more. They wanted you to molt your public image and relinquish to them the pulpy mess you had struggled all along to conceal. They wanted you to overcome yourself. And how could you help but disappoint them? They asked for the impossible; they insisted you be better than you actually were; nothing less would do. And they were willing to wait, with sanguine patience, for the worst to emerge. If you were an All-American hero they were more distrustful than ever. Would so much be expected of a 5'8" Mike Merritt with a flabby gut and glasses?

Take this small exotic beauty with caramel skin, her face immobile as her fingers roamed the switchboard. What did she think of him? Was there a trace of irony in her "I know who you are"? Did he appear smug, full of himself, unconscious of the world around him? Did he expect everyone to know who he was?

Darlene Simmons looked up from the coruscating lights and informed him that Mr. Wexler was off the phone and eager to see him.

Henry Wexler was a grinning man with sparse hair and eyes bright as marbles. Mike proffered a lamer defense against his rapid-fire publicity schemes than he had the night before in fifteen minutes of play against the Lakers. His excuse then was the presence of the mythical Elgin Baylor, whose inspired play in the waning light of his noble career moved Mike enormously. Moved him, in fact, back to the bench and a disgusted coach. Wexler no less ably outfoxed the rookie; he flatfootedly consented to a dozen appearances at schools and stores and supermarkets in three states.

"You'll love Connecticut. Classy people there, really. Classy state." Wexler's glossy face beamed as remembrance overtook him. "Hey, you put in some time in Connecticut, right? So you know what a classy state it is."

Mike supposed it was.

"We're going to make a winning combination," pronounced Wexler, springing to his feet to pump Mike's hand. He concluded with a warm invitation to stop by any time "you feel the urge."

On the street, an electronic clock insidiously marked the progress of heartless time down to the tenth of each fading second, reminding him that the most unpleasant business of the day was still ahead. At four o'clock he was to meet that reporter at MacElroy's Bar, kitty-corner from the Garden. It was now 3:30, a good time to steel himself with a drink.

Mac, with a grin, looked up from swabbing the bar and Mike asked him to bring a scotch to his customary table. There he opened his copy of the *Star* and gloomily scanned the article. It was smeared with his outraged marginalia. When Mac appeared with the drink, Mike made room for it and invited the bartender to sit down.

"Might as well. Getting too old to be on my feet all day. Been doing it for thirty years and I guess I won't stop till I die."

Mike looked at the bartender's fleshy friendly face. "How old are you, Mac?"

"Fifty-nine. That used to be me." He pointed a stubby finger at a faded picture of a boxer hanging askew on the dingy wall. "Fought for five years. Quit one fight too late." He grinned ghoulishly, revealing a wobby and incomplete set of teeth. "Ran into Joe Louis on his way up. Boy was he a hungry fighter."

Mike dropped his eyes to the *Star*, spread in the dim light like a sacred text.

"What you got there?" asked Mac. His moist eyes squinted.

" 'A sober analysis of the shortcomings of Mike Merritt, the Comets' newest bust.' "

"You ought to know better than to read that shit."

"Jesus, Mac, how can I avoid it?" He held up the offending newsprint, complete with photographs of Mike as "headline-grabbing radical" and "smug first-round draft choice."

The bartender looked away as if blinded. "If you got any sense you'll ignore that bastard."

"Don't think I haven't tried. But this is the last straw. I decided I'd better talk it out with him. See what's on his mind."

A look of disbelief crossed Mac's beefy face. "You're asking for trouble."

"He should be here in a few minutes. I called him yesterday."

Mac's silence bespoke his disapproval.

"Goddamn it, Mac, this really upsets me. None of what he says is true. It's just name-calling. Why should anyone stand to have lies written about him? Especially in a rag like this?"

"He's paid to start trouble. Does it every year as soon as the Comets start to fold."

"That's no excuse for this kind of viciousness."

"You're better off taking your lumps, but it's your business." Mac shambled back to the bar.

Mike found out where Rafferty stood back in June when the cream of the college crop was auctioned off in the Plaza Hotel. The pre-selected first choice stood nervously in the wings, awaiting official confirmation, girding himself for a skirmish with the press.

From the claque of sportswriters came applause and good-natured questions and Mike enjoyed the give-and-take until a raspy query reached his ears from lips molded around a filterless cigarette.

"Is it true that college basketball's biggest radical insisted on the most lucrative contract in the history of the NBA?"

"The Comets did all the insisting," Mike replied. "I just signed."

"You don't look too guilty about making three hundred grand a year."

"Is that how much I'm making?"

"You tell me."

"Talk to my agent."

"I'm asking you. Is that what you were marching for a couple years back? For fat contracts from establishment corporations? How does that sit with your so-called radicalism? Or was it just headline-grabbing? Radical today, multimillionaire tomorrow?"

"Times change."

"But principles don't. Provided you got them."

It was not a pretty exchange and Rafferty had to be muzzled by his colleagues, who seemed as repelled by the rumpled reporter as was Mike himself.

The most troubling aspect of Rafferty's recent

insinuations was the distinct impression Mike got that he had heard it all before. From the mouth of his own coach, no less. The words were very nearly the same and the voltage of rancor ran just as high. All that nonsense about wealthy young ballplayers who had forgotten basketball was a game and not a business. His own coach was feeding Rafferty his stale lines—an unseemly alliance but not an unlikely one. The pair were on cozy terms and shared a bilious disposition.

It was five o'clock when a figure made its way into the gloom of MacElroy's. Expecting to see his nemesis, Mike strained to make out the peculiar cast of Darlene Simmons's face—the bushy light Afro, the creamy skin, the nose softly blunted at the tip. He joined her at the bar.

"Oh my," she said by way of accepting his offer of a drink. "A treat from the star."

"Not a star yet, I'm afraid."

"As far as promo goes you are. Like a bestseller. Sell a million before you hit the stands."

"And forgotten a month later. Come sit down."

She trailed him back to his corner. She was tiny, barely five feet tall, with a choppy busy stride. Mac came by moments later with her whiskey sour. She spoke in soft rippling tones. "I like the way you play."

"That's a good one. Nobody else does."

"They don't know the game. They expect thirty points."

"So do I."

"I don't believe it. I see how you move on the court. You look for the open man, you take the right shots, you help out on defense."

"Where did you learn all that?"

"I'm a black girl, my man. I know the game. It's Curry; he's always been that way, jealous of the kids, especially since the big money started rolling their way. Am I right?"

"One hundred percent."

"Also, you're trying too hard. You move like a

dream but you're uptight. You're playing scared." She tamped a cigarette on the table. "Can't be uptight. That's the beauty of the game. Free as the wind and always moving. It's the way you got to be." A flame flared up from a black lighter etched with her initials in gold.

"Let's talk about you," Mike suggested.

"You don't want to know about me."

"Why not?"

"You and I play a different game."

"What's yours—aside from riddles?"

"Survival. Give the beast its due."

"What beast?"

She smiled. "Honey, dey's all kin' beese and dey all be afta yo' ass."

He sighed. "I'm lost."

"I told you before. I'm all kinds of people." She patted his arm with a miniature hand. "You're not such a nasty boy as you think. You just have some growing up to do. You think everybody has to love you. You cut up your own heart and pass out the pieces like souvenirs."

He winced. "That bad?"

"I say it was bad?"

"It sure sounds bad."

"The truth never sounds too pretty. Big man, big heart."

"You're putting me on. Women have accused me of plenty, but being big-hearted's a new one."

"They don't know you."

"And you do?"

She crumpled the butt, blooded with lipstick, into the ashtray. "Maybe I do." She gathered the straps of her purse and buttoned her leather coat. "It's been nice talking to you."

"Shall I see you home?"

"No," she said. "Thanks a lot, but I got business to attend to."

"I'll see you to the door."

"My, he's a gentleman."
Mike plunked a fiver on Mac's gleaming bar.
"What about Rafferty?" the bartender asked.
"Give him my best."

A week later he lay restlessly on his living room couch. His eastern wall was a window. Across the East River was Long Island City—squat warehouses and factories and water towers like little silos on stilts. On Bee's advice he employed an interior decorator to do the place up. The fee bit substantially into his bonus and hardly seemed worth it. The simulated expansiveness ("I'm striving for a concept of space," minced the decorator, accentuated his loneliness and the chrome threw back sterile images of himself.

He paced the polyurethane-glazed floors like a caged animal, looking for something to do, someplace to go, desiring an escape from himself. He couldn't bug Mo again. He called the lawyer nearly every day and met him for a hamburger after each home game. Without Mo Silver he just might hurl himself out his picture window. A great friend was Mo, a believer in Mike Merritt. It was Mo who pleaded with him to be patient, to bide his time. "Your day will come," was his theme. "They can't keep you down forever."

There was the girl, Darlene. He could get her number from the promo office. Hell, she'd be there now. Only artists and athletes had time on their hands in the middle of the week. The rest of New York worked. He could call her up. Dinner, a movie, a drink. She liked him. He knew that as soon as she smiled up at him from her desk. She probably had a lover. What girl didn't? But lovers didn't last forever, that he knew. He couldn't get over her skin, the color of pale chocolate milk, and her eyes like obsidian disks.

"Well, hello there," she said when he called.
"I thought maybe we could get together sometime."
"Sometime?"
"This evening, after you get off. For a drink."

"I don't know."

"Please. It doesn't have to be a drink. A movie, a show—what do you like to do?"

"I like to talk."

"Then a drink."

"You're very persistent."

"You're off at five, right?"

Her sigh was musical, a dreamy moan. "Mac was good to us."

"Mac's it is."

Darlene was there when he arrived. She was nursing a whiskey sour in the same dark corner where they had sat before.

He convinced her to say a little about herself.

"My daddy was a nigger from Atlanta who came North to be free and find a big-city job." She laughed humorlessly. "The joke was on him. He got himself a big-city job all right—cleaning out the bathrooms in Penn Station. Until a couple of years ago you could still see him there, mopping up after bums who couldn't score with the urinals."

She slipped a small hand into her large purse and tore the plastic off a fresh pack of cigarettes.

"Then he found himself a white woman. She taught his high-school equivalency course. He was a real sucker for that stuff. A regular immigrant nigger. This middle-aged white lady teacher loved the way my daddy wanted to read and write. If he made it as a postal clerk someday, that was just fine with her. She invited him to bed and twisted his arm to marry her. Then the lily started to fester. She split two weeks after I was born." Darlene exhaled a musty stream. "She visited us once a week. Awful mother but a great teacher. Taught me and Daddy at the same time—every Wednesday evening. When the lesson ended she kissed us both on the forehead and made her prim fat-assed way downstairs to the cab. I suppose I owe her something. She taught me how to speak like a little white lady. You know what she said when I told her I was going to secretarial school? She said, 'Booker T. Washington must be smiling in heaven!'"

After the third drink Mike took her hand and their knees brushed under the table. He helped her with her coat. At the bar he paid Mac.

They sped through the empty streets of midtown, and then through the curving darkness of Central Park, to the West Side. Darlene directed the driver to a lurid block where men stood below a neon sign, hands plunged in their pockets, each head hatted and gazing toward some distant point, muttering. About him?

The decrepit, paint-splashed stairway conveyed not a hint of the opulence of Darlene's apartment. She led him through a glimmering hardwood foyer into a showcase of chrome and glass and deep pile carpets.

"This is quite a place."

"Some of us niggers live pretty good."

"I didn't realize receptionists were paid so well."

She smiled. "You want to talk salary or you want to have a good time?"

It was an experience that sent him orbiting blissful heavens. Darlene cooed and sighed and gasped at the wonders of his body—so long, so supple, so strong. She hungered after every inch, taking him in with an aria of pleasure that stirred him to superhuman efforts. She grabbed and bit and tore, pumping her small luscious thighs like wings, emitting wild sounds. Then there was a moment of giddy suspension before he spilled into her, sapped of his seed and his strength.

As winter descended on New York with preemptive grimness it was Darlene who saved him from despair. He saw her once or twice a week, not nearly as often as he would have liked, but she was a busy girl with mysterious obligations of her own. She refused to go to his place on the East Side and insisted he call her only at the office. She answered his questions cryptically, if at all, and soon he got the message and abandoned his efforts. Otherwise she was a delight. And she loved the game. After he chalked up a creditable performance she pulled out notes and encouraging statistics on his offensive rebounding, assists, shooting, steals. When Curry yanked him back to the bench she shared his outrage at "that bald-headed fart of a coach."

Although Mike never succeeded in contacting Rafferty, the reporter had suddenly ceased to vilify him in his daily column. Still the rookie read every edition of the *Star* with nervous expectancy, since Rafferty was not likely to make such an immediate about-face without a darkly calculated purpose. Mike braced himself for the inevitable assault. He would have been less anxious if his performance on the court had shown improvement. But Coach Curry continued to ridicule his manifold inadequacies, paralyzing him into ineffectiveness. And the Comets continued to lose. After they dropped seven consecutive games—four to lowly expansion teams—Mike became a fixture on the bench, sent out only to gather a few crumbs after the feast was over.

It was during such an assignment that he first rendered intelligible a chant emanating from the farthest reaches of the Garden, a deep rumbling somehow connected with his presence on the court. For several games he had, against his better judgment, struggled to translate this mystifying noise into a comprehensible message.

Either the hecklers were in good voice or his ears were tuned more sharply to the melody of abuse, but when he was sent in during the fourth quarter the droning gained a clarity it lacked before. The repeated phrase struck him with the obviousness of something suddenly remembered.

Rafferty's right—send back the chump!

He felt a twinge of nausea as he took his place beside Lincoln Moore, the Celtics' heralded sixth man.

"Don't let 'em get to you, man," Moore

sympathized. "They don't know shit."

It was easy for him to say. While Mike's lofty promise was stunted amid the jungle of the NBA, Linc was blossoming like a wildflower, having discovered an environment appropriate to his natural skills. Coming off the bench he threw the fastbreaking Celtics into overdrive. Against the Comets this evening he had racked up twenty, reducing the home team's defense to bumbling ineffectiveness.

Mike lunged clumsily as Moore, waving the ball ten feet from the basket, jerked his ebony head in the direction of a man cutting across the lane, then bounced the sphere behind his back and into the hands of a guard skipping around the key, who cleanly ruffled the net as the buzzer sounded. The Celtics won by 33, handing the Comets their most humiliating loss of the season.

Later that evening, in Darlene's living room, Mike mused morosely. With or without him, the Comets were consigned to mediocrity if they didn't evolve a consistent style of play. As it was they tried to ape the opposition. When the Bulls came to town, they executed plays taken from instruction books. Against the Celtics, they tried to run. They were amorphous, a team without character. Blame that on Curry, who knew as much about basketball as old Jock Ryan.

He contemplated Darlene curled up like a kitten before her monolithic color TV. He felt better just being in the same room with her, neither one of them uttering a word. She understood his silence after a bad game. Darlene felt his eyes on her and puckered her lips in a pantomime of a kiss. He smiled gratefully and turned his attention to the street below.

Oftentimes interesting characters flowed in and out of the joint across the way, called simply "The Club," its name scripted in red neon on a sign fixed over the door. Now, as he peered out, a black limousine slithered into view, coughing up first a plume of exhaust that misted in the wintry air and then three passengers, the last topped by a broad-brimmed hat. The hat tilted up toward Darlene's window revealing an almost expressionless face bathed in lurid light. The man beneath the hat stepped into a phone booth while his companions stood guard.

Moments later Darlene's telephone trilled. She slipped into her bedroom without a word and drew the door shut behind her. Mike crept across the carpet, fell to his knees, and fastened his ear to the keyhole.

Darlene was speaking in the thick slurring tones she ordinarily reserved for jests. "You know I do, sugah," she drawled. Then her tone hardened. "Jes hol' on, honey."

He heard the receiver rattle onto her bedside table. She had caught him—what point was there in hiding? The door snapped open and Darlene glared at him icily. "Get away from this door," she hissed, then slammed it in his face.

He backed away foolishly then returned to the window. The caller emerged from the booth and the limousine swung around to engorge him. Mike made a mental note of the plates as it sped into the darkness.

The bedroom door opened and Darlene approached in her busy sexy walk, her eyes burning into his. Her pouty mouth was grim.

"Next time you do that boy, you're out of luck."

He hung his head. "I'm sorry."

"All right. Now you stop spying on your mama and give her some sweet loving instead."

Darlene had a lover and judging from the rigid set of his broad face and that pair of goons who traveled with him he was no one to tangle with. This man was no mere boyfriend. He was most likely Darlene's benefactor, her sugar daddy. A receptionist's salary didn't finance furs and chrome furnishings no matter how low rents were in the rickety rattraps uptown.

He considered, then rejected, wild and unsavory possibilities. Darlene was a whore and this man her pimp. She was an addict and he her supplier. Stuff for the movies, not for a hard-headed young woman with secretarial skills and a fancy accent.

Still the fact remained that she lived well above her means and the man who kept her there shimmied about town in a limousine padded with bodyguards. Perhaps his hold on her was precisely that, a strangling grip; perhaps he knew things and used them to keep her in line as well as in riches. The poor girl was powerless to help herself, at any rate too frightened to quit the sordid arrangement. Mike knew about the ghetto. He had spent a whole summer there. From Captain Bobby and the other kids he had heard gruesome stories of jealous and insane lovers packing weapons, of vows sealed in blood, of menace and manglings. Darlene mistook him for an Ivy League square, utterly incapable of dealing with the harsh facts of street life. She would find out otherwise.

No doubt about it, once she saw he knew the score, Darlene's defenses would dissipate and she would sail into his arms, sobbing with gratitude, liberated at last from the ogre who ruled her affairs. Whether she knew it or not she wanted him to free her. Hadn't she telegraphed the desperation of her secret life—even if she kept the particulars to herself? The fault lay with him, for being too caught up in his own niggling concerns to decode the message.

The thing to do was shatter the mystery that obscured and protected the stranger with the hat. With only a license plate to go on, a call to the police meant long-winded explanations, fabricated tales of threats and harassment, and worse, divulging his own name. It might reach the tabloids and reward him only with grief. Where else could he turn? There was always Mo, eternally helpful and wise, with advice both canny and shrewd. But he dreaded the lawyer's reaction to his spying, as Darlene had so succinctly termed it. If anything raised Mo Silver's hackles, it was subterfuge, of any description, whether practiced by the CIA, overzealous activists, or love-struck clients.

His lone recourse then was Mortimer Wright, a man of infinite contacts and wide-ranging influence. His ladyish fingertips mastered the circuits of power.

"You needn't bring this matter up with the police," intoned the financier, returning Mike's call. "I have an understanding with the commissioner. Just how serious are these threats?"

"They're not threats exactly, just abusive comments and the like. And I'm kind of curious to know who the man is. There's no reason to give the commissioner the impression I'm in danger."

"You simply would like to know something about your accuser."

"Yes."

"I'll see what I can do."

It was a small lie—no harm done.

Friday Darlene served him dinner in her apartment. They ate in her sparkling dining room on an oaken table scrubbed to a high sheen. The unremitting dead-winter cold rasped harmlessly against the curtained windows. The quiche was good and the hostess delectable in a pastel sweater and diamond earrings that flared in the candlelight like miniscule torches.

Mike uncorked the wine, a fragrant French red.

"I'm sorry I got so mad at you the other day," Darlene apologized between sips.

He shrugged magnanimously. "Entirely my fault."

"You shouldn't have sneaked up on me like that, but I can't blame you for being curious."

"I worry about you, but as long as you know what you're doing . . ."

Her cheeks hollowed around a cigarette. "Does this lady seem like she doesn't know what she's doing?"

"Not in the least. I'm the hopeless mass of confusion."

"It's no good getting down on yourself. Whoever you are is good enough."

"I know some people who might not agree."

"Thinking about that Yale girl?"

Was there a hint of jealousy in her tone? "Patty? She couldn't overcome her preconceptions but there's no crime in that. You're right. You can't change people."

Darlene nodded. "You're learning, lover."

"I've always been an apt pupil."

Darlene circled the table and brushed her lips against his ear. "Since you're being so reasonable I'm going to let you spend the night. No midnight cab."

A breakthrough of sorts, since in the three months he'd known her she had never yet permitted him to sleep over. He thanked her with a kiss.

They made love until daylight cracked the heavy drapes in the bedroom. Then they both dozed off, exhausted, only to awake to a ringing telephone. Darlene grumpily reached a gracile arm to her nightstand. Puzzlement disturbed her sleepy face. "For you."

"Hello."

It was Mortimer Wright. "The car in question is leased not to a man but to a corporation called JOB, Inc. I don't know whether the O is long or short. At any rate, it's an acryonym for one Jasper O. Brown. He calls himself an importer but he is better known to the police as a drug dealer. Heroin, cocaine. On a significant scale, I might add."

"I see."

"Listen, son. If you're in any way involved with this thug—"

"Of course not, sir."

"Just be careful. He sounds like a desperate character. Ruthless as well."

"Yes, sir. Thanks a lot."

"All right, then. Glad to be of service."

Darlene sat up and pulled the flannel sheet up to her soft chin. A storm was brewing in her black eyes. "Who was that?"

"A guy I used to work for."

"What's he doing calling here? I told you not to give anyone my number."

"I didn't."

She sprang out of bed like a cat, clutching the sheet. "Don't you lie to me. Get out! Right now!"

He took her arm. "But, Darlene, let me explain—"

"I'm not interested in your explanations. Get out!" She sat down huffily on the corner of the immense bed, her lips quivering.

"Honestly, I never gave anyone your number. Why would I lie to you?"

"I don't know. I just know I got to be alone now."

"I'm sorry. He won't do it again."

"I don't want to argue with you. Just leave."

"I'll call you later when you're not so upset."

"It better be in a long time. I'm not sure I want to hear from you again."

He slipped into his clothes and out the door. The wind howled through the expanse of empty lots, singing mournfully in the swinging wires. No cab passed for half an hour. Finally he flagged one down. "Straight down to 23rd," he directed the driver.

"Stay on Eighth?"

"That's right."

Damn that Mortimer Wright! How did he get her number and how much did he know? Was the call to Darlene's place a warning to keep away from her? He had never seen her so furious.

Mo Silver's Chelsea apartment was in a red building with a tar-colored fire escape zig-zagging in front and a delicatessen next door. Mike took the five flights three steps at a time.

The door opened to a large young woman in a pink robe. One hand held a towel turbaned around the head of Sheila Martin, Mo's steady girlfriend since he left Yale.

"Hi, Mike. Come in. Mo was just fuming about you."

"Uh-oh."

"Not at you, but that reporter, what's his name."

"Rafferty!" Mo bellowed from the couch by a

window bathed in yellow light.

Sheila grinned and Mike did too. He couldn't help it. Her own smile was so funny, so wide and pleased with itself. Her warm gray eyes crinkled below a wide brow and a few wet black strands escaped from her turban.

"I should have called first," Mike said.

"Don't be silly. As soon as I get dressed I'm fixing an enormous brunch for Mo, I mean for us."

Her bare feet were the least bit ducklike. He enjoyed watching them pad along the floor, leaving behind ghostly traces of baby powder.

The living room was a comfortable mess. The unmatched furniture was so worn it invited you to wear it out more. Next to the battered stereo records were piled four feet high—overflow from the loaded shelves. Books bulged out of an immense bookcase and littered the apartment like clues, bookmarks sticking out like crumpled tongues. Mo held a slim stack of sports pages, gutted from newspapers that lay scattered at his feet like so many husks. Eventually the attorney would absorb every word. Mo was not content to leave any corner of the world uninvestigated. He knew about earthquakes in China, obscure executions in Tehran, arms sales in Africa, escaped murderers lurking in the wilds of Tennessee, starlets twinkling on Malibu Beach.

Mike sank into an overstuffed chair by the crackling hearth. He had grown close to Mo in these rough months. At Yale, the activist had always been a valued friend, but Bee was his companion at arms, his confidant, his soulmate. Mo, five years older and far more mature, was already a man while Mike based in the sunny days of boyhood. Now, as he stumbled into adulthood, he relied increasingly upon his solid, serious, thoughtful friend. He found reassurance in Mo's modest home and in his enduring relationship with Sheila. She was a community organizer; what better match for a politically-conscious attorney? The couple shared a smoldering hatred for those who wielded power corruptly. But they bore only good will to their friends.

Mo's sad intelligent eyes peered into the face of his young client. "No steam pouring out of your ears so it can't be Rafferty or Curry. But something's got you down."

"That's why I'm here."

"Get it off your chest and then wait till you see this meal Sheila's making. It came to me last night in a sort of vision: steak, eggs, hash browns, peas—"

Mike shook his head. "Just not in an eating mood these days."

Mo's glanced lingered over Mike's lean frame. "What do you weigh these days? Two-ten?"

"Twelve—almost."

"Still not enough."

"The appetite comes and goes. Jesus, when I was a kid I ate enough for three. My mom'd make six portions. She ate half of one, my dad ate two, and I ate the rest." He patted his stomach. "Used to be it roared. Now it barely whimpers."

"Travel's hard on it. All the cities, the planes, the irregular schedule."

"That and other things."

"Patty?"

Mike smiled. "Who's Patty?"

Sheila, wearing jeans and a Comets sweatshirt, brought in coffee. "I bet it's that pretty girl who goes to the games with the fur coat."

Mike took his coffee. "I didn't think anyone knew."

"What girl?" asked Mo.

"I've pointed her out at least three times. Teeny, with a beautiful complexion."

"Guess I wasn't listening."

"Oh, really?"

"Basketball's not just a social event, you know."

"Her name's Darlene Simmons," said Mike, "and she's the receptionist at the promo office and I'm crazy about her."

"Great," said Mo. "One of the family."

Sheila's eyes melted consolingly. "Are you having

problems?"

"Yes, in a way. I mean, it's great but there is this other guy."

"Oh, Mike."

Mo shrugged. "May the best man win."

"It must be wonderful," said Sheila, "to have such a sympathetic agent. Are you serious about Darlene? She's very pretty."

"I don't know. I suppose I must be to come barging in like this. I always knew there was another guy. She won't talk about him. He's older and buys her fancy clothes and keeps her in a flashy apartment. He's some kind of gangster."

"Gangster?" the couple repeated in unison.

"Jasper Brown. A drug peddler. He has bodyguards and a Caddy a block long."

"I know of him," Mo said. "Recently paroled from Sing Sing. I'd be careful."

"Does he know about you?" asked Sheila.

"I don't know. He scares me and I think he scares her."

"He scares me," said Mo.

"What are you going to do?"

"*I'm* going to check on the steaks," said Mo. "Talk loudly."

"I don't know, Sheila. You can't imagine what Darlene is like. She's funny and tough and she's younger than I am but she knows so much and she loves the game. I can't get enough of her. Patty—my old girlfriend—was a lot different. Sometimes I got the feeling she didn't approve of me. She couldn't understand my wanting to play ball, for one thing, and she wasn't too hot on the activism. Compared to what Mo was doing my political consciousness was embryonic, but still she didn't approve. Now that I've found someone who respects what I do and why, I see how good a relationship can be—and how important."

Mo reappeared, spatula in hand, grease dabbled on his flannel shirt. "Why don't you marry her?" The seated pair stared at him as if a panhandler had wandered in off the streets. "It's not such a strange idea. People do it all the time."

"All right, Mo. You and I can be next."

Mike laughed. "We could have a double ceremony."

Mo turned to Sheila. "You never said you wanted me to marry you."

"You never bothered to ask."

The lawyer rocked lightly on his heels, thinking. "No, I guess I never did."

Sheila yanked the spatula out of his hand and stalked into the kitchen.

"See what you're missing?"

"Doesn't seem so bad to me."

"I guess not." Mo fell back onto the embattled couch and crossed his thick legs. "Seems to me you've got three choices. One, you continue with Darlene the way you have been. Only you'd better be careful. I mean that. Jasper Brown is more than just a character. He is very real. Don't get in over your head."

"What do you mean?"

"The man is one of the biggest pushers in Harlem."

"Darlene's not an addict if that's what you mean. I considered that myself. She's beautiful and she has a steady job and she's—healthy."

"Okay. She's just his girlfriend. I'm not telling you not to see her."

"I know, I know. The other two choices?"

"They're obvious, I think."

"Forget about her completely or—"

"Marry her."

It almost made sense. He would pull Darlene up from the charred ruins of the "Valley" and install her in his place on the thirtieth floor. An entire wall facing the river and, at night, helicopters sparkling in the sky like fireflies. She could move her furniture right in, if Jasper didn't want it back. No reason for Darlene to be ashamed of a ballplayer, not considering the company she was used to. A pusher—might as well call him a killer.

"You know, Mo, you may have something there. It's a big step but it's got to happen some time."

Sheila appeared suddenly, her hands on her hips. "I don't believe what I'm hearing. The two of you mooning about marriage like a couple of teenyboppers. I'd like to know when Mo Silver contemplated marriage for one second."

"I only suggested it as a logical possibility." Mo escaped into the kitchen and returned with plates and utensils. Next came a platter loaded with steaks, and another with eggs. Gemmy peas heaped in a bowl glistened under melting butter.

Mike swallowed and his stomach felt cavernous. "That looks awfully good."

"Now you're talking."

"I'll get the hash browns," Sheila volunteered.

It was noon and the sun was growing paler. Mo stuck Mozart on the record player and the sweet notes lilted, then died, trailing a wake of melancholy silence. How simple it was! He would meet Darlene in Mac's and spring the proposal. He could barely wait to see the expression on her face. The honeymoon would have to wait until the season was over....

Mo forked another steak on his plate. "What do you think of this breakfast brainstorm?"

"Brainstorm is the word."

He gave Darlene the rest of the weekend to blow off steam then called her Monday at the promo office. A strange edginess cut into her honeyed words. She didn't sound overjoyed to hear from him; still she agreed to meet him after work at Mac's.

He fretted nervously all day. At the Comets practice session he was worthless. Another rookie, whom Mike usually owned, pushed him all over the court. Curry, for once, was easy on him, however, doubtless because Mike's gaffes on the court gave him satisfaction enough.

He arrived at Mac's at 4:30 and quickly drained a scotch and water. How should he do it—come right out with it, blurt the fateful words as soon as she took off her coat? Was it all right to propose in a bar? Maybe if she was feeling affectionate she would want to go to her place. There he would take her hand, staring soulfully into her bituminous eyes. The dropping-down-on-one-knee business was absurd, so chuck that. Her beautiful face would soften and her bosom would heave and her arms would be around his neck, clinging, while she purred in his ear. Then he would assure her patiently that he was in earnest. If she liked she could move in with him today, although he doubted she'd go for that. Women took time adjusting to things. She would want to poke around his apartment and see what it needed. As for the wedding, he preferred a very simple ceremony—if there must be any kind of to-do at all—his mother, her father. Mo and Sheila. Too bad Bee wasn't around. What religion was she? He would leave the honeymoon up to her. Maybe the West Indies or Hawaii.

The doorway was darkened by two figures. The small silhouette was Darlene's; the second he remembered vaguely but couldn't place. It was of average height but its breadth filled the doorway. Darlene made her way through the gray light of the bar.

She plunked down across the table from him. Her nose and eyes were red.

"Darlene, you've got a cold. Take your coat off. Otherwise you'll get overheated."

She shook her head. "I can't stay."

"You will after I tell you what's going to happen to us."

"Nothing's going to happen to us."

"No, listen—"

"I'm going to be married."

"How'd you guess?" he said, insanely.

"Me and Jasper."

He froze. "What are you talking about?" he

managed at last.

"He's right there waiting for me so I got to make it fast."

"Oh God, Darlene."

"Let me explain. When Jasper found me three years ago I was nobody, turning tricks on 26th Street. East Side. There's a little hotel. No fancy call girl, you understand, but for twenty bucks you could have this fine meat and for ten I'd give head."

"Oh God, Darlene."

"You wanted to know about me. Here's your chance to hear it, 'cause I'm never saying it again. One night some bastard beat me up and wouldn't give me the ten and I was crying and hating myself. You can't ever know what that is like, selling yourself. Well, a big black Caddy pulled over to where I was and swallowed me up and inside was this fine-looking man, black as your heart, and dressed like a duke. I was scared. I thought maybe he was some bigtime pimp gonna claim me for his stable. He asked me how old I was and I said seventeen. Then he hit me, stung me right across the face. And I started crying again. Haven't you got no shame, he said. What's your poor mama thinking now? And I told him I didn't have a mama and he said where'd you learn to talk like that. And I told him. And then he asked me where I lived and I said nowhere. I've got no place to go to, I said, and he said then you'll be my girl. And I thought better him than these stinking honkies. And now I'm his special girl, dig. Only the best clients get me, and they pay two hundred for it. And nobody hurts me either."

He stared, speechless.

"Now you know and remember I never wanted to tell you and it's nobody's fault but your own for asking. Jasper helped me when I was nowhere. When I was black and I was white and I wasn't either. Jasper told me I was somebody and he gave me pride and made me feel I belonged. I never belonged before and now I do. I belong with Jasper. It has to be that way, honey."

"But, Darlene, it's special with us, you said so yourself. Nobody makes you feel like I do. Marry me instead."

Tears filmed her huge eyes. "Baby, you got to understand. You and me are different people. We got different places to go. How're you going to show me off to your fancy Yale friends and later, when you become a lawyer, how you going to feel with me as your wife?"

"Let me worry about that. If it was up to me, we'd be staying in my apartment right now, and we'd be together all the time. You're the one who won't be seen in public with me, who hides from my friends. The only people who matter are the ones who'll see we have something special. The rest can go fuck themselves."

"Honey, you don't even know me."

"Only because you won't let me. Why does everything have to be such a mystery with you? I know all about Jasper. Who he is and how he makes his living. He's a killer; for all he taught you about being black he's killing his own people off with drugs. He's no better than some fucking Klansman."

Darlene stood and touched his arm. "You don't know what you're saying. 'Cause you ain't seen anything yet. Everything's always been real easy for you. Jasper is a man and you're still a boy. You're a nice boy, when you're not like this, and that's how I want to remember you, so I'm leaving now."

The busy little legs carried her right out of his life. She was Jasper's wife and the prime filly in his stable, entertaining his friends at two C's a shot. She was gone.

He needed a drink. He made his way over to the bar which Mac pretended to swab. "Scotch, Mac. No water."

"Hurts to lose a looker like that, don't it?"

"Yeah."

"Don't look now but a buddy of yours just strolled in." The bartender folded his stumpy arms on the bar and nodded in the direction of the door. Encased in a drab trenchcoat and crowned in a shapeless hat, a cigarette drooping from his lips, stood Matt Rafferty. One side of his mouth hooked into a sardonic smile as he wheezed onto a stool beside the rookie.

"This your regular drinking hour?" he demanded.

Mike said nothing.

"Not that I don't understand your being here. I mean things haven't been going exactly your way, have they? It's funny but for a while you had me fooled, just the way you fooled everybody else. But the NBA ain't the Ivy League, is it, kid?"

"Shut up, Rafferty," said Mac.

The reporter's washed-out eyes centered on Mike. "They paid you what, a mil, mil and a quarter? Take the money and run, kid. It's yours—they can't take it back even though they wish they could. Go back to Illinois and be a Great White Hope." Rafferty paused to let the dead cigarette fall from his lips and popped in a replacement. "Then again, you got some powerful friends in this town."

"What are you talking about?" said Mike.

"Don't pull that shit with me, Merritt. I fell for it once when you were supposed to meet me here."

"You didn't show."

"Yeah, I wonder why that was?"

"So do I."

The reporter's laugh was raspy. "I bet you do. You're not only a fake, you're a liar as well."

Mike shrugged. "If you've got it in for me it's your business, I suppose."

Rafferty turned to Mac. "Tell me something, friend. You've known me a long time, right?"

"Long enough."

"Ever known me to stop giving the business to a guy when I had the goods on him? Ever wonder why all of a sudden this guy's name practically disappeared from my column?"

"Figured maybe you thought better of it," the bartender growled.

Again Rafferty laughed mirthlessly. "Sure I thought

better of it. After my boss told me to lay off because certain influential parties didn't want their crybaby roughed up. Isn't that right, Merritt? You overrated lummox."

Mike's response was involuntary. Suddenly his drink was all over Rafferty's face. The reporter gasped and sputtered and would have fallen off his stool if Mac hadn't snatched his lapels with a big right hand. "Looks like you've had too many, Matt. Better take off. Drink's on the house."

The reporter righted himself then slid onto his feet. His face was scarlet and he jabbed a finger at Mike. "I'm going to ruin you," he said. "I'm going to run you out of town. I know all about you—everything. You know where I was today? At the promo office. I heard that little nigger receptionist talking to you on the phone. I know who she runs around with. And I know all about that fag Mortimer Wright and—"

"Pack it up, Matt," MacElroy advised.

"I'm going, goddamn it. But I'm telling you now, Merritt. You'll live to regret this day." He spun on his heel and careened out of the bar.

"I don't know, kid," said Mac, watching the reporter leave. "You're not making anybody too happy these days, are you?"

8

When the basketball season ended Mike Merritt breathed a long sigh of relief. He could try to forget, at least for now, the humiliation of the cold bleak winter. He would attempt to come to terms with the awful discovery he had made about the nature of existence: his own existence, anyhow. He had discovered that the soul was not the benign instrument of redemption his mother believed in; it was instead the medium of suffering and pain. Darlene. Jasper Brown. Fat-ass Alex Curry. Rafferty. The screaming spectators who filled the Garden to vent their frustrations and failures in a virulent chorus of hatred for one Mike Merritt. These forces had, like tumors, eaten away at the core of his being. But if they had weakened him, they had also tempered the steel of his heart and heightened his awareness of himself as a free, if lonely, agent in a vast world of darkness. He had no answers—only nameless apprehensions and regrets, and one question: Why?

After a week on a sun-sapped beach in the Caribbean, on the honeymoon he and Darlene never took, he returned to his vacant apartment only to confront, yet again, the void. He began to read, all day, every day, to pass the time. He hadn't picked up a book since college but now he read history, novels, philosophy; he read newspapers and magazines and bestsellers; he read Freud and Wordsworth and Ring Lardner. Words and ideas, like tiny spiders, crawled across his mind and he couldn't sleep at night. In the library once he picked up the *Confessions* of St. Augustine. He glanced through the book and laughed: I was born in the wrong century—and into the wrong religion. Dear Lord, please save me from myself—but not quite yet. He laughed again. Why?

Then he thought of Darlene: his dark mistress. the devil's handmaiden, the delight of his dreams, his partner in despair. Where is she now? Why had she abandoned him? Why?

A brown basketball bounced through his brain: tap, tap, tap. He clutched the ball and it grew until it filled his mind and floated into the gray sky. He clung to it and it carried him above the clouds and out into the darker regions beyond all knowing. Why? . . .

One afternoon Mike climbed the wide white steps of the Public Library at 42nd Street and Fifth Avenue, carrying a stack of books under his arm. His head down, he strode toward the center door. He heard someone call his name.

"Mike! Mike Merritt!"

Some flaky female fan, he moaned to himself. Hadn't she heard? He was overpaid and overrated and, some said, his career was just plain over and done with. He was going to ignore her, but she called out again, insistently. "Mike, wait!"

He turned to see Patty Holmes running up the steps behind him. "Mike, how are you?" she asked breathlessly, clutching his arm, her golden hair shining in the afternoon sun.

Mike broke out into a grin. "The last person in the world—"

"You wanted to see?" she wondered aloud. She hesitated.

"The last person I *expected* to see—ever again. I mean—after our last encounter."

"That was ages ago," she said. "I graduated last month myself and already I feel years older. But let's not talk about last year or last week, okay?"

After the first flush of recognition and remembrance, and the idle pleasantries that accompany such reunions, an awkward silence settled between them. But neither wanted to leave the other. They stood there, Mike shifting his books from arm to arm, Patty fumbling with her purse.

Then, almost in desperation, Mike asked, "Are you free for dinner?"

"Yes," she said.

As they walked down Fifth Avenue exchanging exclamations about the beautiful weather, Mike observed Patty closely. She seemed different, much older, and he wondered what had happened in the last year to change her. She wasn't any less aristocratic, or any less beautiful. Her leggy stride still turned heads and her finely chiseled features had grown even more attractive. She was dressed in a gray suit that was perfectly tailored to her lithe figure. But he felt that a subtle transformation had taken place within her and he found himself determined to find out exactly what it was.

"Let's take our time," she suggested when they were seated at Rinaldo's, one of Mike's favorite restaurants. "Unless you have somewhere to go this evening."

"No," Mike said. "We have a lot of catching up to do."

"So you've been reading?"

"Yeah. Food for the mind. Everything from the *Congressional Record* to Hemingway. And St. Augustine. In fact," he said, his brow knit, leaning toward her conspiratorially, "I'm thinking of joining the priesthood."

She laughed. "Never in a thousand years. I'd stake my sterling reputation on it. Father Mike!"

Mike wore a sinister smile. "I understand there's a fortune to be made from indulgences. You can be my first customer."

"Bless me, Father, for I have sinned," she whispered.

The waiter brought their drinks: scotch for Mike and chablis for Patty.

"To the Public Library," he toasted.

"And to St. Augustine," she amended.

Their glasses clinked melodically.

After they had ordered another round of drinks Patty trained her frank blue eyes directly on Mike. "You know, I do have a confession to make. I'd like to clear the air."

He touched her hand. "I'm all ears."

"Well," she began, "first of all, I'd like to apologize for being such a bitch about your decision to play basketball. If that was what you really wanted to do, I should have supported you. I was wrong."

"No apology—"

"Yes, an apology is called for. I know this past year has been hell for you. I read the newspapers. In fact, I watched some of your games on TV."

"Oh God." He put his hand to his face. "You needn't have subjected yourself to that. For what I'm paid to play the clown, I don't expect my friends to waste their time watching me."

"Come on, Mike. They didn't give you a chance. Mitchell said—" She stopped in mid-sentence and looked down, her delicate hands planted firmly on her wine glass. "Which brings me to my second confession. Mitchell Farris."

"Patty."

"Just let me say it. Please." She paused for a moment to summon the courage to continue. "As you know, Mitchell and I were friends for a long time—ever since I took his class my sophomore year. He's an art historian, Mike, and a good one. I learned a lot from him. He'd take me to museums and shows and introduce me to visiting artists and critics. It was an education—the kind I'd dreamed of. And he's—" Her hands traced the smooth outline of her glass. "He's really a fine man. And we had an affair." She looked directly into Mike's dark face. He seemed so much taller than she had remembered, so much more handsome.

"It didn't start until you and I broke up. I had been with him before, occasionally. And sometimes I was stupid—really stupid about it. Like in Philadelphia. I never told you before, but I was with Mitchell the day of your game. I'm sure you never suspected anything—and I never had the guts—"

"You don't have to explain."

"I want to, Mike. Anyway, I knew he was attracted to me and that he wanted to start something, but I never gave in—until last summer. And by the time school was in session I was practically living with him." She smiled, but her eyes misted. "It was so convenient. He's a Fellow in Trumbull and I was in Pierson, so we were right across the street from each other . . . and I didn't see any reason not to—I mean, maybe it wasn't love, but it was something. And I learned so much from him." She bit her lip. "And then it ended. He took off for Italy. He gathered up a boxful of my things—you know, toothbrushes and slippers and books—and dropped them outside my door in Pierson with a note. 'Love and kisses. I'll write soon.' That sort of thing. I didn't know what to think. I mean, I like to think I had given him a lot—an awful lot. And then he left me, just like that."

Mike took her hand. He squeezed it. Tears fell on her ivory arm.

"Just like that," she repeated. "I never knew what hit me. That was six weeks ago. So what am I supposed to do?" She accepted Mike's proffered handkerchief. "Thanks."

"Do you want to hear something crazy?"

Patty blew her nose. "Crazier than my story of a spoiled bitch who got in over her head?"

"Almost." He sipped his scotch. "I'm a recently rejected lover too. I won't go into the sordid details, but I was that close"—he held his thumb and forefinger a half-inch apart—"to asking a girl to marry me when she told me to go to hell. She married some lowlife character the next day."

"I'm sorry, Mike," Patty commiserated. "Did you love her?"

"I think so. I *thought* so anyhow. Past tense. I never think about her any more." That wasn't quite true, but

Mike thought he should say it.

"I can't imagine that about Mitchell—not quite yet. But ask me in a month." She smiled. Her eyes were red but full of hope. "Maybe we've learned our lesson."

"We're both pretty good students," Mike said.

That evening Mike decided to marry Patty Holmes.

He sat in the darkness of his living room looking out at the dangerous black water and the distant scattering of lights. He had to take a wife sooner or later. Why not now? And why not Patty? She was beautiful; she was sensitive. She could be loving and she would be a valuable partner in the enterprise of life. And if Mike Merritt entertained the idea of a political career—which these days knocked quietly but insistently at the back door of his mind—then Patty was the perfect wife. But weren't her parents Republicans?

He poured himself a drink and threw off his shoes and sprawled full-length on the big couch. But could he forget Darlene—just like that?

He had never seriously considered marriage until Darlene, until she altered his life with her dark charms and untamed spirit. In her he saw everything he had ever imagined in a woman and he wanted to possess her. But she did not want to be possessed—except by her past, except by Jasper Brown.

Basketball promised nothing but a pair of bad knees. Five years tops. Assuming he survived even that long. And after that? Politics? Not a bad life. Provided you maintain your integrity. That's not impossible, is it?

And Patty. He needed a wife and there was no one better suited for him than Patty. They had been there before and, although it hadn't been perfect, it had been good. And it could be better if they worked at it. And there had been no one else really. If you didn't count Darlene. Could Patty be as good as Darlene? But what's *good*? Good looking? Good in bed? Good cook? Good mother? Or some platonic Good, some angelic perfection that answered to the name of Woman? It had to be Patty. And, he felt, it had to be soon. Time to grow up, Merritt, he told himself. Take risks and accept responsibilities. Plan ahead. Ask her.

For the next several weeks he dated her regularly. She even agreed, most of the time, to spend the night with him, and it was different, better than before. She was no longer the reluctant ice princess who had to take a shower every time she had sex. Farris must have taught her a trick or two. Their lovemaking was tender and passionate. She did not fuck with the delicious abandon of Darlene, but she soon learned what satisfied him and assiduously put that knowledge into practice.

One evening they lay tightly entwined, their bodies almost liquid with exhaustion and fulfillment. Everything was going so well. He was right; they were right; the time was right.

"Patty," he whispered into her ear. "I love you."

"Mmm-hmm," she replied, hugging him with all her strength. "I know, I know. And I love you, Mike."

"Marry me," he said huskily.

She put her warm mouth to his ear. "Yes, yes, yes!"

"What?" He sat up, surprised. He'd expected her to give him a maybe, or ask for time to think about it. But a flat-out yes?

The gray light from the street filtered in through the open bedroom window casting a silver glow over the bedsheets and the two lanky bodies joined in love. "What?" he repeated.

She giggled. "I said yes, handsome. Want me to spell it out for you? Y-e-s. Yes."

"Jesus! When?"

"Today. Tomorrow. Yesterday. Whenever you want. I love you, Mike. Of course I'll marry you." Patty put her arms around his bare torso. "You've been thinking about it for a while, haven't you? I knew it. I made up my mind when I saw you at the library. That's the way it's supposed to be. I'll be good for you, Mike—I know I will. I think we'll make a good team."

"As long we have a better record than the Comets, I'll be satisfied," he said.

"Poor losers make good winners. We'll be okay—won't we?"

"By the way," he asked, "are your parents still practicing Republicans?"

A week of frantic phone calls later they were married at the Marble Collegiate Church on Madison Avenue with their parents and a few dozen guests attending the simple ceremony. Afterwards everyone gathered for a reception at the Holmeses' townhouse on East 65th Street.

There John Paul Holmes, Jr., Yale College '29 and Law School '32, presided austerely as his wife, tall platinum-gray Katharine Canby Holmes, supervised the Chinese help. The hosts provided a bar and a buffet and the guests grouped in coveys to chatter and drink and eat and eye the subdued decor of the vast living room.

Bee Crosby, just back from Europe, stood at the bar, his Italian boots brilliant, his elbow perpetually bent. He surveyed the scene with crapulous condescension. He ordered another martini and stalked toward a lonely figure in a simple print dress at the edge of the crowd.

"How's it going, Mrs. M.?" he asked.

Evelyn Merritt, startled from a moment of benign contemplation, looked up as her son's friend weaved toward her. "Bee!" She smiled and said, "Not many familiar faces around here. Beautiful house."

"Yeah," Bee acknowledged. "Beautiful house and beautiful people. Rich anyhow." Then his tone shifted. "So our two favorite lovebirds have finally tied the knot. Had to happen sooner or later."

"When are you going to get married, Bee?"

"Me? Married? Not before the end of the century. Got too much on my mind." He lit a cigarette and took a drink of crystal gin. "'Sides, what woman in her right mind would hook on with me?"

"Now, don't talk yourself down," Mrs. Merritt chided. "You have a lot to offer a young lady. Mike says you've been writing some very interesting stories and articles. Who knows—one day we'll see you on the cover of a magazine. Then they'll be knocking down your door."

"Not bloody likely," Bee replied. "They'll never break into *my* closet."

Mike, in his darkest blue suit, and Patty, in a long white gown, roved the party, posing for pictures, accepting pecks on the cheek, and listening to grave advice from old friends of the family.

Evelyn Merritt beamed proudly as her son and daughter-in-law approached.

"How are you doing, Mom?" he inquired, bending to kiss her.

"Lovely, simply lovely." She turned to accept a soft kiss from Patty. "Bee and I have been saying what a beautiful couple you two make. I just wish I had a camera." She smoothed her dress with nervous hands. "Patty, I'm so happy for you."

"Thank you. And I'm glad you could be here." She kissed the brimming woman once again.

Then her gaunt, white-haired father loomed owl-like over her shoulder, a faint trace of a smile on his lips. He placed a wide hand on her arm. "Have you eaten anything, my dear?"

"Oh, Daddy, I don't know if I could. I'm still full of butterflies."

"How are you, Mrs. Merritt?" he asked, bestowing a gray glance in her general direction.

"Fine, thank you. You have a lovely home here." She gazed at the paintings that dotted the blue walls. "Beautiful pictures."

"Patricia advises us on all of our art purchases," Holmes acknowledged.

Mrs. Holmes appeared, leading a white-coated waiter with a tray of champagne. "Evelyn, you must try the champagne," she insisted, taking a long-stemmed glass from the tray.

"You *must*," Bee echoed.

Evelyn Merritt considered the bubbly golden liquid.

"Thank you," she allowed hesitantly. "I suppose there's a first time for everything." She took a serious sip and sent a quick glance heavenward.

Mrs. Holmes awarded her daughter and new son-in-law similar glasses and took one for herself. "To our families," she toasted. Then she said, "John, have you shown Evelyn the house?"

"Not as yet."

"Evelyn, my dear, would you like to see it?"

"I'd love to."

"We'll only be a short while," Katharine told her husband. "Do see that everyone gets something to drink."

"I think I'll help myself," Bee muttered, wheeling toward the bar.

The two women disappeared into the kitchen. The bride and groom exchanged urgent whispers.

John Paul Holmes adjusted his horn-rimmed glasses as the couple huddled. He cleared his throat. "So do you expect to win more games this year, son?" It came out like a cross-examination.

Mike regarded the man with the to-hell-with-it-all smile of a newlywed and said, "I expect to win them all, sir, but I'm no longer surprised when I lose. We'll be better this season." He looked down into his bride's eyes. "I have high hopes."

Then Mo Silver burst upon them, balancing a plate of sandwiches and a fragile glass of champagne. Sheila was with him and she showered Mike with kisses. She took Patty's hand, her wide face one big smile. "Hi, I'm Sheila. Congratulations. I wish you all the luck."

"Thanks," Patty replied. She immediately warmed to this open-hearted woman with the frank face. "I'm glad you came, Sheila. Hello, Mo."

The robust young attorney saluted her with his glass. "To the best people in New York."

"Glad you could show," Mike said. "Mo Silver, meet Mr. Holmes, Patty's father. Mr. Holmes, Mo Silver. And Sheila Martin."

"Miss Martin. Mr. Silver. Pleased to meet you both."

"Hi, Mr. Holmes." Sheila pumped his hand. "Nice place you've got here."

Mo set aside his platter of food and wiped his big hand on a napkin. He shook the older attorney's hand. "Nice to meet you. Your firm represents Crane Industries, doesn't it? The government roughed your boys up a bit on that one."

A thin smile etched across Holmes's long face. "Indeed they did, Mr. Silver. This time around."

"I went to law school with one of your associates. Steve Wayne. He says he lived with the case for two years."

"Yes, Mr. Wayne. He's one of the brightest young men I've seen in a long time. It's no joy, those first years," Holmes remembered. "We partners depend more and more on our associates. A talented lot." His gray eyes filtered through the spectacles and took the measure of the stout, brown-suited younger lawyer. "Who are you with, Mr. Silver?"

"Roth and Donatelli, downtown."

"Civil liberties," Holmes said, his legal antennae twitching.

"Very lively," Mo assured him.

"It sounds at least as exciting as my son-in-law's career."

"If not as lucrative," Mo countered, winking at Mike. He retrieved a sandwich and took a bite.

Mr. Holmes excused himself to oversee the distribution of the food and spirits. He slipped back into the party like a pale shadow.

"Daddy doesn't like to talk about losing cases," Patty teased.

"Who does?" Mike asked.

"Two things about Mo," Sheila said. "He never loses a case, and he never misses a free meal."

Mo wagged the remnant of his sandwich at her. "You don't know what you're missing. Best tongue you've ever eaten."

"Patty, could you show me to the bathroom," Sheila pleaded. "I need a break from this man."

The women left Mo and Mike to themselves. "I like your suit," Mike commented, admiring the subtle dark pinstripe.

"My uncle in Brooklyn is a tailor. You're looking fit. Recovered."

"And dreading the idea of camp when we get back from our honeymoon."

"Have you been working out at all?"

"Christ, no. I haven't picked up a basketball since I missed my last shot against Detroit. I went 0 for 5 that game."

"You'll come back fresh this season. I know you'll turn things around."

"I sure as hell hope so," Mike said with a solemn nod. "How are you and Sheila getting along? Haven't seen you two for a while."

"Me, I'm tired of butting my head up against a brick wall every day. Jealous of you because you're getting married. Growing up, I suppose, and growing older. Sheila, she's great. I got her another wok for her birthday."

"The world's best-fed champion of human rights."

"Yeah, she's good for me," Mo said. He looked closely into Mike's face. "You know," he began, "it's none of my business, and I'll only ask this once, but, well, have you really put Darlene Simmons out of your mind? I mean, this isn't some kind of desperate move, is it?"

"I've wondered about that myself," Mike said. Then he shook his dark head. "But, no, I'm sure this is for the best. Patty and I—" He looked at the floor. "Patty and I are right for each other. I should have realized it all along."

"Hey, Mr. Sliver!" Bee returned, a fresh drink in hand.

"Bee." Mo extended a beefy hand. "You're back

from the Old World. I've been reading your stuff in the *Voice*."

"Yeah, I'm flapping my literary wings." Mo's hand enveloped his own. "Glad to know somebody out there is reading my immortal prose."

"It's plain to anyone who looks at what you write that you've got talent, Bee."

"Thanks for saying so, at any rate."

"All I know is what Sheila says." Mo smiled at Bee. "And Sheila says—and I quote—'that boy can write up a storm.'"

Bee's world-weary eyes traveled from Mike to Mo and back to Mike. "All right, you guys," he said with a crooked smile. "Jesus, a fellow can't be melancholy for long in this crowd. I'll have to meet this Sheila person. She sounds like an astute critic."

"I'm looking forward to the day you sit down and write a book," Mike said.

"And I can't wait until it comes out in paperback," Mo added.

As he began his second season with the Comets Mike purged the demons that had haunted his rookie year. Rafferty might as well have been dead, for Mike banished the reporter from his thoughts. As for Darlene, the pain had dulled sufficiently to allow him to remember her with more fondness than regret; he would never get her out of his mind, although she, like last season, was a part of his past. He must concentrate on his game and his new position with the team: all else was distraction. This year, he promised himself, it will be different.

After the Comets' first home game in November Mike showered and exited the Garden. It was a bitterly cold night, the wind whipping viciously around the concrete arena. He clutched his coat tightly and ran across the street to MacElroy's Bar. He hadn't seen Mac since his encounter with Darlene and Rafferty. Inside the bar it was warm and dark. The silvery bottles reflected the dull light against the long mirror. Mac was wiping the bar.

When the bartender saw Mike he gave the athlete a wide, uneven yellow grin. "So you remember your No. 1 fan after all, huh? Pull up a stool, kid, and have one on the house. Welcome back."

"Thanks, Mac. It seems like ages."

Mac poured a generous shot of Johnny Walker Black Label. "Yeah, last time I saw you, you were with your colored girl. Pretty, but—no offense—I was glad to hear you got married to that Holmes lass. Saw her picture in the paper. One class filly. You known her long?"

The liquor went down smoothly, warming his insides. "Since college. A few years."

"Well, you gotta grab 'em before they marry those rich old bastards. These young women don't sit around on the front porch any more like in my day. No, sir. Don't suppose a handsome fella like yourself had much trouble, though. Probably have to fight 'em off with a bat, eh?"

Mike looked into the bartender's battered but friendly face. Sometimes Mac reminded him of his dad: he was a ruddy hard-working man with a bright outlook on life, rough when he had to be but reluctant to hurt anyone or anything. "I don't worry about the other girls any more," Mike said.

"Sown all your wild oats?" Mac winked. "I got a few more to sow myself, but I ain't found the right field to plow. A guy my age don't get so many chances. . . . But anyhow, I heard the game tonight. You put it to the Celtics—but good. How many points you get?"

"Twenty-five. Best night ever." He took another belt of scotch. It seemed to coat his soul. He felt fine.

"What does old Alex Jesus H. Christ Curry think of that? You been playing up a storm so far. He'll get his, I say. And Matt Rafferty—come playoff time he'll be singing another tune, huh?" Mac laughed. He waved the wet towel in Mike's face. "Just remember old Mac never gave up on you. Just takes time. Everything takes time. Have another drink." He refilled Mike's glass.

"This is my last," Mike said. "Patty'll be waiting up for me." Four games into the season, he had won the starting position and was averaging twenty-one points and thirty minutes a game. Curry knew he was working hard; he had to see the difference. No complaints, no comments, no wasted motion. Mike Merritt was learning all over again how to play basketball.

"Sure did a job on that boy Moore," said Mac. "Wish I could have seen it. Wonder what our buddy Rafferty'll say about that?"

"All I want him to do is to print the truth," Mike said. "I'll let the standings tell my story. Still don't know what got into him last year. One strange guy." Mike shuddered at the thought of the vitriolic sportswriter.

"Truth is," Mac continued, "Comets need a big man. Am I right?" Mike nodded and took another slug of scotch. "Everybody knows it. Everybody but Curry and the front office boys, that is. Hawkins is a great guy but his day is over. Used to be he could stand up to the best of 'em—Chamberlain, Russell, Bellamy—before he gave up the ghost. But hell, that was ten years ago. Can't figure it. They could solve a lot of problems with a class big man. Sure you don't want another drink?"

"No thanks, Mac. Got to go." Mike got to his feet. He accepted the bartender's wet hand.

"Listen, Mike, you come back. You know you've got a friend here. And I'd like to meet that lady of yours sometime."

"I'll bring her by."

"With one of them little bundles of joy, huh?" Mac winked again.

"See you later, Mac."

"Yeah, keep your nose clean, kid."

His taxi sped across town and then up the avenue. The scotch mingled with his own high spirits and he sat back mellowly as the vehicle rocked through the cold streets. There was nowhere else in the world he wanted to be but here in New York. In time it would be his town: if he scored enough points and pulled down enough rebounds and won enough games. Patience, he reminded himself. One day . . .

Then his key was in the door and he stepped into his apartment. Looking around for Patty, he felt as if he had finally earned the right to live there. The gleaming furniture, the picture window, the paintings and prints that Patty had chosen for the walls—he was home.

They had been married for almost three months now—three good months. She worked at the Hartman Gallery across town; it kept her busy—and happy. When he was in town they frequently went out, discovering restaurants and nightspots where they could be alone among the teeming crowds. He went to gallery and museum receptions with her and occasionally dined with her parents. And they made love almost every night, learning the pitch and rhythm of each other's body, melding their passions into one mutually satisfying experience. They decided to have children immediately. There was plenty of space in their lives for lots of kids.

"Patty!" Tonight he was eager to possess her. He was aching with need. He called again. There was no answer. Maybe she was working late at the gallery.

He went into the bedroom and there he saw her, lying face down on the bed, unmoving. "Patty." She turned over. Her eyes were dark hollows, her cheeks flushed and stained with tears.

"Oh, Mike," she sobbed, reaching for him. She grabbed his neck and pulled him down on top of her. "Oh, Mike, you'll hate me!" She wept loudly. He held her.

"God, Patty, what's wrong? I'm here. What's the matter? Patty?"

Between sobs, he pieced together what she was trying to say. She had been to the doctor. She thought she might be pregnant.

"Patty, why didn't you tell me?"

For several minutes she clutched his arms, her head buried in his chest. "I didn't want—" She stopped and looked into his eyes. "We wanted a baby so much. I love you, Mike. I'm sorry."

"What in God's name is it? Tell me," he demanded.

Patty gazed fearfully at her young husband. His dark face hovered above hers. "You'll hate me, Mike." She collected herself. "The doctor said today that I couldn't have any children. I can't have a baby. I can't—" She collapsed, sobbing.

"Patty," Mike said gently. "Honey, don't cry." He held her to him. "Stop it now. Patty." He cradled her head in his hands and rocked her gently back and forth, smoothing her hair. "Don't cry. Don't cry."

She was silent for a moment, breathing heavily but quietly. Then she looked up at him. "There's more, Mike."

He was stunned. What the hell more could there be? She was sterile. They could never—

"I knew before we were married. At least I had a good idea. But then, last week I missed my period. I was hoping . . . that's why I never told you. I hoped there would be a chance. But the doctor today—" She broke off, her shoulders racking violently.

Black confusion and pain overwhelmed him as, slowly, Patty's confession washed over him. "Why didn't you say something before we were married?" he demanded. "Patty!" He pulled her face to his and stared severely into her bloodshot eyes. "Why didn't you tell me before? Why?"

"I love you," she cried. "I didn't want to lose you." She fell back onto the bed. "It'll never be the same, God. I'm sorry. I'm sorry, Mike."

Mike sat on the edge of the bed, his head in his hands, his mouth set tightly. He said nothing.

"I need to be alone tonight," Patty said. She took his arm and tried to look directly at him. He wouldn't look at her. "I'll be all right if I get some sleep."

Mike went to the bar in the living room. He poured a tall drink and gulped it down. The team was flying to San Francisco the next day but he did not care. The scotch splashed into his glass. He swallowed most of his second drink. Then he threw his tie on the floor and flopped onto the sofa. Patty's cries echoed in his brain and he downed another shot of liquor. The dark river flowed like ink and beyond, among the distant yellow lights of Queens, he imagined a million households all sleeping peacefully, safe from the icy blast. He heaved himself up and stumbled to the bar for a last, numbing glassful. Outside, the city was caught in the chilling grip of the cold windy night as Mike fell asleep, fully clothed, on the couch.

By December the Comets were a few games over .500—for the first time in recent memory. And Mike Merritt, according to the pundits, was much improved. Clint Dixon, the third-year guard obtained from the Bullets, was magic with the ball—and he and Mike quickly developed a smooth rapport on and off the court.

Mo advised Mike to concentrate more on rebounding: the scoring would come by itself. So Mike learned to spark the fastbreak and, as Mo predicted, his shooting percentage increased. All the Comets lacked was a dominating center, someone who could control the other giants in the league. Old Lester Hawkins gave his lumbering best, but that wasn't nearly good enough. But even with Hawkins, the team stood an outside chance of making the playoff this year—if they stayed hot and healthy through the spring.

The turnabout in the Comets' fortunes thrust new demands upon Mike's offcourt time: department store openings, news conferences, commercial endorsement offers, public commitments ad nauseum. Time spent on the road and in front of the cameras added up fast. It meant fewer and fewer hours at home. But neither Patty nor Mike fought the front office on that count. Since he had learned she was sterile they slowly but steadily grew apart. The passion that had bloomed wildly between them now wilted almost as quickly.

On the night of the New York Comets' annual Christmas party at Toots Shors Patty feigned a headache. He rode crosstown in a cab, silent and alone.

As he stepped into the restaurant's banquet room the first face he saw belonged to Alex Curry. The balding florid-faced coach wore a bright plaid sport jacket, a dark purple shirt open at the neck, and a pair of maroon pants. Looks like he raided some poor pimp's wardrobe, Mike mused.

"Join the party, Mike!" Curry called, an alcoholic smile plastered on his rosy face.

"Sure, Coach. That's why I'm here."

"And where's your better half? She's not going to miss the best time of the year—besides championship time, that is?"

"I'm afraid so, Coach. She's not well this evening. Excuse me, I need a drink."

"Let's hope it's nothing contagious," Curry shouted after him with a chuckle.

He headed for the bar where he brushed elbows with Clint Dixon.

"Hey, bro, have a merry and a happy," Dixon said, a handsome smile breaking through his pitch-black beard.

"Same to you." He turned to the bartender. "Double scotch on the rocks, please."

"Where's the lovely missus tonight, friend? I hope she ain't sick."

"She'll be okay. Too cold for her tonight, I guess. Excuse me, Clint."

As he turned he bumped into the rock-like form of Lester Hawkins. The big center peered down at him through a pair of thick glasses. "Mike, my man."

For all his glaring deficiencies on the court, Mike couldn't dislike the veteran center. He had a heart of gold—and a mouthful of teeth to match. "Hi, Lester."

Hawkins frowned. "You look down tonight." His

big black hand clamped over Mike's shoulder. "Cheer up, man. Can't be that bad."

"I'm all right," Mike replied. "Guess I'm thinking of Thursday's game. We've got to whip Philly if we want to stay up with Boston."

"It's a long season," noted Hawkins, nodding his big square head wisely.

Drink in hand, Mike made his way through the party, past the elaborate table of food, toward one of the darker corners of the long room. He didn't want to talk to anyone. He didn't want to explain his wife's absence. Maybe I shouldn't have come at all, he thought. Maybe Patty really wanted me to stay home with her. But, hell, I've offered to enough times—only for her to insist that I go ahead with my "plans for the evening." I never have any "plans" and she damn well knows it.

Mike was tempted to fling his glass at the nearest wall and run, but he stopped short. Staring out a window was Darlene Simmons, her slight figure almost invisible against the cold black glass.

As Mike approached her she turned. She seemed not to recognize him at first. Then she gave him her well-practiced smile and the gloom disappeared from her manner, if not from her eyes.

"Hi, Mike. Merry Christmas and all that."

He noticed faint gray circles beneath her eyes—those eyes. He remembered now: falling deeply into those eyes the nights they made love, dreaming about those eyes every night, longing for those eyes during the worst days of his rookie year.

"Hello, Darlene."

"Where's—?" they began simultaneously. They laughed. Neither one of them really wanted to kow.

From the shadowed corner in which they stood Mike looked across the room. It was crowded with Comet teammates and their wives and girlfriends as well as the front office brass and their wives with their hair piled high above their furs. There were fifty or sixty people there, talking and laughing loudly. Too loudly, he thought. He looked at Darlene. "Shall we?" he asked.

"I'm with you."

Later, in a dark room in a tall hotel near the Garden, they lay together beneath a thick blanket, their naked bodies coated with a patina of sweat and sex, their hands gently, almost dispassionately, exploring each other. They spoke barely a word. It was a raw confrontation—and a rare communion of need and fulfillment. For an hour they slowly, silently made love, each swimming in the flesh and the soul of the other.

"Guess what?" she teased, sitting up so that the blanket fell away from her creamy body.

He stared at her small round breasts, at the dark puckering nipples that were suddenly exposed in the cold room. "What?" he said, planting his hands on her hips.

Her small hands rested daintily on his shoulders. "You're getting twenty-five percent more offensive rebounds this year than last. That's quite an improvement."

Mike sighed. Rebounds! "Yeah, and seventy-five percent less loving." His hands moved from her waist, over her stomach, to her breasts. He smiled. "But maybe I can improve my average."

"I'd say tonight you got a good start, my honky friend." She bent over him and kissed him hard on the mouth. He felt her tongue move insistently against his own as he ran his hands over her upturned nipples. She arched her back and forced her breasts against his palms. "Oooh, Mike. What you do to me."

"What *you* do to me," he whispered. His fingers ran the length of her arm. He grabbed her hands and put them to his mouth. He kissed her palms and each of her fingers.

"Mike, honey."

"Hmmm?"

"Before we get hot and start digging on each other again." She embedded her small fingers in his darkly abundant chest hairs. "Which can happen any second now." Her eyes found his. "Tell me what's happened with you and Patricia Rockefeller. Then I tell you what's with Jasper and me." She brought her pert nose to rest on his. "Then, tiger, you and me we make jungle love."

"There's not a hell of a lot to tell. Simple fact is—she can't have babies. And she knew about it before we were married, but she never told me. That's been enough to bring on the Ice Age with us. I think it made us realize that there's nothing between us. There was once—for a while—I thought. I honestly did."

Darlene lay down against Mike's body. She put a hand on his neck. "So what's going to happen? Just curious. Gotta ask."

He shook his head. "Who's to say? I can't leave her, though. Not right now. I don't want to leave her like that. We've got time to decide. I guess neither one of us is in a hurry." Mike stretched his long arms. "So what's with you and your man Jasper?"

"He and I—we have our disagreements. But he helped me once and I can't forget that. He picked me up off the street when I was nothing and he put me back on my feet. I owed him something—so I married him. Instead of you. You made me mad." She smoothed back the hair which fell over his forehead. "I live in the same place. He sleeps there more often than not." Then she leapt on top of Mike and grabbed his neck with both hands, emphasizing her point with a mock strangulation. "And if he ever caught you with me he'd kill you!" She laughed. He did not; his eyes narrowed quizzically. She released his neck. "Just a joke, honey."

"I'm losing my sense of humor about such things," he said. "It's a sad business, Darlene. Men and women."

"Or men and men," she teased.

"Or women and women," he replied, poking her in the ribs.

Darlene laughed. "I wouldn't know about that." Then she whispered in his ear. "But I think I'd like to try it sometime. I hear it's nice."

Mike sat up. "Do you have anyone in particular in mind?"

She pushed him back down. "Don't be so eager." Her smile filled his mind. "I just want you. Right now." She pushed her mouth against his and kissed him. "I don't care. I don't care," she whispered as her mouth explored his face. "I don't care any more about any-body. Any-body but *you*, baby." She kissed his eyes and ran her hand down his torso. "And I don't want you to care about anybody but me—from now on." Her tongue cut a hot swath over his chest and stomach until it reached his rapidly hardening penis. She lovingly licked it and then took it in her mouth.

Mike reeled in pleasure. She's everything Patty's not—she's everything, he thought. "Oh God, Darlene." He let out a long loud moan as he came. He reached down and gathered her to himself and hugged her. They kissed again, his semen still coating her mouth. Lapping desperately at each other, they clung together tightly. "Oh, baby, let me hold you. Let me love you."

"Shut up and do it, then, Mr. Man. This mama's too hot to talk about it any more."

9

In Mike's third season the Comets jelled. It was a gradual, halting process, and at times it seemed they wouldn't make it, but after the All-Star game (Mike's first) they reeled off an eleven-game winning streak and blazed to a fourth-place finish in their division, drawing the Celtics in the opening round of the playoffs.

In the days leading up to the contest the Comets became the darlings of the press and the cameras, as fashionable as this year's jeans and nearly as heavily promoted. Mike was startled to see his face, blown up to enormous proportions, plastered on Times Square billboards and riding the flanks of buses. No one but Matt Rafferty seemed to recall that the "quiet leader" and "articulate spokesman" had been the biggest bust in the league a mere two seasons before. That was showbiz.

To the further astonishment of New York fans—whose love of basketball had been chronically thwarted by anemic teams—the Comets captured three of the first six playoff games. At La Guardia Airport five hundred diehards waved and screamed good-bye as their overnight heroes boarded the shuttle to Boston to conclude the series on the Celts' parquet floor.

No one said much on the brief flight. Clint Dixon and Lester Hawkins, the aging center, played poker with a rookie. Gordy Wallace, acquired in midseason from the Bucks, studied stock reports, his thick fingers thrumming a fugue on a calculator no bigger than a matchbook.

The Comets had evolved into a team and Mike had emerged as their leader. Forty minutes of playing time, game after game, had honed his skills to the intense rhythms of the NBA. He ranked among the more versatile men in the league, a forward equally at home under the boards or beyond the key or doubleteaming on the fullcourt press. He wasn't Linc Moore, nor would he ever be, but he was scarcely less valuable to his team. The multiple dimensions of his play counted for a lot in a game dominated increasingly by swelled egos and slam-dunk prima donnas.

Off the court, too, he seized the reins of command. It was Mike who carried the team's grievances to the front office, who pressured the big wheels to make at least a few of the trades that turned the Comets around. None of this sat well with Alex Curry, who grudgingly kept the forward in the lineup, but it earned Mike the respect of his mates. They looked to him to defend them against the bosses and the papers as well as to sink the last shot in a tight game.

The plane touched down and they marched solemnly through the airport, past curious faces and pointing fingers, into a bus that sped them to a downtown hotel. There they rested through the afternoon. Game-time was set for eight. Mike Merritt and the Comets were big news and the network televising the playoffs wanted a prime-time show. To Mike it seemed he'd come full circle, waiting to confront Lincoln Moore. As if, he mused in exasperation, there were no other men on the court. If some fans would watch tonight's contest out of love for the game, to most it was still theatre, contrived along allegorical lines, with heroes and villains and underdogs and a theme: the Great White Hope vs. the Natural Man.

"Just remember," barked Coach Curry in the lockerroom. "If we were the Phoenix Suns nobody would care."

Mike was nervous as a doughboy primed for his first battle, pumping his knee, kneading an old bruise, observing Curry's bald spot reflected like halite in the mirror. Next to Mike the diminutive trainer Joey Murphy wrapped tape around Clint Dixon's thigh; on his other sat Gordy Wallace, petrous and calm, his big jaw working steadily. He had legs like redwoods and planted them beneath the boards like a man staking his claim. His prodigious strength and uncanny instinct for grabbing rebounds freed Mike to roam the court as a third guard, searching out openings, engineering plays.

"We've been lucky three times against these guys," Curry was saying. "But if we're not careful they'll eat us alive. And they'll do it with the break. Don't try to run with them. That's what they're waiting for. Run with them and you're dead. Simple as that. Merritt, I want you to see the ball first few times up. Make sure it gets worked around. Nobody starts chucking. No shots without Wallace underneath."

You played them all year and faced them six times in ten days and you knew everything they did, but still they loomed as an unknown foe. Don't get rattled. Can't let them blow us out, Mike fretted.

"If I see anyone standing around, I don't care who, he's coming the hell out. Dixon, that means you. No prancing for the cameras tonight and no showing off for the broads."

"Can't help it, Coach," said the glamorous guard. "I need to make people happy."

"Then you'll do it from the fucking bench. Merritt, you're sticking to Moore so you can't help out with Mulloy. That means it's up to you, Wallace. Make him feel you under the boards. He's afraid of contact so give him some."

Mike blew on his hands. The lockerroom was freezing, an old Celtic trick. When Boston came to Madison Square Garden the Comets used refrigerated basketballs that almost wouldn't bounce and plummeted from the wobbly rims like boulders.

"Those bastards down the hall," said Curry, "are laughing. They think they got the easiest game since basketball was invented. If Russell was still with 'em you'd hear that hyena laugh right now."

It was a miracle they were still in it. Curry was, as

always, the monkey on the team's back. His style was humiliation and he hated to let the young guys play. If we lose, thought Mike, it'll be because we have to doubleteam Mulloy. Curry wouldn't unload Hawkins. He was a good man in his day but that day had ended and now he was deadwood. The refs let him get away with murder, ignoring his swinging elbows and fists, and the center still set a bruising pick, but the last operation had made jelly of his knees. They were lumpy and scarred. Mike felt a twinge of sorrow as he glanced at the man's handsome bowed head. He played in pain rather than quit. A prisoner of his whopping salary, Les had lived too fast and planned too little.

I hope he doesn't embarrass himself out there. I hope we all don't embarrass ourselves out there.

They warmed up before an already chanting crowd. The Celts strolled out moments later and the spectators roared.

In the clutch of seats reserved for the players' wives, Mike spotted Patty. She'd been a trooper this season, catching nearly half the home games and actually volunteering to fly up for this one. Darlene was out there too, with Jasper Brown. Jasper was betting on the Celts, Darlene had confided glumly, as if it sealed the Comets' fate.

"Good luck to us, brother," Clint Dixon whispered as they walked toward the center circle.

Mike nodded grimly. They were going to need it.

Through the first quarter they hung within two. Mike hit a pair from the key, Wallace drew a couple of fouls inside, and Dixon beat his man on a twisting drive. The jarring picks Hawkins set in the high post sprung the second guard free for short jumpers which hit the mark. It was smart team play of the sort that had brought the Comets this far. The Celtics' baskets came more easily and quickly. Mulloy cleared the rebound and pitched out to Moore who found his guards streaking downcourt. Twice after the Comets scored on snappy plays Moore caught them flatfooted and rifled the ball upcourt to speedster P. J. Honey, who left Dixon at midcourt and breezed in for the easy bucket.

The fastbreak. It could demoralize a team that had to labor for each basket. The temptation was to try it yourself, after you saw the Celts rack up so many easy ones. But to do that you had to run with them—which was tantamount to suicide.

The Celts took the jump to begin the second quarter and cleared off one side to let Mulloy exploit Hawkins and his gelatinous knees. His teammates were powerless to help their center without leaving a man completely free or sagging into an impermissable zone. His face twisted with effort and pain, Hawkins manfully stood his ground. He tried to slow the kid with a gouging hand to the hip but Mulloy was snaky and slithered free, spinning in for the dunk. Three times the Celtics fell into the same bizarre formation and three times Mulloy scored.

Curry called time. "Dixon, next time they pull that stunt you come around and take the ball from him. He handles it like a bear."

But Mulloy had already left the lineup. In his place was a six-eleven beanpole with an outside shot. The Comets had hardly glimpsed him all season. He set up outside and Hawkins lumbered after him. Then the beanpole flared back into the low post, Hawkins hobbling in pursuit. Wallace came over but not in time and Moore threaded the needle with a pass.

The Comets were down by nine, kept alive by meticulous teamwork, constant motion, and Clint Dixon's sparkling drives. Halftime score was 59-52.

"Coach," pleaded Mike in the lockerroom. "Put York in there. Les can't keep up. He's hurting." The center was in the training room, receiving cortisone injections.

Curry's eyes ignited and little muscles pulsed in his blue jaw. "You been telling me how to run this team all season, Merritt. Hawkins is a great center. He carried this team for ten years."

"Coach, he can't do it."

"Bullshit. He'll get going."

Mike was about to say more but Dixon grabbed his arm. "Be cool, bro. York ain't gonna make any difference. They're only up by seven, we just gotta stay with 'em."

Through the third quarter they did better than that. Mike found his range and sank three in a row; Dixon snatched the ball from P.J. Honey and took it all the way; the other guard, Barkum, dropped two behind Hawkins's granite screens. Wallace rebounded with a cowpuncher's abandon, clearing a space with his powerful hips and well-placed elbows.

With a minute to go in the quarter the Comets edged into the lead. Still the Celtics controlled the game. Linc Moore had been relatively quiet so far. He threw a few dazzling passes on the fastbreak and once he stripped Mike sailing into the lane, but he rarely threw up a shot. Soon he would call for the ball and soon Mulloy would go to work again on Lester Hawkins.

The Comets tried to pour it on. They gambled on a fastbreak but Moore filched a floater at midcourt and took it in himself for two. Barkum unleashed a twenty-five foot bomb that didn't even nick the rim. Mulloy plucked it out of the air and caught Honey racing to the hoop. Then Wallace passed up a ten-footer and Hawkins heaved one up. It caromed off the hoop like a bullet and fell into the hands of Honey well behind the key.

"For Christ's sake," Curry fumed as the quarter ended. "You're nailing your own goddamn coffins. Lester, the next time you take a shot like that you're back in Mississippi sharecropping. And none of that Jerry West crap, Barkum. You're in this league on a prayer not a chucking scholarship."

They trailed by five as the final quarter began. Boston Garden rocked with noise. Something that sounded like a car horn honked an atrocious tune and Mike nearly swung at a photographer who flashed a bulb in his face.

Wallace jumped center since Hawkins couldn't get off the ground. Boston took the tap. Four Celts parked in the corner and Mulloy squared off against Hawkins. Dixon swooped in but Mulloy found Honey slipping across the lane. Two points. Clint tried too hard to get back the basket and a whistle blew. Offensive foul. Dixon ranted and stomped.

"What did you call me?" demanded the ref.

"Bloodsucker," interpreted Mike.

"That ain't what it sounded like," said Linc Moore.

"Open your mouth again, Dixon, and you're out. Two shots, Honey."

He sank the freethrows, then Wallace hit a short jumper for the Comets. The Celtics fell into their pattern. Honey found Moore who flipped to Mulloy who beat Hawkins inside. Mike missed a jumper from the corner and Linc Moore unleashed the break. The next time up Barkum's man ignored him completely and doubleteamed Lester Hawkins. The flustered center slapped off the guard with an elbow but it was a mismatch and the foul was called. Then the beanpole reappeared. He lured Hawkins outside and shot right over him. Lester waved as if at a plane taking off. On the other end the enraged center called for the ball and bulled into the lane. He shook the backboard with a mighty dunk then crumpled to the floor, screaming. Time was called and Curry and Joey Murphy scuttled off the bench to a mounting chorus of boos.

"Jesus, Lester," said Curry. "What'd you do that for?"

"Twenty seconds, Coach," yawped the ref. "Get him out and put somebody else in."

Another time out to reassemble the troops. Curry spoke quickly. "Down by seven with five minutes. We got to try to run with 'em. We can do it."

Mike couldn't believe his ears. The coach was crazy. He named the replacement for Hawkins. Instead of the tough rookie forward York he chose veteran guard Hal Pecan. "Give us some speed and at least one cool head out there. Wallace you take Mulloy. Merritt, we need you inside on Wallace's man. Dixon, take Moore."

"But, Coach—"

The buzzer sounded.

The next five minutes were disastrous. Moore worked his will on Dixon, who was a tall guard but no match for the rangy forward with his long arms and Nijinskian legs. The Comets never had a chance to run. With Wallace chasing the beanpole or Mulloy—at one point the Celts deployed both—rebounds were as scarce as diamonds. In three minutes the Celtics ran up twelve points and the Comets were through.

It was a prematurely hot day in June. A salty breeze stroked the canted pane in the cramped office of Mo Silver, whose feet were propped on his desk.

"I don't know, Mike. I'd feel a lot better if you'd sign another multiyear contract. If not for five years, then for three. What if you get hurt—tendons, cartilage, or worse?"

"I don't want to commit myself."

"But three years. Surely you'll stick it out that long."

"Probably, but what if we really put it together, then I'm locked into these terms."

"You broke?"

"No, but—"

"Is it Patty? Is she anxious for more?"

Mike shook his dark head. "I wish it was that. I wish she'd make some kind of demands, I wish—oh what's the use? I prefer a one-year contract that's all. The illusion of freedom."

His lawyer sighed. "If that's what you want, that's what we'll get you. Just wait till the Comets take it all, then you'll have so much money you won't know what to do with it."

"I'll find something."

"Now let's drop this money talk and get back to the team. Don't you think Dixon shoots too much on the prime-time games?"

Mike grinned. "No comment."

"All right. Candid answer please, how far you guys going next season?"

"Definitely the playoffs again. Last season was no fluke. We proved that, I think. Maybe past the first round. Those damned Celtics. We need a big man but that son of a bitch Curry has them so bamboozled they won't trade for one."

"Still have it in for Curry?"

"He cost us the series, Mo. I won't admit it to anyone but you, but it's true."

"At least he let you play. After what he put you through the first season I didn't know if you were going to make it. You ought to be proud of last season."

"I'll be proud when we win."

The phone pealed and Mo reached for it. He cupped the mouthpiece with a hairy hand. "For you. Comet office."

"Mike. Ed Walters."

The Comet president. Here comes the squeeze. "Hello, Mr. Walters. To what—"

"How do you feel about coaching, Mike?"

What? "Why, I don't know . . ."

"Curry's out. You've talked enough about what the teams needs. Here's your chance to practice what you preach."

"But I want to play."

Walters laughed softly. These corporate guys laughed as if they had learned how from a book. "We're not ready to put you out to pasture yet. Player-coach, I mean."

It was too good to be true. First unload Hawkins and pick up Johnson from LA. Maybe gamble on a college kid. . . .

"So what do you say, Mike?"

"Sure. I'd be honored." Mo raised a speculative eyebrow.

"Great. We'll talk terms later. My best to Mo."

"You look like you're in shock," said his agent.

"Ed Walters wants me to be player-coach."

Mo rose out of his seat to pump Mike's hand. "Looks like you'll name your terms after all. Now it seems to me that you've got to unload old Lester Hawkins and go for Johnson in LA. . . ."

Back in the Pan Am building, sipping coffee as the afternoon turned cloudy and sullen, Mike watched the crawling traffic below and contemplated his good fortune. He had wished for Curry's departure a hundred times, and finally it had come about. Better yet the Comet organization was entrusting the fate of the team to him, an All-Star after three seasons but still only twenty-five years old. It would not remain a secret for long. Matt Rafferty must already know—his nicotine-stained fingers still rested on the pulse of the Comets and, in particular, on the feeble pulse of Alex Curry, who was sure to raise hell. Mike felt no triumph in that regard. Curry was getting on in years and might have a rough time signing on with another team. On the other hand if he went out like a docile, company man the organization would take care of him. As long as he didn't meddle with the team any longer, Mike had no quarrel with the deposed coach. Now the Comets were going places; visions of a championship danced in his head.

Patty would be pleased. A new job, more money. All the fine things. Had he earned them or did they come of themselves? In any case he took his wealth in stride. More was within his grasp than the grasp of others. Talent. Big deal. What did talent amount to if you didn't make something of it? And what was his talent? Hard work? Being 6'6"?

He was glad he had chosen a career in basketball. A career of pounding up and down the hardwood floor below the glistening faces and the blue veil of undulating smoke and the burning lights; of jostling under the backboards, among big bodies in perpetual motion. For that he endured the frustration of losing and afterwards—in the stinging shower or the next day—the aches. It was basketball and he loved it, loved to play hard, loved to compete. But all the while he was loving it he was preparing to leave it, getting ready for another career—whatever it might be. Even now he pursued other interests, his job with Future Leaders for one. At banquets he gave speeches and shook hands. Was that directing him toward his life's work?

He hadn't told Mo yet but law school was out of the question. He was learning too much outside the classroom ever to go back. Patty agreed. Such a move might launch their marrige into calamitous seas, after they toiled so hard to reach a point of relative calm. Had the initial romance fled for good? Too often the old disapproval flickered in her steady blue eyes. Her sterility became moot, unspoken. Much else was also left unsaid. Still they were accustomed to each other and both kept busy, that was the main thing. Not a marriage made in heaven but not quite a catastrophe either, as long as she didn't know about Darlene. They were, as Patty said, "a good team." The irony wasn't lost on either of them and perhaps that explained their compatability. They understood each other. She didn't watch him play every night the way some of the wives did, but she was in the stands as often as not and she never missed the big series, against the Celts, the Lakers, the 76ers. At the gallery she had a serious career of her own. What should he give *his* life to? Again he came back to that question.

One answer offered itself. Recently, and privately, he had toyed with the idea of entering politics. He still felt ignorant—one of the great advantages of a Yale education; it reminded you how ignorant you always would be—but he was studying. He went about it methodically, the way he went about everything. In college he'd been an indifferent historian, mostly Bs, here and there an A when something caught his fancy. A thinker he was not. Politicians, however, were men of action, and there he couldn't fault himself. From Jefferson and Wilson and Roosevelt, and even Huey

Long, whose biographies he consumed avidly, he gained insight into governing on a grand scale, noting its limitations, its virtues, its dangers, its seductive power. Democracy, though a collective enterprise, depended on just a few leaders. He shed his athlete's modesty long enough to admit he could become one of those few. He possessed the qualities of a vote-getter, he had friends, he had admirers, he had a name, he had money, he had connections. A law degree might help, but disaffection with legal types ran high these days; he could turn that shortcoming into an advantage.

Frequent talks with Mo and gilded memories of the student movement convinced him he also had ideological substance. Everywhere you looked people were decrying the old liberalism. Yet America owed its genius to progress, improvement, enlightenment, reform. Those principles hadn't died, but they had been flayed into rhetoric by the garbled insinuations of the recrudescent right wing. Not that Mike wasn't a realist. You had to pay the electorate its due, you had to tell people what they wanted to hear. But with that came responsibility—to the downtrodden, the short-changed, the neglected. F.D.R. served as his model here. You did what was necessary to win votes, but once the power was yours, you must wield it effectively, direct it toward the common good. There was a fine line between ruthlessness and idealism. Combine the two artfully and you became a statesman.

In retrospect, his years at Yale and his activity off the court took on a political bent. Mo had given him a political consciousness. Wright had educated him in the practical uses of power. He must accept the obvious: there were those born with the gift of leadership. He would be, at twenty-five, the coach of a professional basketball team. On the surface it might not seem like much, but it meant leading men, responding to their needs, as well as goading them into giving their best. He would come through, prove his ability to work with things and people as they were. In others, like Mo, the iconoclastic streak was too severe; their lofty principles couldn't accomodate the nasty side of things. A man such as Wright, conversely, harnessed the unseen currents of influence the way Edison harnessed electricity; but it was backroom stuff, kingmaking, wheeling and dealing, power dispensed and accrued in secret, around heavy oak tables with a dozen matching chairs and weighty ashtrays supporting expensive cigars.

How did you make the two work together, the men with the money and the men who understood the public good? Wasn't it up to fellows like himself, who for reasons that couldn't be explained, and ultimately didn't matter, earned the respect and confidence of both camps, alchemizing repellent elements into pure, democratic gold?

He even had a sort of plan for injecting himself into the political stream. He would begin as a private citizen, using the centipedal branches of First New York to aid the city that had adopted him. The Youth Center was the ticket. He had already done a bang-up job at Future Leaders, had in fact altered its entire orientation, so that now it benefitted the poor instead of the privileged. A promotion was due. With a bigger budget and a freer rein he might get that Center under way. Then, perhaps, a Congressional seat. Strictly temporary. He would represent the East Side, a community which demanded little from its Congressmen beyond clamping down on escalating taxes. Patty through her gallery had connections with his neighbors. He would throw a fund-raiser or two, low-key affairs. If he served with distinction he would then train his sights on a Senate seat. Once ensconced in that elite brotherhood his future would be limited only by his talent and blind luck. And he had plenty of both.

He daydreamed until five o'clock then snatched his jacket off the door and bolted out of his office. The pretty but dim receptionist looked up from breathing on her freshly rubied nails and actually, God help her, batted her lashes. He took a cab home.

It was an excited Patty who rushed to greet him, the color radiant in her lovely face. She planted an unexpected kiss on his lips and led him by the hand into the living room.

"Hey," he laughed. Maybe she already knew.

"How about a cool drink, handsome?"

"You're a step ahead of me."

It was a pleasure to watch her at the bar. The girl had become a woman. Put to rest was the affected maturity of the frightened virgin, and the rankling priggishness. She had transformed their apartment into a luxurious home without consulting magazines or her friends or her mother. Above the marble fireplace hung a Rothko she spotted last summer at an auction. At first it gave him the creeps but now Mike loved to look at it, three enlarged bricks of earth-deep colors, totems of a dark but luminous death-vision. Also a sound investment, as sound as the treasury notes and money markets Wright hawked like a fruit vendor.

Patty poured too much water into his scotch but that was all right. It was nice, what you expected from a woman. They sat side by side on a black sofa that was long enough for him to sleep on.

"I have wonderful news," she said.

"So do I."

"This is fun. I have two things, so you go first."

"Looks like I'm going to be player-coach next season. Ed Walters called today when I was at Mo's office discussing the contract."

"Darling, that's wonderful. I'm happy for you." She kissed him again and drew his hand into her lap. "Do you want to hear my news now?"

"You bet."

"First, the Hartmans have offered us the use of their cabin in Vermont. I thought maybe we could go up for two weeks. To get away from the city and be by ourselves."

"Terrific. When can we go?"

"You want to? I hoped you would."

"Never been to Vermont."

"It's beautiful and piny and Laura said they have a lovely cabin she and Leo designed on a little mountain and there's a lake and a rowboat."

"No more, please. It's like telling a starving man about food."

"Does the first of the month sound all right?"

"Sold."

She put a slender arm around his neck. "Now for the next news, although it's not really news. It's been going on for a couple of weeks, since I spoke to a woman who comes by the gallery a lot. She told me how she and her husband went to a wonderful agency with lovely children and—"

He stood up. "No."

"Please, Mike. Let me finish. I went to two places and they have such beautiful children and it's so sad—"

"I don't want somebody else's child. I have all the adopted kids I need at Future Leaders. It's got to be *our* flesh and blood, Patty."

"But, Mike, it can't be. And so many children desperately need families. They need to be cared for and we have so much to give."

"Hook up with Future Leaders. You can care for twenty kids at a time. You'd be good at it. Organizing trips to SoHo—"

Tears glazed her glabrous cheeks. "You don't *have* any love to give. That's why you won't adopt a child. It's got to be Mike Merritt's child. It's got to be *you*. If we adopted a child it might interfere with all the love you give to yourself."

"Let's not forget who's sterile."

He winced from the horror imprinted on her face. He heard a choked moan, then ice rattling, and then feet pounding lightly on the floor. The bedroom door slammed.

She was right. It had to be himself. Was that such a crime? It was human nature. The father born again in the son, the body struggling against time to preserve a unique soul. You took in another man's child and you were reduced to performing a function. You shared your name and your wealth and yes, goddamn it, your love, but the child couldn't give you back to yourself. There were genes to be passed on and rejuvenated and—fuck this mumbo-jumbo. What was he talking about? What did he mean to say?

Shaking with remorse he burst into the bedroom. Patty welcomed him with trembling arms, answering his apologies with her own. It had been too sudden, she should have consulted him from the start. They would talk about it later, give it more thought. Maybe when they were in Vermont, far away from the frenzied city.

"We still love each other, don't we?" said Patty. "We can work out our problems."

"Sure we can."

"It was good we married, wasn't it?"

"Sure it was," said Mike. "It was good."

The next two weeks they put aside all talk of adoption and focused instead on their upcoming vacation. It would be a time to mend their wounds and return to the bedrock of their love. At Mike's suggestion they altered their plans slightly, agreeing to invite Bee up for the second week. It was a long time since Mike and his former roommate had shared their special communion. He thought back nostalgically to the thousands of hours they had spent together at Yale and wondered if some of the old memories couldn't be recaptured.

With this in mind he arranged to meet the fledgling writer at a midtown restaurant. The place was dark with a ceiling as plush as the carpet. Both were red, and joined by mahogany beams. Spotlights touched the tables with muted light.

Bee licked the last drops of his fourth martini and summoned the waiter with his eyes. A nervous kid scurried over to take the glass.

Mike carefully measured his friend's face, illumined gently in the dull light. It wouldn't show for a while yet; it would take a few years before the nose became veiny, the eyes liquescent and blurred. His chin hadn't yet crumbled and his flesh wasn't scarlet, but the drinking had already taken its toll.

"You're nervous as a rabbit, Bee."

"It ain't easy being Queen for a Day."

"Why just a day?"

Bee laughed shortly. "I don't know if I can hold on much longer."

"You need a break."

"You said it. I don't know what to do with myself."

"Fed up with writing?"

"No, I'll never be fed up with writing. But I'd like to get away from all this sexual politics stuff. After a while it wears thin, even for me. Thing is I don't know where to turn. I don't want to go back to reviews. I could move to the glossies and make more bread but it'd be the same story. Hack work. What I'd like to do is try my hand at something serious—a novel. I don't know if I have one in me." He held up a warding hand. "Don't say it. There's only one way to find out."

"It's true."

"I know. I could wangle a contract right now since I've got something of a name."

"So you have something in the works."

"That's the trouble, I don't. Or maybe I do but it's not at all clear to me. I'm scared to put it on the line, risk being serious. What if it's a flop, what if it gets killed in the reviews?"

"That I can sympathize with, after my rookie season."

Bee stared intently at his friend, his pale eyes beseeching. "Do you think I'm a good writer, Mike?"

"The best."

Bee smiled thinly. "Don't say that. It's funny but it hurts."

"You expect too much."

"This from the man who will be king. The richest graduate of the class of '72."

"Why don't you take the risk then, give it a shot. Go for broke. Head for the hills—say Vermont. That's where writers go, isn't it? Get yourself a little house with a lake and a grove of trees. Leave the booze and the cigarettes and the flashy parties behind. They'll get along without you. Cart your talent and your typewriter out to the country.''

"A pretty fantasy. But it takes money."

"If you had a chance would you do it?"

Bee's eyes narrowed shrewdly. "What have you got up your sleeve, buddy?"

"Patty and I have the run of her boss's place for a couple of weeks. And we'd like you to come up."

"Three's a crowd."

"Not necessarily. We're spending the first week alone. You come up the second. Patty's all for it too. Think of it. A week furlough from smog and noise and filth and insanity. The cabin's on a hill with a lake. We can camp and have cookouts and swim all day."

"A boy scout this boy ain't. I spent six hours in summer camp before they sent me packing. Not that I wasn't overjoyed to go. Up at four to greet the mosquitoes and then a dip in the freezing lake. Organized tree-climbing and volley ball, pissing in smelly latrines. It was like prison."

"No rules at Camp Merritt. Your time is your own. Patty says there's an extra room with a little balcony. You can write there all day if you like. We'll leave you alone."

"And miss a whole week of partying?"

"You'll survive."

"You tempt me, *amico*."

"It's been a long time since we really talked about things, Bee. Where we're headed with our lives and all. Remember how it used to be: the all-night bullshitting sessions, the long walk out to East Rock, the—"

"All right, all right. You're breaking my heart. I'll join your little bungle in the jungle. But the booze and the cigarettes are coming with me. And my nasty disposition, too."

10

July bludgeoned the city with roiling heat and the Merritts packed off to Vermont in a rented car. Next to Mike, gathering sun on the seat, were the essays of Emerson, untouched since his Yale days, the collected writings of Thoreau, some poetry, and Patty, studying the map through owlish sunglasses. They sped along the Hudson to Lake Champlain and crossed into Vermont just above Burlington. A short spell on the interstate brought them to a scenic state highway at the foot of the Green Mountains. For an hour they spun along, for the most part in silence, murmuring their pleasure now and then when a brook purled into view, or another fold of blue peaks nudged back the horizon.

"Turn here," directed Patty, her words almost lost in the eddying rush of scented air. They were on a hogback; behind them sank the marigold sun. Mike, unused to power brakes, crunched his foot to the floor and they nearly fishtailed into the next world. They recovered and bumped along a private road, gravel sputtering metallically between fender and tire. Their progress was paralleled by a mountain rill, which mirrored like black stripes the slim trunks of pines.

"There it is." Patty indicated an A-frame crowning the verdant summit.

"Wow."

A short driveway ran up to the lodge. Below, basined by this mountain and its sister peaks, sat the lake, brimming like a vast drink in an earthen bowl. They giddily inhaled the crystalline air and then unloaded their bags, a tent, a portable stove, hiking boots, and an old kerosene lamp Patty had disinterred from her parents' basement.

Their quarters proved spacious and handsome. The living room was amply furnished and overlooked the lake. A flight of stairs smack in the middle led to a pair of bedrooms, triangulated by the inverted V of the roof.

An inspection of the kitchen uncovered canned goods and a note, held to the refrigerator by a magnetic bottle opener, encouraging the couple to use whatever supplies they could find. Mike left Patty to settle them in and headed to the nearest town for provisions. New Snowdon, five miles away, reminded him of Williamsburg. Past the clapboard houses huddled crookedly along Main Street were two bright gas stations, a movie theater with an aged marquee, and a shopping center. At the supermarket he picked up milk, corn, potatoes, chicken, and steak. He purchased two bottles of wine at the liquor store and couldn't resist the fresh bread displayed in the bakery next door.

Back at the lodge he tracked down Patty. She was in their bedroom, unpacking. She had changed into shorts and a lemon-colored sleeveless top. He watched with pleasure as she efficiently placed his clothes in a drawer. The perfumed woods, the sparkling lake, the falling sun—the excitement of new surroundings—flooded him with desire.

She turned from the bureau and smiled. "Something on your mind, stranger?"

"You."

"What about me?"

"Come here."

"In a minute. Let me put a few more things away." She bent back to her task.

He crept up behind her and circled her small shoulders with his long arms, cupping her breasts. She leaned back on him, her eyes closing, lifting her chin. He nuzzled her smooth throat and his hands dropped to her waist. She snuggled against him contentedly. "Mmm. This is nice."

They kissed tenderly, again and again, until her breath quickened and her arms cinched around his neck. He carried her to the Hartman's quilted bed. Insects looped in and out, dancing with their reflections on the windowpane as evening hooded the sky.

"I'm famished," said Patty.

Mike insisted on fixing dinner. "In remembrance of my old boy scout days." He dressed potatoes in foil and tossed two chicken breasts into the oven. Patty grabbled in a drawer for a corkscrew.

After dinner Mike hunted in the adjacent shed for firewood. He found a pyramid of thick logs and bundles of newspapers. Three editions of the *New Snowdon Press* and a hefty log were soon blazing in the hearth. The flames crackled and filled the living room with smoky warmth.

"Wouldn't it be lovely to have a place like this for a retreat?" said Patty. She was sitting on the sofa, draped in one of Mike's sweaters. She had pushed up the sleeves and they bulged hugely around her elbows.

Mike's head was in her lap. "Just what I was thinking. The city can wear you down, especially a farmboy like me."

"Hardly a farmboy."

"A small town boy, then."

Patty traced the line of his nose. "Miss it?"

"Not Williamsburg but the space and the big skies and the lazy days."

Patty raised her coffee mug. "I propose a toast. To you."

"To me? Why?"

"Because you're wonderful. So wonderful that I spend too much time looking for faults."

He chuckled. "Don't look too hard."

"I'm not taken in entirely. I wonder what it is you're afraid of. As far as adopting goes, for example."

"For example."

"You're deathly afraid of rejection."

"Who isn't?"

"But you seem to expect it."

This time he regarded the subject with equanimity. Patty wanted to talk it out and it was her right. Besides, he had done some thinking on his own. "What if we were to adopt in a couple of years, after my playing days are through? That's not just a way of putting you off. The season takes too much out of me. Too much time, too much energy."

She nodded soberly. "He'll need us both and he'll need us often."

Crickets clicked and timbers creaked and orange flames licked the stone fireplace. Was a lifetime of this possible: a marriage of true minds, of kindred spirits twilled into something durable, weaving together circumstance and time? Probably not if he continued to see Darlene. In her arms he achieved bliss but the toll might prove severe. Aside from the obvious impediments there was the price of passion itself, the tiresome trysts with their recent undercurrent of hysteria. The result of drugs; Jasper kept her well supplied. It amounted to a yoke more cumbersome than wedlock, bereft of the dimmest glimmer of relief. His marriage could be resuscitated by the healthy instincts that had birthed it, but this affair, conceived illicitly, must always be illicit, and sooner or later would taint him for good.

"What are you thinking?" his wife asked softly.

"That I love you."

She clapped her hand over a yawn. "All of a sudden I'm awfully sleepy."

They awoke to a pink band of dawn, rimming the hills opposite above the wrinkled sapphire lake. Hand in hand they skipped down a root-filled path to the swatch of sand. They stripped off their clothes and plunged into the frigid water. Within moments their lungs rebelled. Gasping for air they quickly shivered back into their clothes.

A rowboat rocked lightly against a dock fingering into the water. Mike loosened it from its moorings and they set off.

The lake was bow-shaped, nearly a mile across at its widest point before funneling symmetrically into a channel walled on both sides by the tree-covered mountain bases. Then it widened again and was dotted with tiny green islands. Every hundred yards another dock fingered into the lake. In boathouses sleek outboard jobs swayed and shifted like racehorses in stalls.

Mike enjoyed the strain of rowing, the steady rhythm, extending his arms till they tugged at their sockets. Patty perched near the prow, like Lorelei on the reef. The lake was empty; the whole crinkly expanse was theirs. The dipping oars pushed ripples toward the shore.

"When should we go camping?" Patty wondered, shielding her eyes against the climbing sun.

"When Bee arrives. So he can be alone to write. We could take an overnight trip. Climb one of these mountains, then hike along the ridge. There's bound to be trails. I'd like to follow that stream, too, the one by the road. Maybe we can locate its source."

"And we can picnic on these little islands."

"It's going to be an eventful vacation," said Mike.

"Yes. So much is going to happen."

The week passed lanquidly. They were up with the dawn for an early swim, then hiked in the woods. The best time to explore was early morning, when the chameleon sky blushed from pink to orange to violet to blue and their neighbors slept on deeply in the cool fragrant air. Evenings the couple warmed themselves by the fire, watching the lake dissolve into the comforting blackness of night, and the flickering image of flames in the window.

Patty read Eudora Welty and Flannery O'Connor and Mike pursued his casual study of the Romantics. He browsed in Thoreau, tasted a couple of Emerson's lectures, tried Whitman, and then returned to Wordsworth like a prodigal son.

The reading and his surroundings evoked fresh memories of his boyhood. The steaming sun, the heavy corn-growing air, the pungent, nostril-filling odor of the soil. Williamsburg was hardly Vermont or Grasmere: there were no mountains or crags, no gushing rills; the landscape was as monotonous as the lives of its inhabitants. Its resemblance to lovelier regions subsisted chiefly in what it was not. Williamsburg was not the city, that cauldron of boiling smells, sights, sounds, and schemes, that exotic mingling of luxury and squalor, grandeur and fetid death. New York seemed an organism pulsating toward indeterminate ends. Was its final purpose increase or contraction, growth or decay? Or was it both, did growth and decay nourish each other and thus create an atmosphere of unchanging variety? Like humanity itself, which could never get better or worse, but only endure, clinging to the shadow of its past and a frail dream of the future? Was society too complex to admit improvement, like a broth so laden with spices that no single taste emerged?

Suddenly this notion bothered him; it threatened his inherited vision of America, and its principles of enlightenment and progress. Did history deny such principles? Instead of advancement was there only repetition? What was the alternative? Taking the cue from his reading, which said, "Look to nature, look to things not human," he did exactly that and concluded that the alternative to repetition was rejuvenation. Death conquered all—death in the form of disappointment and disillusionment—but from death sprung new life, new hope. The expired river would flow again, when the first soft drops of rain pelleted the mountain and trickled down the slope, gathering substance and force, filling the empty bed that had been carved ages before, in patient anticipation of refreshment. The same truth held for systems of government, which also in the course of events ran dry, but could be renewed, reclaimed, refurbished. Cynicism and deceit, the offspring of a government whose ruling consideration was mere self-preservation—again the dreaded repetition—drained the body politic of its vital fluids. But the channels of progress remained. The dry riverbed was still a bed. The cycle might begin anew.

"I'll never forget seeing you at the Public Library with all those books under your arm," Patty said, breaking a lengthy silence their last evening alone. "It's what made me love you, I think."

"Not my looks?"

"Don't be vain." She lapsed back into silence, pondering. "It changed my image of you so much. I never doubted your intelligence but I hadn't a clue to the inwardness before. It was so nice seeing you with that earnest look on your face."

Mike held up his tattered anthology of poems and prefaces. "Reading pulled me through. Those were rough times. I felt I didn't have a friend in the world and each book was comforting, another voice."

Patty struggled with a thought. "It was that girl, wasn't it, who upset you so. It wasn't just the basketball."

"She was part of it," Mike admitted.

"Do you still think about her?"

"Do you still think about Mitchell Farris?"

"Yes, but not in any special way. He's just a memory, a person I knew and learned from. Is that how you feel about Darlene?"

The name on his wife's lips sent a jolt through him. "Yes." And at that moment he knew he was done with Darlene for good. Their trysts were merely repetitions and by his new reckoning must end.

Patty's somberness lingered on her mobile, perfect features, then she burst into giggles.

"What's so funny?"

"For some reason—maybe it's the wine—I was thinking about that time I was so drunk and silly. You know, that summer you were in New York."

Mike improvised from the page he was reading:

"Five summers past; five summers, with the length
Of five long winters! and again I hear

Those hiccups, spilling from your loosened tongue. . . ."

"It's unbecoming to gloat."

"What gloating?"

"You knew I was terrified of you. I had to chase away my nerves."

"I was terrified of *you*. I thought you pegged me for a hick, a hayseed. And you were this princess—"

"Please don't say that. I hate that word."

"I didn't mean anything by it."

"Bee always called me that. He knew I hated it but he said it anyway."

"He takes things too far sometimes, but it's all in good fun."

"I used to think so, but now I'm not so sure. He acts so strangely these days. At the wedding he was so aloof and sardonic. He resented it. He resented *me*. He still does."

"Oh, I don't know. He was just back from Europe and things were still a bit strange for him."

"Darling, that's just evading the issue. I've known Bee as long as I can remember. We were never really close friends, for all the time we spent together. And with the tree of us, it's you he cares for and performs for, not me. He doesn't even admit he's gay to me. How often has he come over since we were married? Hardly ever, if you think about it."

"He's got his own life to lead. And things to do. I see him some. Not enough maybe, but compared to roommates even best friends are virtually strangers."

"If we weren't married you'd see him a lot more often." She paused. "I've never known anyone to be so gloomy as Bee."

"Even Mo?"

"Mo's not gloomy, he's just serious. Bee's morbid. Even those jokes of his. It's some kind of compulsion, pretending not to take anything seriously, even his own writing."

"He has high standards."

"He hates himself."

"It's not a crime to downplay your own accomplishments."

"Even if it's an excuse for avoiding new things? He just mocks everything. I don't mean to sound spiteful. I worry about him."

"So who's being gloomy?"

"You're right, I suppose. Bee's a good friend. And he *is* funny. I hope his vacation does him some good."

"What do you say we measure his weight and his blood pressure as soon as he steps off the train? Then each day we can monitor the changes. Like with cattle. We'll put him on an experimental diet too. All meat one day, then no water—"

"I hate you."

He tossed his book onto the floor. "Well, I still love you. Even if you're undeserving."

The next morning they drove to New Snowdon to meet Bee's train. The town was quiet. A few families in their Sunday best emerged from the Congregationalist church and filled the luncheonette across the street.

The train pounded down a steep grade and halted with a shrieking of steel. Bee stepped off in a flannel shirt and workboots. A rucksack was strapped over his shoulder. He carried a typewriter in one hand and with the other tapped the platform with his black umbrella.

"Yoohoo, Bee!" Patty called. Mike touched the horn.

Bee smiled winningly and hopped into the back seat. "The prettiest pair in all of New England, Matty and Pike."

Mike swung out of the station.

"How was your trip, Bee?" asked Patty.

"Ten hours in the twenty-fifth circle of hell. Two bucks for a roast beef sandwich that was positively blue. The drinks were outrageous. Good thing I brought my own. A one-story Windows on the World or The Great Train Robbery, take your pick."

"Philistine," Mike hissed.

"Who, me? I live for my art. And the countryside was lovely."

"That's better," Patty approved. "Isn't this a pretty town?"

Bee sniffed. "I smell churchgoers."

"This isn't Sodom," Mike advised. "People up here have faith."

"Have pity on this poor pillar of salt. I was denied your Middle-American roots. Snowburg take you back to Lincolnburg?"

"Yeah, it does. Williamsburg's not so picturesque but the feeling's the same. Remember, small towns are the backbone of the Republic."

"A week of lectures," moaned Bee. "I'll get cabin fever."

Outside town they picked up the now-familiar road to the cabin, ribboning along the hubble-bubble of the stream. When he stepped out of the car Bee breathed the pure air just as his friends had done, and gazed serenely at the lake. "Can't wait to see my little garret."

"You'll love it, Bee," promised Patty.

They tramped inside. Mike and Patty pointed out the kitchen, the bathroom, the fireplace, then led their guest upstairs.

Bee let out a whistle upon entering his room. "What a view!" A desk faced the lush downslope and the sparkling lake and the rising hills beyond. The balcony was small, composed of cedar slats with a table shaded jauntily by a tilted umbrella.

"A year in this joint and I might turn out *Walden III*."

"How about lunch first?"

"Yes, a drink would be fine."

"You'll have to setttle for Dago red."

"I'll settle, I'll settle."

After the meal Mike guided Bee on an expedition through the backwoods. They followed a twisting path down to the stream and sat on the cushiony bank, within reach of the tingling spray. Black branches, torn from the upstream pines by the swift current, snagged against polished boulders. On the riverbed pebbles glittered like doubloons.

"Tomorrow Patty and I are going on an overnight hike so you ought to be able to get some writing done."

Bee studied the serrated edge of a leaf. "I haven't thanked you yet for inviting me."

"We're glad you could make it. We both wanted to see you get away from the city."

"It's not so bad. After all, it's treated *you* pretty well."

"True enough. But I won't stay there much longer. Not once my playing days are through."

"Then?"

"Eventually, Washington, D.C., I hope."

Bee cocked an eyebrow. "Congress?"

"I'm thinking about it."

"Mo's doing?"

"No, as a matter of fact. Of course he's influenced me but not overtly. Subliminally. I've been doing some studying on my own. Reading."

"Great Books about Great Men?"

"Nobody knows me like you do. Other things too. Poetry and fiction and straight history. What I should have been doing in school. Trying to catch up. You were always reading, weren't you, for all the pot and booze and the screwing around. You didn't need the classroom."

"Classrooms made me nervous. Killed the life out of books."

"Thought anymore about that novel?"

"No, but I've begun a story. Inspiration struck one night so I got a few thousand words down. Haven't looked at it since. I figured I'd get back to it up here. I'd like to read some of it to you."

"When?"

"After you come back from your camping trip and after I've written some more. It's a painful business, writing. Patience and time. It isn't like basketball. A lot of good writers don't get anywhere till they're twice my age."

"Hell, you've already done some fine work. Who knows where you'll be in ten years?"

"Drunk in a gutter most likely."

"That's up to you."

Bee lowered his gaze to the ground. "I know. Sometimes I think I might be trying to do myself in."

"Why? You've got talent and you're the brightest guy I've ever known. When you tore off that paper freshman year—remember that?—I was amazed. And you're getting better all the time."

"Better at the same old thing. Better at being caustic and elegant. But I'm not sure there's a place for elegance in a shabby time."

"It's when the world needs it most. And don't all writers complain about shabby times? *'O tempora, O mores,'* 'It was the best of times, it was the worst of times'?"

"That's some Great Books course."

"Fancy words never sound right coming out of my mouth. Maybe because I'm so big. It's a damned affliction sometimes but it's the way it goes. Not that I'm trying to pull that Young Man Lincoln crap any more. I've outgrown that, with your help. No more wide-eyed innocence."

"I'm not putting you down, Mike. I respect what you've become. What you're doing with your life. Your energy and perseverence. Maybe I'm jealous."

"What for?"

"You're a millionaire at twenty-five. You never fail, you have no weaknesses. Two hundred years of American history filling the stands and yelling, 'Go, go go!' You'll probably be President some day. Admit it, admit you're already thinking about it. That's why you read all these books, not so you can represent a bunch of lead-headed East Side snobs in Congress. It's the great Republic that's ringing the chimes in your

Apollonian head. The Gettysburg Address and 'We have nothing to fear.' What do you read? Emerson, Thoreau, Henry Adams?"

"Among others. Go on, though, I'm interested."

"Sure. The American cadence, the rhythm of power and freedom and Manifest Destiny. You're bound to succeed because you're an antique, a throwback. Horatio Alger Revisited. Henry Ford, Harry S. The rest of our generation is like me—going crazy with nothing to do and nothing to believe in—and you're like Adam awaking to his dream of Eden. Crosby self-destructs with a crummy imitation of Rimbaud and Merritt struts through the countryside like Johnny Appleseed, sowing the old values. Your fellow citizens can't wait to vote for you—I guarantee it. You'll get a hundred percent of the vote. And once they see you in the White House they'll crown you President for life. Just so you can remind them how great everything is, that the dream's still alive. Andrew Jackson Merritt."

Mike smiled. "You know my fantasies pretty well. But that's just one side. It's practically a caricature. I've got problems too, you know, and fears and worries and weaknesses, just like everyone else. Maybe more since I can't make my mistakes in private. Hell, I've been famous since I was nineteen." He skinned a twig with his thumbnail.

Bee lit a cigarette and buried the match in the dirt. "What are these mysterious weaknesses and fears? What is it you don't tell anyone?"

Mike looked squarely into the pale inquiring eyes of his friend. Bee craved to hear about his failings the way Patty craved his love and Mo craved his assurance that the Fight was still on and Darlene craved—what did she crave? Perhaps if he knew he would be content to keep on giving it to her. How could he resist a plea to parcel out another bit of himself?

"Well," he began, "for one thing I haven't been honest with Patty. There haven't been many other women, just one in fact, but I out and out lied about it just last night. I'm going to end it, though, as soon as we get back. I can't go on this way. I've been selfish too, as far as Patty goes. She's a great girl, Bee, and she deserves a lot more than I've given her. But I'm going to change all that. Being out here has really brought us closer. Our marriage has been a partnership so far, an arrangement, and I never realized how much that hurt her. I've been cruel and made her feel inadequate."

"Sexually, you mean?"

"Sort of."

"Sort of?"

Mike eyed his friend. "Now you're asking me to tell her secrets."

"Sorry. Withdraw the question, your honor."

"No harm intended—no harm done."

"Is that it for your secrets? I mean, a little hanky-panky is nothing to immolate yourself for in 1975. People expect it."

"Not Patty."

"That's her problem for being uptight. Surely there's something else." Bee sounded urgent.

"Well, there's our little romp freshman year."

"So you're ashamed of that."

"I just meant it's a secret. Nobody knows. Unless you've told."

"Ask me no questions and I'll tell you no lies. Don't sweat it. Before long people will apologize for being straight. Flings with fags will be the rage."

Mike tossed a piece of bark into the stream. It lolloped in the rush of water then swept past. Jays preening atop a pine flitted away, their sweet mocking chirrups fading into the black wood. A faint rustling nearby revealed a rabbit, his ears daggered back and quivering like antennae. He pounced into a low bush. The endless activity of nature, things pursuing their instincts, their rightful course. What was his rightful course, to clam up or to come clean?

"All right," he said. "There's one thing I've never told anybody although one other person knows. A woman. The stepmother of my old girlfriend Diane."

"You tupped her."

"There's more."

"Go on."

"Her husband was on a scholarship committee. Yale had already accepted me but I couldn't afford the loans. Jesus I wanted to go! I felt I deserved it. My dad died the summer before and if he'd been alive the loans wouldn't have been any problem. The scholarship was my only hope. It was called the College Fund. Mrs. Davidson promised it to me if—"

"You slept with her."

"Funny thing was her husband wasn't on the committee at all, although I won the scholarship anyway. She knew all along I would win and I should have known too but you get desperate and you'll do anything. Maybe I *did* know but I had to do something final to kill my ties with Williamsburg, make it so I could never go back. My dad went back and he was never the same. Still there was no excuse for cheating like that. There were other kids who needed the scholarship a lot worse than I did. I had offers from fifty colleges—basketball scholarships, full rides. Mrs. Davidson made me give Diane the brush-off too. Just to hurt her. Those two really had it in for each other. A bad scene all the way around."

"So that's why you were so serious as soon as you stepped off the train. You had to prove yourself worthy."

"I still do."

Bee put a hand on his old roommate's shoulder. "It doesn't damage you in *my* eyes. You're still my hero."

"And the secret's safe with you, right?"

"As safe as it could ever be."

Mike lay back and cradled his head on his folded arms. "I'm glad I told you. It feels good to get it off my chest. The worst thing I've ever done. There's a fatalistic little voice inside that says I'll pay for it yet. But I have no idea how or when."

"Hey, it's not as bad as all that. You got to Yale without any help and besides *she* came to you. If you hadn't banged the dame, somebody else would have. Maybe she needed the loving."

"She sure did. But Diane—that was the worst part."

"Where is the little pixie now?"

"Married to the new coach at Whitman High. Guy we went to school with. A bozo and a half."

"All's well that ends well."

"As long as it's ended. Now we better check up on Patty."

"Can't leave the squaw alone. Not with white savages roaming the hills."

Patty was sunning herself on the lawn in front of the lodge. Her hair was damp from an afternoon swim. the week in the country had agreed with her. Her blue eyes shone against her tanned skin. She smiled brightly. "Which one of you is going to fix dinner?"

Mike and Bee each pointed at the other. Bee threw up his hands. "I suppose it's time I contributed to the team." He stepped off toward the house.

Mike sat crosslegged next to his wife.

"Have a nice talk?"

"A good talk anyway. I think he's glad he came. He's been working on a story and he wants to read it to us."

"How exciting! I'm glad he's here. And I'm glad we're here too. I don't think I've ever felt this close to you and I like it a lot."

He took her hand. "I do too."

"Don't you think we have something to offer—to children, I mean?"

"Planning a brood of Anglo-Saxon marvels?" Bee stood smiling with two glasses of wine.

Patty blushed. "Bee—"

"Come on, Patty. Don't be so sensitive."

"You just surprised me."

"How's lunch coming along?" Mike asked—too quickly.

Bee wagged a finger. "Now what are my best and

prettiest friends hiding from me. A little sprout on the way?"

Patty shut her eyes.

"Not yet," said her husband. "Just thinking out loud." He handed a glass to Patty and took the other for himself. Bee dropped onto the grass. "When *are* you two going to people the earth with little Mikes and Pattys? That's why you got hitched, isn't it?"

Patty gave her glass to Mike and ran inside, her damp tresses roped around her neck, her long legs flashing brown in the sun.

"What's gotten into her? My jokes ain't the best but they're not that bad."

"It's nothing. But I'll check on her anyway."

"Poor Princess Patty."

"Can it, will you? You've said enough."

Mike found Patty lying tearfully on the bed. He touched her shoulder. "He didn't mean anything."

"It's not him, it's me."

"There's nothing wrong with you. It's just the way things are."

It was a quiet uncomfortable meal. Bee chewed silently, not looking at his hosts.

Patty spoke up. "Bee, Mike says you're going to read to us from a story."

"Depends how it holds up to the light of sober analysis. I haven't looked at it since I wrote it. It might not be any good at all. You two still planning to hit the nature trails tomorrow?"

"Yep," said Mike. "We'll take off at dawn and you'll have the run of the place."

"Good. Maybe I'll get something done."

As promised Mike and Patty were up and out of the house at dawn. They stowed the tent and the stove and the kerosene lamp in the boat and set off. They breakfasted on an islet on the far side of the channel, then rowed to the farthest edge of the lake, mooring the boat to the trunk of a tree. They climbed a ridge, following a marked trail. The vegetation was thistly and deep. It was rough going since the incline was severe and periodically they rested. The view atop the mountain justified the effort. It was the highest elevation for miles, some four thousand feet, and afforded a vista of their own summit, topped by the A-frame. Beyond were imbricated hills, violet below a shining sky.

Patty had recently acquired a camera and she shot half a roll, zeroing in on the lake, which reflected the sun like foil. A speedboat, towing a skiier, spoiled the vision, so they moved on. The mountain sloped down over a town they didn't know existed and Patty photographed the patchwork of roofs and the rolling hills and the foreshortened tops of the pines, a hispid green carpet tinged with blue.

Mike waited for her to finish then pointed north. "I don't like the looks of those clouds."

"They're awfully dark. Ominous."

"And they're really moving."

"A storm?"

"It may just pass over, like a sun shower, or miss us entirely. But the wind is blowing them south. We could set up the tent right here by the rocks. This is pretty secure."

"I'm exhausted anyway and it'll take a while to get dinner ready."

They set up the pup tent and then the portable stove. The kerosene lamp took some fiddling with, but before long it produced a warm vibrant glow. Mike built a fire with twigs and leaves and branches scoured from the trail.

The clouds piled in rapidly. They were heavy and purple, sagging over the peaks like the gravid bellies of great cows. When the rain came it was thick. Dark droplets formed on the tent like splotches of black paint. Luckily, the tent was sturdy and withstood the squall. Their location too was good; the wall of rock provided adequate protection from the gusting winds. But the crepitating rain and the cold made it impossible to sleep and there was hardly space to breathe, since they had stashed all their paraphernalia inside.

The rain let up at dawn, but the sky stayed dark. The dispirited campers decided to make their way back to the lodge, reversing yesterday's tracks.

By the time they reached the boat it was noon and clouds gathered for another downpour. Mike was confident they would make it if they hugged the shoreline until they reached the channel, which they could cross in minutes, nosing along the shore all the way back. The first warm drops fell as they rounded a bend which put them in sight of home. Mike sent Patty into the house when they docked and stayed behind to make certain the boat was secure. The rain fell harder now, swelling the lake into lapping waves.

Patty greeted him at the door with dry clothes. She had changed into corduroys and a Comets sweatshirt.

"Thanks. What's Bee up to? Writing?"

"Hardly." His friend held a glass full of amber liquid. "The muse deserted me some time ago, I'm afraid. I was worried about you two. Thought maybe you drowned last night."

"Getting plowed, I see."

"I'm scared of the rain."

"Mike, get out of those clothes, please. You'll catch cold."

In the bathroom he slipped into the dry togs. He poured himself a shot of brandy from the uncapped bottle in the kitchen and carried it into the living room.

The wind scratched against the enormous window and mist rendered the downslope and the lake blurry. Hard-slanting drops lashed the cabin like pebbles. Patty sat near the unlit fireplace on the arm of a chair and Bee stood by the window, tracing expressive arcs with a cigarette, sipping his brandy. A single light pulsing from a table lamp cast a block of light at his feet. In the dusky glow Mike saw Bee's eyes were moist. "Yes," he was saying, "a question of fertility. This morning I was blossoming with ideas. But then I sort of dried up—"

Mike interrupted. "Anybody bring in logs for the

fire?"

"I'm afraid they all got soaked," Patty said. "There's a leak in the shed."

"Oh no."

"What do we need with a fire?" said Bee. "We have our own ignescence."

"I thought the fire was your idea."

"Ideas come and go. That's what I was telling Patty while you were changing. As regards writing."

Mike fell onto the cushion next to Patty. She gripped his arm tightly, her nails sinking into his flesh. He smiled at her but she didn't smile back.

"Hey, Bee. You going to read to us tonight?"

"No, children. Daddy isn't going to read you a bedtime story."

Mike was surprised. "Why not? We're game."

"Because what I wrote isn't any good, that's why. I reread what I wrote in the city—about three thousand words—and it was so bad I burned it last night in the fireplace." He gestured vaguely with his cigarette. "It didn't even read like my own writing. I don't know what the hell I was pretending to do. The style was adopted, if you know what I mean."

Patty's nails sank deeper. "I think I do," he said.

"I'm sure you do, Big Boy. Anyway I decided if it doesn't come naturally it better not come at all. You read any Keats, or isn't he part of the Future Dictators Great Books course?" It came out like a taunt.

"A couple of poems, mostly sonnets."

"The letters, man. You got to read the letters. Little Johnny says that if it doesn't come like leaves to the trees it better not come at all. Where was I? Oh yeah, I sacrificed to the hearth the paltry pages I had and decided to start from scratch. I was pretty depressed by then, as you can well imagine, so I poured myself a refreshment or two and stared moonily at the view. And a lovely view it is through that magic casement."

"At faery seas forlorn?"

"Bingo, Adonis! Well, this fairy got pretty forlorn

himself looking at all this loveliness, none of which touched his blank pages, and so decided to bag it, but not before cranking out a thousand words for the *Voice*. Hack work, but it pays the bills."

"What did you write about?"

"A trip to the country, what else? I riffled through your portable library and found a book of essays. *The Basketball Player's Guide to Purple Prose*, or was it *The Statesman's Directory of Essential Quotations and Noble Sentiments*?" He stubbed his cigarette into a metal tray and lit another.

"What the hell's wrong with you, Bee?" said Mike.

"What do you think?"

"You've been drinking too much," said Patty.

"No more than I have to."

"Why do you punish yourself?" she asked.

"Haven't you heard? This fruitcake's a masochist. That's what you mean, isn't it? A little taste of the old dominance and submission."

"Christ, Bee."

"You know that's what you think. Don't pull that good-guy riff on me."

"We're your friends."

"More like enemies within the gate. Patty, maybe you and I have a special understanding. We both seem to have trouble giving birth to our best intentions, a fellowship based on incapacity, you might say."

She gasped faintly and her fingers tore into Mike's arm like talons. "Listen, Bee. Maybe you better say what's on your mind."

"No secrets at Camp Merritt, eh? Did you tell wifey about the fun game we played yesterday?" His eyes darted to Patty. "We told secrets about ourselves, see, like one of those touchy-feely groups. I want to play some more. It's like telling ghost stories around the campfire, only we haven't got a fire." He sprawled on the sofa, his cigarette cleaving the air like a wand. "My secret isn't much of a secret, really. And Coach Merritt here got a taste of it himself one night, many cold moons ago, when Yale was still boys-only and our big healthy stud was desperate for some loving. Broke my heart, he did, the way he's broken countless others—all female though. I have the rare distinction of being his only experiment with the other half. As far as I know."

"That's enough, Bee," Mike said.

"Why don't you shut me up? Knock out my lights with a single blow and impress the little lady with your muscles. I'm in the market for submission, remember. My pain is my pleasure."

"What about our pain," said Mike, "is that your pleasure too?"

"Two points, Coach. But all aggression is ultimately self-aggression—isn't that what Rabbi Freud says? The more I hurt you the more I hurt myself."

"Why, Bee?" said Patty. "Why do you want to hurt yourself?"

"We're not up to that yet, Princess. We're still at the confession stage. Later we discuss the why."

"I don't want to hear it," said Mike.

"Unless you throw me out into the rain you're going to have to."

"You're drunk."

"I'm always drunk. My only lucid moments come when I'm drunk."

"Your cruelest too?"

"The truth is cruel."

"And you've got a monopoly on the truth?" said Mike.

"Not the way you've got a monopoly on lies."

"Bee," pleaded Patty.

"You know, Princess Patty, I never thought you had it in you to keep this hunk of manhood satisfied. Now I know you don't."

Mike stood up. "I just may have to throw you out after all."

Bee grinned up at him. "Please do. Maybe I'll drown."

Mike turned to his wife. "We better go upstairs until he calms down. He doesn't know what he's saying."

"You're really anxious to split this scene, aren't you? Just when I'm getting to the good part."

"You're trying to ruin a good friendship. That talk we had yesterday was confidential—"

"There's somebody else, isn't there?" Patty cried. "That's what Bee's talking about. There's another woman. It's that Darlene! You still love her!"

A stingy smile crossed Bee's face.

Mike went to touch her but she drew back. "Patty, honey—"

"Tell me! Is it her?"

"I'm never seeing her again. It's only been a couple of times. I know it's no good now. I love you, Patty. I love you like I've never loved anyone."

Patty's face was drained of color. "That other night. You lied. I asked you and you lied." Her face fell into her hands.

"I'm through with her, please believe me." He turned to Bee. "You can stay the night but then you're getting the hell out of here and out of our lives. If you weren't such a little runt I'd knock your teeth down your throat."

"I'll pack now." Bee slowly mounted the stairs.

"Patty—"

"Please don't say anything."

"Don't hate me. We'll talk after he's gone. It's not like you think."

"Just go away. Please."

The bastard. His best friend. He climbed up to Bee's room. The writer sat at his desk, a container of pills open beside him, his image in the blackened window swallowing from a glass.

He turned from the desk. "Here to finish me off?"

Mike grabbed the pills. "Looks like you beat me to it. Downers?"

"Relaxants."

Mike cracked the window and sent the container into

the blackness.

"What else have you got?" He tore open Bee's shaving kit. "A regular medicine cabinet. You are a sniveling little masochist. Well I won't gratify you by slapping you around. Is that what your boyfriends do?"

"Mike—"

"Did you think Patty would leave me and I'd move in with you?"

"I love you. I always have. I'm sorry." Bee still faced the window.

"Jesus, Bee. Pumping me with all those questions, storing up ammunition. What's happened to you?"

"I can go now, if you like."

"No. Tomorrow morning I'll take you to the station. It's my fault too. I dragged you up here."

"I'll apologize to Patty."

"Save it for tomorrow. I don't think she feels like talking to either one of us right now."

"So you love her."

"I married her, Bee."

"She'll forgive you."

"I hope so. I'm not sure I deserve it."

"Will you forgive me?"

Bee fumbled nervously with a match, then lit his last cigarette. Reflected in the window Mike saw the ghost of the boy who had met him at the station in New Haven with an empty suitcase and a black umbrella. A hopeful boy smiling sunnily through his own loneliness, a third-generation Yalie who would sire no more Yalies, with a secret that by rights should have been no secret at all.

"Yes, I forgive you."

Then Mike climbed downstairs to seek forgiveness for himself.

11

Pivoting at midcourt, he strained to control the ball as his opponent's arm snaked around his waist. He flapped an elbow to ward off the steal. As he did, he felt a foot between his legs. He put the ball to the floor and lunged across the line only to trip over a foreign sneaker. Pitching forward, he crashed to the floor and slid out of bounds, leaving a wide sweat-streak on the hardwood surface. The whistle shrieked and he struggled to his feet and bent over beneath the dazzling lights of Madison Square Garden, his chest heaving. A bolt of pain seared his knee.

These were the final minutes of the deciding game of the NBA finals. The New York Comets and the Los Angeles Lakers had taken the series to the wire.

At twenty-seven, Mike's black hair was cut short and his dark eyes had settled deeper in a lined face that reflected the total seriousness with which he regarded the basket from the freethrow line. For what seemed to him the millionth time he bounced it three times and arched the leather sphere cleanly through the air. The Garden erupted as the ball sliced through the white net. The squat, black-striped referee tossed him the ball again. He had another shot. With studied precision he tossed it too through the hoop. The mob of twenty thousand went mad: the Comets led 91-90 with five minutes to go. Mike had scored 29 points, twenty so far in the second half.

For two years now, as player-coach, he had pleaded and prodded and pulled and pushed his team toward this moment, investing every competitive ounce of energy into making the New York Comets the winners they had never been. This season they won the division and survived two preliminary playoff rounds, whipping the Philadelphia 76ers and then edging their nemesis, the Boston Celtics. This was the Comets' year, Mike Merritt's year. He felt it in the bones that now ached like an old man's.

On the Comets' next possession he called a time-out. They looked a bit sluggish and they couldn't afford to lose their slim lead. They couldn't let up—not now.

Clint Dixon jogged up behind him and planted a friendly hand on his ass. "Good shooting, Coach." Mike looked into the bristly face of the celebrated guard. Dixon flashed his heartbreaking smile. "We're gonna win this one," he declared. "We're with you, Coach." Except for occasional flareups of showboating, Clint had tempered his style of play to match Mike's demands. The coach learned to let him loose against certain teams and in one game earlier this year he had poured in 50 points. In the playoffs he had been superb. When he had his game together, Clint Dixon was dangerous.

The men on the bench rose to let the starters sit down. A ballboy threw towels over the players' massive shoulders. Mike grabbed one and wiped his face. The boy stuck a small chalkboard in his hands and Mike squatted in front of the bench, among the long black legs and pungent white socks of the men whom he'd spent the past two years molding into his idea of a basketball team.

He, like Dixon, was flushed with excitement but he forced himself to remain outwardly calm. They were leading by only one point. It came down to a question of will. That much he had learned as a professional athlete and coach. You've got to stick with your game plan, lean on your strengths, exploit the opponent's weaknesses. You must not crumble as Curry had done when the pressure became too great. You had to trust your own instincts and you had to trust your players.

Perspiration sluiced down their faces as they focused on their young coach. Mike scribbled on the miniature chalkboard. "Dwayne," he barked, pointing to the seven-foot man-child who swallowed up two seats on the bench, a towel wrapped tightly around his huge neck.

Dwayne Tremont joined the team the year before as a first-round draft pick from a small college in Tennessee, after Lester Hawkins had been put out to pasture. This season, under Mike's tutelage, the giant had come into his own. He provided a ton of muscle under the boards and a nearly unstoppable shot inside. With Tremont and Wallace to snag rebounds Mike and Clint Dixon directed the Comets' lightning fastbreak. Dwayne Tremont inclined his enormous head toward Mike.

"Dwayne—I want you to stay at the low post." He marked an X on his blackboard. "We'll work the ball into you for a layup or a pick and roll. They won't expect it. They'll be looking for some fancy footwork. Clint, you and I will draw the action away from Dwayne on the other side of the lane and look for the outside shot. If you feel hot, pop it. We need every point we can get no matter how we get it. Gordy, you and Bobby pass the ball. Keep it moving."

Gordy Wallace, the muscular forward, and Bobby Barkum nodded. Their jobs were unspectacular but vital, and well appreciated by Mike. It was a five-man game.

"And, Dwayne, remember you can't block up the lane for more than three seconds." The team laughed. The kid had a tendency to linger where he didn't belong.

"On defense, keep pressing," Mike continued. "All we need are two or three turnovers and we've deprived them of possession—the best defense possible. They're tired and we've got to take advantage of that. And watch the fouls. Tremont and Wallace have only one left. We can't afford to lose you guys. Clint and Bobby do the fouling if necessary. So, for God's sake, you two, keep your hands to yourselves." Dwayne grinned at Gordy. Their teammates chuckled nervously. Spirits were running high. They could taste victory.

Mike sensed it too. This young team had come a long way. The buzzer blared. "All right, guys. Let's play defense—and trust to God and Dwayne Tremont."

The Comets scored quickly on a pass from Barkum to Tremont. They relentlessly pressed the Lakers for twenty seconds before Johnson, the Los Angeles center, stuffed a last-second shot. Then Merritt hit a long jumper from his corner. The Lakers marched downcourt and bagged two more.

"Defense!" Mike shouted angrily. Sometimes his players were like two-year-olds; he had to hold their hands every step of the way; he had to pound the fundamentals into their heads for every game; he had to hover over them like an overzealous mother.

Dixon brought the ball over the halfcourt line and rifled a pass to Dwayne who hooked into the basket. His shot thudded against the glass. Johnson plucked the basketball out of the air and one-handed it the length of the court where a teammate hung beneath the basket, his arms outstretched. LA led 96-95.

"That's your man," Mike stormed, glaring at Barkum. "Wake up!" His insides boiled. The pressure was as much physical as psychological.

Striding downcourt, Mike glanced up into the faces in the stands. He caught a glimpse of Patty's shining hair among the shouting, stomping fans. The roar sent a chill through his tired frame. He remembered the same mob cursing and booing him just a few years ago. New York's biggest bust, they called him. Go home, Merritt, you stink. You suck. Now he couldn't distinguish the words and he didn't care. He long ago had given up playing the game for anyone but himself, and his team. The mob could go to hell.

Patty, he knew, felt uneasy at big games like this one, but she came because he needed her. She sat like a shy flower among the other wives and followed her man with sky-blue eyes, quietly absorbing the spectacle that was his life. Or a part of his life. She preferred the reflective inner man she had seen in the mountains to the big boy in the short pants under the hot lights. Well, this was his last season. Soon they would adopt a child. She looked forward to the time when their life would be like that first week in Vermont, before Bee came, when they had discovered the source of their love. Then, after Bee—once the whole truth was out, once there were no more lies—they had stitched up the frayed fabric of their marriage and made it stronger than ever. She knew his ambitions, his fears. And he knew hers. Wherever they went from here it would be together. She didn't want anything more from him than that.

Dixon cut around his man toward the basket as Mike shouldered through the crowd in the lane. Dwayne lumbered to his position with Wallace floating toward the other side, ready to help out with a screen or a tip. Then Barkum streaked in from the top of the key. Clint flipped the ball behind his back to Mike who had worked himself free. Mike faked and scooped the ball to Barkum who, behind a double pick by the two big men, hit a soft jumper for two.

"Press!" Mike called as the team turned from the basket. "Press!"

Dixon and Barkum harassed the Laker guards, waving their arms like windmills. The inbounds pass spurted free, bouncing toward Mike who patrolled the midcourt stripe. He dove for the ball, batting it toward Dixon who drove for the hoop. Encountering a Laker hand in his face, the guard passed off to Tremont who took one magnificent stride and stuffed it. The Comets led 99-96. The Lakers called a time-out.

The players gathered around Mike at the bench. A wave of desperate energy cut through his exhaustion. He craned his neck for a look at the flashing clock on the great inverted black pyramid hanging from the distant ceiling. "Same game plan," he wheezed. His knees ached but he willed the pain away. The ballboy threw him a towel. "Keep pressing. Don't foul." His dark eyes ranged over the faces in front of him. What the hell was there to say? All they had to do now was play their guts out for sixty seconds more. "A minute left. For Christ's sake every guy stick to his man. When we get the ball work it inside and everybody keep moving. Pass the ball. Hit the open man. We can wait for the percentage shot. Don't get stupid. Look," he said, his voice barely audible amid the din of the arena, "it's the same stuff I've been saying for the past two years. We're almost there. We can take it all. Any questions?"

There were none. The buzzer sounded. The arena crowd jumped to attention and roared even louder.

The Lakers took the ball in for an easy field goal. The Comets methodically set up their offense. They fell into their pattern, passing off, constantly moving, setting picks, darting beneath the basket. Mike worked to spring Tremont free to take a high pass for a layup. He stepped behind Johnson to screen for the seven-footer. Dwayne read the play and pivoted around Mike and across the lane, his arms upraised for the lob. Dixon controlled the ball at the key. He launched it above the big man's flapping hands. Tremont leapt high, caught it, and slammed it through the rim on his way back down to earth.

The fans began spilling onto the court. Police pushed them back. There were ten seconds on the clock. The Lakers trailed by three. Mike had seen stranger things happen. Like the time his rookie year when, with his team ahead by five points in the last minute, he threw up two twenty-five-footers and missed them both, and lost the game for the Comets. He now commanded his team to hustle back to the Lakers' basket. "Don't foul!" he added. Los Angeles could score once, but they mustn't be allowed the three-point play.

Seconds later Johnson dropped in a hook from five feet, with Tremont riding his back. Jesus! Mike cursed. At the whistle the young giant shrugged and slowly stalked toward the bench, hanging his huge head. At Mike's signal York came into the game.

Johnson, the lean LA center with the highest shooting percentage in the league, stepped to the foul line. He had one shot. He took a deep breath and considered the goal, the ball cradled chest-high in his long fingers. He sent it softly on its way and it bounced crazily off the hoop. Wallace jumped for the rebound and wrapped his arms around it. The big forward stood there, motionless, protecting the ball with his body as the clock ran out. The klaxon sounded. The Comets had won.

MacElroy's was relatively crowded for a change. Mike had never seen more than three or four people in the bar at any time. As a tribute to Mac, and as a treat for his team, Mike threw a late-night party there for the Comets. It was a players-only affair, a chance for them to savor the championship privately.

After the series there had been press conferences and receptions and local talk-show engagements—enough to make Mike already sick to death of the public cost of his achievement. This was a chance to relax with the team before they dispersed to their homes for the summer. And, since he had announced his retirement from the game—over the front office's vociferous pleas and mind-boggling money offers—it would be his last function as a New York Comet.

Mac beamed, his sodden towel working in fast motion, as the twelve players and Joey Murphy, the trainer, filed in. "Hey, hey," he called. "What is this? You boys know I don't serve riffraff here." His gap-toothed grin betrayed him.

Mike edged through the knot of players. "Give my boys something to drink, Mac, and be quick about it." He reached for the bartender's hand and clutched it tightly. "These guys are world champions, you know."

Mac's mouth went slack; his chins piled one on the other. He feigned ignorance. "I didn't know—"

"Cut the crap, Mac." Joey Murphy's head barely

topped the mahogany bar. "Gimme some rye. You know how I take it."

"Straight up," responded Mac. "You've only been drinking here for twenty years, Joey." He winked at the big player-coach. "Some guys never change." He reached for a tall brown bottle and poured the trainer a shot, plunking glass and bottle down on the bar.

Murphy clambered onto a stool and took the shot neat. He wrapped a gnome-like hand around the bottle and poured himself another. "See about these kids here, will ya, Mac."

Bill York, the veteran sixth man from Wisconsin, called for a beer.

"Vodka gimlet," one of the rookies volunteered.

Dwayne Tremont mumbled something about a bourbon and 7-Up.

"Black Russian," Clint Dixon ordered. "And I do mean black."

The team exploded in raucous laughter and Mac did his best to match the dozen drinks with the dozen thirsty men. He hauled out the Johnny Walker and poured Mike a double on the rocks. "Cheers, Coach."

"Thanks. For everything," Mike added.

"My pleasure, kid. Look, I hope this isn't the last I'll see of you. Just because you're giving up basketball doesn't mean you got to become a stranger."

"Sure thing, Mac. I suppose I'll be around the city for a while. There's still a lot to be done here."

"You're not going to get a mansion up in Westchester, huh? Rub elbows with the big mucky-mucks and high-rollers?"

Mike grinned. "Not this kid. Patty and I have thought about a country place some day, but . . ."

"Yeah, I grew up in the city, but Jesus I sure wouldn't want to today. Wouldn't want my kid to either." Then Mac abandoned the gloomy subject. He pulled his Polaroid from behind the bar. "Say, I want a picture of all you guys. I wanna remember this historic—"

The battered telephone at the end of the bar jangled. Mac threw his towel onto the bar. "'Scuse me," he muttered and waddled over to answer it.

"Tell her I'm booked through September," Dixon shouted amid the laughter of his towering teammates.

Mac scowled and clamped his fist over the receiver. "Mike, it's for you."

Who the hell? he wondered. The players hooted.

"They can't leave him alone."

"That stud won't quit for a minute."

"We won't tell your wife, Coach."

"How can one guy handle it all?"

MacElroy shook his head gravely. "I think it's that colored girl," he told Mike. "She calls every once in a while. Maybe I should've told her you weren't here."

"That's all right, Mac. I'll take it," he reassured the bartender. Darlene? Why would she be calling him here? He hadn't spoken to her for over a year. He took the phone and regarded it warily, then he spoke. "Hello?"

"Mike, honey, is that you?"

"Darlene?" He plugged his other ear with a finger against the noise of the party and planted himself in a dark corner behind a jutting architrave on the far side of the mirror. He could barely hear here.

"Oh, Mike, I'm glad I found you. Honey, I miss you so much. I've got to see you. Got to . . ." Her voice trailed away.

"Darlene? What is it? You know you shouldn't be calling me here. I thought we agreed—"

"I need you. You can come over now, honey. No one is here but me. All alone. Your little girl. Like we used to be. Mike . . ." She whined like a dying kitten.

"Is something wrong, Darlene?" She did not answer. "Darlene?"

"Mike, honey . . . where are you?"

"I'm here at Mac's. What's wrong? What's going on?"

"Mama done flied 'way, chile. She done gone like a

bird an' she ain' nevah comin' back no mo'. De angel come an' done take her 'way up to de sky wid Jesus. Lawdy, it de Jedgment Day fo sho'." There was a weak giggle. "Dass right, chile, yo' mama done gone t' meet Jesus an' she sho' nuff one happy niggah lady. 'Cep' she ain' no niggah lady, chile, cuz she be white. Ain' dat right?" Darlene gave out a strange growl. "Dass right. She be white."

"I'm on my way, Darlene. Just stay there. You hear me?"

"Mmm-hmm," came the eerie response.

He hung up the phone and dug for his wallet. He slid a fifty-dollar bill on the bar and headed for the door.

"Hey, Mike!" Mac called, waving his camera. "What about the picture?"

"I'll be back," Mike said with a half-hearted smile. "Gotta take care of some business."

"She in trouble?" the bartender queried. But Mike was already out the door.

He took a taxicab through the hot thick drizzle of the black summer streets. Darlene sounded in terrible shape. How long had it been? He calculated the months. After his Vermont vacation Mike had terminated the affair, slicing their connection cleanly and, he thought, for good. His marriage had to be preserved; while it rarely achieved the ideal, it was a better match than most. He and Patty were suited for each other—like the finely wrought steeples of Chartres, each with its own charming imperfection, they aspired in unison toward something greater than themselves. The issue of adoption had cut a yawning gulf between them, but that too would be mended with time.

For Darlene, though, there was no more time. Several weeks after he told her they were finished he received a tearful call that brought them together once again for a meeting at Mac's. They sat silently as if mourning the loss of an old friend, but Mike did not give in to her pleas. She hated Jasper, she cried; he made her quit her job and kept her locked up in the apartment; he fed her drugs to make her docile; he did not love her any more and she doubted he every really had; he used her like he used everyone else; now she was merely his whore, a despondent prisoner of the devil himself.

Mike's visions of rescuing his black princess from her ghetto garret had dissipated completely. A boy's dreams. An unreality that could never be more than fantasy. Sometimes he was amazed by his own naivete. How had he ever believed that he, Mr. Lily-White All-Everything, could, merely by proffering a pale hand, lift her up from the slough in which she was mired? He had once offered to marry her, and she had declined. "We're different people," she had said. Indeed, Mike now agreed, we are different people.

But how could he forget the soul-quenching rapture which he had known in Darlene's arms? She was like no other woman and that is what had kept them together: her spontaneity, her wild energy, her sexual wit. And yet, even in the earliest days when she lapsed into her dark and dangerous moods he shrank from her as from an avenging lioness. From the beginning they had bucked the odds. Now her life apart from Mike was a complex fiasco of tensions and drugs and degredation. She needed him desperately and she despised him for it. At their last meeting she begged and cajoled and threatened him. But by then it was too late. And now, it was more than late: it was impossible.

The black rain sheeted violently from the night sky as he unfolded from the cab and ran into Darlene's building. Stairs came with more difficulty these days and he took them one at a time. He paused at her door and for a chilling moment terror seized his mind. he knew he should never have come. She was a part of his past, and even if she weren't dead she no longer lived in him. He had done all he could for her; it was no good, his being there. But she was in trouble, he reminded himself, and perhaps he could help her. At least he must try. He knocked softly on her door.

"Hello, lover," she cooed. Her hair fled wildly from

her face in furious matted clumps and the once-lustrous cheeks had lost their sheen. In distant grottoes her aqueous eyes hid fearfully from the light. She wore a white blouse unbuttoned nearly all the way to the waist and tight blue jeans. "You're all wet, tiger man. You come on in and sit down and get comfortable." Her erect posture was gone, her busy stride replaced by a listless shuffle; and her musical voice was no more than a dreary dirge.

He followed her through the doorway into the vast gaudy living room where the nineteen-inch color television flickered obscenely. "What's wrong, Darlene?" The words emerged painfully from his dry mouth. "You sounded like you were in pretty bad shape when you called."

"Things get bad and then they get better. Time heals all, right?" She turned and smiled, standing on tiptoe, her pouting lips puckered tightly.

He allowed her to kiss him on the cheek, then he went to the TV and switched it off. She watched him without a word. He returned to her. "Have you been taking something?" he demanded.

Her tiny round face remained silent as her eyes swam away from him. He took her arms. "Let me see." He yanked back her white sleeve and there he saw the purple pricks of a dozen needles.

"Aw, lover," she moaned, "it's a rainy day and I want to see the sun shine. And I want to see my man."

"I'm not your man any more. Is Jasper making you do this?"

She whirled and threw herself on the overstuffed brown couch. "Jasper doesn't make me do anything I don't want to do, dig? This lady can take care of herself." She reached for a cigarette.

"It sure didn't sound like that on the phone." He sat down beside her. This beautiful young woman; this frail but feisty creature. Jesus, would she end up back on the streets? Or could she straighten herself out and get rid of her drug-dealing husband? But Mike knew the answers all to well. "Where's Jasper?"

"He's gone and I don't know when he's gonna come back. I don't need him. I need you." She took a long drag on her cigarette and tilted her head, releasing a stream of blue smoke that hung on the air.

"You need a doctor," Mike said. "Darlene, you can't go on living like this."

Her eyes were hot coals. "You call this livin'?" she spat. "You have no idea, Mr. Clean." Her soft lips quavered. "Why are you here, anyway? To see how far this mama's sunk? You better go home 'fore that skinny woman of yours starts to worryin'. I know she don't like her man to mix with po' folk."

"For God's sake, Darlene, you called me. Mac says you call there all the time."

Her chin shot up haughtily. "Well, mistah, tha's his honky word agin' mine."

"Talk sense," Mike said, anger rising in his throat. "If you don't need me, I'll be on my way." Then he wavered. "I just don't like to see you like this. I wish there was something I could do."

Darlene cackled. "You're so funny you're sad. Why didn't I give up on you a long time ago? Hoping cost me a lot, you know that? You're one expensive dude." Then she laughed, her creamy face melting into a wide drugged smile. She reached for the black forelock that hung like a loose thread over his brow. "I want you, baby. Why can't I have you?"

Mike took hold of her skeletal wrists. "You need to get to bed. I'll call a doctor."

"Why?" she begged. "Tell me why." Her obsidian eyes danced crazily. "You're no better than me, White Man. The whole world ought to know what I know. And I know all about you." As she slumped back onto the fat couch her blouse fell open, exposing chocolate breasts tipped by winking black nipples.

"You're not making sense, Darlene." Mike pulled the blouse over her chest and lifted her in his arms. She hung limply, her hands grazing his chest, her eyes drowning in his.

"You can have me, Mike. All you have to do is take me."

For a second he considered it. This beautiful black nymph. He had possessed her many times and he could never erase the memory of the sublime and dangerous pitch of their passion. But to attempt to regain what they had once known was doomed from the conception of the idea. Darlene belonged to the days of his thwarted ambition when the illusions of youth had been shattered and desolation and failure lurked around every corner. But now a new ambition had grown up within him: the ambition to be a man. With Darlene he was still a boy—with Patty, a man. His life had achieved an order and direction with his wife; he could no longer justify the follies and excesses of youth. That was repetition. He could not risk it.

After closing the bedroom door he stripped her jeans off and laid her in the bed and covered her. He sat down next to her and looked into her wasted face. The drugs had taken their toll. Goddamn Jasper Brown.

"Let's settle this thing once and for all, Darlene. I loved you once and would have married you if you'd have had me. I still care for you, but now I'm married to someone else and I can't leave her. I won't leave her. You and I must never see each other again."

Angry tears spilled onto the bedclothes. Darlene bit her pink lip until it bled. "That's what I wanted to hear," she rasped. "The pure truth—right from the horse's ass." Her shoulders rocked as she sobbed. "Get the hell out of here."

"Darlene, listen to me—"

From beyond the door they heard someone moving around in the outer room.

"Jasper!" she whispered hoarsely, her face a map of dread. "He's home."

Mike Merritt's spine went rigid.

"Hey, Darlene," Jasper called from the living room. "Where the hell are you?"

A sudden shaft of light cut into the bedroom as Jasper flung open the door. He was shorter than Mike remembered, a compact figure in his ubiquitous broad-brimmed hat and the long coat that almost touched his patent leather shoes. The hat obscured his face so that he appeared a malevolent black shadow against the imposing bolt of light. A devilish hiss escaped his lips. "Goddamn," he cursed. For a frozen moment no one moved. Then Darlene puled, triggering the black man into action.

"Bitch!" he panted. He sprung with baleful eyes onto the bed, his hands shooting to her neck, choking her scream.

Mike lunged over the bed. Gripping the man's shoulders he tore him away and hurled him onto the carpeted floor where he fell with a thud and his hat rolled free. Darlene howled, her eyes filled with hot tears. Mike reached for her with a comforting hand. He saw that she wasn't hurt but before he could turn to meet her raging husband, Jasper was on his back.

He rode Mike like a mad mountain cat, his fingers wrapped around the taller man's face and neck. Mike bucked in an attempt to throw his attacker but Jasper clung tenaciously, his breath steaming fiercely from between clenched teeth. The two tumbled from the bed.

Darlene watched them, paralyzed. She sat up at the head of the bed, her blouse hanging loosely, her hands locked at her face.

Again Mike tried to heave the man from his back. Failing that he buckled his knees and fell backwards, Jasper writhing beneath him. He ripped the hands from his neck and turned to pin them to the carpet, but Jasper swiveled free and regained his feet as Mike, blinded with sweat and shock, struggled to find him.

Jumping clear of the athlete's long arms, Jasper planted himself by the door. Hatless, the black man's face took on a deadly chiaroscuro in the half-light of the room. His teeth flashed in a grin as he reached inside his coat and produced a knife. The blade snapped open.

Mike, on his knees, lurched for Jasper as the knife sliced the air above his head. He caught the man's ankles and yanked hard. Jasper spilled against the wall and slid to the floor, still clutching the glinting weapon. As Jasper fell Mike found his balance and grabbed for the blade. With a desperate grunt Jasper slashed at Mike's right arm. The knife cut deeply into his skin and Mike gasped, pulling his arm away as Jasper whipped the weapon toward him again. Mike bolted upright and kicked. His foot met Jasper's knife-hand and the blade flew across the room, clattering against the far wall, disappearing into the darkness of the corner.

"No! No!" Darlene shrieked.

With all his strength Mike sent another blow at Jasper, this time catching the man in the chest with his foot. Dazed, Jasper's head rolled impotently and he gulped for breath. Mike turned to Darlene. He saw her open the drawer of the nightstand beside her bed. Her tiny hand came out clutching a small pistol. It looked like a .38 and she brought the blue muzzle around, aiming it with unsteady hands at her fallen husband.

Mike summoned his calmest voice and held out a warning hand. "Be careful, Darlene." He took a hesitant step toward her. "Give me that thing. Somebody's going to get hurt."

He glanced over his shoulder at Jasper who was still slumped against the wall, obscured by the shadow of the open door. "You don't want to shoot anybody, Darlene," he advised. But one look at her flashing black eyes and flaring nostrils told a different story.

"No! I'm gonna kill him!" Insane tears streaked her face. "Don't move!" she shouted as Jasper, his long coat flapping over his legs, managed to stand up. He stared at her as if trying to exercise a mystic power over her. She trembled. "Don't look at me or I'll shoot you!"

"Darlene, give me the gun," Mike said quietly.

She turned to her former lover, her whole body trembling. "No," she hissed. "You'll be next. I hate you both."

"Tell him, baby. Shoot his honky ass," Jasper aid with a laugh that didn't disguise his own fear.

"Shut up, you jive asshole," Darlene said. "You told me to use this thing if anybody tried something with me and I'm gonna do it. And you're gonna be the first." She raised the gun.

Before she could pull the trigger, Mike clamped his hands around hers and squeezed tightly. She winced. He jerked her hands and sent the pistol flying. He and Jasper dove for it.

The two men grappled for the weapon, thrashing on the floor like alleycats. Mike's head met the corner of the nightstand just as he found the small gun. Stunned, he tightened his fingers around it and tried to pull it to himself. But he felt Jasper's hands attempting to pry his own from the weapon. He held on, blood flowing from his injured arm. His head felt as though it had been split wide open. He clutched the cold metal object and wrested his hand from Jasper's frantic fingers.

"Mike!" It was Darlene. "Look out!"

Mike rolled quickly toward the bed as a lamp came crashing down where his head had been. Then Jasper Brown was on top of him, pounding at his face. Still gripping the gun, Mike pushed his attacker aside and tried to stand. But Jasper pulled him back to the floor. Again he jumped on top of Mike. Jasper's right hand found the gun while with his left he slapped Mike's face hard. Nearly blinded, rage erupting within him, Mike roared as the gun went off, spitting a yellow flame into the darkness.

"Oh Jesus," Darlene wailed. "Jesus. Jesus." She collapsed on the bed, her face in her hands.

Jasper groaned and held his stomach. Mike slid out from under him and the black man doubled over in pain. Blood oozed from his wound, soaking his coat and staining the thick carpet.

Mike cursed, his head aching and his face stinging. He got to his knees and then to his feet and stumbled toward Darlene. He could barely breathe. He slumped onto the bed. "Darlene," he said, "we've got to call an ambulance—the police—somebody."

"No. Get out. Go away."

He tried to take her hands but she buried her face in the pillow, keening hysterically. She was in shock. He dropped the gun on the floor and lifted the telephone. He held it for a minute and then replaced it. No. No police. His head reeled. "Darlene," he whispered. But she did not answer. She lay still as a corpse. He touched her but she did not respond, not even to move away from him.

He swung over the bed. What to do? Call the police, an inner voice urged. No. What then? Panic seized him.

He ran out to the living room. In the glare he saw that his hands and shirt were smeared with blood: Jasper's and his own. His arm throbbed and his face felt swollen to twice its normal size.

Call the police, the voice insisted. No, he responded. No police. An ambulance then? For Darlene. He peered into the room where the mortal tableau was imprinted in the darkness. Should he call Mo? Mo would advise him; Mo would . . . No. He decided to call Mortimer Wright.

Long minutes later Darlene heard somebody enter the apartment. She turned over in her bed. "Mike?" she chirped hopefully. But it was not Mike.

Two men—white men, one very tall and the other very broad—came into the bedroom. The tall one moved toward Jasper and the fat one came wordlessly at her.

She wanted to scream but she couldn't. Police? The man drew nearer. No. The fat man pulled a long needle out of a brown case. She looked over to Jasper. The tall man plunged a similar needle into her husband's arm. Jasper cried out in pain. He was alive!

"Keep him quiet," the big man barked.

The tall man sent the back of his hand crashing into

238

Jasper's face and the black man lay silent once again. "I thought Mr. Wright said he was dead," the tall man muttered.

"Shut up," said the other.

"Please don't," Darlene whimpered as the fat man, smiling, ripped the sheet from her and took her slender arm. She went slack as the needle penetrated her skin. Again she looked over at Jasper.

The tall man lifted him up and administered another violent blow to the head. Jasper fell lifelessly to the floor, black blood smeared all over his white shirt.

"Find the gun," the fat man ordered as he pulled the needle from his victim's arm.

She dropped back, watching with weary eyes as the men searched the room. Who are they? Clouds formed in her brain and billowed and burst. Dense blackness hooded her gaze. The last thing she remembered was seeing the fat man pick up the gun, wipe it clean with a white cloth, and drop it beside her on the bed. Then she drifted into a ghoul-ridden nightmare.

After dispatching his men to "attend to the situation" at the apartment, he was on the telephone again. "Commissioner Leahy, Mortimer Wright here. Excuse me for disturbing you at this hour."

"Yeah, Mr. Wright," sounded the sleepy reply of Police Commissioner Francis X. Leahy. "What can I do for you?"

Mortimer Wright despised these slinky Irish pols. He hated their laziness, their grossness, their weak brains. Leahy, a lawyer by trade, was the best of the lot, and even he was an incompetent and uncouth administrator. But such people were important—in the short run—and had to be coddled.

"Commissioner, a crime has been committed in your city and I thought I'd alert you personally." Leahy grunted and Wright imagined him fumbling for a pencil and paper. "I hope it is understood," the financier continued, "that my call is off the record—and that I am interested only in justice. The fact that First New York is a potential contributor to future campaigns for public office, assuming you heed the popular cry for your candidacy, has nothing to do with this sad, indeed tragic, case."

"I understand, sir," said Leahy, his interest piqued.

I thought you would, Wright said to himself. "This is the situation, Commissioner. A man named Jasper O. Brown, a notorious drug peddler, was shot and killed. I'm sure you'll find his name in your records. I believe he has been behind bars a number of times. The incident took place in his Harlem apartment. His wife was present—a witness and possible accomplice. My guess is that it was a gang-related shooting. A murder like a hundred other murders which, unfortunately, plague that section of the city."

"Sad but true, Mr. Wright."

"Indeed. No more and no less."

"Yes, sir."

"The appropriate precinct officers have been or will shortly be informed of the crime by an anonymous caller. I would hope that the young woman will be confined, pending whatever action the authorities deem necessary. That, I presume, is the usual procedure in such cases?"

"It is, sir." Leahy paused. "May I ask, sir—"

"That is all I have to say, Commissioner, except to remind you that this conversation never took place."

"Understood, sir."

"Good night, Commissioner Leahy."

"Good night, sir."

Fool, thought Wright, as he replaced the receiver. Already he's imagining himself mayor. Well, if that's what he wants . . . It looks as if the hapless clown in the hot seat now isn't going to last through the next election anyway. No harm in elevating a cooperative police commissioner to that office. It never hurts to have friends at City Hall. Friends of young Merritt's at that, though Leahy and Merritt have not met each other—yet.

In the gloom of his suburban bedroom, Mortimer Wright frowned. Is Merritt worth the trouble? he wondered. Or is he really just another of these vain boys who seem to think the world is waiting for them to reveal their divinity and set things straight. Have I been wrong about him all along?

Mortimer Wright did not tolerate untidiness in the person or the performance. He took it as a personal insult. And Mike Merritt had been untidy: careless, stupid, messy. Damn him—didn't the boy have brains enough to know better?

When he was a youth Mortimer David Wright hadn't been careless or messy. He had known from the very beginning where he was going and how he must get there. His father was a doctor in Bronxville—where Wright still lived—and his mother the daughter of a textile manufacturer in New England. Mortimer was their only child and he received the very best of everything. At Yale the boy was a serious student who knew all the right people. He was football manager for four years, Phi Beta Kappa, Skull and Bones. He came of age just in time to vote for Herbert Hoover who lost to the left-leaning Governor of New York in 1932. He swallowed that bitter pill and determined to do his part to save the country from ruin. The summer after graduation he joined the First Bank of New York as a junior clerk at thirty dollars a week. With the aid of a monthly stipend from Father he managed to survive rather well, and by the time the second great war thundered across the water he was a bank officer well-regarded by his seniors who made certain that they didn't lose him to Roosevelt's Folly. He had no inclination to enlist, however, knowing his duty to be on the homefront guarding safe-deposit boxes and maintaining interest rates and overseeing defense loans to worthy borrowers. Someone had to do it. The war, which he had quietly regarded as a Bolshevist plot from the outset, finally ended and the boys came home and the boom began and he rode the crest of the wave of renewed prosperity right into the inner councils of First New York. Three decades later there was no one who knew more—he was always the thorough student—about the workings of the elephantine corporation, and no one more suited to control the reins of the beast, than Mortimer D. Wright.

And now, after more than forty years with the company—forty years accumulating power—Wright called all the shots.

He sat on the edge of his wide bed. No, he concluded, he hadn't misjudged Merritt, even if the boy had committed an indiscretion this time. There mustn't be a next time, however. He would make certain of that. Then Wright smiled a rare smile. Merritt would learn his lesson. He was ambitious enough, and now he would be far easier to control. The boy would pay the price. He would see the error of his ways and he would never stray again.

Mortimer Wright curled up on his bed. There was nothing more to do tonight. He would talk with young Merritt in the morning.

The scalding shower spat streams of stinging water on Mike's weary body, laving the blood and grit and guilt of the previous night away—or so he hoped. It was now six A.M.

He remembered stumbling blindly from Darlene's building into the black rain-slick street. He sprinted down Eighth Avenue past the dim shops and pool halls and the bleak faces that retreated into shadows from the yellow glare of the lurid lights. A gaunt ghost of a giant, he raced around Morningside Park, a pitch-dark valley of death when the dingy spires of Columbia looming above the damp trees. His lungs heaved and his legs ached from the punishment of the brutal pavement. He ran toward Broadway, halting exhausted and confused at the corner of 110th Street near the noble cathedral which mocked his mad desperation. Panting, he lifted a painful, blood-streaked arm to flag down a cab. The yellow vehicle skidded to a stop at the decaying curb and he dove inside.

"Drive," he gasped.

The cabby tore off down the avenue stealing quick glances in his mirror of the frantic figure slumped against the back seat. "Where to, buddy?" he asked after several blocks.

Mike hauled himself upright. He pulled a soiled handkerchief from his pocket and wiped his battered face. His right arm was black with blood and throbbed hellishly. "Just drive," he repeated.

At a red light the cab driver tossed a clean towel to Mike through a crack in the plastic partition. He gazed at the tall man in the mirror. As he accelerated through the intersection he said: "You're Mike Merritt." Before he got an answer he went on: "A man shouldn't be messin' around uptown. You in trouble?"

He took off his jacket and ripped back the sleeve of his crimson-tainted shirt and wrapped the towel around his injured arm. "I'm all right." He winced as the makeshift bandage rubbed against the deep cut. "Keep driving."

"I'll drive all night if you can pay the fare."

Mike sat back on the black vinyl seat as Broadway careened past. He winced at every rock and jolt of the cab. His mind reeled as his bright visions of fine deeds and noble ideas crashed into the black sun of despair. The poetry that had animated his soul vanished, leaving a gaping void, a pandemonium of thrashing fears.

He heard the cabby clucking through the singing sheets of steaming rain. The man did not disguise his disapproval but, for the next few hours, took his pale passenger on a silent predawn tour of the lip of Manhattan Island. Finally, Mike directed the driver to his home. Then he had stripped his sanguine clothes and planted himself beneath the nozzle that sprayed warmth and cleansing water over his racked body.

After toweling himself dry he wadded up his foul clothing and stuffed it into a plastic shopping bag. He remembered every murder movie he had ever seen and he knew he must destroy the emblem—the evidence—of his deed. For now he had the bundle in the front closet behind a box of winter garments. He could dispose of it later. He must not panic; he must rest and construct his thoughts; he must see Mortimer Wright at the earliest possible moment. He wondered if the police already had discovered the corpse and Darlene and knew the whole story. And how soon would it be before everyone knew? What the hell could Wright do to keep him out of it?

The bleeding had stopped. He placed a clean dressing on the wound and carefully tugged a long-sleeved shirt over it. Then he put on a sport jacket and inspected his form in the mirror. His puffy face was robbed of color, his dark eyes imbedded in gray pillows of flesh. He wouldn't fool anyone. He mustn't let Patty see him like this.

But as he stepped out of the bathroom there she stood, her eyes wide in disbelief as she beheld the ashen figure of her husband. "My God," she choked.

"Rough night," Mike kidded, a wan smile scarring his face.

"What happened to you?" Her voice trembled between fear and anger. As her hand touched his wounded arm he grimaced. "You're hurt."

"I, uh, got blasted with the boys. Fell and bruised my arm. I should have called. We took a suite at the Statler. No funny stuff—just drinking and—"

"Where in God's name were you, Mike?" she insisted. "Don't lie to me."

"I'm not—I mean, you've got to believe me, Patty. There's nothing wrong—really. I got in a scrape and I got out. Everything will be okay. I promise."

"You look like a ghost. Where have you been? I was worried sick all night. I was up until—"

"I've got to see someone now."

"Have you eaten anything? It's only seven o'clock. Have you slept at all? Mike, tell me what's going on. I want to know."

"Patty," he said, lifting his good arm and touching her shoulder, "it has nothing to do with you. I'll straighten the whole thing out today and we'll talk later. Believe me, I'm all right."

"Have something to eat, first, Mike. I'll make coffee and fix you an omelet. You're not going anywhere before you have some breakfast."

The coffee scorched his throat but righted his head somewhat. Sitting at the round glass-topped table, he drank from a candy-bright mug with a white ribbon of steam rising into the cool kitchen air. Patty sat across from him, he hair pulled back from her worried face. She held the loose silk robe closely around her neck and poured herself a cup of coffee.

She faced her husband squarely. "I won't press you now if you don't want me to, Mike," she said, "but I expect the truth when you decide to tell me what has happened. And remember that I'm your wife and I love you—and I'll be here when you need me. Mike, look at me."

The athlete's eyes met hers. "I've never lied to you since Vermont," he said. "And God knows I'm still paying for that one." His hand slid over the tabletop and sought hers. "I hoped I would never have to ask your forgiveness again."

Patty placed her hand in his. Their life together since Vermont had been good. They had strained the dross from the experience in the mountains and were left with the precious ore of the rare communion they had known: when they had discovered each other all over again, when they had purged the secrets of the past. But as she studied the pallid face before her she knew something had again upset the balance. Would this tip the scales for good?

"I understand," she said.

An hour later he walked from his Fifth Avenue home to the First New York Building downtown on Third Avenue, a distance of several blocks. He had walked these blocks hundreds of times, but as he trudged through the spring-morning rush, his face a lump of pain, his arm dangling at his side, his mind a turmoil of defeat and guilt, he saw the people and the buildings as he had never seen them before, through the prism of his own desolation.

The early sun capped the giant offices into which the swarms scurried, purses and briefcases clutched jealously, their faces gray and grim and their eyes dull mirrors of their souls. No one saw the black sky. No one saw it was raining blood.

Mortimer Wright's placid and polished pink face revealed nothing to Mike; it never had. His was a soft hairless visage that belied the steel will and the immense power the man possessed. It was a face that never smiled, an unfathomable unwrinkled face, the face of one who knew more than he would ever tell.

Mike remembered their first meeting in the Yale Club—six years ago—when the man in the silver tie offered him the job with Future Leaders, Inc., when it seemed to the boy that the great world was opening up and innumerable possibilities would soon be realized. . . .

Enthroned behind an immense black desk in a high-backed leather chair, Wright looked up as Mike entered his office. The banker's hand floated like a feather from the papers in front of him to indicate a chair. Mike sat down, breathless, his face a haggard mask. He waited.

After a lengthy moment of deadly silence, Wright said, "Tell me what happened. Exactly what happened."

Mike related the story of the previous night in gruesome detail. As he listened Wright busied himself with the papers on his desk, rearranging them in neat piles and filling his fountain pen. The clean fingers worked effortlessly; the face never changed.

When Mike finished his account, Wright trained his intense gaze on the young man. "You realize that this affair could ruin you completely." It was not a question.

Mike nodded. He felt on the verge of tears, as if he were confessing to his father that he had cheated on a test at school. "Yes, sir. I understand the implications. And I'm sorry. I appreciate all you've—"

"Do you?" Wright regarded him with an arched eyebrow. "Do you realize exactly what you've done—how close you have come to destroying your career? Do you realize the implications of dragging *me* into this sordid mess? Do you realize what I had to do to keep this from the police and the press? Do you?"

Mike's heart sank to the pit of his gnawing stomach. "I think I do."

Wright moved barely a muscle. "I hope to God you do, son. And I hope you realize that this is absolutely the last time you will be allowed any mistakes. One more false step and you will be punished swiftly and finally. You have used up every inch of your rope. Do you understand what I'm saying?"

"Yes, sir."

"I'm disappointed in you, Mike." The financier affected an almost soothing tone. "You are a young man with a lot of growing up to do. You must put your life in order." His hands curled around the perfectly aligned edge of a small stack of papers. "And I mean today."

What had Wright done to keep the incident under wraps? Mike wondered. How much did he owe this man? "Yes, sir."

Wright's fingertips formed a steeple over which he peered at Mike. "We must understand each other on this matter—there must be no doubt in your mind that if this sort of thing occurs again I shall have no mercy on you."

"Yes, sir." The oppressive litany stuck tastelessly on his tongue.

The intimation of a smile slid over Wright's smooth face. "Very well, then." He cleared his throat with a prim hand to his mouth. "Aside from this unfortunate incident," he continued, "your performance both on and off the court has proved, needless to say, a remarkable success. Of course, when you first asked me about overhauling the Future Leaders organization I had serious reservations. The idea of scouring the ghettoes for our leaders took some getting used to. The other board members echoed my doubts. But so far you have proved us wrong."

Mike regarded the banker with uncertainty. What the hell is he getting at now? This subtle fox who had nosed his way into Mike's life almost without the young athlete's knowing . . . and yet Mike knew too well why he had allowed it, why he had sought a wily mentor like Mortimer Wright. He mustn't forget that the man could prove useful in many ways—and that he owed Wright something more now.

"Good to hear," mumbled Mike. His eyes darted across the room. A well-tended plant here, a muted watercolor there, the drapes pulled so as to admit no hint of the outside world, the tidy desk, the enveloping chairs. There was definitely something eerie about this man.

"There is presently an opening in our community affairs office," Wright explained. "It has a budget eight times as large as what you've been handling at Future Leaders. It has also—" a frown puckered the pink face—"failed to ignite even a spark of interest in the community. In certain circles it has become an object of scorn. Recently the IRS subjected us to the embarrassment of an audit—because, odd as it may sound, we cannot find a way to spend what we've got. And I despise the idea of our money lining some bureaucrat's pockets. We pay far too many punitive taxes as it is."

Mike strained to listen. The frail dark form of Darlene flickered across his mind and he wondered where she was now. What had he, with the help of this man, done to her? But he blotted out the image. The past was dead. To repeat it . . .

"Since your playing days are over," Wright was

saying, "I thought perhaps this might be the time for you to draw up a proposal for that recreation center you mentioned sometime back. That is, if you haven't given up on the idea. The job includes the rank of vice president and a comfortable salary and, as I mentioned, a large budget. I would like for you to consider it, at least."

The Center. Was this his chance to build on the ashes of the nightmare? Might he redeem himself by putting his energies to a constructive purpose? "It is certainly something to think about," Mike said. "I haven't yet decided what to do with all the time I have on my hands."

"A busy man is a happy man," intoned Wright. "A busy man has no opportunity to get into trouble."

"It will take time," thought Mike aloud. "Perhaps even a few years."

"That's fine. Frankly, the longer we can stretch it out the better it appears for tax purposes, as long as we can prove that we are working actively on the project."

Mortimer Wright had his reasons—for everything he said or did. "I'll take the job, Mr. Wright." Already visions of a civic jewel flamed in his mind: a monument to the dreams of his boyhood.

"I'm glad to hear it, Mike. The board meets next week. You and your project will be at the top of the agenda."

Mike rose. He needed to rest, to sort out the events of the past twenty-four hours, to regain his bearings, to see Patty. Wright's office had become stifling. "Well, if that's all—"

"There is one more thing, Mike. And that regards your attorney, Mr. Silver."

"What does Mo have to do with any of this?"

"I'm afraid that several members of the board have expressed dissatisfaction with him. As you move up in our organization the rest of us have to be able to place full confidence in you. Believe me, there is no question about your loyalty or your ability or your seriousness.

In every way they match our own. Mr. Silver, however, is a different matter." The financier ran his hand down the blue-striped tie knotted neatly at his neck. "His activities at Yale, as, well, an agitator, alienated more than a few. And even now, although he has apparently toned down, his image does not really suit ours—or yours. More to the point is the fact that First New York employs its own attorneys: Garland, Steele, Stone and Holmes. Surely you see the virtue of a single—"

Garland, Steele. Patty's father's firm. Of course. Let's keep it in the family all the way. But he couldn't let the bastards snub Mo like that. "He's more than just a lawyer, Mr. Wright. He has been an adviser and a good friend, as well as my agent, for several years. It's clear by now that he is a capable and honest man. Perhaps his politics are a bit extreme at times, but as you yourself said, he has learned to—"

"He may continue in any capacity but as your lawyer. I will not presume to choose your friends for you, and as long as no legal matters fall into his hands I have no objection. But on this I must insist. You understand our position."

"Of course I do." Mike swallowed hard. "I'll give it some thought, sir."

"I'm sure you will," said Mortimer Wright.

Part 3

The Candidate

12

The new apartment had been his mother's idea. Why didn't he live as a lawyer should? Why punish himself? Why not a room with a view? At first Mo resisted, but then he realized that there was no reason to stay in Chelsea, not without Sheila. So he took the path of least resistance. He settled for Riverside Drive because it was less offensive—and somewhat less expensive—than most other parts of Manhattan.

The only thing he had kept from his old life was his telephone number. Earlier in the day he had called his mother, but there was no answer. She was probably at the hospital. He would visit his father tomorrow. The thought of the old man shrinking and rotting between the crisp antiseptic sheets of the old Jewish hospital in Flatbush plagued him. Only the slowly darkening day reminded him of the press of time, and as the sun slid behind the gold-crowned trees of the park outside his window he mourned the dead moments of his life and pondered the unborn future.

The smell and feel of Brooklyn where he grew up assailed Mo's memory: the hump of the gritty black street and the wide cracked sidewalks and the old tree and tiny patch of green in front of the house where his mother and father made their home above the grocery store; and the loud shoppers with their squeezing hands and upturned noses; and the slap of a rubber ball on the stoop next door where his cousins and his aunt and uncle lived. Then there was the cool musty back room where he slept and where he read through the night, burning the old yellow lamp at the desk his father built for him; and his mother's favorite dress which she wore in the summertime when they strolled in Prospect Park, his father telling him how proud they were of him and how far he would go and how it was a joy to raise a son like him; and the man's knotty hand on the boy's broad shoulder and the woman's rough but warm hand in his own; and the dreams they shared. They returned to the dark house for pie, which had cooled while they were away, and an icy glass of milk; the electric fan blew the linen tablecloth around their legs, and they ate in happy silence. He remembered the crisp envelope of book money his father pressed in his palm before he went off for his first day at City College; and sitting at attention in the cramped classroom until his back ached as he learned about Plato and Hegel and Marx and Darwin and Veblen; and the rich comforting silence of the library where he camped in a green chair until they ejected him at closing time; and the long walk home through the noisy byways of Brooklyn with a heavy load of schoolbooks and three of four daily newspapers in the canvas bag his uncle the tailor had sewn for him; and the endless winter evenings when his breath froze in front of his face; and the fist of fear in his stomach the morning of final exams. Later, the hot summers at the store stacking cans and carrying old ladies' groceries and the clean white apron as big as his father's and counting the cash and closing the tinkling door at the end of the day and the cold key in the lock and switching off the lights and washing his hands for the big evening meal; and father and son eating and arguing politics and history and his decision to believe no more in the God of his people; and the moment he realized for the first time that he would always be a Jew in the eyes of the world no matter how vehemently he denied it or how stubbornly he ignored it; and the anger in his eyes as he sat before the flickering blue TV and watched Vietnam: the madmen with stars on their shoulders and swaggering Presidents and the stretchers laden with bloodied half bodies and the distant splash of rice paddies which echoed in his dreams. Then the letter from Yale Law School and his father's kisses and his mother's tears as she wiped her red hands on her wet apron; and the day he left home for New Haven like a soldier shipping out overseas with promises to call and to work hard and to eat well and to make his proud parents even prouder and never to forget they loved him and to spend the two hundred dollars his father stuffed in his shirt pocket on a new winter suit but not to tell his uncle who had fitted him with a gray flannel for the fall.

In New Haven the dutiful son was metamorphosed into the conscience-ridden radical who learned that conventional politics and unconventional ideas don't mix. But that discovery neither surprised nor disappointed him: the signs had been there all along, clear enough for anyone to read. So he did what he could, which was more than most, to bring coherence and muscle to the antiwar movement on campus.

He became a public man, linking his life to the Cause, toiling to translate ideas into action. A quiet, possessed leader, he navigated his coalition of students through the rough seas of egotism and violence with an eye fixed unswervingly on a single purpose: to end the war. His steady stewardship did not go unnoticed by national student organizations, but he refused to throw in with the more colorful troublemakers who grabbed headlines with their inspired pranks. He did not trust Hoffman, Rubin, and Company; the scent of incipient fascism lingered over their antics. Instead, he concentrated his prodigious energies on limited but specific gains at Yale: Corporation concessions, faculty involvement, prohibition of intelligence activity on campus, support for minority grievances, nonviolent marches to display the size, strength, and solidarity of the movement.

Law school came second. To Mo it was merely a tedious exercise in memorization and regurgitation, though, despite his careless attitude, he graduated without a hitch. He clung throughout to his love of ideas and his identification with the disenfrancised: the pursuit of power or money never held his imagination or stimulated his best efforts.

But where had his singlemindedness got him? To the Upper West Side with a third-floor view of the park. Alone. . . .

The doorbell's insistent wheeze recalled him to the present. Mike Merritt answered through the call box and Mo pressed the appropriate button to admit him.

The man who appeared in Mo's doorway was older, somehow sadder than he remembered. Slightly stooped, his cheeks swatches of gray, Mike wore a white sport shirt, jeans, and a pair of lopsided loafers, and he carried a brown paper bag. There was a slackness about him which his friend had never noticed before, although the winning smile had not faded.

Mo had last seen him at the final game in the Garden, almost three months ago. A few weeks before that he and Sheila and Mike and Patty had been to dinner at one of Sheila's favorite Indian restaurants and then to a movie, like an oldtime double date. But since then they had spoken only once, when Mo called to give Mike his new address and to ask him over sometime.

"Thought I'd take you up on your invitation," Mike said, freeing a bottle of scotch from its brown paper prison. "The lady at the liquor store thought I was Joe Namath. Gave me a discount."

"Sit down, Broadway Joe. I'll get some ice. There are glasses around here—somewhere." He gestured vaguely at the boxes strung out across the floor. From the kitchen he shouted: "Where the hell have you been recently? Haven't seen your face for months."

"Around," Mike responded. He waited for Mo to return to the living room. "Got an overdose of people after the championship. Been keeping a low profile ever since."

They sat on the new sofa that smelled like a plastic

funeral bouquet, the window open at their backs, the warm breath of dusk whispering into the room. Mo munched on potato chips as Mike finished his double scotch.

"So what happened with Sheila, Mo? You sounded pretty upset when you called—and you don't look so happy right now."

"Why should I bore us both?"

"For Christ's sake: you always listen to my problems—saves me the cost of an analyst. If you want to talk, talk. If not that's okay too."

"You said you have something to ask me."

"That can wait. Is Sheila gone for good? You two aren't getting married?"

"Married!" Mo's brown eyes rolled toward the ceiling and he rubbed his stubbly chin with a big hand. "We're not even speaking to each other, Mike. She just got good and sick of waiting for me to make up my mind. I avoided the issue for three years—long enough, I guess, to make any woman suspicious, if not downright angry. Married? Even if I asked her I'm not sure she'd do it—not now. I really screwed that one up." He scooped the last of the potato chips from the bottom of the bowl. "I blew it."

"I always thought of marriage as a last resort," he continued. "And I thought of it in conditional terms: when and if the rest of the world is in order, then maybe I'll get married. But women don't look at it that way."

Mike chuckled. "Women never see things the way we do, Mo. A fact of life so obvious you refuse to believe it."

"A great pair of feminists we make."

"We can't let them know we know, is all."

"I thought we were supposed to be more enlightened than that." Mo offered the reproach with a smile.

"I don't say we're even close to perfect, but you can't deny the obvious: women want something different out of life than we do—what it is I'm not quite sure. But they never seem to get it and they suffer secret pains that we can know nothing about. They don't want us to know because that would spoil their advantage. But there's nothing wrong with making us suffer a bit too—so we'll know what it's like. Ergo: the noble institution of marriage." Mike opened his hands like a magician producing doves from thin air.

"I've never heard you so cynical."

"Not so much cynical as realistic. You showed me how never to take anything at face value. And I've been married for almost four years now."

"Is that why you've lost weight?" Mo asked.

Mike knew that he still showed the effects of his nightmare encounter with Jasper Brown, that he carried the emblem of his guilt almost as clearly as a scarlet letter. Perhaps he had agreed to see Mo too soon. But he had to take care of an unpleasant item of business. . . .

"Some sort of bizarre reaction to giving up basketball, I guess," Mike said. "*You* haven't given up eating, I hope."

"Not entirely. Although I don't taste anything any more. Sheila used to—well, it was different with her. Now I don't get any pleasure out of food—or anything." He shrugged his considerable shoulders. "Listen to me feeling sorry for myself. Ever since Sheila left I've been getting vaguer and vaguer. She gave *definition* to everything around her: including yours truly. She never lets you forget you're alive."

"Sounds like you should find out her number and call her."

"I know I should. But I also know how she feels. Maybe I should give it a bit more time. At least I could unpack these damned boxes." Cardboard boxes lay scattered like last autumn's leaves across the floor all the way into the naked dining room, sad and brown, the masking tape cracked and curling. "I haven't even asked about you and Patty. Or what you have on your mind these days. You look pretty serious."

"Serious enough. Patty and I are all right. We both keep busy. Out of each other's hair. It's never easy but somehow it works."

"At the wedding I remember I was worried. I wasn't sure you were doing the right thing. I guess I was jealous. Sheila really likes Patty."

"And vice versa."

Mo stared for a moment at the golden liquid in his sweating glass. The graying light descended upon the two men, along with a peculiar silence. "I suppose this isn't a bad place to live," Mo declared, as if staking a claim to the idea.

"Could be worse," affirmed Mike, sipping his scotch. "Why'd you give up your old place?"

"Besides the fact that my mother insisted? I suppose it was too full of memories. I always think of it as Sheila's place more than mine. I've got to get over thinking that way. I'm a one-man show now."

"Where is she living now?"

"How the hell do I know? We didn't even have an argument. She just left. She said I knew why. That was four weeks ago." Mo gripped the glass in his lap with a hairy paw. "I heard about this apartment from a guy at the firm. And that's another situation that's got to change. I'm wasting my time there."

"How so?"

"Civil liberties is just another game, Mike. Like the rest of the law. It's another gesture of the old liberalism, the stuff that got us in trouble in the first place—in Vietnam, with welfare. Too little too late."

Mike smiled wanly. "Looks like you've got a bellyful of problems."

Mo laughed and spat an ice cube into his glass. "You said it, brother. If there were anywhere else to go I'd be out of this city so fast . . . but the trouble is, I don't belong anywhere else. Student activist, Jew, civil-rights lawyer—I'd get lynched if I set foot out of the five boroughs. And I've got my few remaining friends here."

"So, what are you going to do?"

"Hell, I don't know. Wangle some appointment with the city or the state—go for a U.S. attorney spot or assistant DA. Maybe if I made less money I'd feel better. All I know is, it's time for a change."

Mike poured two more drinks. Mo usually never touched liquor except at parties or with dinner. But he was feeling garrulous tonight: he wanted to indulge himself, to grease the gears before undertaking major repairs.

"All day every day I sit there trying to make a crusade out of some poor joker's illegal search and seizure complaint. Occasionally I tackle a real First Amendment case. Sometimes I get the goods on a sleazy slumlord—and that feels good. But by its very existence—as a profit-making operation—the firm is a compromise. I'm not naive enough to think that the DA doesn't face the same thing every day—politics and compromise, I mean—but it seems to me that the ends are so much different in a prosecutor's office. It's not profit but some approximation of justice he's after. It seems a purer goal than money. Maybe I'm all wet," he concluded as he took a slug of whiskey.

"You always told me that you wanted to be able to wake up and look at yourself in the mirror every day."

"I've seen more than a few bought and sold," Mo affirmed. "And thank God I'm not that far gone yet." He shook his great head. "No, not yet."

"C'mon, Mo. You're the one guy who doesn't know the meaning of selling out. That's something rare. The rest of us have to depend on you to hold the line."

"I hope you're not as bad off as you make it sound. You haven't gone over to the other side, have you?"

"Not yet," Mike said with unaverted eyes.

"Let's hope so. You know, I depend on you too. To keep my feet on the ground. You've always been a realist. You've always known the limits. That's why you can accomplish something some day, whereas I'll probably have to settle for little gains here and there. You have a special quality going for you—besides just physical talent. Maybe it's a capacity for compromise, in the best sense I mean, the ability to see the other side of the issue. We both know the dangers, I think, but someone has to be willing to bend a little to get something done." He looked at his friend with frank admiration. "How's that for faint praise?" he added ruefully.

"I know what you mean, Mo. And I appreciate your saying so. But how different are we, really, you and me? Sometimes I wonder."

"Well, if I have something to contribute—a big 'if'— I think it'll be as a watchdog. I'm a patient and steady plodder. I can spot the enemy and hold him off. You, on the other hand, should be right out front—like you've always been—a visible public figure. Bee always said you had a lot of Lincoln in you, which may not be far from true. But you've got to let it happen; more than that, you've got to work for it." Mo's mouth curled into a grin. "I sound like a coach. It's just that I have a lot riding on your future. You've got it all, Mike; you can go as far as you want to."

"You shouldn't put all your eggs in this basket," warned Mike. "Lincoln I'm not."

Just then the telephone jangled, an angry, urgent summons. Mo lumbered across the room to answer it, stepping around the boxes on the floor. The conversation was brief and one-sided, Mo speaking in muffled affirmatives. When he returned to the sofa he finished off his drink with one gulp.

"That was my mother," he said. "My father is in the hospital—has been for several weeks. Cancer. She lives over there. Says he's taken a turn for the worse. I should have been there today."

"Jesus, Mo, I didn't know. I'm sorry."

"I hate going to the hospital. I hate seeing him there.

It's no way for a good man to die."

Mike recalled his own father's death. He wanted to say something to ease Mo's burden, but he remembered all the empty murmurings of his mother's friends, so he kept his mouth shut. He silently refilled Mo's glass.

For a minute the lawyer sat there mute, until the pain of the moment faded. He took another healthy swallow of scotch before he spoke, changing the subject.

"Did you hear about your old buddy Jasper Brown?"

Mike's cheeks burned. "He get nabbed finally?"

"Somebody wasted him."

"What about Darlene? Did she get hurt?"

"She wasn't mentioned in the newspaper. Have you talked to her?"

"I haven't seen her in over a year."

"Surprised you didn't know about it," said Mo.

"I guess I knew it would happen sooner or later."

Mike fidgeted under Mo's intense scrutiny. For the past several weeks the memory of Darlene and Jasper had haunted him, invading his mind every waking moment and twisting his dreams into gory intimations of destruction and death. Wright told him she was confined in a sanitarium upstate. He hadn't yet discovered exactly where, and he remained reluctant to find out. You can know too much, he admonished himself.

"I suppose so," said Mo. "I'm glad you got out of that mess when you did. The police called it a gang killing. I hope Darlene wasn't involved."

"So do I."

"To hell with this gloominess," Mo announced as if to dispel the stormcloud forever. "What was it you wanted to discuss with me?"

"We can talk about it another time," said Mike, panic swelling inside him.

"Why not now? I've unburdened myself about Sheila, and about my dad. Your story can't be half as depressing as mine." Mo's hand found Mike's knee. "If we can't talk to each other, who can we talk to?"

Mike took some more scotch and avoided his old friend's curious gaze. Mo hadn't really changed, even with his recent troubles; he remained the solid, tough-thinking activist Mike had known at Yale. It would take more than a break-up with Sheila and a death in the family to shake him. Yet how would he react to the new rules of the game as Mike proposed to lay them out? And how could Mike pull it off without alienating an already troubled friend? How much control did Mortimer Wright now have over his life—his soul?

"I've taken a job with First New York, Mo. Vice president for community affairs." As he spoke he watched his friend's face. Mo didn't blink; his eyes remained focused fully on Mike and a look of pained recognition passed over his face. Mike continued: "It'll give me a chance to pursue the Youth Center I've been talking about for years."

Mo nodded glumly. "Mortimer Wright."

"Yeah, Mortimer Wright—but so what? Look, it's a job—a chance to make some good out of the bad. First New York has so much money they don't know what to do with it. You can't say the Center isn't a worthwhile cause—better than using the money to tear down housing for some half-assed federal project."

"I suppose I can't disagree with you, Mike. But I don't trust that man. From what I know of him—"

"I'll admit he's a strange guy—but he's giving me the chance to build this thing." Mo's face had turned to stone, but Mike continued. "Think of the kids, Mo. I'm doing it for them."

"I don't doubt your sincerity, Mike. But once you get mixed up with Wright and men like him, you become their tool—whether you admit it or not. I've seen it happen before and I don't like it. I think you can do whatever you want to do without them."

"I want to build this thing. And I can't do it without

First New York and Wright."

"That's a decision you have to make."

"I've made it."

"So what do you want to ask me about?"

"I need your advice."

"I've already told you what I think: steer clear of Mortimer Wright."

"I mean, as my attorney." Mike paused, framing the statement, dreading Mo's response. "I—if I'm to work for First New York I've got to play by their rules. The bank retains Garland, Steele, Patty's father's firm, as counsel and—well, that outfit takes care of all legal matters for the company, and if I'm a vice president—"

" 'If'? I thought it was settled. All wrapped up with a bow."

"That's why I wanted to talk to you, Mo. What should I do? I can't remain your client if I go with them."

"Who says?"

"It's company policy."

"Wright?"

"He mentioned it," Mike allowed. He was sweating now, and sick to death of the whole idea.

"I'm too radical, is that it? A rabble-rouser? Unstable? A Jew?"

"What should I do?" he repeated.

"You've already made up your mind. We're not kids any more, Mike. It's not like the time you missed the ballgame because Wright tugged on your string. What do you expect me to say?"

"I just want you to tell me if you think I'm doing the right thing."

"As simple as that."

"If you want to call it simple."

Mo heaved himself from the sofa and took his drink to the window. Outside, across the park, the gray river coursed on silently over the tops of the black trees. A taxi whizzed by on the narrow street below.

"What's come over you, Mike?" he asked. "Does Wright have something on you? I don't buy your line. And I won't tell you you're doing the right thing, because you're not. There's something going on that you're not telling me."

"What makes you say that?" Alarm crept into Mike's voice.

"We've known each other long enough. I've seen you in action before."

"Maybe I *am* hiding something," Mike blazed angrily. "Or maybe I just want too much to create something that will last. Tell me what's wrong with that?"

"I won't argue means and ends with you, Mike. If you don't need my legal services anymore, that's fine. But don't lie to me."

The room, dark now but for a feeble lamp at one end of the sofa, seemed to crack and split wide open between the two men. Mike put his glass on the table and rose.

Mo was surprised—at himself, not Mike. The signs had been there all along; Mike had too often been willing to take the expedient route. He remembered the first time he had seen Mike Merritt. On the basketball court. Moving swiftly and flawlessly beneath the hoop. Sending twenty-foot shots soaring and snapping through the net. In those days he had believed—it seemed they both had believed—that there could be grace in the world, that action could be a noble expression of human reason. But both men had grown up to see that simple vision shattered. No, he wasn't surprised at Mike. The furrowed face, the stoop, the hesitant manner. A big slice had been cut out of the athlete and what was left didn't allow for their continued friendship. Was it Wright? Was it some woman? Whoever or whatever it was wholly possessed him now.

"We've always kept the bullshit at a minimum in dealing with each other, Mike."

"What the hell is that supposed to mean?"

"Maybe it doesn't matter," said Mo. "Maybe it's for the best."

"Don't make me apologize, Mo. I'm doing what has to be done."

"I wouldn't accept an apology," the lawyer shot back. "I wouldn't believe an apology from you."

"You say that now. Let's give it a few weeks until you get straightened out. We'll talk again." Mike stepped forward hopefully, with a hand upraised to put on his old friend's shoulder.

Mo waved him off. "It's dead. Can't you see? There's nothing more to talk about. Thanks for coming over," he added icily.

Mike hurdled the boxes and made his way to the door. "Call me, Mo," he pleaded.

"Yeah, we'll take in a ballgame sometime."

Mo stood for a long time gazing out the window, the drink sitting forgotten on the sill, the ice melting, diffusing into the amber liquid as the night-domed city buzzed on.

"Do you want a cup of coffee or something, Mike?" Patty's hand rested between his shoulderblades as he bent over the blueprints on his desk.

He grunted affirmatively.

"Is that a 'coffee' or a 'something'?"

"Coffee," he mumbled.

"Do you know what time it is?"

"Mmmm."

"Or what day it is?"

"Mm-hmm."

It was early October and outside the afternoon heat lay like a scratchy woolen blanket over the gasping city. Indian summer savaged New York City with a vengeance.

"You haven't forgotten that tonight is our party."

Mike Merritt looked up at his wife as if startled from

a deep sleep, his eyes dark and distant. "Tonight?" His voice ebbed in confusion. "But I'm meeting with the contractor next week. I can't—"

Patty spun and strode out of his study. He watched her tall figure in a crisp white blouse and blue shorts, her bare feet treading noiseleslly over the carpet.

Their party. Her party. Two hundred invitations had invaded the mailboxes of friends and business acquaintances, most of whom were expected to show up. It was the first such affair they had ever thrown, and, when she had broached the idea several weeks ago, Mike had panicked, hating the idea. Parties gave him a big pain in the ass. But she persuaded him to go along—or at least not to interfere: "It'll do us both some good," she said, "and it'll get your mind off your work for an evening. You'll see."

Mike was too busy to interfere—or even to care. For the past year he had created and nurtured plans for the West Side Youth Center. Before him on his desk lay the blueprints for his redemption, over which he hunched every day like a monk over his sketches for the new abbey.

Once he and Mortimer Wright won over the First New York board of directors, Mike Merritt faced a challenge equal to the physical task of building: how to overcome the social and political lethargy that could block the project. Patience, he discovered, was the prime virtue he must cultivate as he courted black community leaders and city officials and contractors, seeking their advice and approval—which wasn't easy to obtain. The blacks feared this was another white encroachment on their turf. True, their neighborhoods were in trouble, but they had seen too many blocks gutted and leveled and never rebuilt—and too many well-intentioned white folk who built "privately funded" facilities which remained closed to local residents. It took all Mike's discretion and charm to convince them that this project was different. He also had to apply pressure on the city government and his own First New York backers to ensure the validity of his promises to the black community. The Center would be open at no cost for kids age six to eighteen; it would provide sports and cultural activities; it would employ a dozen people, members of the local community, full time. Of course, the Center would also be a highly visible tax write-off for the First Bank of New York, but Mike accepted that particular irony. As long as the dollars were there.

A site was chosen, architects commissioned, and Mike's brainchild was close to being born.

Patty too had become involved. One evening after a particularly acrimonious encounter with a First New York board member, he had complained to his wife: "Why the hell can't they see beyond their fucking budgets and 'priorities'?"

"Maybe they don't understand why you want so much to build it," she said. "Not everybody plays basketball, you know."

"I should build a gallery?"

"I don't mean that. But if you're building something for the kids, why not encourage dancers and artists and musicians, as well as athletes? Maybe if you broadened your base, as the politicians say, some of those old fogeys on the board would be more comfortable with the idea."

"Yeah." It struck him as obvious but canny. "Ballet and basketball. No one can be unhappy with that combination."

Patty's suggestions on the design and function of the project proved valuable, esthetically and politically, and the facilities as mapped out in front of him now strongly reflected her tastes and concerns.

Here it was. The grainy purple and gray hieroglyphs told the story of his future, of his bid for absolution from sins past. Besides the handball and basketball courts, the swimming pool, weight room, and showers, the plan incorporated classrooms, art studios, and a theatre, as well as an administrative office and rooftop patio and garden. The West Side Youth Center: a multipurpose facility which could serve, Mike hoped, as the focus for future efforts to revitalize the neighborhood. Construction was scheduled to begin in November and the estimated completion date was July 1979.

"Do you know what you're going to wear tonight?" Patty returned with the coffee.

"No idea," he said, brushing a stubborn strand of hair from his eye. He took a sip of the strong black brew.

'Well I do," she stated. "And I'll lay it out for you on the bed. You're going to be the handsomest man at the party tonight—whether you like it or not."

"You warned me once about being vain. You're not helping."

"Well, tonight I want you to be vain, Mike. I want you to be proud and happy—and I want you to put that Youth Center out of your mind for a few hours. We're having a party, damn it." She smiled gaily and found the back of his neck with her slender fingers. She kissed him quickly on his cold lips and straightened before he could respond. "We're friends, right?"

"So you've got your party," he said, his hands slipping around her slender waist.

"I've got you—I hope. That's all I really want." She gently raked his shoulders with her nails. "We both need you, Mike—you and me. You're all we've got."

"All right. Tonight I'm all yours." He rolled up the blueprints and stuffed his papers into a desk drawer.

She took his hand and led him into the bedroom. "Before we get dressed," she whispered huskily, "let's get undressed first." Their clothes floated to the floor and they fell onto the bed where they slowly, quietly, hungrily made love for the first time in weeks.

Afterward Patty held him. "Tonight let's be the happiest married couple in New York."

"If you say so."

"Oh, Mike, I've always loved you. If only—"

He put a finger on her lips. "Let's not talk about it—not tonight."

She pushed a pillow against the headboard of the bed and sat up, her golden hair caressing her shoulders. She pulled the white sheet over her exquisite breasts. "You know Mo and Sheila are back together."

"You invited Mo?" asked Mike, his astonishment mingling with dread.

"I invited Sheila," Patty said. "She said she'd come—but she didn't know if Mo—"

"Jesus, Patty, why?"

"Because I hate to see you two feuding like a couple of spoiled kids."

"There's more to it than that."

"I'd say there's a lot less to it than you think. Mike, you're both grown men. And you've been friends for too long to let this thing go on."

"You don't know the whole story."

"Only because you haven't told me. Another one of your secrets," she added bitterly.

"I don't want to talk about it."

"That's our problem—can't you see?—you don't talk to me about *anything*. Anything important. You still haven't told me—"

"Goddamn it," he raged. "I said I didn't want to talk about it."

"Well, I think you'd better get it off your chest one of these days—before it ruins you—and us. I've done all I can to get through to you."

"Patty . . ." The words caught in his throat like angry fishhooks.

They ate a silent dinner before they dressed for the party. Patty donned a clingy black crepe de chine, and she fashioned her hair in a tight bun atop her pale sculpted head. She laid out Mike's darkest pinstripe suit, a starched white shirt, and a black and gold silk tie.

He moped around the house, bumping into the scurrying caterers as they arranged the buffet and set up the bar. Finally, as she emerged from the bedroom, he went in to gird for the main event.

The first guests arrived uncomfortably early and hovered at the bar to wash down their uneasiness. Mike elbowed in for a drink.

"It wasn't my idea to come," a plump young woman told an open-faced young man, "but my boyfriend insisted. He's around someplace. I don't know a soul here."

"Me neither," came the sad reply. "My aunt brought me. She knows Laura Hartman."

The liquor warmed Mike's gullet. Let's have an intimate party, he thought wryly—just our two hundred closest friends.

Across the room at the front door Patty greeted a pair of vaguely familiar faces. Mike turned back to the bar and felt a pair of eyes locked on him. The plump girl stared frankly. He smiled and raised his glass. "Hello," he said.

"You're Mike Merritt," she said, the words enveloped in a worshipful gasp.

"That's right," he said. "Are you having a good time?"

"Oh yes. It's a wonderful party so far." She turned to the young man at her side. "Mr. Merritt, I'd like you to meet—" Confusion and embarrassment clouded her face. "What's your name?" she whispered to the young man.

Mike shook the youth's hand and excused himself, urging them to enjoy themselves. The living room was filling up as he made his way to Patty's side.

"What's that smirk all about?" she asked as he approached.

He shook his head and snaked an arm around her waist. "I just met two of our two hundred nearest and dearest. You want something to drink?"

She eyed him uncertainly. "You're incorrigible. Yes, why don't you fetch me a highball, like the obedient husband you so rarely are." Her hand caught his sleeve as he turned to go. "Thank you."

Returning a moment later with her drink, he encountered an older couple who held his wife in affectionate greeting. "Mike," she said, "come here and meet the Finnegans."

Bob Finnegan published the glossy weekly *Manhattan* and collected art. His wife Betty chaired two clubs and crocheted in her spare time.

Mike took the man's hand firmly. "Bob." Then the woman. "Betty." He softly enclosed her fingers in his.

"He's marvelous, Patty," Betty Finnegan declared. "Much more beautiful than his pictures."

For the next hour Mike squeezed scores of hands and stoically endured the chitchat and backslapping. Then Sheila Martin arrived—alone. Mike was both relieved and disappointed; he had almost welcomed the chance to see Mo again.

Sheila, wearing a long skirt and sandals, smiled sardonically and kissed Patty Merritt. "I brought me," she said. "My recalcitrant roommate had to work late tonight."

"He could stop by later," Patty suggested.

"Thanks for trying," Sheila said. Then she turned to Mike who stooped, somewhat embarrassed yet genuinely pleased to see her. "Hi, Mike." Her tiptoe smile culminated in a smack on his cheek. "Long time."

"Too long. How's Mo?"

"Fat and fidgety," Sheila replied with a disarming smile. "Busy. Always busy." She shruged frankly. "I tried my damnedest."

"What's he doing these days?" Mike pressed.

"Still with the firm—anxious to get out. He's talked to some political people about a DA appointment. That won't come through for at least a year, though, if it comes through at all. Meanwhile, I'm trying to pin him down on a date for our rendezvous with marital destiny."

"That's wonderful!" Patty exclaimed.

"You mean, that's difficult," said Sheila. "But, without making any predictions, I'd say we'll get our act together at the first of the year."

"How's his father?" asked Mike.

"He died two months ago."

Mike was not surprised. His father had taken just nine months to die. *Just* nine months . . . against the greater wash of time it wasn't so long, but, as he remembered it, the months had stretched into an infinity of suffering for Hugh Merritt. He saw for a moment the ashen corpse of the once vital man; he heard again his mother's solitary weeping and relived his own empty gropings for an answer to the riddle of life and death. It seemed so long ago, so far removed from the present. And yet the needle of shame was as sharp as ever and now it pricked his conscience.

"Mike," interjected Patty, "you never told me."

"It wasn't my place," said Mike. "I'm sorry, Sheila."

"The past year as been tough for Mo," Sheila continued. "But he's surviving."

Mike escaped into the crush of the party, leaving the two women engaged in serious conversation. The packed living room rocked to the rhythm of a hundred dialogues, each barely audible amid the discordant festive welter. He was conscious, as he shouldered through the room to the bar, of partygoers' glances and whispers. Although he had lived a largely public life for more than five years it still irked him to see that surprised, expectant, possessive look in a stranger's eyes. He smiled and nodded at acquaintances, many of whom he had met just within the past few minutes, and quickly moved on. How many parties had he attended since his first days in college, through his career as a professional ballplayer, and now as a corporate functionary? He remembered the surge of expectation he had felt when Bee took him to the Yale Club their freshman year: the scrubbed faces of the scions of old families, the gleaming punchbowl, the thrill of his proximity to tradition and wealth, Bee's sarcastic deflation of the whole thing, then getting drunk, really drunk, for the first time in his life. The cold nights had seemed not so cold, the skies not so dark, the possibilities not so limited in those days.

"J & B on the rocks," he told the bartender. Then, drink in hand, he turned to see Bee plowing toward him through the knots of people. He brightened. His old friend had been keeping to himself in recent months, holed up in a West Village flat writing a novel he was reluctant to talk about. Mike hadn't seen him since the past summer.

Immaculate in a tweed coat, pleated gray pants and brown knitted tie, Bee looked fit but tired. The spark of deviltry had returned to his eyes and, as he smiled, his face shone confidently. "Mr. Lincoln!"

Mike greeted the writer with a two-handed grip. "The Hermit of Hudson Street. Am I glad you're here. Now this is really a party."

"Can't stay long," Bee said. "Keeping strict hours these days."

"It must agree with you."

"It gets the job done. I've given up pills, pink ladies, and people—not to mention parties, though I wouldn't have missed this orgy for anything."

"Can I get you something to drink, in honor of your brief descent from the mountain?"

"Club soda with lime."

"So you've really given up booze?"

"At least for the duration. It disturbs the routine that I've finally established."

Mike poured his friend's drink. "So you've turned serious on us."

"To tell you the truth," said Bee, accepting the glass,

"nothing much seems terribly funny to me these days. It's a serious business, this writing." He shook his tawny head. "There are days when I sit there like a retarded parapalegic and can't decide whether to take a crap or not. Then there are days when I fly along at a thousand words an hour straight to the heart of the idea." He waved an elegant hand in dismissal. "But forget my frettings. Where's *your* fine head at these days? Still in the clouds?"

"I've got to wrestle with a bunch of builders next week. Construction starts next month on the Center."

"Altruism and energy, the Merritt Formula for success."

"It's just a job. Somebody has to do it—should have done it years ago."

"How's Patty holding up? She looks like a million bucks."

"She keeps busy too, at Hartman's. And she had a number of ideas for the Center. It's really half hers too."

"You know," Bee began, his clear blue eyes awash with affection, "you two people have been pretty good to me ever since that disgraceful performance up in Snowburg. And I've never thanked you for that."

"For Christ's sake, that was years ago. We've forgotten all about it. Besides, you got me to read Keats's letters, so it wasn't all bad."

"So how is our 'Man of Achievement' faring on his autodidactic adventures?"

Mike drained his scotch. "I don't flatter myself that I've achieved negative capability, but I sure as hell sometimes wish I were a poet—or at least a man like Keats with total self-knowledge. I can't say I know myself yet, so I'll have to settle for doing what good I can with my 'society' rather than my 'wit.' "

"If you ask me, you've a good measure of both—more than most." Old love and well-worn hope filled his gaze. "I still say you'll be a great man some day, if you'll let yourself—if you find the appropriate medium for your talent. Still think about politics?"

"I can't say that I don't, but the Center absorbs most of my conscious hours. I'm not sure how many votes I could pull down for dogcatcher."

"You haven't got any more skeletons in your closet?" Bee queried with a wink. "Your secrets are relatively safe with me, you know."

"I'm not sure I like you better sober," said Mike.

"Can it, brother. I'm reformed and I'm gonna stay that way. Booze just fuels my unnatural desires."

As they spoke Mike noticed a bespectacled man who stood near Bee, half in and half out of their conversation. The man cleared his throat and Bee turned to him. "Stephen," he said solicitously. "I'm sorry." With a sheepish grin he introduced Mike to Stephen James. "Patron of the arts and purveyor of fine taste," he exclaimed, "and good friend."

Mike sensed he was something more. James was a well-dressed, graying, So-Ho type with a strong friendly hand. Mike couldn't help liking him. "Please make yourself at home," he said expansively.

James scanned the handsome host from head to toe. "Thanks. Didn't mean to horn in on a private conversation. But Bee's told me so much about you—I had to see for myself."

"Stephen has an eye for the finer things. He's a painter."

"A dabbler," James corrected. He nodded toward the Rothko that hung over the fireplace. "That's painting. I'm a student and an appreciator."

"He's modest is what he is," Bee countered.

"You should talk to Patty, my wife," said Mike. "She has the eyes in this family. Have you seen her, Bee?"

"She was holding court in the dining room last time I looked. She's already met Stephen." Bee finished his drink. "We better be going." He looked to his escort who agreed.

Mike watched them push toward the door and felt a twinge of jealousy. He had often wondered what sort of men his friend chose for lovers. Alone now, he faced a gaggle of strangers gushing with gratitude.

"I must have seen you play a hundred times at the Garden," one man observed.

"This is a beautiful pad," cooed a young redhead in a strapless, backless, and almost frontless evening dress.

"Marvelous taste," another woman chorused.

"Say, Mr. Merritt, my firm is looking for a young man like yourself. . . ."

Where the hell is Patty? he wondered, surveying the party for a glimpse of her. He imagined her cornered by a dozen admirers. He remembered the college party where he first saw her, surrounded by those admiring drones. Perhaps she welcomed the opportunity for the attention she rarely received from him. Perhaps she wanted this party to fill their home with the life it seemed to lack with just the two of them. Where is she? He craned his neck.

Not spotting her, he slipped to the bar where he got another scotch. When he turned again to face the party a tall bronzed woman of about fifty, wearing a revealing maroon gown, stole up to him. She smiled and deep crowsfeet met the faint wrinkles on her tanned forehead. Her voice was a sexy rasp. "Mr. Merritt. I'm Janet Harper." A jeweled bracelet dripped from her thin wrist and her hand felt firm and athletic in his. For a moment her longing eyes were Nancy Davidson's.

"Pleased to meet you, Miss Harper." Was he supposed to know her?

She put her cocktail down and lit a cigarette. Smoke spilled from her lips as she spoke. "Mrs.," she corrected. "My husband Rudy is an old friend of Mortimer Wright's. Mortimer speaks very highly of you. I get the impression you're a young man with quite a future."

"Thank you very much." A tight smile cut across his

face and he blushed. This lady was coming on strong. He glanced past her quickly for a sign of Patty.

"I'm hoping that sometime you and your wife will join my husband and me for dinner. I've met your wife—and I'd love to talk to you." Her slim fingers found the sleeve of his coat. She was an attractive woman, trim, sensuous, her eyes dancing seductively.

"We'd be happy to," he said, though he doubted he'd ever make the effort. "I hope I live up to your expectations."

"Oh, I've no doubt you will," she said. She squeezed his arm. "See you then."

Clutching his drink he plunged into the tangle of guests in search of his wife.

After Bee left, and as the party swelled and tittered past midnight, Mike's tolerance for the whole affair diminished further. He surveyed the scene skeptically: two hundred faces, less than half of them familiar, congregated here for liquor and facile conversation and to be seen. What if they knew the secret he carried locked up and darkly deposited in the deepest recesses of his mind? Even a glimpse of the truth would, he guessed, upend their cynical senses: some would be titillated, some sympathetic, most shocked. Indeed, the idea of exposing himself gave him a perverse pleasure. He was known to the world at large as one who played by the rules. He imagined that if they knew the truth they would simply reshuffle the moral deck and continue the game without him. He would be frozen out. But he wondered if he might not prefer it that way.

He sighted Patty across the room with the Finnegans. He caught her eye and signaled her to meet him in the kitchen. "What do you say we get the hell out of here?" he asked her.

A lock of wheat-colored hair fell in front of her ear. She whisked it back with a knowing, exhausted smile. "Wouldn't that be impolite?"

"Sure, but I don't know if I can take any more come-ons from bored middle-aged socialites."

"Has someone propositioned you?" Patty asked, piqued. "Who?"

"Bee and Sheila were the only civilized people here. The rest are total strangers."

"Most of them are our friends."

"God help us, then. Let's step out, Patty. Just for a while. Nobody will miss us."

"If it'll get you away from these panting bitches," she teased. "I'm with you."

It was a breezy but temperate night, the moon a pale yellow disc when it could be seen among the tall structures along the avenue. They stepped into the night among the glaring lights of the busy streets. Taxi cabs sped recklessly by, careening perilously close to the toes of eager pedestrians who shouted and scurried against the stoplights. Once she took his arm as they negotiated a busy intersection, but she dropped it when they stepped onto the sidewalk.

Always in a hurry, she thought. Everyone. Mike. What's the rush? Slow down and let's talk. Something needs to be said.

She wasn't quite sure what it was, but between them existed a dense wall of foreign experience, never to be breached even in their rare intimate moments.

Her long legs carried her lithe frame quickly along the crowded walk. A stylish old man who bumped into her smiled with his white mustache and begged her pardon. She thought about her father. Where was he tonight? At home, in his study, drinking brandy, reading a fat Victorian novel. Solitary. Alone with his powerful, barely restrained contempt for the rest of the world. So cold sometimes.

She glanced at her husband who marched sternly ahead, lost in one of his moods. Like her father. So damned distant. What was he afraid of?

All she knew was that Mike's secret had been eating away at him. For months now. Ever since that night last year. Where had he been? Why wouldn't he tell her? How awful could it be? But she never pressed him. She said nothing that might close him up to her forever. She spoke less these days about adopting a child. But she yearned for him to trust her, to tell her. Even if the truth brought down the final curtain between them—and that was her greatest fear—she needed to know the truth.

They walked for a half-hour, matching strides through the warm night past darkened shops and noisy bars attended by packs of scrubbed young people who wore tight jeans and talked loudly about cars and football and getting laid. The patches of black sky overhead were clear. They covered block after block, absorbed in their private silence, observing the nighttime fragments of other people's lives.

Before they realized it, they had reached Gracie Park. In the distance among the ebony tree trunks twinkling rectangles of light indicated the mayor's mansion. Mike led Patty to a bench. There they watched the denuded tops of the trees serrate the gibbous moon.

"We should go back soon," she whispered as she nestled in the solid crook of his arm. If only I could make him fall in love with me all over again, she thought.

"If you say so," he answered. "In a minute."

"Are you angry that I asked Sheila?"

"Of course not, I'm glad to hear they're getting married."

"Me too. I like them. They're good people. I wish we could see them more often—like we used to." He continued to stare into the darkness of the park. "What's wrong, Mike?" she asked finally.

"I just wanted to get away. All those people, in our house—"

"We invited them."

"Maybe I'm paranoid."

"I know you better than that. You're not paranoid—you're chicken."

He laughed, turning to look into her night-veiled

face. "I suppose you're right." The rebellious forelock fell over his brow. His arm tightened around her slender shoulders. "Chicken, huh?" he repeated as if it were the punch line of a joke he had to remember. "Sometimes you surprise me."

"How? Tell me how?"

For a moment it seemed as if the city had vanished, leaving them in a quiet tenebrous forest. Patty reached for his hand; it was cold but he yielded it to her.

"Someday," he began, standing up and pulling her gently to her feet, "this will all be over—the project, I mean—and I will have paid back some of what I owe and we can have a real life together. Like we should have from the beginning."

"Why someday?" She stood beside him, her cool face reflecting the glow of the moon. "Mike, why don't you tell me what's really on your mind? We never talk any more. Married people should talk."

"I wish I could answer you. But so much—it all depends . . ." What could he tell her without telling her everything, without destroying himself, without ruining what was left of them? "I just don't know, Patty. I can't say."

"One day, Mike—tonight or tomorrow or a year from now—you'll have to answer me."

"I know."

They caught a cab on Lexington Avenue and sped back to their building. The party to which they returned had not missed them, it seemed. It must be a good party, he thought, if no one wants to leave. He wondered if a romance or two had been born—perhaps between the fleshy girl and the egg-faced boy he had met earlier, or maybe Mrs. Harper had found someone else. As he and Patty unobtrusively reemerged into the ranks of bent elbows and gay smiles he felt like ordering them all out and away so he could retire and get up tomorrow refreshed for work. But no, he considered, he couldn't do that—it would be impolitic, impolite; it would spoil Patty's evening.

13

After the dedication of the Center the following summer, Mike resumed his duties as vice president for community affairs at the First Bank of New York. His office was in the upper reaches of a towering edifice on 56th Street beyond a maze of cubicles where his assistants, eager smoothies with Harvard MBAs, toiled over budgets and tax schemes. Mike's first assignment was to assess last year's ad campaign, a tedious chore. He slogged through reports, condensations, and synopses of minutes recorded at free-for-alls between in-house "experts" and outside consultants. Picayune details inspired rabid conflicts. Should they go with roman type or italics on subway posters? Blue lettering on a red background, or black on white? Did the portraits of bank managers feature enough conspicuous blacks—or were there too many? Was it wise to picture a white woman smiling at a Puerto Rican man? Idiocy, all of it, and yet millions were spent. The bastards must be laughing.

After two hours of this one bleak morning in November his receptionist buzzed. "Mr. Maris is here. He doesn't have an appointment, so—"

"Send him in."

Mike first met Jeff Maris at Yale. He was a year behind the All-American and among the most active members of the radical coalition organized by Mo Silver. After graduating Maris returned to his native East Side and promptly signed on with the Democratic Party. He was appointed to a local planning board, then held a minor post in Abe Beame's administration. In 1976 he won election to the State Assembly, and was re-elected two years later. Mike followed his progress idly and a touch wistfully, especially now that his own career had reached a standstill. At a fund-raiser hosted by Maris in 1978 Mike was pleased to learn that the assemblyman knew about the proposed West Side Youth Center. Thus an incidental friendship took on new life. Maris periodically called him for news of the project and commended Mike's work in several interviews over the next year. He repeatedly urged him to run for office, promising to manage the campaign should he decide to take a stab at it. The party was on the lookout for fresh faces and Mike, with his celebrity status, his corporate nexus, and his compelling physical presence, was an attractive prospect.

At first glance Maris wore the contented look of the privileged class. But there was an underlying toughness about him that made you look again. The firm set of his mouth, although the lips were a trifle thin, and the steady light in his gray eyes, suggested both inner reserves of caution and a capable mind. Maris was a man of action with a ruminative streak, like Mike himself.

"You've rescued me from tedium," Mike said after they shook hands.

"For good I hope."

"Not too goddamn likely. Have a seat."

Maris smiled. "You haven't heard my proposition yet."

"If it'll get me out of this straightjacket I'll agree to it right now." Mike sat on the corner of his desk, arms crossed over his loosened tie.

"Just what I was hoping you'd say. In three weeks I'll have a staff lined up."

"For what?"

"Your campaign."

Mike shook his head. "Congress is out. Green looks

tough and to tell you the truth my heart isn't in the silk-stocking district.''

"I agree. I'm talking about the Senate. Whiting's seat."

"Ask me in ten years."

"When do you turn thirty?"

"January."

"Why wait?"

"Jeff, I'm not ready for the Senate. I've got to get some experience—like you've got."

"You mean you don't have any ideas. I can see that. After all, Whiting's a real pro."

"Are you kidding? Whiting's a cocktail politician. Have you ever read his foreign policy statements? He warms his chair on the committee and shakes a lot of hands, but that's all he does. He's a pawn of the oil companies and the Republican machine."

"And you wouldn't be?"

"Damn straight. I'd support the needs of this state— especially when it comes to federal assistance for the city. It's a crime that we're paying the taxes we do and get nothing in return. And Whiting doesn't care in the least. He just wags his tail and salivates at the bullshitters at the top. In eighteen years he hasn't once produced a piece of legislation that would have bailed out the city. As for the upstaters, tell me how he's going to see them through a recession if he's nothing but a lickspittle and a mouthpiece for the robber barons? You know what I'd do?" Mike was on his feet, pacing.

Maris shook his head.

"I'd levy a killer impost on gasoline—fifty cents a gallon, maybe a dollar. Once we cut down gas consumption we'll prick the balloon of inflation. That's where all our money's going. The government pays OPEC the going rate for oil and the consumer pays only half that. No wonder the feds are going broke. But you can't just raise the price of gas. All that does is beef up the corporations—and Exxon doesn't need any more of our money. So, like I say, you drop a tax on it. Some of it funneled back to the communities that fork it over in the first place—in rural areas, say, it'd go to subsidize the farmers and free them from the clutches of the banks—some to cover the cost of the oil we import. The rest I'd pour into mass transit. The work force is there to build a comprehensive rail system. Hell, in England and Japan they have trains that run 130 miles per hour. With our technology we can do the same. And we can put plenty of people to work to get it done. After gas prices become prohibitive, the car manufacturers will be forced to lay off even more workers. Already three quarters of a million auto workers are without jobs. So we have those guys building the railroad and then we show 'em how to run it. Fuck cars, they ruin the air, they cause more deaths than war, and they destroy the small towns. Without cars people would walk again and live ten years longer.

"Next thing, rebuild the cities. Rebuild the ghettoes, room by room the way Norman Mailer said when he ran for mayor. And let the poor do it themselves. Which means the minorities. Because like it or not that's still our biggest failing. We're a racist nation and we always will be. The melting pot rap is dead as a doornail. The minorities don't buy it, and we don't buy it. We've fucked them over too many times. We sent them to Vietnam as cannon fodder, then put them on the dole. Who needs welfare? On that one, the Republicans are one hundred percent right. Not only because it empties the pockets of the poor working devils, but because it cripples the fellow in the ghetto. Give him a job that means something and he'll be glad to work. Only don't expect him to clean your toilet. The best we can do right now to atone for what we've done to the poor is to let them go their own way. But we have to help, that's the wage of our sin. We've treated them horribly for so long that it's become like a necrosis. Our moral tissue is rotting and you can smell the odor of death. I played ball with black men. I coached a team that had only one white face, and it was mine. For a long time I felt nothing but guilt. I'd look at these guys carrying names that weren't their own but the names of slavetraders and slaveowners and think, Jesus they've been robbed of their identity. Then I decided, Fuck that, Merritt. These guys don't want your pity. You can shove your pity up your ass. If anything they feel sorry for you, because you have to live with your own degredation. You understand what I'm saying? It's time we stopped grinding out the doubletalk about the American Way. I don't say it with pleasure because most of my life I bought that line like nobody's business."

"Where do you stand on defense spending?"

"I don't like piling hardware onto the Doomsday Machine, but I don't think we can scotch it either. It keeps our allies from getting nervous because they're frightened to death of the Russians."

"And you're not?"

"Why should I be? I look at their position and it seems like ours, only worse. Because in the paranoia department they put even us to shame. The Russians don't care about ruling the world. Unless they're crazy. Ruling the world is one big headache. Look at Rome and now Britain; every country they used to own is stampeding London with immigrants. And they can't accomodate them. It's not a Soviet empire the Russians want. They're just scared stiff that the rest of the world is closing in on *them*. That's why they expand their borders. That and the fact that they're still looking for a warm-water port. From a pragmatic point of view all this mutual paranoia is a bummer because with the wrong character in the White House or the Kremlin the whole planet will go up like an exploding cigar."

Maris was excited. "Listen, Mike. Big Jim Callahan has opened the primary. It's up for grabs. He told me so himself. He's not backing anybody and he said some pretty embarrassing stuff about Moskovitz and Palermo who're telling everybody in town that they're in it for sure. The party's in lousy shape. If I thought I had a shot I'd put in a bid myself, but I'm not there yet. I'm still too young. And nobody knows who the hell I am. You, on the other hand, are famous. The press loves you, the city loves you. You've got ideas and the voters'll listen. I can arrange a meeting with Callahan anytime you say. All you need is his clearance and you're off and running. He's a Tammany type but no fool and he's willing to give new guys a chance. I've got contacts through Albany with all the upstate Democratic clubs—"

"Why me?"

"Because you can win—with a professional staff. I can think of a dozen good campaigners, experienced and industrious as hell, who are just itching to get on with a guy who has promise."

"I don't know."

"Think about it. Take a look at who your competition's likely to be. You already know the score with Whiting. All you have to say is yes and in three weeks I can get you a staff. Which I'll manage."

"It would be a lot more gratifying then poring over these inane reports."

"That's the spirit. There won't be any formal declarations of candidacy until late spring. But I'd like to get an early jump. To establish our legitimacy. It still gives you plenty of time to think about it. Talk it over with Patty. Take a leave of absence from this vault. Promise me you'll give it serious thought."

"All right," Mike said. "I'll think about it."

"We're going to go far," said Jeff Maris. "I can feel it."

The press called him "Big Jim," but no one other than longtime intimates dared use that name to his face for, beneath nearly three hundred pounds of political flesh, the state chairman did not need to be reminded how big he was. He carried his weight as if it were a physical emblem of the power he wielded in voting booths and back rooms across the state.

He had held the chairmanship over twenty years, after a career that took him from the Manhattan wards to Washington where he served briefly as Postmaster General. Callahan had started out with Tammany Hall as a precinct captain and now he pulled the strings across the entire state. Ward heeler or county boss or governor: his yea or nay could make or break them all. Power was his livelihood and his passion. He'd seen them all—F.D.R., Robert Wagner, Bobby Kennedy—and, like the despised GOP pachyderm, he never forgot. His endorsement, which Mike and every other Democratic candidate sought, was equal to as many as a million votes and, more often than not, the election. Now seventy-five years old, Callahan remained near the peak of his powers, an anachronism in modern American politics, an old lion whose growl made younger men jump through *his* hoop. . . .

The cabby pulled over to the curb in front of the white rectangular tower of the Sheraton Centre. He was saying: ". . . But the Comets were class. Now it's just a bunch of niggers out there. Ya know what I mean? Let's see—that'll be six-seventy, Mr. Merritt."

Mike strode across the sparkling lobby. He felt the stares, as he always did, from the people idling about. His stomach dropped with the swift lurch of the elevator, and he breathed deeply. The doors eased open and he stepped out into the silent hallway. Like a nervous bridegroom he fiddled with his tie and smoothed back his dark hair. Then he knocked on the door of Callahan's suite.

A big gray-faced man with a suspicious-looking bulge beneath his ill-fitting black suit admitted him. With a nod with man led Mike through a series of rooms. A vase of bright flowers on the coffee table was the only touch of color or life in the place. The bodyguard brought Mike to a closed door. The man knocked and entered without waiting for a reply from within. Mike followed him.

The master bedroom was almost as large as the living room, with four tall windows facing Sixth Avenue from where the sounds of the cold glaring night rose to penetrate the glass. A mammoth canopied bed dominated the room. And there sat James J. Callahan in his black pants and starched white shirt and suspenders, pulling a long black sock over his big pink foot. His fringe of white hair was cropped close around the gleaming dome of his head. He looked up from his garters. Without standing he shot a wide smile at Mike and extended his fleshy hand. "Happy to meet you, son. Goddamned fund-raiser at nine," he grunted, "but you can have a few minutes. Here, pull up a chair."

"It's my pleasure, Mr. Chairman, and an honor."

"Care for a drink, my boy?" Mike nodded and the Chairman commanded Alex, the bodyguard, to pour the bourbon. Callahan took an eager gulp before he addressed the young man who sat holding his drink on his lap. "Smoke?" he offered as he opened a wooden chest on the night table. It was full of long black cigars.

"No thanks," Mike said.

"Still in training, eh?" queried the Chairman with another smile that split his florid face. "I suppose that's for the best. I've cut down lately myself—only fifteen a day. Used to smoke thirty or forty. The wife hates 'em, but for an old man they're one of the few pleasures left."

Callahan returned his attention to the garters. He adjusted one, revealing dark pink marks where the elastic had cut like teeth. "So what do you want from me?"

Mike was taken aback and no words came to him.

Callahan laughed. "For fifty years I've been dealing in half-truths. It was my business. Now I'm an old man and I've got this cockeyed compulsion to call things by their proper names. Tell you, when you feel the end is near you want to flush out all the crap. Of course there's just too much of it and not nearly enough time to get it all out. Especially if you're in this racket. But just to appease an old geezer be honest with me, all right? It'll make me feel better. Almost like I'm in an honest profession. Nobody comes to see me except when they want something. A pretty face I don't have and I don't spin delightful conversation."

"I'm thinking of entering the primary for Whiting's seat and I'd like your go-ahead," Mike blurted.

"Do you know what the voters want?" the Chairman asked as he slipped into a pair of shining black shoes.

"No more than they do, but I don't mind telling you, Mr. Callahan, that it's not my intention to run on a middle-of-the-road Democratic platform, the kind that's in fashion these days. I think the party and the voters are in serious trouble, and I think they're being fed a line. It pains me to see the Democratic party become the spokesman for the status quo. I suppose in one sense there's no getting around it, since we're the party of government. Still, that's no reason for us to defend a shoddily managed economy and shabby ideas. The oil shortage is serious business and we're all culprits, American consumers that is. I say put a tax on every purchased gallon. I also think Democrats have been pretty damn cold toward the coalition that put us in power. The poor, the minorities. Which isn't to say we can simply push the old New Deal populism. I agree with the Republicans that we have to stimulate production, only I think they've got the wrong kind of production in mind. The two-cars-in-every-garage days are over. We need public-works projects; we need to rebuild the cities before they crumble into ruins; we need a mass-transit system to tie the country together instead of relying on interstate highways that swallow up gas like air in a closed room."

The Chairman laughed. His head rolled back and his mouth fell open wide and a meaty palm slapped his thigh. He regarded Mike with a keen eye. "Sounds as if you've put a little thought into the race. And that's rare enough these days—believe me." He scooped up a black tie from the bed and wrapped it around his fleshy neck. "Today the hotshots jump in, pretty head first, without much thought to what, if anything, they stand for. I don't like that. Not that I'm a great believer in ideas. Not any more. Not after fifty years in this game." The Chairman knotted the tie with ease, despite the big blunt fingers. "But a candidate has to believe in something—if only in himself. And I have a feeling that you have no problem believing in yourself, Merritt."

A smile touched Mike's lips. "I figure this year is as good as any to begin. I think I've got a lot to offer—to the party and to the state."

"How old are you, son?"

"Thirty in January."

"That's mighty young. Some people stand in line for years to get a shot at the Senate. They put in a lot of time and pay a lot of dues." He lit another cigar. For a moment he contemplated the blue smoke that filled the room.

A tough old fart, all right, thought Mike, and he enjoys it—making people squirm. But the young man held his ground. "I don't doubt that."

"I'll tell you something, Merritt. This country's heading straight down the tubes. And you know who's taking us there?"

"The Republicans?"

"Don't kid yourself. The whole damn caboodle of 'em. Every politician in the game. Now, I happen to be a Democrat, so it's clear where my loyalties lie, but face-to-face with a young fella like yourself, new to politics, I can speak my mind. There hasn't been a politician worth his weight in shit since F.D.R. And not because of the New Deal either. Hell, that didn't rescue this country from the Depression—it was the goddamn war did that. In 1940 we were still sliding around in the muck. But F.D.R. understood power. He knew how to keep 'em hopping. If it took diddling with the Constitution to put his men on the Court, so be it. Principles? They went out with the ancient Greeks, who spent most of their time buggering each other anyway. Don't take me for an ignorant man, because I'm not. I've read a book or two. It was enterprise built this country and kept it going, and I'm not talking exclusively about money-making either. I'm talking about ideas, ingenuity. Now this line you're handing me, it's not bad. I've heard it before, maybe a dozen times. But that doesn't mean it has no value. What I like about it is that it thrusts us back on our own resources. It uses what we've already got. The skeleton of a railroad system is there. Also a great work force. Put us all back to work. I like it. Reminds me of the TVA."

"So you can support me and my platform?"

"Support? You're speaking a dead language. Support is Sanskrit. I have no objections to your running and I think you have an idea or two and we'll leave it at that."

Mike lifted his glass and took another swallow of the rich liquor. That's something, he told himself. He's not against me. "I'm willing to take my chances."

"Can't fault a man for that. I remember when I quit college. My old man thought I was crazy. And I remember a lot of cold nights working my precinct before I could stay in the Presidential Suite." The memories seemed to mellow him and an ash from his cigar dropped unnoticed onto his pants. "I took a chance. But it paid off. I was a young man then too." In his eyes were power and knowledge, accumulated over five decades on the front lines. He had been a tough character in his day, but now there was less of that and more of the old man who saw in the young man's eyes the ambition that had once been his own. "Don't base anything you do on me, my boy. If you want to run, go ahead and run. I may endorse you or I may not—I've got a thousand of debts to pay and ten times as many to collect—but I'll see what I can do for you, unofficially."

"I appreciate that—Jim," Mike blurted. He had expected much less. For a moment he saw Ralph Davidson where Callahan sat. And he remembered his desperate hopes of long ago. The scholarship. Nancy Davidson. Yale. The Comets. Darlene. Mortimer Wright. How many times had he sold himself now? And how many more times would he offer himself to the highest bidder: voter or banker or lover? And why the doubts now? He pushed them aside. He could not give up his dream; he would be like the kid again. Perhaps he had lost a bit of himself over the past ten years—but he had grown up some as well: he had learned how to survive.

Callahan tossed down his second drink and smacked his lips. Alex was there to refill the glass. "I know you appreciate it," the Chairman announced, a slur slipping into his speech. "And I know that I like you, son. It doesn't take me long to size somebody up. Christ, I've been doing it all my life; I pride myself on being able to judge a man on the first meeting. You've got brains and ambition—and you need both to get elected statewide. I'll keep my eye on you, don't worry about that."

Mike knew the old man was true to his word. Maris had spoken of Callahan's reputation for spotting newcomers and not allowing them to become enemies. He was smart that way. But if crossed . . . Mike guessed that few ever turned against the Chairman and survived.

Mike made ready to leave, but Big Jim talked on. The two men discussed the upcoming party dinner, a week away. The Governor would be there. Did Mike know the Governor? No. Callahan would introduce him. What about the state House Minority Leader? No. Mike would meet him. Useful friends both. Big Jim reeled off a long list of names for Mike, useful friends all: county leaders, state senators, committee chairmen, borough presidents, former government officials, rich Manhattanites, Jews, Catholics, Harlem Democrats, lobbyists, labor leaders, judges. Yes, it's who you know, Callahan chuckled. And he knew them all. He had made them all.

As he worked on his third bourbon the Chairman's drink-flushed face went slack but his eyes remained narrowed as he regarded Mike. "By the way, who's managing your campaign?"

"Jeff Maris."

"I approve," Callahan said. "I don't like youngsters who think they have to buck the system like a bunch of rodeo ponies. This isn't Russia, you know. All we old folks want is to know our opinion still counts." He said it with another wink, but his black cigar was pointed at Mike. "Hell, I don't care how long your hair is—I can work with anybody. I worked for Stevenson, for the Kennedies, even for fag writers who wanted to be politicians. There's room for everybody and as long as you're a good Democrat, I'll give you the shirt off my back. It may not fit but . . ." An expansive gesture with his hands, spilling the bourbon from his glass, indicated he was fully aware of his bulk and proud of it.

Callahan paused and exhaled a gulp of smoke. "How about money?"

"Well, I haven't officially declared, but we have enough to operate on right now," Mike said. "Before I go is there any special advice you could give me?"

Big Jim wheezed. "Advice? Jesus, I can't remember the last time anybody asked me for advice. Two things come to mind. First, don't let those media shysters stick your face in too many places. They'll tell you different but don't believe them. There's such a thing as overkill. Let's take a regular Joe, guy with dirty hands and bills steaming out of his ass. He gets up in the morning and what's the first thing he sees after his wife's ugly mug? The effing newspaper. With your goddamn picture. And you're smiling like under the table Gina Lollobrigida's sucking you off. Next he squeezes onto the subway, between the muggers and the drunks, and stares at a poster with your smiling face. Then, walking to lunch at his favorite greasy spoon he sees you again, wrapped around a lamppost, maybe, or covering a bus. At last he makes it home. Another day, another dollar. He relaxes with a brew and turns on the tube. What does he see? You again, smiling. Fuck this guy, he figures, he's already made my life miserable. Why vote for him?"

"What's the second thing?"

"No nooky. Big good-looking buck like yourself probably has broads itching to get into your pants. Live and let live, I say. But get caught and you're out. Maybe not in the city but in Newburgh or Buffalo they'll ream you good. So keep your hands to yourself and your wife."

"Of course. I love my wife."

Big Jim grunted. "Sure you do. Everybody loves his wife. Nobody screws around. That's why life's perfect. Now that I think about it, there's also that business with Mortimer Wright."

"Sir?"

"I don't like that little queer and I never have. He's a cold fish. Whiting got to the Senate on Wright's money and now it's you. Republican, Democrat—doesn't make a bit of difference to him. Remember that. If you can squeeze money out of the tight-fisted bastard, more power to you. But just make sure it's your hand on his nuts and not the other way around."

A week after his meeting with the party chairman, Mike made an appointment with Mortimer Wright. The banker kept his youngest vice president waiting for half an hour in the anteroom but greeted him cordially, paternally.

"What can I do for you, son?"

"I'd like a leave of absence from the board."

Wright was surprised, although he scarcely gave it away. The tremor that came over his smooth pink face resembled that caused by a stone skimming over a pond. "If you're having problems surely we can work them out."

"No problems, sir. I've decided to enter the Democratic primary for the Senate."

"Setting your sights a little high, aren't you? Miller has a pretty firm hold—"

"Not against Miller. Whiting."

"You plan to challenge a three-term Senator?"

"I think his time is up."

"Perhaps so. But his support is strong. As a matter of fact I myself have been a generous contributor to his past campaigns."

"I understand that, sir. And it's unfortunate. But I still plan to run against him. Of course there's a primary to win first. I have already assembled a staff and I've gotten the clearance of the State Chairman."

"Callahan? You did all this without consulting me?"

"I didn't want to broach the subject until I had assessed my chances. It would have been premature."

"I see. And how do you expect me to react to your challenging an incumbent who has the endorsement both of this corporation and myself?"

"I expect you'll have little compunction about releasing me from the board."

Wright smiled. "Quite so. And do you also expect First New York will back you overnight?"

"I don't expect you to back me at all."

Wright was bothered. "Don't misunderstand me. I don't question the seriousness of your intentions. Nonetheless I cannot help feeling this constitutes a bite at the hand that feeds you. Need I remind you of your personal obligations to me?"

"Of course not. But my decisions are my own to make. I hadn't the slightest idea of the extent of your support for Whiting until I spoke with Mr. Callahan.

And I can't let a regrettable coincidence affect my intention to run."

"Yes, of course. Still, a more circumspect route . . . a Congressional election perhaps. Or a post with the city. That could be easily arranged."

"If you don't mind my saying so, sir, I would prefer to proceed without any arrangements of that nature. I'd like to strike out on my own. I believe I have served both you and the board honestly and well. I've made some mistakes and been humbled. But I also believe I've learned from them and have earned the right to run for office."

Wright tipped his small frame back in his leather chair. His eyes left Mike's and fastened on the ceiling. His gaze swooped down and a meager smiled creased his face. "It sounds as though your mind is made up. I wish you luck. And if you should lose there will still be a position for you with us."

Mike stood up and took Wright's hand. "I appreciate that. But I don't intend to lose."

Wright watched the graceful giant make his way out of the office. So the boy wants to buck me. A good sign, actually. He hasn't lost his ambition. Could he win? Very possibly. Merritt cut a most attractive figure, almost hypnotic. He was bright and energetic and hungry. Still, there was Whiting, a popular Republican who shared that party's responsible support of untrammeled enterprise and sane taxation policies. Merritt's outlook had a dangerous component of populism. Witness his grandiose gymnasium scheme. Still, if Wright required his services, the prospective Senator would come through. The boy wasn't a fool. And his youth could prove a plus. He was only thirty now and could well have as many more years to do Wright's bidding in Washington. As for his being a Democrat, it might prove a blessing in disguise. Yes, an errand boy from the misguided opposition camp might be just the ticket to subverting the unclean tactics of demagogues out to snaffle corporations—those pillars of the empire. Besides, since Roosevelt had died, along with his anarchic notions of government, the two parties had edged closer together, like a long-estranged couple. Nowadays, in fact, party affiliations seemed almost arbitrary. This fellow Carter was no *homo populi*. Yes, the idea of Merritt in Washington was not disagreeable. The only issue was his reliability. That messy business with the Negroes was most distressing, and it had happened less than three years ago. Had he learned his lesson in such a short time? Perhaps this Senate race would constitute the final test.

Wright punched a button and commanded his secretary to bring in her pad. In trod Ethel Pruney, his personal amanuensis of twenty-five years. In his rare jocular moods Wright referred to her as his second in command, his senior vice president.

She perched birdlike on the edge of a wing chair, holding a pencil in her liver-spotted hand.

"Take a letter to Senator Whiting. Dear Tom: I must apologize for not bringing this matter up with you in person but we are both busy and I, anyway, am of the old school and firmly believe the intimacy of a letter exceeds that of awkward blurtings over the telephone. Frankly, I'm afraid that circumstances prevent me from tendering my support in the upcoming election. . . . Please read that back, Miss Pruney. I suspect it's too wordy."

It amounted to nothing less than a new lease on life, a new beginning. The old mistakes were remediable if only you managed to transcend the state of mind that had led you to make them. And, already, he had taken the first and most difficult steps. He had won his freedom from Wright and First New York. He had stood on his own two feet. Ahead of him now stretched the road to the Senate. Since the frightening night uptown Mike had lost the taste for battle, but now he felt it rush through him like a fresh transfusion. There was much to do. A primary to win. Opponents to be studied, probed, bested. Then the real challenge—a popular three-term Senator, a Republican stalwart bolstered by big dollars.

Patty, to his pleasure and relief, wholeheartedly supported this latest venture.

"It's already made you happy," she said at dinner. "I can see it in your eyes."

"And you'll help? I don't have a chance without you, you know."

"If you can take a leave from the bank, then I can take a leave from the gallery. Will I have to make speeches too? I don't think I could stand all those expectant eyes. What if I sound like a know-nothing?"

"Then you'll prove a fitting partner for me. You'll be wonderful, Patty. I know you will. And I'd like us to adopt now, too."

Patty pushed her plate away. "This is awfully sudden."

"Sudden? You've wanted it for five years."

"And you said you were too busy. Now we're both going to be busier than ever. How can we take a child along on a campaign? That's silly, it's worse—"

"All right. Then after the election."

"Like after your career."

"Honey, you can't have it both ways. You don't want a child now, you don't want one later. Do you want one at all?"

"I don't know."

"Why not?"

"You've changed a lot, Mike. Sometimes I feel I'm livig with a stranger. When we were working together on the Center it was different, but even then it was like a team, instead of two people caring for each other. I felt like you were my coach. I don't think our relationship is strong enough. I'm not sure we could provide a loving home for a child."

"But I'm over that now. Can't you see? I'm a new man. I'm free of Mortimer Wright and that dungeon of a bank. I'm nobody's lackey now. You know who I'm going to call? Mo. I want him to help me draft a platform. And he'll be my lawyer again too."

"Sheila says he's busier than ever now that he's with the DA. Besides, what makes you so sure he wants to have anything to do with your campaign?"

"He won't turn down a chance to build a responsible platform. It's his civic duty."

"Will he see it that way?"

"Whose side are you on, anyway?"

"Mike, the games are finished. Life isn't like playing in the Garden. This talk about sides—"

"Patty, I don't think you understand. To you I'll always be a jock."

"That's not it, Mike. That's not it at all. You're being so naive about this. You hurt Mo very deeply and you've hurt me too. And now you think that just because you're no longer working for Mortimer Wright everything's forgiven."

"Then what does it take?"

"The truth."

"About what?"

"That night."

"Nothing happened that night. There was a scuffle, that's all. A bunch of basketball players drinking and celebrating in a bar. We got carried away—"

"Oh, Mike. Why can't I believe you?"

He stood up. "That's a question you have to answer yourself. Right now, I have a call to make."

He retreated and dialed Mo Silver's home.

"Mo, I'm putting together a campaign for the Senate and I want you, as my lawyer and adviser—"

"I think you've got the wrong party," Mo replied flatly.

"No, I haven't. Listen, Mo, I'm through with Wright. Finished. I told him to fuck himself—"

"Which is precisely my advice to you."

"Don't you see? It's not the way it was before. This is the chance we dreamed of. A statewide campaign—"

"I'm not interested. You sold out a long time ago. And it's too late now to buy back in."

His ears rang from the receiver slammed at the other end. Why was Mo so shortsighted? I made my share of mistakes, maybe more than my share, but all that's over. Bee will join the campaign. He still owes me one. Could it be too late to get on the right track? For someone else maybe, but not for him. The good things were just beginning. That was what mattered, not a night long ago when events had overwhelmed him. His destiny belonged to him again. And soon enough they would all see it.

14

I've imagined this scene for ten years, thought Bee Crosby. Why does it seem so unreal? The campaign headquarters was a madhouse. All this body heat, the place may go up in flames, like an overstimulated engine. Phones shrilled into one another like mewling birds and girls in MERRITT hats and MERRITT badges leaped to answer them. Sweaty young pols—hyperkinetic or crazed?—shouted in each other's ears, flapping mimeographed sheets.

"Bee, man, you're late! The boss wanted to see you half an hour ago." The young man did not wait for an explanation. He grabbed Bee's arm and pushed him through the panoply of campaign workers. "Woodruff's already here." He left the speechwriter at Mike's door.

Bee knocked then stepped into the small office. Mike, exhausted and wan and glossed with sweat, was stretched out on the long couch, his feet dangling. Filling an easy chair was a burly man with a round face. Glasses with boxy lenses magnified searching dark eyes. He had wispy eyebrows and a spongy mass of reddish hair. He got to his feet and stuck out a hand. "Bee Crosby? Rod Woodruff."

Mike scowled. "Goddamn it, Bee. Where the hell have you been?"

"Nice to meet you. Sleeping. I was up until four working on your speech." Bee settled in front of Mike's desk. "Where's the ringleader?"

"Jeff's in Buffalo."

"Actually," said Woodruff, "your timing's perfect. We were just getting into the serious stuff."

"Does that mean I missed the fun stuff?"

"I was just explaining to Mike that it was smart to hold off on the media assault until right before the primary, because you've got to build a viable foundation first. There you guys have succeeded. With the primary four weeks off, though, the time is right to make a big splash. Mike has expressed some skepticism, but maybe I can get your support."

"Shoot."

"First, some background. My years in the game have taught me that virtually no candidate has an uncontestable strength. Which is to say there are two sides to every issue, unless you singlehandedly prevented a war or stopped a house from burning down. Otherwise, candidates break down into weaknesses and contact points. A weakness is an obvious thing—you killed somebody or raped an old lady or were on the take. Things that obviously don't apply here. So we're left with contact points and that's where the game is won or lost. A contact point is potentially either a weakness *or* a strength, depending on how you handle it. Contact points are the heart of the matter because they work both ways. The candidate uses them to score with the voters, his opponent uses them as a means to detract from the other guy's credibility. You following me?"

"Not at all. But go ahead. I'm slow on the uptake."

"Whiting's positive contact point is experience. He tells the voters he's been a distinguished Senator for eighteen years. He sits on big committees, he knows how to work with powerbrokers and Presidents. Okay, he contacts the voter that way. We, on the other hand, say: This guy's had eighteen years and hasn't done a damned thing. He's cultivated powerful friendships but only to serve himself. He's been in there too long. Get him out. For us there are three basic contact points. Youth, visibility, and appeal. For youth we say: This new fellow is young and eager, bursting with ideas. Visibility: He's already a national figure, a champion, a fighter, he knows how to get what he wants. Appeal is easy because we don't have to say a thing. We just show this beautiful hunk—forgive me, Mike—and we're scoring points. Now Whiting will reverse all these positive things, you see. He'll make *negative* contact. He'll say this guy's barely thirty, a kid. He's got no experience of any kind of government office, let alone the most prestigious legislative body in the world. Next, on visibility, he'll say this guy's a jock, not to be taken seriously. Appeal: Mike's irresponsible. He's got too many connections in the chic world—artists, gays, the ritzy liberal establishment. In the city it's fine but in Port Jefferson and Hamilton people resent it."

"You talk about Whiting," Bee said. "What about the primary?"

"The primary's in the bag."

"But we'll still run TV ads, won't we?"

"Sure. Strictly as test runs. To see how they go over. My personal opinion is that almost anything we do will go over like a dream. The camera will eat Mike up. It already does. I remember watching you with that armband, Mike. Way back then. Right then and there I pegged you for a comer. What a beautiful stunt! I only wish we could get you in front of the camera in a bathing suit. You'd get every female vote in New York State."

"Rod, I wish you wouldn't talk that way. This is a senatorial election."

"You bet it is. That's why we have to pull out all the stops. If I did what you want, if I put you up there in a pinstripe reading quotations from Woodrow Wilson, folks'd turn the channel so fast they'd hear it in New Zealand. Look, your opponent isn't Whiting. Nobody ever liked that old geezer. He just played the game without making any costly mistakes. He toed the line and since nobody better came along he kept on winning.

Your opponent is apathy. Most people just don't care. You've got to turn people into voters and that's why you can't write off TV. TV gives you the same credibility as the broads shaking their boobs and their fannies and the cop shows and the soaps. You can't take the tube lightly. It's the only connection most poor benighted souls have with the outside world. You know what voters want?"

It was a question every so-called expert asked and had his own answer for. It was like asking, Do you know what will save mankind? Bee shrugged, Mike shook his head.

"They want you to beg them for their votes. You have to love 'em with your eyes and implore them to push the right lever. It may not mean much to them but they have to be convinced it means everything to you. Make every last one of them feel like a kingmaker. Because the vote is theirs not yours. Used to be you could walk up to a fellow and ask for his vote straight out, like old Harry Truman did. Can you do that now?"

"No?" Bee ventured.

"Of course not. Nobody'd believe you. They wouldn't buy it. They want to see somebody just a bit slick and shifty. Like it or not it's what people expect of politicians. But you have to be careful. When they stick that camera in your nose a lot will be revealed. People think the camera's a kind of trickery. But it isn't so, not at all. It's the Great Seeing Eye, the Great Revealer. Guy watches you on the tube and he knows how close you are to your mother, what kind of kid you were in high school. It's like plugging into his nerve-endings. Once an image is formed in his mind he's going to have trouble shaking it. That's why these pre-primary ads are just a dry run. We have the demographics people spot-check the audience, like the Nielson ratings, and we find out what goes over and what doesn't."

Mike was troubled. "Instead of all this hocus-pocus why can't we just have a debate? Like we did three weeks ago—all the primary candidates."

Woodruff's faint eyebrows disappeared into his forehead. "You're not serious."

"Of course I'm serious."

"Whiting may be a lousy Senator, Mike, but he's not an idiot. He won't go within fifty miles of a camera trained on your face. It'd be suicide. What do you have on him, eight inches? You're thirty, he's over sixty. The worst matchup since Lindsay and Proccacino."

"There's more to this than appearances. Candidates should debate. The voter has the right to see us face-to-face, fielding questions under pressure, addressing the issues. Democracies depend on open, straightforward dialogue."

Woodruff cocked his head toward Bee. "What's this guy interested in? Principles of democracy or winning elections?"

"If I'm not mistaken, he thinks the two are related."

"Mike, don't get me wrong. A debate is a great idea, super. I'd love to see it. No clowning around, no spicy ads, just two sober servants of the public interest tackling the great issues of the day. But you have to face facts, you can't hide from reality. And in this instance reality dictates that Whiting would just as soon expose his dingus on 42nd Street as step in front of a camera with you."

Mike sat up. "After the primary, when I start to gain on him, he'll have to debate. I'll *make* him debate. Until then, just do whatever you think needs to be done. How much time will I have to put in at the studio?"

"Just one day. We'll film three ads, then splice 'em up to give us twice that many. It's all we need. I'd like to get your wife in a couple of them too. She's a lovely gal. Never knew a pretty woman who didn't like the camera. So we're agreed? You want me to go ahead and put together the act?"

"Yeah. Thanks a lot, Rod, for joining us—and for putting up with me."

All three of them got to their feet and shook hands. Woodruff said warmly to Bee, "You seem to have a real feel for this. I'd appreciate your lending a hand."

"Delighted to help."

"Great."

The long-time friends watched the media wizard leave.

"So, Bee," said Mike, "you going to fuck him?"

"Aren't we testy today." Bee sagged back behind the desk and spoke into a box. "Sarah, could you wiggle in with some coffee, please?"

"I asked you not to make fun of the girls."

"They love it."

Sarah entered the room moments later. She did indeed wiggle, and the look she gave Mike was somewhere between worshipful and loving. But the candidate hardly noticed.

"Now there," said Bee, "is a girl with contact points."

It was like being on the ocean floor. Bright ceiling bulbs shelled in aluminum shimmered on waxy fronds sprouting from symmetrically placed tureens. Patty had her own name for this health-food restaurant. She called it the Smoker's Greenhouse, a name inspired by the dense exhaust produced by cigarettes poking from the mouths of lunching women—office slaves and executives and shoppers fueling up for another foray into the swirl and stampede of Bloomingdale's. Now and then fragments of conversation burst like bubbles above the din.

". . . slept with him but he never called . . ."

". . . *so* competitive. I *know* she resents me . . ."

". . . he said, 'Stop acting like a woman and act like a lawyer' . . ."

". . . bottom-line analysis of substantial market gains . . ."

". . . but why does everybody have to be so *special*? I

306

like a normal average guy . . ."

Mrs. Holmes's angular features suddenly appeared among the incoming faces. Patty waved. Picking her way carefully through the tightly packed tables, her mother looked as regal as ever. At fifty-eight she retained the erect posture she had passed on to her daughter, and, though her hair was gray, it was not the fuliginous gray of a weary matron; it was, if such a thing were possible, a lustrous gray, like a rain cloud. To disguise her wattled throat she wore a high-necked blouse ringed with ruffles.

"You're looking awfully peaked, dear," Mrs. Holmes began.

"The campaign is tiring. Such a rush all the time. By comparison the gallery was totally uneventful. I don't know how I stood it."

The waiter plunked down two cups of coffee. Her mother struggled with the thimble-sized cream container. She had lost some of her dexterity. Blue veins mapped her translucent hands. "I can never open these things. My nails—"

"Here." Patty tore off the seal.

"Thank you. Couldn't you take some time off. Running around like this every day . . ."

"But I love it. I'm learning so much. Did you know that almost every City Hall official comes from the East Side when only a miniscule percentage of the population lives there? There's also a calculated move to expel all but the well-to-do from Manhattan. There's even a timetable for it. So many highrises here, so many hospitals and old neighborhoods destroyed there. It's terrifying."

"Are you getting enough sleep?"

"Mother, I'm perfectly healthy. I walk five miles a day meeting people. It's a wonderful change. I never used to visit Queens except to go to the airport. I never saw the South Bronx at all and it's just as much a part of New York as Tavern on the Green."

"What were you doing in the South Bronx?"

"Talking to people. There're *people* there, inside all those horrible buildings they show on the news when the President strolls through shaking his head. Families. There's so much to this city that many people never see."

"Meaning me."

"And me. And thousands like us."

" 'Like us.' Is there a label for us too, as there is for all the other minorities?"

"Mother, I'm not labeling you. I'm certainly in no position to do that. I've spent my whole life in a dream. All the time I was at Yale people tried to inform me about these things and I was too caught up in my own little world to pay the slightest attention, I ran and hid."

"From radicals, you mean."

"Yes. Revolutionaries. They want to plant bombs in every suite at the Waldorf and give ostrich-skin purses to welfare mothers. Then they're going to kidnap the chef from the Four Seasons and make him cook hamburgers."

"Excuse my ignorance, Patty. My generation was brought up differently. We were thankful for what we had. We didn't want to give it all away."

"Who said anything about giving things away? What makes you think anybody *wants* what you have?"

"Well, I don't see my radical daughter giving up her Fifth Avenue apartment."

"That's not the point."

"What is the point? Please enlighten me."

Patty sighed. "Only that we all share responsibility. Especially now when our resources are dwindling." She stopped abruptly. She had already made this speech eleven times this week—at churches, synagogues, the Brooklyn Women's Art Society. And here she was delivering it again to her mother, who was innocently forking a mushroom omelet into her mouth. "I'm sorry. I guess I don't know when to step off the dais. I never imagined I'd get so involved."

"You haven't touched your sandwich, dear. Have you thought about what the future holds? As the wife of a Senator?"

"We talk about it." Although not too often. But this information was better left uncommunicated. "I can continue my own work in Washington. Perhaps I'll start up a gallery of my own. I think I'm ready for that now."

"What about—the child?" Her mother always assigned a definite article to what remained no more than a possibility.

"There isn't time for us to do anything now. It would take a major change in our schedules—"

"Patty, that sounds awfully cold."

"I didn't mean for it to sound like that."

"I'm sure you didn't, dear."

Does she blame me for not being able to bear a child, or is she secretly pleased? It entitles her to a kind of superiority. I lead a more active life but she's more successful as a woman. Is it my fault my ova won't stay where they belong? What am I supposed to do? In Africa or someplace they'd tie me to a stake and forbid all men to touch me. Daughter of the devil, transgressor against nature.

"You're just tired," Katharine Holmes continued. "I saw Mike on television the other night, being interviewed. He looked tired too." Her favorite theme.

"The whole world's tired. It's five billion years old."

"That's no reason to miss your sleep."

"Compared to Mike I'm in hibernation. You wouldn't believe how much energy he has. Everyone tries to stay up with him and they practically collapse."

"It doesn't surprise me. Not after seeing him race up and down that basketball court."

"Wait until after the primary. Then, assuming we win, the real racing around begins. We've only made quick trips outside the city so far, because most of the

Democrats are concentrated here. For the general election we'll barnstorm the whole state."

"Perhaps the wrong Merritt is running for Senator."

"Very possibly. How's Daddy?"

Mrs. Holmes frowned. "He's become a very cantankerous old man. It still upsets him that they're trying to ease him out of the firm."

"Hasn't he had his fill of it by now?"

"It's all he knows. He'll die before he retires. That may very well be his intention. He has nothing to retire *to*. It might be different if he had—"

"Grandchildren," Patty finished.

"I'm sorry."

Patty shrugged. Two mentions per lunch was her mother's average. "Why don't you two travel, maybe move to a warmer climate?"

"Not your father."

"What about you?"

"I have things to keep me busy. I wouldn't want to force your father into anything."

"You should think of yourself."

"I can be happy anywhere. My life is in this city. There's no reason for me to leave it."

She and Daddy put Mike and me to shame, Patty thought. Would our marriage be more stable if my husband were older? Fifteen years separated her parents. In one sense they were never quite in step. On the other hand, they didn't constantly wage ego battles. Every disagreement wasn't a matter of life and death. They accepted each other and their common lot.

"Patty, I'm thinking of getting a new highboy. You have such a nice eye and it would be lovely if we shopped together. I can't remember the last time we did. For the wedding, I suppose."

"All right, Mother. Maybe just after the primary would be best. I can take off a couple of days then."

"That's fine, dear. I had better be going now. We're having people over for dinner this evening and I haven't made a single preparation."

Thus ended their weekly lunch.

Back in the apartment Patty stepped out of her heels and sank onto the living room sofa. The foliage of Central Park filled the wide window like a picture. Pictures, pictures, sometimes they were oppressive, like a silent reproof of what her marriage had become. Her mother was right. She was tired. Tired of forgiving Mike, tired of apologizing for herself, tired of loving someone who could not love her in return. "He's the most attractive young man I've ever met," Mrs. Holmes had once said. "Perhaps too attractive." Which meant, a man so handsome could care only for himself. "You don't understand him," Patty had replied. And, in fact, she had not. But neither, as it turned out, did Patty. Vanity was supposed to lead to indolence, not this frenzied pursuit of honor and fame. What had he been like as a little boy? Now and again he gave voice to recollections. The long hours in the driveway, the state championship. Where had he gotten his ambition? Certainly not from his Godfearing mother. On the several occasions Patty had seen her, Evelyn Merritt seemed the embodiment of pious resignation. Not a bitter woman, but one in whom the lights of fancy had long ago dimmed. All joy for her must have expired with her husband's death. On that question too Mike was a closed book. He answered her queries vaguely. "He was a great father. He got me interested in sports. He wasn't much of a reader but a pretty deep thinker." What did he think about? "I couldn't say. He kept his thoughts to himself and I was a kid and too selfish to ask. About his job, I suppose, and how it was getting him nowhere. He hoped he might own the hardware store someday but he knew Old Man Thompson would outlive him." Hugh Merritt had been a talented baseball player but had given up the game at Evelyn's insistence. It was the chief sorrow in his life, his deepest regret. Yet the Merritt household was a happy one. About that Mike was clear.

A close family, not well-to-do, but with high standing in the community. "Church on Sunday, roast beef for dinner," Mike said. "Good law-abiding Christians." At sixteen Mike was a celebrity, a star on the court, a fixture in the local papers. At eighteen his name rang in every corner of the state, from Chicago to Cairo. College recruiters swarmed the modest clapboard house. The phone rang constantly. But high-school senior Mike, with his customary purposefulness, was saving his stuff for the Ivy League. He left behind Main Street for Wall Street. A deliberate journey. Did his present station match his boyhood aspirations? How could he even know? He didn't slow down long enough to ponder such questions. Seven years of marriage and she couldn't begin to understand him. It was frustrating. Some things she made sense of. He was a competitor for one. Not fiercely aggressive—he was too self-contained—but nonetheless out to win. Power, Achievement, Destiny—those were his words. He didn't often speak them, but she deciphered them in the scribblings tucked away in his desk. She was ashamed of looting his papers but she had no choice. He gave so few outward clues. Was it possible that underneath the vigor and the charm lay—nothing? Did she search for things that didn't exist? Perhaps, as Bee claimed, his character had been formed in the dark mills of the national consciousness, was traceable not to his boyhood but to the tumultuous history of a people. Such notions disturbed her. They were frightening. It made Mike a kind of specimen.

She had never seriously considered divorcing him. You couldn't spend your life in search of perfect love. In all probability it wasn't there. Besides, she was accustomed to living in fine style and couldn't bear to give it up. How many husbands would unblinkingly consent to spend half a million on a painting, instead of pouring it into real estate or some other sure-fire investment? In that respect we have a fine partnership, she thought. Mike's content to leave it at that. She still prayed there might be more between them, but she hadn't done much of a job of convincing Mike. Love didn't rate next to fame and glory. Not that Mike's odd quest was trouble-free. Sometimes she woke up in the early hours sensing his absence. She slipped on a robe and found him in the kitchen with a glass of milk, like an ulcerous old man, or reclining on the sofa, illumined gravely by the predawn light, staring dully at the wall. "Go back to sleep, Patty. I'll be with you in a few minutes." It was no time to argue. At breakfast he sipped his coffee tiredly, his eyes avoiding hers. He would stand for no talk about quitting the race. "What would you have me do instead? Take up space in that bank? I mean to win, Patty, and I mean to be in the Senate come January." She didn't doubt it, and out of a loyalty she could scarcely explain to herself, she did all she could to help him.

Lately she wondered if he had married her for convenience instead of love. Did he ever love me as much as he loved that other woman, Darlene? He was in the market for a wife. His first choice turned him down so he came to me. Good old reliable Patty. She used to hate the thought of Darlene; now she felt a strange compulsion to meet her, to find out what she was like, what secret she held. Part of the blame for this rocky marriage, Patty knew, was her own. After Mitchell Farris flew out of my life I was hurt and alone and the prospect of similar affairs—the curse of the single woman—seemed too terrible to face. After all, *I* called to *him* that day outside the library. I was the one who jumped for joy when he proposed. I could have said no, or given the matter more thought. I could have let him walk on with his armful of books and struck out on my own, looked elsewhere for comfort and love. Which probably would have been better for us both. Everyone said we were the perfect match. We were meant for each other. Why didn't they wed our yearbook pictures and let the two of us go our separate ways? And the lies. Mine and his. On that count perhaps we were well-suited. He couldn't give me his heart and I couldn't give him a child. Still we tried to get closer.

Those early years she went to the Garden and even learned something about the game. She almost missed those days now. She sat in a row with the other wives. All but Patty shared the competitive urgency of their husbands. "Come on, ref, that clown was all over him," or "Patty, honey, when is Mike going to put my man in? He's dying on the bench." The warmup drills were effortless. The announcer's nasal voice filled the arena just as the lights dimmed over the crowd. During the playoffs the whole second half of *The Star-Spangled Banner* was lost in noise. On the court Mike's eyes were never still, flicking from his own players to the positioning of the other team and the clock on the inverted frustum. After he scored a basket he looked almost grim, backpeddling to the midcourt line. Basketball bloomed in a wonderful vacuum, like painting.

Her thoughts were broken by the panicky rasp of the intercom. "Mr. Crosby is here to see you."

"Send him up." This was odd. In New York one always called first. Killers and rapists lurked everywhere, seemed to hang in the air, like the fumy smell of the buses.

Moments later the bell chimed. "Bee! What a surprise."

"I should have called first. I was in the park and I had an impulse to stop by."

"I'm afraid Mike isn't in."

"I know. I came to see you."

"Well, come in. I just got back myself. Would you like coffee or tea or a drink?"

"Coffee, please. If it's not too much trouble."

"I was just going to make some." One of the gracious lies she had learned from her mother. "Have a seat. I'll put some on."

"I'll watch. I'm afraid to be alone with your paintings."

She laughed. "Afraid?"

"I feel reproached."

In the kitchen she scooped grounds into the percolator and set it on the electric coil. They chatted at the small table. They were all so weary these days; everyone connected with the campaign. Mike's hours were extraordinary.

"Rodney Woodruff came by today," Bee said.

"What's he like?"

"Television is the all-seeing eye. Let the housewives fall under Mike's spell."

She smiled. Women loved him. At fund-raisers they stared at him shamelessly, even with her at his side. Hungry eyes devouring his marvelous body and the handsome face, curiously gaunt for one so powerful and fit. His eyes were set deeply, like the buttons she, as a little girl, pressed into the faces of snowmen. (The indentations hardened into icy sockets. It made her think of God shaping damp earth into flesh.) Mike was oblivious to individual women—that part of his life seemed over; she no longer worried about adultery—but the collective love of women affected him greatly. Water bubbled in the glass nub. She shrank the flame and watched the drops blacken. "Did Mike insist on a debate?"

"Woodruff said it was out of the question. Whiting would look too dumpy and old. So it looks like commercials. You'll be hearing from Woodruff yourself, I suspect. He wants you in the ads too."

"Really?"

"He says you're too pretty not to be in them."

"And all the housewives won't mind? Milk, sugar?"

"A little of both, please. That's a good point. About the housewives."

"Mike's going to win, isn't he?"

"He always wins."

"He says it's the only thing he knows how to do."

"It's a significant talent."

"Only to all those strangers who worship him."

"They understand him better than we do." Bee blew lightly on his coffee, which shivered in a crisis of ripples.

"He's such a public person. He can't bear not to be a hero."

"His cloth is cut from the Stars and Stripes."

"What comes next?"

"The Presidency. You'll be the First Lady."

She laughed. "I'll set a terrible example. But I mean after all this winning. Or when he loses."

"That's looking a long way ahead."

"Not that far. It seems to me that it's all happening very quickly. Like watching a movie speeded up."

"Yes. Spying on fate."

"Bee, what's wrong with him?"

"I don't think it's wrong—"

"I don't mean that. Something else. He's terrified of something."

"Nervous strain, the campaign . . ."

She shook her head. "Maybe it's apparent only to me. But he's slipping away. At first I thought it was just from me. But he's losing himself too. One night, years ago, after the Comets won, there was a celebration. Mike didn't come home until the next morning. I've never seen him look the way he did. All the blood drained from his face. As if he'd seen or done something—oh, it sounds so melodramatic. Anyway, he wouldn't tell me what happened. He just pushed me away. Sometimes I feel like covering my ears and shutting my eyes and just waiting for it all to explode."

"Maybe I do know what you mean," Bee confessed. "That's why I came here. To ask you. I thought it was *me*."

"Does anybody know him? Does he know himself?"

"I don't know." They laughed, then Bee said, "For the first time since I've known him I almost don't care. Do you understand what I mean? I love him, of course, but I don't care. He used to matter so much. He was always so beautiful to watch. On the court or in a crowded room or standing in a bar looking for you. Every step so sure. This flawless figure striding through things. But now he's like a clock run amok."

"And it can only go so fast before it stops or falls apart."

"Yes."

"Are we all stepping stones? Is he going to use us all and then let us go? The way he did to Mo?"

"I don't think he wanted to do that."

"But he did it."

"Yes, he did it. Mortimer Wright made him."

"But how? Mike knew it was wrong. It was his choice."

"Maybe it wasn't."

"What do you mean? Wright has something on him? Back to this awful melodrama."

"Melodrama can happen."

"What could he possibly have on him?"

"Could be a thousand things. I try not to think about it. It might be better if you didn't either."

"He's my husband. And he's your best friend and even if you say you don't care you do. I know you do. I have a feeling Mo cares too. I'm tempted to call him. He's a wonderful person. So kind and gentle. Mike was upset for weeks after he let him go. He really hoped Mo would join the campaign. He called him a dozen times. Almost as if he couldn't run without him. I think he wanted Mo to redeem him. Now he things winning this election will redeem him."

"You mean, the collective approval of the people will absolve him."

"Something like that. Bee, he's so driven."

"And now he's on the brink."

"Yes," said Patty. "Of something."

He did not sound angry; mystified was more like it, with an admixture of caution. Still, he agreed to see her. Another man would have had her go to his office in order to intimidate her, but Mo Silver wasn't that way. She could understand why Mike had been so desperate to persuade him to join the campaign. With Mo on your side you felt safer.

At the downtown luncheonette she spotted him instantly. He sat at a booth with a newspaper spread before him. He looked up and gave her that sad sweet smile. His hair was thinning toward baldness. She remembered the curly mop of his Yale days. He half-rose but she gestured him back into his seat.

"Can I order you some coffee?" he asked.

"Please. How's Sheila?"

"The same. She still thinks there's more good in the world than bad."

"You disagree?"

"I'm skeptical."

"I suppose Mike had something to do with it."

"He didn't help."

"You must hate him."

"I'm too busy to hate. Hating gets in the way."

"Is there any way I can convince you to reconsider joining the campaign?"

"Patty, for me that would be an act of pure cynicism. He stands for everything I detest."

"He's changed, Mo. He really has. He's not a pawn anymore. If you could only hear him. . . ."

"I've heard him often enough. I don't deny he talks a good game. And I don't doubt he'll talk his way right into the Senate. Maybe beyond."

"Can't you forgive him?"

"Forgive him? I'm grateful. He disabused me of some of my flightier notions. He woke me up."

"You have every reason to be bitter. He treated you

like a bastard. But it wasn't easy for him to fire you. Afterwards he agonized for months. It was the last thing he wanted to do. Wright forced him into it."

"He's a grown man. He makes his own decisions. He knew where his loyalties and commitments lay. He knew who could get him what he wanted."

"Have you followed the campaign at all? Did you hear him during the primary debate? Have you read his platform? This election is his mission. There's so much good he can do. He really did tell Wright off. He has nothing to do with him, or next to nothing. He said he didn't want his support or his money. I wish you could see him talking to people. There's so much sorrow in him now. We went to Bedford-Stuyvesant last week and he was almost in tears. We were in an apartment. It was a terrible place. You could smell rusty pipes and the toilet was backed up and there was an enormous family without a father. And Mike saw this little boy, he couldn't have been more than four, and he was bitten by rats and there was this awful sadness in his eyes. All of us just stared except Mike. He picked him up and held him. He has powerful hands, you know, and he snatched up the little boy and he held him and said, 'This isn't going to happen anymore.' It wasn't a promise, it was a declaration. And you should have seen the poor mother. She looked at Mike with such love. And then we went to the playground. There were boys throwing old tied-up socks through a hoop and Mike said, 'How come you guys aren't using a ball?' And then we found out they couldn't afford one. So he jumped into the car and came back with three basketballs and he gave them to the boys and then played with them. And soon all kinds of boys were there, dozens of them, and they all knew who he was. And he didn't once mention that he was running for Senator. He played with them for hours and missed three appointments. Jeff Maris, he's the campaign manager, said, 'Mike, don't forget that talk at Chase Manhattan.' You should have seen the look on Mike's face, as though he couldn't believe his ears. He said, 'What the hell's wrong with you, Jeff? Fuck Chase Manhattan. They can just go fuck themselves.' Don't you see? He's not the same. He's not who he was before."

"Patty, I'd like to believe it. But I can't. Maybe he's not evil, but it's just himself he's thinking of. It's always going to be Mike Merritt he's looking out for and no one else."

"I know there's something wrong with him. There's something awful he's not telling anyone that's eating away at him. I haven't told anyone else this, but we're having troubles. We have for a long time. At times I hate him. More than you do, I think. He can be cold and cruel and selfish. But he's a wonderful candidate and a caring one. I'm not asking you to like him or approve of him as a man. I can't even do that and I love him. But in office he'll do fine things."

"He'll win. He doesn't need me. He's got the primary all sewn up and he'll whip Whiting."

"I know it, but he needs a different kind of support. He talks about you all the time. He says it's your campaign and not his. 'Without Mo I'd be nothing, a corporate shoeshine boy. It's my name on the ballot but these are Mo's principles.' He says that to anyone who'll listen."

"Sounds like he's already co-opted me. He doesn't need me in the flesh."

"Why can't you forgive him? I don't believe it when you say you don't hate him. Otherwise you could never be so cynical. I know you, Mo. You're not this way—so implacable. It's not just Mike. It's a chance to do good."

"Then let him do it. He'll beat Whiting and he'll go to Washington and he can be the next Robert Kennedy. He shouldn't need a pat on the back from me."

"But he does need it. And it wouldn't be so hard for you to do it. All you have to do is visit him at headquarters or call him up and tell him you're with him, that you know he's doing good things. The things you always wanted him to do. It would make him so happy."

"Patty, I'm moved, I really am. But I can't do it. Because I know as soon as Mortimer Wright lays down the law, Mike'll jump. Just the way he did before. He wanted to do good then, too. But he has too many debts."

She saw there was no hope. "Well, thanks for listening to me anyway. For letting me rattle on like this. And think about it, please, Mo. Think about whether it's principles holding you back or bitterness. Promise me you'll think about it."

"All right, Patty. But I can tell you now that nothing could change my mind about him. Nothing at all."

Bee was keeping a campaign journal. He wasn't convinced it contained anything of value, but he owed it to himself to write, and since his days were consumed by the effort to win an election, his thoughts ran that way too. He recorded his impressions of the chief personalities, jotted down descriptions of the places he visited, and kept a daily account of the candidate's progress. Thus the night of the primary he wrote:

Maris, Woodruff, and I gathered at the Merritts' dishy pad to watch the returns. Patty kept our coffee mugs brimming and plied us with pastries. She was calm, confident, almost serene. Her husband, on the other hand, was in a state. He couldn't keep still. He swallowed the Persian carpet with lengthy strides or stared out the picture window at the lights winking on across the park. Woodruff, in an attempt to soothe him, reminded Mike that the primary was in the bag. Here, to the best of my recollection, was their exchange.

RW: Take it easy. Every time you bounce out of

your seat my coffee spills. How can a guy with almost 50 percent of the vote in a four-man race be so nervous?

MM: I don't have any votes yet. That's just a poll. And polls are meaningless. Look at Alf Landon.

RW: That was before polls meant anything. It was a crude business then. There's no way you can lose.

MM: Overconfidence can lose elections just the way it loses games. (He grabbed a newspaper off a table.) Look at this. Hortense Merk gave eleven talks last week, we gave only seven.

RW: So you missed the Divorced Lesbian Atheists and the Fascist Anti-Defamation League. Maybe the retired bellhops.

MM: You can laugh. But there're a lot of voters out there we never talked to.

RW: Merk won't get over 12 percent of the vote. Nobody takes her seriously.

MM: She served ably on the city council.

RW: So she's got your vote.

MM: What about Palermo?

RW: He didn't even get the endorsement of the Scalutti family, since he squealed on Three-Fingers before that committee in '71. All right, give him Nassau. But that's it.

JM: Which leaves us with C. Irwin Moskowitz.

RW: Another Jewish momma's boy.

MM: He's got the mayor's endorsement.

RW: The kiss of death. Like an endorsement from Spiro Agnew.

At ten o'clock the first returns came in. Mike took the city, every borough. Fifty-one percent was the estimated total, with 33 percent for Moskowitz, and the peanuts split between Palermo and Merk. Palermo, as predicted, took Nassau County, with 43 percent. Mike won 37 percent. Suffolk was the same. In western New York, he and Palermo each garnered 31 percent. Moskovitz got 25 percent. Maris's pull in

Albany was good for 48 percent there. The final tally gave us 48 percent, to Palermo's 34. A splendid win. We shook hands all around and pecked Patty on the cheek. Mike declined to write a speech and didn't even ask me for any ringing phrases.

Then we trucked over to headquarters to take calls from the losers and to greet the hoplites. By the time we arrived the assembled troops were cheering and dancing and stomping and generally whooping it up. Newspapermen were there from three states, as well as correspondents from the AP and UPI. The major networks and the locals all had sent crews. It must have been a hundred degrees from the burning lights. Mike shook hands with each campaign worker then took his place on the makeshift platform. He seemed as tall as any two of us, like Michelangelo's David. He silenced the roar and then he spoke.

"This is your victory more than mine. And it is not merely three estimable opponents we have defeated but a failure of imagination and conscience. There is a dangerous strain of extremism infecting us all, poisoning our hearts and nourishing our hatred. The principles that for generations have made our party great are now threatened with ruin. They are threatened by the cynicism of the silent princes of power and the pawns whom they put in office. They are also threatened from within, by those of us who think the days of reform and compassion have died and do not deserve a new life. They are threatened, finally, by fear. We have lived through a decade of apathy and self-absorption. We have lost touch with our high aim of bettering conditions for all Americans. But now, as a new decade dawns, with new hope in the offing, we can change all that. For it is the prospect of change that makes democracy work, that overcomes together petty differences and dispels selfish grievances. It is change that bids us all to grow. And with growth comes willingness to learn, *courage to forgive, strength to defeat the haunting memories of past mistakes.*

"Tonight we have won and we'll celebrate. But tomorrow we'll be back at work. That is the sum of our victory. We have won the right to work harder, to take our cause further, to meet more people in this great state, to offer our ideas to a wider audience. Our victory now becomes our responsibility. It was thrust upon us this evening and we will not take it lightly. And in November we'll carry our ideas and our cause to the greatest legislative body in the world, the proudest forum in this land. Our journey then will have only begun. For it will not end until we have reclaimed America."

There was at first silence and then came the wild, cathartic racking screams. I think everyone knew he was speaking off the top of his head, for his eyes were fixed on a distant point, as if he saw none of us, or perhaps all of us in some abstract way only he could understand. He was looking, I suppose, into himself. Mickey Nagle from the Times *shook me by the shoulder. "My God," he said. "He's going to win. He's going to be President."*

A woman operating a camera for ABC had to call someone to take over for her. She was shaking with a kind of grievous rapture.

Behind the platform, where we honchos stood, Maris whispered something to Woodruff whose round head was nothing but a grin bobbing below his mossy hair. Then Maris stepped over to Mike, who was talking to reporters, and the candidate bent his ear. The wonderful smile—it begins at his chin and ends with a glitter in his eyes—embraced us all.

"What's going on?" I asked Woodruff.

He answered in a kind of sing-song, like little girls do when they're jumping rope. "Whiting's going to debate. Whiting's going to debate."

Onward marches the Merrittocracy.

15

The television studio was cramped, smoky and hot like a poolroom, and Mike Merritt's campaign entourage huddled at one end of what was euphemistically called the waiting room, an off-white, fluorescent-bright box with a tattered green sofa, cracked plastic chairs, and overflowing ashtrays that hadn't been tended in months.

"Remember to look one of two places, Mike: squarely at the camera or squarely at Whiting. Keep your hands folded when you aren't speaking. No sudden movements." Rodney Woodruff gripped his silk tie in a white fist and his wild reddish hair stood electrically on end.

"Yeah, pretend you're a Notre Dame tackle," Bee chided with an easy smile that belied his anxiety.

Mike sat on the sagging sofa, a loose-leaf "issues" notebook open on his lap, nodding impatiently. His stomach churned, and his mind buckled beneath the weight of facts, figures, and formulas he had absorbed for this debate, cramming for the past week like a college freshman before a final exam: this after months of intense statewide campaigning in the face of polls which showed him six points behind the incumbent.

Now, as he girded for the single most important confrontation of the campaign, a tidal wave of exhaustion washed over him. After two hundred and fifty days and scores of cities and towns across New York, his quest for the U.S. Senate—a frantic whorl of new faces that were always the same, of cold 4 A.M. showers and bright stage lights and drinks in stale hotel bars, of labor committees and Rotary lunches and teas, of flabby florid men and the swapping of shoddy promises, of buses and airplanes and rented cars, of the vast weary landscape of a populous state (from Buffalo to Schenectady to Jamestown to Hamilton to Ithaca to Binghamton to Albany to Huntington to Yonkers to Oswego to Watkins Glen to Rochester to Massena and back to the city: from the Lower East Side to Flushing to Staten Island to Harlem to Brownsville to Forest Hills to Riverdale to Ozone Park), of the dull silence that greeted his ideas wherever he spoke, of the high school gymnasiums and veterans' meeting halls and shabby Democratic clubs and posh private living rooms, of speeches and press conferences and visions of a better society for all citizens—climaxed tonight with his face-to-face duel with Thomas Whiting. He barely heard Woodruff's pep talk; he heard instead sounds culled from the memory of days past: the howling of a baby in the brazen July sun, the screams of teenage girls, the throaty hellos of rich divorcees, the staccato shouts of angry Puerto Ricans, the garbled diction of party bosses, the clang and chug of mammoth factories, the whistles and cheers of the race track, the wheezing of crowded buses through congested streets, the cruel howl of the wind off Lake Erie, the squawking of gulls on the beaches of Long Island.

"Remember, you've got to take the offensive from the start," Woodruff was saying. "Make him defend his record. Don't be afraid to step on his toes, but be gentle about it. Take your time and relax."

Mike felt the media wizard's thick hand on his tensed shoulder. "*Relax*," he repeated. Woodruff consulted his watch. "The old man should be here any minute."

The stuffy room seemed to shrink and breathing was difficult. Droplets of sweat popped through Mike's pores. He watched Bee pacing impatiently. A young campaign aide appeared with a coffee tray, then melted away. Mike gulped the tepid, inky liquid. Woodruff fiddled with his glasses, glancing anxiously at the candidate whose pale lined face was a map of the territory beyond fear. Bee lit a cigarette and flopped down beside Mike on the dilapidated couch. A thick silence cloaked their thoughts as time ticked slowly, agonizingly on. Fifteen minutes to air time and still no sign of Whiting.

Mike flipped through the pages of his briefing book but the neatly typed words blurred, paragraphs coagulated on the glare of the paper. There was a rock in the pit of his stomach; he felt as he had so many times before playoff games: tight, sick, cold, dull, numb, gray.

Patty would be watching the debate tonight at her parents' place. He imagined John and Katharine Holmes sitting, stiff-backed, in their austere living room in front of the television, their lips tightly sealed, their faces drawn. Holmes, a longtime Republican, had already told Mike that, regretfully, he must vote for Thomas Whiting. "I might suffer a stroke if I pulled the Democratic lever," the venerable attorney said. "Sorry, son. I wish you the best." And Mrs. Holmes? Patty guessed she'd vote for Mike simply because he was her daughter's husband—and Patty deserved a victor. He could see the three of them now, watching the last few minutes of the evening news, adjusting the color and the volume, sipping drinks, Mother and daughter discussing how tired and frayed the candidate was and how a vacation after the election might do him a world of good.

And would Mo watch? Mike had received no word from the assistant district attorney, not even after Patty's plea for support. *If only he could see the faces I've seen: the poor kids and old people and working men and the housewives with their squealing babies. If only he'd bend a bit. How much would it cost him? Isn't there more at stake here than petty personal grievances. Why doesn't he take a look at the larger picture—as I have?*

Then there would be the millions who casually tuned in, as if it were a game show or soap opera, just to pass the time. Mike longed to capture their imaginations, to inspire them with the zeal he had acquired during the campaign, to show them the tangible stuff on which to build their hopes. Whiting would show himself for what he was; it would be up to Mike to draw the contrast and to exploit his opponent's obvious weaknesses. But would the people see what he was aiming for? Would they realize that his purpose was greater than merely winning an election, that he was imbued with a vision, that he could lead them to the threshold of a new world?

A gray crewcut, a pair of horn-rimmed spectacles, a pointed nose, and a striped bow tie poked through the door. A finely modulated voice issued from between the man's long thin bloodless lips: "Mr. Merritt?" Then the slight, erect figure was in the room, approaching the candidate, a clipboard in one hand, the other extended. Mike rose and shook hands with the man. "Morgan Crane," he announced. "I'll be your moderator tonight. Welcome to WXNY, Mr. Merritt." He in turn greeted Rodney Woodruff and Bee. "Have you been apprised of the format of our show, gentlemen?"

"Basically," Woodruff replied. "Look, where's Whiting? We've been sitting on our asses here for half an hour and there's no sign—"

Morgan Crane's raised hand cut Woodruff short. "Mr. Whiting arrived ten minutes ago. He's been upstairs in the network president's office. They're old friends."

"Great," said Bee. "I suppose he's lining up his own camera angles—so they can capture that noble profile just right for his fans."

Crane gave out a gurgling chuckle. "The advantages of the incumbency," he said casually, "but let me assure you, gentlemen, that I'm in full control of the program once we're on the air. And I want to see a fair and full debate just as much as you do."

"Where's the men's room, Mr. Crane?" Mike's need was evidently powerful for as soon as he received the somewhat complicated directions he fled.

The newsman turned to Woodruff. "Hasn't the makeup girl seen Mr. Merritt yet?"

"We've been squatting in here on our thumbs, like I told you," Woodruff groused. "For Christ's sake we haven't even seen the janitor."

Crane studied the watch on his bony wrist. "Twelve minutes to air time. I'll send her right in. Is there anything else you gentlemen need?" he asked as he turned to leave.

"How about eight percentage points in the polls and a toasted bagel with cream cheese," Bee suggested.

"I can see that this is going to be a lively show tonight," Crane crowed. "Good luck, gentlemen."

When Crane was gone Woodruff turned to Bee. "How do you like these bastards? 'The advantages of the incumbency.' I hope our boy puts the screws to old Whiting but good."

"Don't worry, Rod," Bee said. "Mike's got the fire in his eyes. It's gonna be hot."

After a brief session with the makeup artists who powdered his nose and brow and brushed his suit and straightened his tie, Mike was admitted to the studio where everyone awaited him.

Technicians and cameramen wearing space-age headsets milled around as he stepped over bundles of snake-like cables and wires taped to the floor. Morgan Crane called to him from behind a desk set up between two gray lecterns that stood in front of a blue curtain. Woodruff and Bee stood to one side and the former grabbed the candidate's sleeve for a last word.

"Don't let 'em spook you, Mike. Play it like we planned," he advised. "Remember who you're in this for."

"Good luck, kid. We're all rooting for you. Boola-boola," Bee added with a grin.

Mike moved toward the stage.

"Jesus," Bee exclaimed when their man was out of earshot. "That Whiting looks like everybody's grandfather."

Thomas Ward Whiting, at five-eleven, a trim tennis-playing seventy years old, stood chatting with a pack of smiling, confident cronies. His imperial silver mane and sharp Protestant-blue eyes struck one first, then the marble chin and seriously drawn mouth. He wore his gray flannel suit with authority. After all, as a young executive for a men's clothing store chain he had personified the product he was selling: success and good looks. He became sales director at thirty-two, vice president at thirty-four, and president at forty. He married well enough to retire at forty-five and sail around the world—twice—before he began dabbling in politics. As Republican Party chairman of Westchester County he impressed his peers, including Mortimer Wright, and was groomed for the Senate. He won handily over a liberal Congressman and never faced significant opposition, within his party or in the general elections, for three full terms. He sat on the foreign affairs committee in the Senate when he wasn't sitting in a deck chair in Palm Beach. But, despite his affinity for golfing and yachting, he courted his constituency with the ardor of a young lover. His staff was among the best on Capitol Hill—shrewd, computerized, tough—and they did their homework for him. They made sure he was never without a position on any issue or without a joke for any audience, and they briefed him when he wanted to be briefed and kept their mouths shut when he didn't. In short, Whiting was a practiced professional politician who knew which side of his bread was buttered, and by whom.

He saw Mike Merritt approaching and disengaged himself from his coterie. The two had never met. As Morgan Crane scrambled from behind his desk to join them at center stage, Merritt and Whiting shook hands. They stood enveloped in the hot glare of the television lights.

"Thanks for agreeing to debate, sir," Mike said stiffly. "The voters deserve the chance to see us hash it out face-to-face."

"Sure they do, my boy," Whiting said, flashing his

paternal smile. "You've made a fine showing for yourself in this campaign. I wish you all the luck."

Mike blushed, embarrassed and confused at the ease with which the older man spoke to him. Never having met him, he had thought of Thomas Whiting as the jelly-spined puppet of Privilege; he had believed most of the harsh rhetoric he had used in criticizing the doomed incumbent. But now, as the man stood with a friendly hand on Mike's arm, a conspiratorial glint in his clear eyes, Mike suddenly regretted the hyperbole and invective of the campaign.

"Well, sir," he found himself blurting, "you're the toughest opponent I could ask for."

"Good, that's good," Whiting continued, patting the young man's shoulder, glancing over at Crane who now joined them.

"Gentlemen," said the congenial reporter, "it's a pleasure to work with you. Are you ready to take your places? We have four minutes." He directed Mike to the lectern at the right of the desk. Whiting stood behind the one to the left. Crane conferred briefly with the director.

"Two minutes," a voice called from behind the phalanx of cameras and lights.

Morgan Crane cleared his throat and his Adam's apple bobbed spasmodically. "Any last questions, gentlemen?" he asked. Both men indicated there were none. "Very well. Good luck to you both." The teleprompter was wheeled up for Crane, but he ignored it, shuffling through the papers on his clipboard instead.

"One minute."

For an instant Mike was back in Madison Square Garden craning to see the scoreboard in the smoky vault of the arena, the roar of the crowd pressing on him as he shouted to his teammates. Then he was running down the court, cutting under the goal, losing his man behind Lester Hawkins's mountainous pick, taking a pass from Clint Dixon, launching the leather sphere through the murky air for the basket . . . falling back, falling as he watched the ball snap through the net, falling, still falling, falling into Darlene's arms as her face bloomed before his eyes: her ivory smile, her shining close-cropped hair, her black eyes . . .

"Ten seconds."

He stole yet another glance at Whiting who faced the camera, his face a mask of statesmanship, and panic leapt into his throat through his open mouth.

"Five seconds."

But a quick wave to his right caught his eye. Bee smiled and blew a kiss at him. Woodruff motioned for Mike to stand up straight. The candidate acknowledged them with a shrug. He brought himself to his full height and stared into the black eye of the camera at center stage.

"Three . . . two . . . one." The tiny red light on the center camera flashed on. They were on the air.

"Good evening, ladies and gentlemen. Tonight WXNY brings you, live, a debate between the two major candidates for the United States Senate from New York." Crane explained the rules of the debate. "Each candidate will give a five-minute introductory statement. Then I shall ask questions of each candidate who will be allowed a two-minute response, followed by a minute's rebuttal by his opponent. Finally each will have five minutes for a closing statement. We will begin, based on the flip of a coin, with Senator Thomas W. Whiting."

"Thank you, Mr. Crane," Whiting began. "For the past eighteen years I have had the distinct honor to represent the state of New York in the United States Senate. During those year the world has become smaller, the pace of life faster, the quality of our environment diminished, the price of bread outrageously inflated, the position of our nation in the world seriously endangered. And what has been the cause of these changes, some of which were unimaginable two decades ago when I began my public career? Well, I'd like to think Thomas Whiting has *not* been the cause." He paused and dispatched an ingratiating smile.

"No, ladies and gentlemen, the cause of our present national woes is no one man, no single party, no easily identifiable villain—the cause, I fear, is the lack of stable leadership in Washington: the kind of leadership that puts nation and state above party, principle above politics, the good of the people above popularity.

"Please note that I said 'stable' leadership—for our nation's capital is teeming with men and women who are leaders—who would lead us down a dozen garden paths, who would lead us into a second Great Depression, who would lead us into a war we are ill-equipped to fight and win. Many faces appear overnight and are gone just as quickly, tampering and toying with our system of government to bend it to their own ambitions.

"But there are a few of us—and I rank myself among the few by virtue of the trust you have shown in me over the years—who have been in government long enough to discover that the true power in Washington derives from the people.

"Being a United States Senator from New York is a lonely, serious job, but it is not without the unique satisfaction that comes from serving the people of the most energetic and varied state in the Union. I believe that I have fulfilled your trust in me these past eighteen years. I believe I have many more years to give to the service of my state and my country. And I am confident that my record, which is and always has been the basis upon which I ask you to judge me, speaks for itself.

"But I have spoken thus far only in general terms. Allow me now to address myself briefly to the specific issues which confront us in this crucial election year.

"First and foremost, you are concerned about inflation. Let me say, without exaggeration, that every vote I have cast in my public career—on the budget, on foreign aid, on military spending, on aid to our cities, on taxes—has been a vote against inflation, which I consider to be the greatest threat to our survival as a free people. Second, you are concerned about our national defense. Let me assure you that Thomas Whiting takes a back seat to no one in his efforts to ensure that the United States remained a first-rate world power with the capability to turn back the threat of war with any nation on earth. And third—as I see my time is running short—no one in the Senate can match my record on federal concern for New York City, one of our greatest national resources and the queen of our cities; or on my concern for Israel, our staunchest ally in the troubled Middle East; or on crime, the scourge of our cities and towns; or on energy policy; or on human rights for all citizens whatever their race, sex, or religion.

"In conclusion, ladies and gentlemen, I trust that two weeks from tonight you shall renew the compact first achieved eighteen years ago when you saw what Thomas Whiting stood for and elected him as your representative to the United States Senate. Thank you."

"Thank you, Senator Whiting," Morgan Crane intoned. "Now we shall have an opening statement from Mr. Michael A. Merritt."

"Mr. Moderator, Mr. Whiting, fellow citizens of New York: It has been for me, and for my wife Patty, a particularly enlightening and enriching nine months on the campaign trail as we have crossed this state on our crusade to restore a sense of reason and compassion to government."

As he spoke Mike found his reserves of composure and confidence. "While we respect the achievements of Mr. Whiting's generation of political leadership, we cannot overlook the legacy of fear and cynicism which that generation has bequeathed to us, nor can we ignore the results of their expedient policies. We have for too long trusted them, only to be disappointed time and time again when, despite the noble pitch of their rhetoric, they revert to base instinct when formulating public policies that increasingly frustrate our true national purpose.

"And what is that purpose? Our government was created to provide a structure for the establishment of a workable social contract, for the pursuit of personal freedoms, and for the defense of these complementary goals from threats within and without. Today, the social contract has evolved into a monolithic, impersonal bureaucracy on the city, state, and national level. Personal freedom has been interpreted as the privilege of the wealthy and powerful to exploit the poor and helpless. And defense has become the refuge of the fear-monger who sees threats to 'national security' in every expression of individualism at home and in every effort against tyranny abroad.

"How then are we, as individual citizens, to reverse this process and restore the principles I have outlined? Well, I prefer to avoid the generalities to which Mr. Whiting so fondly clings."

All his fears melted away as he stepped boldly now toward the heart of the matter. His voice assumed an edge of authority as he talked of the issues to which he had dedicated himself.

"The needs of our state parallel the needs of our nation, so I shall speak first in terms of what will directly affect New York. An increased gasoline tax would have the greatest impact on our state. Money raised with a fifty-cent tax, or more, on every gallon could be funneled first into expansion and improvement of public transportation for our cities; second, into food production, as fuel and equipment subsidies for our farmers; and third, into the development of alternative fuel sources. Besides decreasing gasoline consumption, and thus our dependence on foreign suppliers of oil, this tax will improve the quality of our lives. It will also ease inflation and could, as I hope to discuss in more detail later, help to decrease unemployment.

"I also propose a national commitment to rebuilding our cities. Dollars, while not the cure, must be invested without strings in poor neighborhoods to allow those citizens to build from within. I envision a commitment to urban revitalization as strong as our commitment twenty years ago to putting a man on the moon. Hand in hand with his restoration of freedom and dignity would be a similar commitment to a national healthcare policy.

"I propose that we maintain and improve our military capability without succumbing to profiteering and pork-barreling and without sacrificing sanity for the illusion of security. No one today denies the awful necessity for powerful and complex weapons systems; but no one today should slacken in the effort to negotiate arms limitations and to enforce them vigorously. No, let us not tie up our precious human and natural resources in a race to beat the Russians to the grave.

"In the course of this debate I hope to outline in greater detail the ideas which have inspired my candidacy. And, in conclusion, I must point out that my positions on the issues in this year's election are based on the proposition that the people of New York are a sensitive and stubborn lot who, as history has proved, can achieve anything in which they wholeheartedly believe."

Except for the muted shuffling of cameras and crew the studio was weighted with an expectant silence as the debate proceeded.

Crane: "Senator Whiting, in your opening statement you claimed that every vote you have cast in the Senate has been a vote against inflation. What concrete examples can you give us of your strategy to revitalize the economy? For instance, do you support the Kemp-Roth plan?"

Whiting: "Every vote cast in the national legislature affects, directly or indirectly, the state of the economy: whether it's on an appropriations package or a peace treaty. And in my eighteen years on Captiol Hill I have, I believe I can say without exaggeration, never voted for a bill that would damage the economy. Military expenditures are, of course, the most roundly criticized, along with certain social programs which the Democratic administrations of years past have instituted—and I have been selective in my support of such measures, weighing immediate military and social needs with long-term effects.

"For example, I opposed the B-1 bomber on the basis of its cost versus its benefit. I supported the grain embargo on the Soviet Union, despite the short-term hardships it imposed, because I thought it necessary at the time. I also supported the proposed MX missile system, with reservations and with the hope that it will be amended to cut the total dollar expenditure, because, unlike the B-1, this system will more quickly begin to earn back the original outlay. I oppose the administration's plan to bail out a major automobile company—until the Senate was assured that the money would save jobs and promote research and development of more efficient cars. These are just a few examples of the approach I have taken when voting on my legislation that comes before the Senate.

"About the Kemp-Roth bill: I have strong reservations about the concept of this legislation. Primarily, I don't see that tax cuts are the answer to inflation because the further down the income ladder you go, the less effect such tax cuts, even ten- and twenty-percent cuts, really have. However, some provisions I find attractive, such as the encouragement of inner-city industry, and providing certain tax *incentives* to stimulate production. However, I think you'll find that once the bill emerges from a House-Senate conference committee it will have a very different face on it."

Merritt: "Without denying the Senator's good, if somewhat confused, intentions, I think we should remember that his economic conscience is not working overtime. He has the third worst attendance record in the Senate and has missed over thirty percent of the roll-call votes in the current session. While conceding that his votes are cast only after considering *all* the implications, we must point out that voting is but one of the duties of a legislator. His other functions include attending committee hearings, introducing bills, and acting as an ombudsman for his constitutents. On these three counts Senator Whiting is especially lax.

"I challenge anyone to name an important piece of legislation the Senator has introduced in the past five years. Since he represents the second most populous state in the nation he holds an especially important and influential position. But, sad to say, he has not taken the lead in shaping the economic policies of this country—instead he has taken a back seat, when he has condescended to warm his seat at all."

Mike's blood raced as he pressed together his moist palms; he had Whiting on the defensive now. . . .

Well, it wasn't Lincoln and Douglas—or even Kennedy and Nixon—but our boy did his best and had at least as much to say as his venerable opponent. Woodruff was pleased, his scarlet beaming smile locked on Mike throughout, tabulating all the skipped heartbeats in the audience, counting all the votes won every time the big black cameras focused on Mike. Afterward he hugged the candidate in his powerful arms and kissed him on the cheek with a shattering, spit-slinging smack. I merely shook Mike's hand and nodded affirmatively as he queried me with that haggard but handsome tilt of his head.

Whiting knew the score too. Like the godfather in the movie he clasped his opponent's hand solemnly, as if one of them were soon to face a tin lizzie full of machine-gun-toting Keystone Cops in some Brooklyn back alley, and whispered something which Mike wouldn't repeat. Then the Senator glided out of the studio with his Republican lieutenants and into history.

Rod and Mike and I went out to dinner at a trendy but cheap Lincoln Center restaurant, with the media genius picking up the tab. The two of them had a martini apiece; I stuck with iced tea (day by day it's less difficult, though sometimes I want a drink so badly I'd sell my Yale degree—in Latin, mind you—for a sniff of sherry). Anyhow, we were all in great spirits. We could feel Victory flapping her wings above us and enjoyed the breeze.

Television loves Mike even if he disdains the tube. Woodruff caught on to that from the start. Who knows: maybe Mike would have won the primary even if he'd hitchhiked across the state and talked with people about History and the Future and Great Ideas as he wanted to at the beginning. But I don't think he'd have a prayer against Whiting if it weren't for Woodruff and the all-seeing Camera Eye. People have to see Mike to believe him—and to believe in him. The commercials, the few that I've seen, have been simple, basic fare: showing Mike looking regal and concerned. But that seems to be enough. He's got that presence or charisma or animal magnetism that gets those eyes popping and tongues flapping and feet stamping—and it comes over beautifully on film.

In person, especially these last days of the campaign, he's not the same hot property. I'm not sure what it is, but he has erected a barrier of impenetrable reserve which no one can breach—not even me, and I used to be able to break down all his defenses (for my own selfish purposes, I admit). Patty claims it's even worse now than when she first spoke to me about it weeks ago. I don't have to live with the guy, thank God, so I don't know what he's like at one A.M. after a long hot day of campaigning, but I can imagine him lying there in bed, his jaws tight, his eyes open and empty, his fists clenching and unclenching, unable or unwilling to rest for a minute for fear—for fear of what? Of something he's done? Of what he's become? Of new responsibilities? Of old obligations? Of losing? Of winning?

He told me a few days ago that after the election he wants to fly out to Illinois. He hasn't seen his mother for a couple of years at least. I told him that was a marvelous idea, that I'm sure she'd love to see him, that I've always thought she was a fine lady (in her own Godfearing way: I didn't tell him that).

"I've dreamed of her a lot lately." When do you sleep? I wanted to ask. "And my dad," he said. "After all these years I've almost forgotten what he looked like. I always remember him in the hospital, when he was really sick and shriveled up and I hated to be there. But in my dreams he's like he was before, when I was small and he'd talk about when he used to play baseball and basketball and he seemed like a giant who had lived three or four lifetimes before I was even born. Now I remember things I thought I had forgotten about those days. How he and Mom fought—in their own way, muttering in the kitchen because they didn't want me to hear—over getting a TV set.

"He wanted to watch the ballgames and fights; she thought it was a tool of the devil, an excuse for idleness. We couldn't really afford it, but we got one anyway. I was glad Dad won out because I'd get to see the shows all the other kids would talk about at school. But Mom was strict—she'd never allow me to watch it during the week. But on weekends Dad and I watched every baseball and football game we could, and she wouldn't say a word.

"Just a couple of nights ago I dreamed I was a kid back in our living room in Williamsburg and I was watching the television and Mom and Dad were on, like the Honeymooners *or something, and they were arguing. I couldn't hear at first so I turned up the volume—and they were arguing about me. Mom was warning him that I'd lose faith in God if they didn't watch out and Dad said I'd be all right if they let me do what I wanted. He said I could be a great ballplayer. Then they stopped fighting. Mom just gave up and Dad turned to me as though he could see me from inside the TV. 'I know you can do it, son,' he said. It scared me. I turned it off. I don't remember what happened then, but I know I was scared."*

He paused, then asked me: "Do you think it means anything, Bee? I never believed in hocus-pocus but it seemed as if they were trying to tell me something."

I told him that it was a guilt dream, that he ought to visit his mother like he planned. Just a function of all the tension, I said. He seemed to believe me and thanked me for listening to his problem—as if he had never unburdened himself with me before, as if we were new roommates freshman year in Vanderbilt. I've never seen him so keyed up, almost in tears. That was last week when we were preparing for the debate. I haven't spoken to him alone since.

Now I wonder how he'll hold up during the final two weeks of the campaign. Perhaps the debate will shore up his confidence. He has to know how good he was—everybody else does. Maybe that's what he needed: just the way he needed the respect of his opponents when he played basketball. It occurs to me that he's never been sure—as an athlete or as a politician—just how good he really can be. All the bullshit hyperbole in the press: the lavish praise or ignorant criticism. He's always been overly sensitive to that stuff, but he's never trusted anyone else's opinion about his performance. Now he's laying it on the line for the voters to judge.

The campaign has been tough on all of us. Woodruff is probably the least affected: he whirls through twenty-hour days like a dervish. Jeff Maris is driving me nuts, pushing, pushing, pushing toward Election Day, the mad general marshaling his troops into the gaping maw. Patty, though she still glows, gives off a feebler light; she is taciturn and goes now wherever they point her without question, though with all the enthusiasm she can muster. Even the girls who pour the coffee and lick the envelopes pour with less flair and lick with less vigor.

Me, I'm just tired. No more or less cynical about the whole thing because I didn't have any illusions to *start with. From the beginning I expected Mike would win. Not just because he has the potential to be a better Senator than Whiting, but because he lives closer to the core of the public unconsciousness, because all his life he has drifted ineluctably toward a special destiny. He is, perhaps, the only man left in this shabby time to whom it is possible to assign such an old-fashioned notion of destiny. I've felt it all along, ever since our first days together when he was a nascent Titan with a mind and a soul as open as those Midwestern skies under which he first drew breath. He's neither greater nor smaller than his own aspirations, or ours for him, but by the very nature of his calling, he'll always stand apart and alone—and that's no small price to pay for the chance to touch greatness.*

Meanwhile, as Mike reaches for his brass ring, I'm anxious to lunge for mine once this political endeavor is over. For the past nine months I've not had a chance to breathe, let alone think, and yet my book has been building itself in the unfathomable reaches of my mind like a coral reef under the turbulent surface of a faraway sea. This journal has kept me writing (I discovered during my "exile" that a writer has to write every day, for each day lost is irretrievable) and sustained the confidence I have fought so hard to gain. Talent? Nine out of ten guys you see weaving through the man-packed streets of this town have talent. I don't know or care if I've got any. All I care for now is the work left to be done—and there's plenty of it, once we establish the Merrittocracy.

16

Matt Rafferty twisted the knob angrily. The images of Merritt and Whiting died with a quick explosion, like filament breaking in a bulb, and his dingy apartment, at 81st Street on the West Side, fell entirely dark but for the red tip of his cigarette. . . .

He had been sure his editor was joking when he took him off basketball, four years ago. It was his life, always had been, even as a kid growing up in Jersey City with dreams of becoming a sportswriter. Baseball players were arrogant and favored heroes. Footballers too got their share of glory. But back in the Forties nobody talked basketball. It was a gym-period game, a form of conditioning, never a serious sport. When he came to the city in '51 the only basketball talk he heard concerned the point-shaving scandals at City College. Thus, the day twenty-six-year-old Matt Rafferty, with sportswriting experience in Elizabeth and Trenton, presented himself at the offices of the newly founded *Star*, requesting to cover the Comets, he was met with jeers and snickers and looks of disbelief. He forced a smile and assured them, yes, he really meant it. The editor shrugged and said since the guy they had now preferred the trotters Rafferty could have the job.

In the following years basketball came into its own. The league eased its quotas and the great black players, Russell and Chamberlain and Baylor, showed the country a new kind of game, a Watusi ballet that was fluid, swift, and clean as a Marine drill. The Comets weren't much but they had Lester Hawkins and Hal Pecan, sons of the segregated South who ran and leaped with the abandon of men sprung from cages. Only the few thousand faithful ventured to the old Garden to see the show, but these all understood the game—in its sublety, its precision, its grace—and they came back again and again. It was a small but devoted following and every member read Matt Rafferty's column.

Then, in the late Sixties, something happened. Another league came into being with franchises operated on a shoestring, offering prodigious salaries to any kid who could pop from twenty-five. Basketball was big business. Before long there were more gawky seven-footers than the world had ever seen, nurtured, pampered, and gushed over like prize pandas. And the game itself changed. Gone were the stoic Negroes who lived in the shadows of other athletes, big tough men who held a history of anger in check and fought their battles on the court. In their stead flourished a generation of pipsqueak rebels with million-dollar salaries and complaints against the world. With the aid of the liberals they corrupted the game, spreading the word that basketball was the "urban art," the "city game," the death-dance of the ghetto restaged on the hardcourt. Restraint gave way to riot, deliberation to disorder.

When the Comets drafted Merritt, Rafferty almost wept. It was a mockery. The leader of a second-rate squad that mauled a string of Ivy League patsies became the highest-paid performer the game had ever known. True, he was not a belligerent ghetto-child, but he was worse, a glamour boy, a showboater, a grandstanding weekend radical with one eye focused uncertainly on the rim and the other fixed firmly on the cameras. He was introduced as a hero, crowned and fawned over at the Plaza, before he logged a minute of playing time. Hawkins and Pecan, the Comets' sole links to the heyday of the sport, were ignored like idiot children in a family of aristocrats, and Merritt was proclaimed their savior. Merritt would reshape the team in his own image. Rafferty could sense it. The reporter warned Alex Curry, who got the message, but before long the matter was out of his hands. After one disgraceful season, another that was mediocre, and a single good year, Merritt, at age twenty-five, replaced Curry as the Comets coach. He fired Hawkins, and then Pecan. And Matt Rafferty himself, the first genuine basketball writer the city had ever seen, was deprived of his column and put on the crime beat. It was a betrayal he never forgot.

Rafferty stared at the blank television. The debate was a charade. Merritt, the bastard. He would win again. With lies and fulsome displays of compassion and populist ardor, Merritt had roughed up Whiting. A year ago, when the ballplayer announced his candidacy Rafferty had cackled with glee. Merritt was overstepping his limits and was sure to come crashing down. How could anyone take him seriously as a candidate? He had come through as a coach, the reporter grudgingly admitted, although his success was born of luck and the obvious decline of NBA competition. But Merritt in the Senate? The very idea was preposterous. Yet he captured endorsement after endorsement, chiefly from the rattle-brained liberal press, and then, wonder of wonders, waltzed to victory in the primary. And tonight he had sneaked by Whiting, the pride of New York Republicans, while a chorus of smarmy "analysts" sang his praises over the air.

There was more to Rafferty's anger than simple dislike of Merritt, though God knew that came easily to anyone with even a sliver of sense. A greater cause offered itself. Not just Merritt must be thwarted but everything he stood for. A perilous future was descending, a miasma of weakness and dishonor.

This country had seen enough imposters to whom victory came without struggle, without sacrifice, who got what they wanted for the mere asking. America had fallen into the hands of handsome do-nothings who tinkled martinis and twaddled about unity. Of course the fabled melting pot looked to be made of gold when viewed from the dizzying heights of their penthouses, but when you stuck your nose deep enough, when you explored every nook and cranny of this filthy town, then you saw the great pot was in fact a cloaca, with the most disreputable slime edging its way to the top. Like Merritt. Somehow he dazzled them. But then they were fools; they worshiped qualities which shrewd men instinctively distrusted. Merritt was good-looking and glib and when he smiled the ladies smiled back. He was sincere; he was committed. He was everything that meant nothing.

Take Merritt's relationship with the queer writer Crosby. No one ever thought to question it; no one cared to expose such filth; no one anymore, except Rafferty, clung to the old moral values in a new, corrupt age.

Matt Rafferty thought about things. He was naturally curious. That's what made him a reporter and a damned good one too, even if the *Star* took him off sports. He had persisted in telling the truth about Merritt after the Comets started to win. When a notion made its way into Rafferty's fertile mind he was loath to relinquish it. And recently he had gotten a notion about Merritt and his connection with that drug-dealer who was gunned down in Harlem. After all, it was a fact that Merritt had been screwing the wife. If the cops had done some investigating they would have questioned him, but in their customary half-assed way they didn't bother to nibble below the surface. Then, of course, there was Mortimer Wright, pulling more strings than a puppeteer. He and Merritt made quite a combination. The banker paved the way with his pelf and Merritt strutted along, untouchable, like some kind of god, sowing his rotten seeds. Now the pair was headed for the Senate. There was talk about the White House. Something had to be done.

Rafferty reached for the bottle at his feet. He tipped it but only a few drops dribbled into his mouth. He would have to get another. He slipped on his jacket and left the apartment. The street was dark and the cool October air wafted laughter from lighted windows. What was there to laugh about? What was more dangerous than laughter when you could feel the tremors of a world nearing collapse? Where had seriousness gone?

The liquor store was closed. And this the city that never slept. Damn, he needed a drink. The bars were still open on Columbus but his idea of a fun time didn't include shelling three bucks for weak scotch in a roomful of funny boys wearing alligator shirts. Where should he go? For some reason, MacElroy's joint near the Garden popped into his head. He hadn't been there in years, not since Merritt had bullied him with the halfwitted MacElroy's approval and assistance. What the hell, he had money in his pocket. He'd take a cab there. Maybe he could get a rise out of Mac.

He flagged down a taxi on Central Park West. The cabby made good time. Rafferty rewarded him with a dollar tip.

"Have a good evening, sir," said the cabby. He belonged to the new breed. Make New York fun for the tourists, like Disneyland.

The bar was nearly empty and this gave the reporter pleasure. He didn't like crowds and it was good to know hard times still plagued the barman, who had shown his true colors on the infamous occasion when Merritt had flung his drink.

Mac's face had mysteriously lost its jovial excess. The pillows of flesh had thinned and aged brittle bones showed through. He gave Rafferty a speculative look. "Long time, Matt."

Rafferty plunked onto a stool. "How's my favorite has-been fighter?"

"I'm still here, so things ain't great."

"Your buddy Merritt isn't cutting you a piece of his

cake?"

Mac pushed him a drink. "Fat chance. He comes around, though. I'm proud as hell of that kid. I kind of feel like I got something to do with where he is."

"And that makes you proud?"

Mac shook his head. "Still have it in for the boy, don't you?"

"I don't forget."

"No, I guess you don't. When you stopped coming around I figured you was still mad at me. But hell, Matt, it was nothing. Like Mike says, you got to forgive."

"Who are you, his campaign manager? He's telling lies. Just the way he always has."

"You won't change my mind, Matt. I think he's the greatest. After the Comets took it he brought the boys here. Hell, another team would have gone to '21,' but not Mike's boys. He don't forget his friends." Mac pointed a thumb over his shoulder. "There they are, the champs. Took that picture myself."

Rafferty cast a scornful eye at the framed, dated group photograph. He dropped his eyes, then something made him look again. He craned his neck and squinted—his eyes were going bad but he wasn't about to wear glasses. "Where the hell is Merritt?"

"Huh?"

"Merritt. Where the hell is he? He's not in the picture."

Mac gave the photo a careful once-over. "I'll be damned. He ain't. I'll have to get another one just of him. Funny I never noticed. And nobody else did either. You make a good reporter."

Rafferty wasn't listening. He was puzzling over the date. It stuck in his mind like a thorn. June 15, 1977. "How come he's not in the picture?"

Mac tipped his head ceilingward, thinking. "Lemme see now."

"You've got to remember. How could you forget?"

"Give me a minute." He smiled as remembrance dawned. "He hadda leave. He got a phone call and he hadda take off. I remember 'cause he laid down a fifty."

"Answered the phone himself, huh?" Rafferty tried to sound casual.

"No. I took it myself. This is my bar. I answer the phone. No matter who's calling."

"So he was expecting the call."

"Wouldn't say that. As a matter of fact he was kinda mad about it."

"Wife, huh?"

"No again. It was that gal he used to see, the colored gal. She was in trouble. She was always pestering Mike, even after he married that lovely Patty. I tell you he brought her in once? He said, 'Mac, you think I'd go off and marry a girl without your approval? What kind of son would I be then?' "

"That colored girl? You mean, uh, what was her name?"

"Darlene. You're slipping, Matt."

So Merritt had still been seeing her! And June 15th. . . did it match the day Jasper Brown was killed? Rafferty could hardly contain himself. Glee washed over him like a summer shower. Oh, Jesus, let it all be there. Let that be the date. It had to be. Sure, she calls Merritt. He races over. In barges the husband with a gun. Merritt's strong as a bull. He snags the gun, wastes him.

Rafferty ordered another drink to calm his shaking insides. The girl—what the hell happened to the girl? Why didn't she squeal? Or did they quietly take her away then snuff her on the sly? But who . . . ? Why, Mortimer Wright!

"You all right, Matt? You look like you got some kind of chill."

"Yeah. I had a fever a couple of days ago. Still shaking it off. Give me one more scotch and I'll be all right."

Two days later Rafferty stumbled out of bed with a hangover. It was, he could tell, a bitter day. The cold sun lit his chaotic studio through the grime of his geminate windows. Noises from the street rose through the thin acrid air—a racking engine, a yipping dog, a garbage can banging onto the sidewalk. He grabbed a squashed butt from the ashtray, straightened it between ochrous fingertips, then struck a match. The stale smoke silted down his throat.

He hated showers but today there was no choice. The needling spray woke him up a bit. Drying before the mirror on his medicine cabinet he contemplated indifferently the sallow folds of his face, the pouched glassy eyes, the cruel lines etched by time. He ran a comb through his damp thinning locks and his grooming was complete. Let the pretty boys like Merritt primp all day; Matt Rafferty did his best work just the way he was. And today he had serious work to do, very serious work.

He set to boil last night's coffee, which muddied a pot on a crusty back burner, and took a piece of bread out of the refrigerator. It was all he needed to start the day. The rest was gluttony, and a waste of time. He'd grab a couple of hotdogs later.

He donned his overcoat and exited. On the corner a man soaped his car while another watched and a girl leaned in a doorway. Damned Puerto Ricans. Ought to ship them all back to San Juan. They charged up north like a pack of wild animals, squatting fifteen to a room, never leaving except to rape, rob, kill and collect their welfare checks.

Anarchy reigned in the IRT. The defaced cars rattled and screeched and the lights blinked on and off so fast he felt queasy. But Rafferty was late and even the mayor's limousine wouldn't get you to the DA's office faster than the subway.

He had an appointment with the new assistant prosecutor. Man named Silver, with an interesting past. A radical who got wise and threw his weight with the law. Judging from their chat over the phone yesterday Silver was a tough customer. Still there was a slight trace of the sap about him, not discernible to most perhaps, but Matt Rafferty was not most men. A filigree of sanctimoniousness ran through Silver. A reformer. Put three guys like Silver together in a round room and they'd form a coalition and file a protest to make it square, with a quotation here and there from *Das Kapital*. They'd present the whole package to the walls and the ceiling. Don't you understand, they'd say. It isn't fair. It isn't right.

He was interested in Silver because he went back a long way with Merritt. Leave it to the blind fools in New York to overlook such an obvious fact. Silver was in the DA's office and he was sitting on a firecracker. Only maybe he didn't know it. That's what Rafferty intended to find out.

The Manhattan District Attorney's office was the reporter's kind of place, one of his many homes away from home. The peeling walls, the scarred furniture. It was a place of business. Rafferty liked the man who ushered him into his little box on the corner of the third floor. A rare response for the reporter, who wasn't in the profession of liking men. Good reporters made few friends.

"What can I do for you, Mr. Rafferty?"

"Well, that isn't so easy to say. But my paper likes to keep up with the new boys, over at City Hall, and down here, because readers need to be informed about these subtle changes in, uh, city management. Some new fellow takes over a desk and maybe he's not on his toes, maybe he's there to sweep shit under the carpet, and that isn't right. New York needs honest men in positions of responsibility."

Mo Silver smiled. "If you're here to lecture me on

civics, I'll have to ask you to leave because I've inherited a full docket and I've got work to do."

Rafferty poked a Lucky into his mouth. "All right, Mr. Silver. Fair's fair. You said something about a loaded docket. Now you wouldn't be able to tell me, off the record, of course, if one of those cases has anything to do with that nigger gunned down in Harlem a few years back. Name of Brown, Jasper O. Bigtime dealer, pusher I should say, because this nigger did a lot of pushing, shoving in fact. Took over a chunk of territory from the Mob from what I understand."

"Yes, I'm familiar with the incident. Drug-related killing. The police cleared it up pretty quickly."

"Any idea why no charges were brought?"

"Usual reasons, I suppose. No suspects. No hard evidence."

Rafferty took a long drag. "I get a glass of water around here? I'm not feeling too chipper this morning. Afraid I tied one on last night."

Mo Silver got to his feet. A big guy, Rafferty observed. Blocky but not fat. Thick in the shoulders and the arms, deep through the chest. "There's a cooler outside. I'll bring you a cup."

The reporter took the opportunity to examine the office. An army-green cabinet held the files. Was the Brown case in there? He pulled open the top drawer. The files were arranged alphabetically. There was nothing there. Not yet. Rafferty had a plan. He heard steps and sprang back into his seat.

"Here's your water, Mr. Rafferty."

"Appreciate it." He drained it and crumpled the paper cone into the trashcan. "Now let's suppose you came across something in the old police files. I'm speaking of you as a DA, because I know you guys go over police reports. It's not news that the cops have a way of missing little details. It ain't easy being a cop. They get bogged down like anybody else and, well, they're not the brightest characters on God's earth. So a new DA, from the new school, the school that says you don't let sleeping dogs lie, decides to investigate some recent gangster killings. After all, this is the Manhattan DA's office and everybody and his sweet sister knows that Manhattan DAs consider themselves real gangbusters. So you go through this old case and maybe, just maybe—I'm speaking hypothetically—the report looks funny. What would you do?"

Mo Silver toyed with a pencil and looked the reporter squarely in his watery eyes. "Why, I'd ask to see more. Request the complete file. Reports from the on-duty cop, from the medical examiner's office, and so on. Maybe call the cop in for an interview."

Rafferty lit a fresh smoke with the butt of the last. "Look, Silver. There's no point in our sparring like this. I'll give it to you straight. Brown didn't die because of any drug deal. It couldn't be, you see, because the operation continued just like before. Only a slight change in personnel. Gangster killings aren't like business deals. You know, one guy's out, another guy's in. Very smooth. After our man Jasper bought it Harlem should have gone crazier than ever, niggers sniping each other and slitting throats like there was no tomorrow. The big man was gone and there wasn't any replacement. His territory was up for grabs. But nothing happened."

"Are you telling me I should reopen the investigation?"

"What do you mean reopen? There never was any investigation."

"In any case, I can't proceed simply on whimsy or your theories about the organizational structure of Harlem drug operations."

"Is that why you won't reopen the case? Or are there maybe personal reasons?" He paused to let that sink in and gauged the lawyer's reaction. Silver remained impassive, but Rafferty felt the heat of wheels whirring and humming in the big head.

"I'm listening, Rafferty."

"Let's talk cases. A certain party was screwing a colored girl who used to work in the Comets' front office. I knew it all along, maybe you did too. That's immaterial. But he was screwing her and she happened to be mistress and maybe whore to Brown, who kept her in a dishy pad uptown. Furs and antiques and parquet floors. A regular black Princess Grace. Kept her in style, probably in smack too. So he finds out she's two-timing him and—since we're not talking about a nice, well-mannered, law-abiding citizen—he decides to waste the other guy. Only it backfires and he ends up with his own brains on the shag carpet. Now, you know damn well who that other party was and you're keeping your mouth shut because he's an old buddy of yours. Hell, you used to be his agent. Even if now there's bad blood between you. That's what people tell me anyway. Yeah, the killer might just be a famous man in town. And if word ever got out it would blow his ambitions sky-high, might put him behind bars for ninety-nine—"

Mo Silver stood up. "Get out of this office."

"Now wait a minute, Silver."

"I'll give you to three before I have you forcibly removed."

Rafferty jumped to his feet. "All right, Silver. I'm going. But remember what I said. I got enough info now to sink your pal Merritt and maybe you too for conspiring to obstruct justice."

Mo pushed him out and slammed the door. He fell back into his chair, shaking. It was ridiculous. Merritt was an unprincipled egotist but he wasn't a killer. Could he have killed Brown inadvertently, or in self-defense? Which would mean he had been cheating on Patty. That Mo could believe. Still, to kill a man and not breathe a word of it to anyone—not even Mike was that cold-blooded. The lurid picture Rafferty painted was just a bluff, the work of an inflamed, unbalanced personality, stuff for tabloids like the *Star*. Nonetheless the reporter's accusation about police negligence might be justified. Would it hurt to examine the police file? It would clear Mike and set Rafferty's impossible claims to rest.

It had worked like a dream. Silver had gotten just as riled as Rafferty had figured, especially when he hinted at a cover-up. It never failed with these idealistic types. Just give them the scent and they were off and running. Rafferty doubted that Silver himself was involved. There had been talk of a falling out after the Comets won the championship. Merritt had let his lawyer go and the two had become enemies. Further proof was Silver's absence from Merritt's campaign.

Now it was a matter of biding his time. The reporter had a contact in the Commissioner's office. As soon as Silver requested the file Rafferty would know. And then he would be ready to strike. Once he got ahold of the file he would have Merritt dead to rights. Probably the file contained nothing damaging on the surface, but if you were on the lookout for details there was bound to be something—perhaps something that wasn't there but ought to be.

Three days later his contact came through. The assistant DA had requisitioned the Jasper Brown file. It would be sent to him the next morning.

Rafferty placed a call to Mo Silver's office.

"Yes?" the attorney's voice came over the line testily.

"Can I meet you this morning, Silver? I've got some pretty vital evidence—"

"I don't believe you have a shred of evidence."

"Now don't get angry. I apologize for what I said about you covering up. I got carried away. I just want to see justice served."

"What have you got?"

"I'd rather not talk over the phone. Listen, let me make up for shooting off my mouth. I've got a tight schedule, but if you can meet me tomorrow morning at

9:30 I'll buy you breakfast. It's urgent.''

Silver sounded resigned. "All right."

Rafferty named a coffee shop on lower Broadway.

The next morning Rafferty showed up at the DA's office at 9:10. He approached a security officer he recognized.

"What can I do for you, Mr. Rafferty?"

"Where's Mr. Silver?"

"He's gone."

"Listen, Scotty, I need a big favor from you. The other day I was talking to him, the new guy, and I left some papers in his office. I have a story due tomorrow. If you could let me in there to look around for myself I'd be grateful as hell."

The guard was skeptical. "I don't know. We're not supposed to let anyone up there except by appointment."

"I realize that. I promise you I'll return the favor. The *Star's* thinking of running a profile on guards down here. Big double-column spread. I'll put you in there."

"Yeah?"

"With a picture."

"No kidding?"

"Give you my word."

"All right. Hell, the office ain't even locked. It can't hurt. I'll give you ten minutes."

"Thanks a lot, Scotty. Next month, I promise, you'll be in the *Star*. You know we're running color pictures these days."

Once inside Silver's office Rafferty picked up the phone and called his contact.

"You send that file over yet?"

"It's on its way. What's the rush?"

"By messenger?"

"Yeah, we keep a couple of kids around."

"They have passes or do they have to be cleared?"

"Nah. The security chumps know 'em all. They let them go right through."

"Great. Thanks a million."

Rafferty rolled up his sleeves and pulled a sheet of paper out of Silver's desk. He opened a law book on the desk and pretended to look busy. A few minutes later the messenger arrived.

"You Mr. Silver?"

"That's right."

"I heard he's a husky guy."

"Yeah, well I had the flu."

"Got something for you." From underneath his parka he pulled out an envelope. "Here, you got to sign."

"Let me see." Rafferty took out the file. On the protruding edge was typed "Jasper O. Brown." He scrawled Silver's name on the receipt. After the kid left Rafferty waited a couple of minutes then footed out the office and down the stairs.

"Find your papers, Mr. Rafferty?" the security man asked.

"Yeah. Thanks a lot. They would have had my ass if I hadn't."

"When do you want me for that interview?"

"Tell you what. Call my office next week and we'll set up a time."

"Great. You know I got a couple real good snapshots my wife—"

"We'll talk about it later. I got to run right now."

"Sure thing."

Rafferty scuttled toward the door.

"It's a real good picture she took at graduation from the academy," the guard called. Rafferty raised his hand but didn't turn around.

He raced over to Broadway and found a Xerox place. The clown took forever to get the few documents copied, stopping after the second page to take a phone call from his wife. Yes, he had taken her watch to the jeweler's. No, he had forgotten to stop by the pastry shop. . . .

"Hurry up, will you?" Rafferty shouted. "I've got places to be."

The copier cupped the receiver. "Take it easy, buddy. I usually don't handle anything except by appointment. I'm doing you a favor."

"What are you, a goddamn brain surgeon? A chimpanzee could do what you do and get the job done a hell of a lot sooner."

"Call me later," the man told his wife, glaring at Rafferty. "All right, wise guy," he said when he was finished. "That'll be a buck."

"A dollar to copy four lousy pages?"

"Minimum fee. Read the sign. You have any idea how much it costs me, energy-wise, to operate a single machine for even a minute?"

"All right, all right," Rafferty growled. "Here's your dollar. But don't expect to see me in here again."

"I ain't holding my breath."

Rafferty scanned the photocopies and, satisfied they were legible, stuffed them into his shirt. It was nearly ten. Silver must be back by now. The reporter raced back to the DA's office and dropped the envelope on the unattended desk of the security guard with a scribbled note. Then he caught a cab home.

Uptown in the sanctity of his apartment he perused the documents. A cover sheet named the victim, and the cop who found the bodies. Then came the ME's report. Brown had been shot before he was drugged. There was a brief confession signed by Darlene Simmons. Attached to this was a note recording her recent death in an asylum upstate. What had she died from? Something fishy there.

Rafferty paced his cramped apartment, thinking. What if Merritt shot Brown? The bullet wasn't fatal; it was the work of an amateur. Crime passionale? Then, let's see, he would have panicked. Maybe he figured the nigger had bought it. His next step would be to call his lawyer. Silver would advise his client to call the police,

358

turn himself in docilely. Obviously no such thing had happened. Had Silver helped cover it up? It didn't ring true. Why not? The drugs, that was why. A killer dose of heroin administered by professionals. Coincidence? A contract put out on Brown the very night that Merritt shot him, the real killers arriving on the scene moments after the shooting? Unlikely. What then? Had the girl assisted? She too was an addict; she'd know where to slip the needle. But why were no charges brought against her? She confessed, then was whisked out of sight. And she didn't name Merritt. Which means she was bought off. The cops must have struck a deal with her. Take the entire rap and you'll never see the inside of a jail cell. But why? Why would they make such a deal? Why risk their careers to save Merritt? Unless—unless they were under orders. From the top. The Commissioner, most likely. Again, the question was why. Who was pulling the Commissioner's strings? Mortimer Wright? How did he get involved? What if Merritt called Wright instead of Silver and Wright sent over his boys to finish the nigger off, maybe drugging the girl at the same time. Not enough to kill her, but enough to short her circuits. Then the cops arrive on the scene, find Brown dead, his wife in a stupor. Book her for the shooting. Wright and the Commissioner work out an arrangement. There it was. All he lacked was evidence. But, if he played it right he wouldn't need evidence. In fact, the dearth of evidence might work to his advantage. Its very absence signaled something amiss. A cover-up. The police file was barren. There was never an adequate investigation.

Rafferty sat at his rickety table, facing the wall. Rust from the pipes blistered the cracked paint and the stale dry odor of steam tickled his nose hairs. At his feet was a box overflowing with clippings from newspapers and magazines, all concerning Merritt. The file had not fallen into idle hands. This, the reporter exulted, was the icing on the cake. He need only write that he had obtained an official file indicating misconduct in the highest reaches of the police department and whatever followed would see print. Besides, he knew he wasn't far off. He might have missed a detail or two but the substance of his theory had to be on the mark. It would be convincing enough to trigger an investigation which, for now, would keep Merritt out of the Senate and eventually land him in the slammer, where he rightfully belonged.

His typewriter was a little black portable with a temperamental paper bail. Things came out crooked. That was all right. He had a crooked subject. It was the story he was destined to write. If you wrote out of hate you needed a grand polymorphous villain, substantial enough to absorb all that abuse and still seem real. No simple news flash, this, but a major expose, a morality play. A story crying to be written, freighted with truths the world needed to hear.

The election was days away. Time was closing in. And out there, crouching perhaps in the abandoned apartments across the street, or huddled in doorways, or speeding silently, at this very moment, up Central Park West, lurked his enemies, who would stop at nothing.

17

Mike was resting on the "campaign couch" when Jeff Maris burst in with a smiling Rodney Woodruff on his heels and a press release in his hand. "Here it is. We're in front."

Mike sat up and grabbed the paper. The *Times*/CBS poll gave him a two-percent lead. "I'll be damned."

"It's ours, Mike," said Maris. "The timing couldn't be better. We're peaking. By election day we'll be up by five."

"I can't believe the debate didn't help Whiting."

"Maybe now you'll trust your advisers."

"It doesn't make sense. I didn't blow him out. I tried to get him on every point but he was too damn slippery."

"You may not have won the debate," Woodruff pointed out. "But you stole the show. Good thing we went with the dark suit. It made you look more aggressive."

"I was afraid I'd overdone that," Mike confessed. "I came down hard on his absenteeism."

"Hard but clean," said Maris.

"Still, a grandfatherly guy like that . . ."

"Great grandfather, lousy Senator."

"He's not lousy," Mike reproved. "For a Republican his performance has been good. I'd say he's the most responsible man in his party."

"Faint praise," said Maris. "I thought he was condescending as hell. 'Perhaps if Mr. Merritt had the benefit of my eighteen years of proud and able service . . .' Rod, you think we could run a private poll on that? Maybe half a dozen questions about personality differences?"

"I'm still not convinced we're in front," Mike said. "Or maybe we are today but in the voting booth minds will change. After eighteen years you get used to a man. People trust Whiting."

"Which is why we have to push," Maris said. He looked at his clipboard. "There's the meeting in Albany this afternoon. They're still unhappy about the gas tax and they can't promise their districts will come out in full force till it's cleared up. Just pound the farm subsidy into their heads. Also I tacked on two brief meetings with citizens groups. Businessmen in Troy and the PTA in Schenectady."

"I met with them already."

"They want to see you again."

"Excellent," said Woodruff. "I can run a quick poll before you talk. Pre- and post-TV. I'll have to dig up the stats we came up with last time."

The phone trilled. Maris picked it up. "Who? Mr. Silver?"

Mike lunged. "Give me that. Yes, put him on. Mo! How are you?"

"I have to see you, Mike."

"Are you in trouble? If there's anything—"

"When can you get away?"

"Right now, if you like."

Maris shook his head emphatically and waved as if to flag down a runaway vehicle. He opened his mouth to protest but Mike silenced him with a raised hand.

"—on Varick Street," Mo concluded.

"I'll be there." Mike broke the line and dialed the receptionist. "Get me a cab, please. Right now."

"What's going on?" Woodruff asked.

"I don't know."

"Mike," Maris pleaded. "The schedule."

"I've been waiting to hear from Mo all campaign.

362

I'm not going to put him off because of the schedule."

"Trouble?"

Mike shrugged and grasped the doorknob. He parted the ranks of bustling workers with Maris in tow. "Call as soon as you know what's up so I can patch up the appointment log."

Chance synchronized the arrivals of the estranged friends. Mike stepped out of his cab at the precise instant Mo turned the corner of Varick Street. The candidate stuck out his hand. Mo hesitated a moment before taking it.

"I'm glad you called, Mo. It's been a long time."

"It has. You're looking good for the final week."

The bar was a businessmen's den. Fortunately it was well before noon so there was no press of hands to grab, no punches on the shoulder to endure, no garrulous hearty quips to smile through. The pair found a table in an embrasure and were entirely alone but for two solitary drinkers stationed like bookends at opposite corners of the bar, each lost to his glass and his contemplation of ruin.

Waiting for their drinks they talked cautiously. Mike asked after Sheila, Mo after Patty. Then their orders came. Mo fingered an ice cube. "I'm afraid it's bad news I have, and I'm partly to blame."

"What is it?"

"Jesus. Where to begin?"

"You're making me nervous."

"All right. Last week your old buddy Rafferty dropped by my office with some pretty wild accusations about you and Jasper Brown. He claimed to have evidence that you were involved in his murder. He accused me of covering it up. Apparently he thinks I still work for you. I told him it was all bullshit and finally threw him out. I didn't believe any of it for a minute, but the business about an inadequate investigation interested me. I was curious. Maybe there was something there. So I sent for the police file.

"A couple of days later I agreed to meet Rafferty. He *had* to see me that morning. He claimed to have more evidence. It was *urgent*. He couldn't talk over the phone. Damn, that was stupid of me! I had the file coming—what did I need with Rafferty? There's no question the man's a lunatic. He's working out some kind of obsession. Anyway, I showed up and he wasn't there. I waited around for half an hour, then went back to my office. A guard downstairs handed me the file. There was a note: 'Thanks, Buddy.' He must have a contact on the force who told him when the file was coming. He knew before I did. He's got to know somebody in the Commissioner's office or the mailroom or somewhere. Some security idiot let him into my office and when the messenger came by Rafferty snatched the file. He must have photocopied the documents. He's right about the case being mishandled. There was no investigation, no attempt to explain the most obvious discrepancies. They didn't look hard enough to see anything amiss. The file is bare but what's there is interesting. For one thing your old girlfriend Darlene was dispatched by unnamed authorities to an institution upstate. A recent entry lists her death. No cause given."

"Darlene?" Mike was ashen.

"Yes. I wonder about that. I wonder about it all. She made a point-blank confession under who knows what kind of duress. Jasper's death is strange too. There was a gunshot, serious but not fatal, and then someone pumped him full of heroin. Why both? Were they related attempts? But there's not a hell of a lot I can do. Whatever evidence there might have been is sure to be gone by now, and in Harlem there's no such thing as a witness. In my younger days I would have launched an investigation of the police but that's a hopeless proposition. With no fresh evidence there's no case."

Mike felt claustrophobic. The shadowy place was threatening to cave in. The walls strained at their panel facing and the bar buckled like a battered rampart. He would be buried up to his nose in the dust of plaster and wood, blizzard-thick motes clogging his notrils like smoke in a burning house. Was he losing his mind? He gulped his scotch. Darlene, Wright had killed Darlene, snuffed the flame inside that beautiful body, turned her heat to ice. And Mo had just said something about Jasper. Drugs had killed him, not a bullet. Did Wright pay contacts in Harlem to finish him off, or did he unleash his own trained killers? He almost laughed out loud. Wright was as guilty as he was! He would go to jail too. It wouldn't be so bad for the old bastard. His life was mostly behind him. Suddenly his glee was eclipsed by terror. Wright might not be implicated at all. Mike was alone in this. It would come down to his word against the board chairman's. No question who would win that contest. Mike did his best to meet Mo's deep gaze. *He doesn't know. He hasn't said I did it.*

"What I'm worried about," Mo was saying, "is Rafferty. I'm sure he'll use that file to implicate you in any way he can. Even if nothing's there he can twist the facts to make it seem otherwise. And you know how some of those rags are—the kind he writes for. They'll print anything. I tried to get a warrant but it was no go. Judges fear reporters. I've already written a denial and it'll be published as soon as Rafferty's story hits the stands."

"There's no way to stop him?"

"He's too cagey. He may already have sent it off. And the papers will pull out the First Amendment argument. Of course the responsible publications won't touch anything he writes but the others will claim it's unbiased reporting from a respected professional."

Mike had regained his senses. His mind was working rapidly. Could Wright have fouled up? But Mo said there was nothing damaging in the file. Still, if he knew where to look . . . Had he stumbled across the cabdriver who had taken him on the all-night tour of the city? Were there witnesses in the building? "Mo, I don't know what to say. The election's less than a week away and you know how tight we're running. All that crackpot has to do is sway the minds of a few thousand people out there."

"Mike, please accept my apologies. I was a fool, irresponsible and unthinking and God knows what else. I never should have let the bastard into my office. He had it in for you and I knew it. I guess I was curious. I haven't been your biggest fan myself these days."

Mike met the eyes of his former agent and mentor, the source of his own political consciousness. "It's not your fault, Mo. You couldn't know he wasn't being honest with you. I've given you reason enough not to take anyone at face value. If I were in your position I would have welcomed any insinuations Rafferty had to offer."

"I'm sorry as hell. If it costs you the election I could never forgive myself. I wish I could make it up to you."

"There is something you can do."

"What's that?"

"Vote for me."

Mortimer Wright was beginning to feel the effects of old age. His office was heated to seventy-two degrees but the dampness of the sodden November day seeped into his bones. He felt a light chill. He pulled the sleeves of his sweater over his cuffs, recoiling from the touch of his own skin. It was flaky, dry as the hide of a snake, and cold. His father's flesh had been similarly cold just before his death at age sixty-nine, a milestone Mortimer Wright himself had reached just last week.

He was willing prey, these days, to recollections from his young manhood. Life had a splendid purpose then. The country was in a shambles. Many of the good families lost their wealth in the crash and with it their position and stability. More discouraging yet were the cowardly defections: Communism, Trade-Unionism, and Roosevelt's cabinet claimed many an able mind.

Dr. Horace Wright openly mourned these betrayals. He was a fine man, perhaps too fine, particularly in his ideology. He chose the physician's livelihood because he could not bear all the imperfection around him, the weakness and disease. His son inherited his diagnostic bent but at Yale his passion ran to politics and management. After Mortimer graduated, Father urged a career in business. Better to work behind the scenes: anonymous efforts on behalf of the common good might go untrammeled. Out on the hustings the same efforts were unfailingly diluted by compromise. Mortimer remembered his father's words, uttered in that soft yet commanding tone. "In a noble democracy, that of the Athenians for example, such compromises did not occur because while all citizens might vote, not all men ranked as citizens. The unworthy did not affect public policy. We are the greatest nation the world has yet seen but we have not learned from history the imperatives of an ordered society, guided by its principal men." Those ringing phrases! "The imperatives of an ordered society." "Principal men." Where had such fluency gone?

Wright peered at a sepia photograph he kept in his desk. Father, dressed in a gray suit, his fingers gripping the wings of his chair, closely resembled son. You could not tell that his eyes were blue but they were large and arresting nonetheless. The taut modeled cheeks were beginning to sag from decades of selfless work and deep thought. May I die as he did, as quietly, as honorably, as certain that I have acted as I should. This last thought came involuntarily. He shuddered and tugged again at his cuffs. I have done things Father never dreamed of but only because I had to. The country was different then. The enemy was not both ubiquitous and invisible. Irrationality was the exception rather than the rule. Fortunately Father had not survived to see the horror life had become. Why, compared to the present state of affairs the anarchic Thirties had been sane as a

Victorian tea party.

This decline was especially painful to one who had accepted the task of nurturing strong leaders. Thus far Wright's endeavors had yet to put a man in the White House. Whiting was able and loyal, a hard worker with firm principles, but he lacked panache. He had never seized the collective imagination of the vast unwashed electorate. Party leaders commended him, flattered him, embraced him, yet invariably passed him over as their standard-bearer. Merritt, now, was a different story. His political ideas verged on the outrageous—he no more understood his country than the rest of his benighted party—but he possessed the spark of leadership. And he was educable.

Wright had felt a father's grief when he learned Merritt was carrying on with a prostitute and addict. But to dismiss him then and there would have been an admission of abject failure. Besides, the banker was a generous man with an eye on the larger picture. He could forgive a minor lapse. Since then Merritt's behavior had been exemplary. He proved a sterling candidate. Beginning as a dark horse he had quickly galloped ahead of the primary pack and now threatened to overtake a three-term incumbent. The debate had made the difference. A tactical error on Whiting's part. Was it vanity or desperation that led the old goat to lock horns with a man half his age?

Wright looked at his watch. Merritt was due any minute. It would be a pleasure to see him again. Privately he was wounded when the young candidate spurned his assistance. He had sacrificed much for him—had murdered for him, thereby jeopardizing his own security—and was not about to put on blinders while Merritt mounted an assault on the Senate. The young were callous and myopic: they rejected the wisdom only old men could give.

The specially muted tone on his intercom sounded repeatedly before Wright answered it.

"Mr. Merritt is here."

"Good. Send him in." Wright put away the photograph.

Merritt's appearance startled the banker. He hardly resembled a man with victory within his grasp. Wright had seen him look like this only once before, after the Negro affair. He was ill-groomed and wan.

Wright stood up and offered his hand but Merritt didn't take notice. He stood rooted to the carpet before the desk. He stared at the banker for a long minute then said, "You killed Darlene. You killed Jasper, then you killed Darlene."

"I don't know what you're talking about."

"You told me you put her in a rest home."

"I did."

"You didn't tell me you were going to kill her."

"Be sensible. She was beginning to fling absurd accusations. Her ignominious life dictated her demise. Indeed she fared better than most of her kind. She was well-provided for. Her surroundings were comfortable. Considerable expense went into looking after her."

"How could you do it? She was beautiful." No longer hostile Merrit was shaking, evidently rent with grief for his departed Negress. It was pathetic to behold, a huge mountain of a man rumpled and tearful.

Wright grew angry. "What's gotten into you? By rights you should be languishing in prison. Instead you're days away from a Senate seat. One does not dissolve into"—he brushed a hand toward Mike—"*this* because a whore has perished."

Merritt was near collapse. "Sit down, my boy. Do you need a drink?"

Mike fell into a chair and buried his face in his hands.

Wright picked up the phone. "Miss Pruney, please bring in some scotch."

"Mr. Wright, it's only ten—"

"Did you hear me, Miss Pruney?"

Within moments the withered secretary wheeled in a

cart. She uncapped the bottle. "That's quite all right, Miss Pruney. We can manage for ourselves," the banker said.

"Pour yourself a drink," Wright instructed Mike. "Then tell me what this is all about."

When Mike had finished Wright said, "The story will never see print. I have connections with every newspaper in this city. We supply each of them with substantial revenue. They will not relinquish that revenue merely to peddle a few inconsequential lies."

"What if he has evidence?"

"There is no evidence. Silver admitted as much. And if there were it would not matter."

"He could go to the police."

"Who will not listen to him."

"What if he goes outside of New York? This race has drawn national attention. Rafferty could find a taker somewhere. He could take it to the television networks."

Wright absorbed this argument passively. The boy had a point. He coldly appraised his protege. "For a year you have not come to see me. You have not once asked for my advice on any matter pertaining to your candidacy. Now, when you are in trouble, you expect me to bail you out as if I were a Mob overlord."

Mike shook his head. "I don't expect anything from you. I'm through, finished."

"You're giving up?"

"I don't have much choice. Even if the police don't investigate the election will be lost. There'll be a scandal. Who knows, maybe Mo'll decide to prosecute."

"Have you considered paying a visit to Rafferty?"

"I'm sure he won't talk to me. Why should he?"

"Perhaps you can persuade him to reconsider."

Mike laughed harshly. "Not Rafferty. He'd rather die than pass up a chance to destroy me."

"Still, if you can convince him to talk we can get

some idea what's on his mind. He claims to have evidence. It wouldn't hurt to know what it is."

Mike was skeptical. "If he thinks I'm a murderer he won't let me near him."

Wright disagreed. "I know these Iago types. It's glory and power he's after. Beg him to talk with you, break down over the telephone, admit you're licked. It may go to his head. He may even be induced to accept payment. No, most likely he would use it for blackmail. He strikes me as thoroughly dishonest. Impossible to do business with."

"I suppose I can try."

"It seems to me that we must do something. Any action is better than none."

Mike got to his feet. "I'll think about it. I have to think about a lot of things."

"Don't worry. You'll be in the Senate come January. And we'll resume our work."

"How can you be so certain?"

"At my age one can hardly afford not to be certain."

Merritt staggered out. Wright picked up his phone. He dialed a number only he knew, a number kept secret even from Ethel Pruney.

"Yes, sir?" came the gruff voice.

"Mr. Merritt has just left my office. Monitor all his lines. I expect him to place a call to a Matt Rafferty. When he does, get back to me and I'll have instructions for you."

"Yes, sir."

Wright once again pulled out the treasured photograph. He observed, for the first time, sadness in the sepia eyes. Why should Father be sad? What could he possibly have done that was not honorable and good? Was it not merely personal sadness but sorrow drawn from the tragic sum of life? Healing, fixing, correcting—a sad business, really. You could never fix enough, or correct everything. Some wounds would not heal. Father, like son, had dedicated himself to a task that required too much. Wright traced the frilly edge of the picture and held it at a distance from his eyes, sifting it to find the angle at which new depths would be revealed. Then his head pitched forward and he cried silently in his own arms. O Father, forgive me. For I have besmirched myself.

It was the moment he had waited for, the fruit of seven years' labor. A prince of the establishment was coming to beg. Diligence and an eye trained unblinkingly on the truth had won Matt Rafferty the power to ruin Merritt. The bastard had sounded desperate over the phone, so desperate that the reporter dug up his old revolver. You could never be too sure. He would have to keep Merritt at arm's length, across the room, in case he made a leap. His papers and the ten-thousand-word article were safely locked in his desk and under the chair where Merritt would sit was a tape recorder. Not a word of this conversation would be lost. Merritt would knot his own noose and twist slowly, luxuriantly, in the wind.

At three o'clock sharp the buzzer rattled and Rafferty let Mike into the building. He unlocked his door and resumed his seat by the window. A knock sounded.

"It's open," Rafferty called.

Merrit was a sight. His hair was uncombed and his suit looked as rumpled as Rafferty's own.

"Well, well. The villain of the piece. Come in. Not as nice a place as you're accustomed to, eh, Merritt? Not all of us have millions to throw away. I understand even the niggers uptown live like kings these days."

Merritt said nothing, but stood, enormous and crazed and haggard, filling the doorway. He stepped in slowly, like a man half-awake.

"You sounded eager enough over the phone. I've got a story to cover."

Mike dropped his big frame into the seedy couch. His voice, when he spoke, was a croak. "I want to talk about . . . what you know."

"I know all kinds of things. What would you like to hear first? See, I'm a reporter and I think in stories. One story I know, for example, concerns a big stud who wasted a couple of niggers. He had help, of course. A fag named Wright. The richest little killer in town. And, let's see, there was a cover-up. And also—this is the good part—the guilty party is getting primed for a Senate seat! I hear he's even got the personal congratulations of the President for the fine way he handled himself in a debate! Hard to believe, isn't it? Only in America, I say. Fact is stranger—"

"The story's written?"

"You bet. It wrote itself. Every reporter lives for the big story that writes itself. Took years before I found one. It's going to break you, Merritt. It's going to put you where you belong, behind bars. For life. If you're a model inmate they may parole you. Not after the first seven years, I don't think, because what you did was just too coldblooded for that. Over two years of silence. If you'd confessed right off, it might not look so bad. But you were goddamn arrogant about it and judges don't like that. And the fact that you came within a hair of conniving your way into the Senate—well, it's not a pretty picture."

"You have no right. Leave it up to the authorities. To the DA. It's his case, not yours."

"Up to Silver? You're kidding me, Merritt. He's another one of your boys. He won't prosecute. No way I'll do that. This is public information. The public has the right to know how you deceived them. They need to learn a lesson about spoon-fed pretty boys who mow down anyone in their way."

"Give your article to the state as evidence. If you publish it first you'll prejudice the jury. They'll throw the case out on circumstantial grounds."

"You're reaching, Jack. So they'll give it a change of venue. It doesn't make any difference to me. When my story hits the stands they'll be screaming for your neck.

The only votes you'll get will be votes for the chair. You betrayed them all."

"What do you want, Rafferty? What do you want from me?"

"I want to see you burn. You've always been a no good shit. I've had my eye on you for a long time. You should be flattered. There's nobody who knows you like I do. I followed you at Yale, when you were pulling those stunts. I never missed a game at the Garden, even after Wright paid off those bastards at the *Star* to can me. I watched you like a hawk. I've seen a lot of guys like you come and go. But you were special. You were the top of that sleazy line. I predicted it all. The money rolling in, the rich little Daddy's girl for a wife. It was all there. And then when I found out about Wright clearing the way for you it sewed everything up. But nobody'd believe me. Nobody'd listen! They'd call me a cynic or jealous. Jealous! Of you! But now the public will thank me. Because I wasn't taken in. Not ever."

"Please, Rafferty. I'm begging you—turn over your story to the DA. Please don't print it."

Rafferty shook his head. "Not on your life. Not for a million bucks."

Mike got up heavily. "There's nothing else I can do, I suppose."

Rafferty heard the click as the tape wound to its end. Merritt was too dazed to notice. He was about to say something more but didn't. Then he disappeared, stoop-shouldered and slow, out Rafferty's door.

On the street Mike walked past the car that had trailed him. "Mr. Merritt!" the driver called. Mike didn't hear. He continued toward Columbus Avenue.

"Should we go after him?" the driver asked his burly companion.

"Nah. Let's just get this guy like the boss said. Big Mike'll take care of himself."

The pair bent their bodies out of the car and slowly mounted the stairs to Rafferty's apartment. The door was locked. The tall man rattled it. "Open up!"

"Who is that?" called a raspy voice from within. "Go away! I'm calling the cops."

The fat man pulled out a pistol and shot through the lock. The reporter was reaching for his own revolver when he whirled around and saw two huge men—one very tall, the other very broad—and a cold muzzle trained on his belly.

Been at a remove from things the past few days. Working on an acceptance speech in imitation of the roof-raiser Mike reeled off after the primary win. Maris insists the Senate victory will propel Mike to the top of the party and thinks a speech directed at the nation is in order. Who am I to disagree? I'm the boy's biggest booster.

Everyone is feeling flush except for the candidate himself, who, I'm told, is acting very oddly. Maris called me two days ago. He was frantic. Mike was scheduled to fly to Albany but was nowhere to be found. Apparently he saw Mo Silver somewhere downtown and then took a powder. Mo refused to discuss the nature of their meeting. I told Maris that I knew nothing and proved to be no help in establishing the candidate's whereabouts. Six hours later Mike turned up in Washington Heights, of all places, wandering the streets. The fellows Maris had dispatched to find him said he wouldn't get into the car. The pressure must at last be wearing him thin. Victory is within smelling distance but hovers yet beyond reach. . . .

With the election one day away we are clinging to a slim, barely measurable lead. Three percent, according to one poll, dead-even in another. Maris's contacts in the Bronx and Brooklyn are pounding on the doors of Puerto Ricans and blacks. If we can get enough of the vote out we might just crawl over the top. Mike, after holing up for a couple of days, has changed moods yet again. Now he's campaigning insanely. He hasn't spent any of the last four nights in his apartment. He's on the streets at all hours. Nobody's sure where he goes. One of our black workers claimed he saw Mike in a bar on 125th Street with three dozen men gathered around. There is talk of his collaring whores and squatting on benches next to the rummies in Madison Park. I don't know what to believe, but that's all for the better. It has a legendary ring to it and I don't for a minute question Mike's sincerity. This election has already transcended the banal plateau of mere obsessiveness. Its meaning for him is positively religious. Every promised vote is like a conversion, and every vote lost taints his soul. I've tried repeatedly to get him to look at the speech I'm writing—pruning I should say; it grows smaller and smaller—but he's incommunicado. Everybody tells me not to worry. Which makes me worry.

Today the city has struck a rare attitude of repose—or is it watchful calm?—a suitably solemn backdrop for the approaching shift in seasons. Harsh winds borne across the Hudson cough against my loose panes like the wolf who huffed and puffed and blew the house down—crude counterpoint to the heavy rumble of trucks pulling out of their stables on West Street. It ought to be a jubilant day. Mike defeated Whiting last night. His name is bannered across this morning's Times. *(Has that ever happened to a writer? I doubt it. The best they ever manage is a front-page obit near the bottom with a ghoulish photo, like a death mask.) At headquarters he accepted my congratulations but rejected my speech. To the hoplites he uttered a few choked words of thanks, as if it pained him to acknowledge victory. He avoided the newspeople altogether although they had assembled in droves. I counted representatives from twenty papers including* Le Monde *and the* Manchester Guardian, *and* Là Corriere della Sera.

Can it be the vestigial strain of a rigorous campaign has unhinged him? Last night ought to have been his finest hour, the kind of occasion that makes him soar. But throughout he was somewhere else. "Out to lunch," Woodruff said. The thread of an old dialogue runs through my head. That portentous exchange with Patty before the primary. Is Mike closeted in a secret hell of his own devising? As for Patty, she gamely stood at his side, but confusion was written all over her face. I could read her thoughts: There is so much love here, and it is all for him, so why isn't he happy?

At any rate the trek is over. New York has a new Senator and a good one, I think. He'll work hard, as he always does. Before long he'll distinguish himself. And then will emerge talk of the Presidency. It's inevitable.

I'll provisionally close this journal with an interesting coda buried in the nether pages of this afternoon's Star. *Earlier this morning, Matt Rafferty, the reporter who gave Mike so much grief during his playing days, was fished out of the Hudson near Hyde Park. Apparently the unlucky fellow had been there for days. The police issued no statement but announced an investigation is under way. I wonder if Mike has heard.*

Part 4

Return

18

The decaying towers of Manhattan behind him now, he plunged through the Lincoln Tunnel in a rented sedan, and a two-minute eternity later he emerged in New Jersey where, after a confused hour of circling the web of concrete highways, he spun onto I-280 and sped west.

Great gray factories and refineries and warehouses jutted from the marshland, and the metallic dawn sky hung low and heavy. Newark, which he bypassed at a distance of several miles, lifted its blackened claw into the morning as the suburbs disgorged their harried citizens. He needled ahead in the opposite direction against the floodtide of commuters. Brick churches and frame houses and choked gas stations and gaudy shopping malls dotted the roadside now and the traffic dissipated into a trickle as he got farther from the fountainhead. Soon he achieved the raw countryside, bare-limbed against the weak assault of the November sun.

An open road atlas, with the interstate highway system staining the pages like exposed veins, lay beside him on the seat along with the soggy paper cup from which he had consumed his first dose of coffee for the day. His tie had fallen like a dead serpent onto the floor. He carried no luggage; he hadn't had time to pack.

He was running: running hard, running scared, running home. The news about Matt Rafferty had broken and the edifice of lies and secrets he had built to sustain his ambition was about to collapse. Everything he had fought for and won in the election had been washed away in a freakish moment of revelation.

Last night Patty had invited Bee over for an intimate "family" dinner—just the three of them. She broiled steaks and Bee told campaign war stories. He was able, for the first time in months, to relax with the two of them, his wife and his one-time alter-ego. With the election successfully concluded, he thought, as the three of them sipped wine, perhaps now I can get down to the business of life without the cloud of the past obscuring everything I do. Rafferty had been bluffing; he had never published his story. I was a fool to get rattled. . . .

The wine loosened Mike's tongue: he drank several glasses and kept trying to fill Patty's and Bee's. Bee allowed himself two glasses and no more. Mike talked about how their lives would be different in Washington, busier and better; and he outlined his great plans.

"We're in the vanguard of our generation," he declared with some of the old book-reading fervor. "We've stepped into history now and there's no turning back. So shall we step boldly or timidly? Shall we engage the great issues or shall we skirt them out of expedience?" He spoke as if in a trance, still stumbling through his dreams, grasping for a hold on the reality which continued to elude him.

He invited Bee to go to Capitol Hill with him on his staff. "You'd be the best damn speechwriter they've seen in years, I'll bet," he exclaimed, his wine-tinged face aglow with the unbridled ambition of an eighteen-year-old, as if he had just climbed down from the roof of Vanderbilt Hall in the first flush of the day with the key to the secret door within his reach. Knowing and unknowing. Innocent and corrupt. His soul as pristine and as scarred as the land from which he had sprung.

Bee tabled the offer, pleading fatigue and post-election mental paralysis, promising Mike he would consider it.

Later, as the conversation waned, Bee asked Mike if he'd heard about the demise of his old nemesis Matt Rafferty. He thought it a grisly but predictable end for the reporter who had tried to destroy a young athlete's career. In fact, Bee had thought him long gone, a victim of his own hatred and bile. He assumed Mike had read the story in the paper, but at the mention of the man's name Mike went pale and somber, almost furious, his knuckles white as he squeezed his napkin and wiped his purpled lips.

"The guy probably stuck his nose where it didn't belong," Bee joked. "Maybe the Mob caught him going through their wastebaskets."

Bee mentioned Rafferty's murder as if it were a bizarre footnote to the new Senator's history instead of a swift rewriting of his whole future. But Mike knew better: in death Rafferty had accomplished what he could not in life. The game was over for good; there was no time left.

After Bee left and Patty retired, he sat in front of the fire, numbed and afraid. He had worn a mask of cruel indifference the rest of the evening but that fell away when the others were gone. The fire spoke to him from the lip of hell as he gazed madly into it. Wright had ordered the reporter's execution. That much was clear. The newly elected Senator was, then, an accomplice to yet another brutal killing. An accomplice? A humorless smile knifed across his face in the flickering light. He was much more than that. A murderer. Who had killed Darlene if not he? Others had poisoned her with drugs, but he had written her off long before that; he had willed her death even as he loved her, for how could he not know that his folly damned them all. And who had killed Jasper Brown and Matt Rafferty if not he?

Repetition: the failure to learn. Once he thought he had it licked, that he knew better. After Vermont when the world looked cleaner, the choices more stark. What had happened; how had he slid back into the slough? He had allowed events to dictate; he had parceled out pieces of himself and not retained claim to the whole. Darlene. Jasper. Rafferty. The litany of his crimes. All his reading, his building, his winning were forfeited to his ambition, his lies, his lust. A lesson unlearned. Overreaction. Death. The farflung fragments of his crippled will.

He looked in on Patty before he left. She lay on one side of their bed, her shoulders rising and falling peacefully. Then, without a word, he stole away in the early hours of the morning. At Seventh Avenue, in the bowels of a highrise hotel complex, he rented a car. He used a credit card; he signed his name; he knew they would find him sooner or later, but he didn't care. He folded his tall frame into the driver's seat and headed west.

He imagined blue-clad policemen, their eyes shielded by shiny black visors, their wide waists heavy with weaponry, bursting into his apartment with a warrant for his arrest. They would find only a distraught Patty, ignorant of her husband's whereabouts. He cursed himself for abandoning her, but he drove on.

Fifty miles outside the city he spotted a diner and pulled off the highway. He ordered a black coffee and fumbled with his change under the matronly cashier's baleful scrutiny. Returning to the car he wondered what he had looked like to her. Did she think him a fugitive? Had he made the early papers? As he slid into the seat he examined his face in the rearview mirror. A blue stubble sprouted on his pale jaw and his eyes were suspended in fear under a darklined brow. Of course, anyone could see: he wore his guilt as plainly as his shirt. The coffee keyed his nerves and ate away at his fatigue. He had a long way to travel.

By late morning he crossed the Delaware River into Pennsylvania on the smooth ribbon of road which took him through the stately Blue Mountains and down into the Susquehanna Valley. Evergreen forests hugged the rugged breast of the land and he rolled on, past signs that announced the towns he left behind: Stroudsburg, White Haven, Freeland, Milton. He then ascended with the Appalachians to where the clouds gave way before a revivified golden sun that limned the rigid peaks against the ultramarine sky. The highway kept on coming and he took it on its own unbending terms, pressing forward just above the speed limit with a wary eye glued to the mirror for cops. After more coffee and a spongy hamburger at a squalid roadstop he raced onward, emptying his mind as he drank in the cold fast air through his open window. At the desolate junction with Interstate 79 he cut south toward Pittsburgh. He hooked around that city as it gave up its ghost to encroaching dusk and he picked up 70 at Washington. Chasing the dying beacon of the day, he brushed by a dust-caked Wheeling, West Virginia. Then, once over the Ohio River, the flat endless plain stretched before him like an empty plate.

Basketball: the rough-stitched fabric, the sharp drumbeat, the bold color scheme of his life. That's what the recruiters had sensed when he was still a skinny rail of a kid; he and the game were smoothly meshed, without friction or opposition of any kind. Basketball was then the sum of his existence, the first form of self-expression and fulfillment he knew. In college he had startled everyone but himself with his singlehearted achievements. But the greater surprise and greater satisfaction had come in the pros. Five long years of his life for a brief moment at the apogee of Sport. He remembered the men with whom he had forged a steel-strong union of common purpose: the swift, skilled, swart men of the New York Comets. Sweat and guts. Curses and cajolery. Big money and bigger dreams. A winning team.

He shivered in the frigid gale of memories.

Jail: the dim-lit, urinous, last-stop congress of criminal flesh. His tongue stiffened in his mouth like a dried-up dirtied sponge at the thought of it. The night in confinement with Robert Goff after the demonstration had been more than a lark. The reality of New Haven had come sharply alive for him that night. He remembered the dank walls and rust-governed locks and the silent sleeping men who shared their imprisonment. He had emerged a hero the next morning, sentenced to a lifetime of celebrity, but he never forgot the old Negro and his ruptured dignity who had taught him the secret depths of the black man's pride.

Now, at nightfall, he barreled across Ohio. He rolled up his window against the bone-aching chill of onrushing winter. Roadside neon signs blasted their promises across the darkening landscape and he drove on. Then the curtain of black velvet swiftly and finally fell over the highway and it was deep, forbidding night and he was alone. He followed the white painted line, then, that jumped at him in the glare of his headlights. The line beckoned him forward in place of the western sun; the line spun on and on, curling around invisible hummocks and sweeping under bridges and thrusting itself into the night. The black highway hummed beneath him. Trucks rumbled and roared past his vehicle. Speed obsessed him now and nothing else. He pushed on at seventy, then eighty, daring the unseen forces of the law to stop him, recklessly eating up the miles and spitting them out behind him. Columbus loomed before him but fell to his relentless siege and sank away in his wake as he drove on. Then Springfield, Ohio. Then Dayton where the noisome rubber wastes clung to the night air. Then, at Richmond, he was in Indiana.

It had been over a dozen years ago, he recalled, that he left Williamsburg for Yale. He remembered now: the train pulling out of Chicago, the stiff-backed coach seat, the sandwiches his mother packed in a brown paper bag, the beautiful mystery of those first miles on the longest journey he had ever taken, the promise of knowledge and glory in faraway New Haven. He remembered the girl who had taken the seat next to him—her bold eyes, her acne-scarred face, her giggle when he allowed her to feel the muscles in his arm. She couldn't have known that his mind was already a thousand miles ahead of him and that even then the seeds of ambition were germinating in the pit of his consciousness. He remembered his fantasy: the return trip ten years later with a beautiful woman on his arm and his pockets stuffed with cash and his name a household word; he'd treat everyone in Williamsburg to hamburgers at the Maid-Rite.

Twelve years ago he had left his hometown with Nancy Davidson's scent in his nostrils, with images of her butter-smooth thighs open to him, her tremulous cries of delight, her eyes misted with desire, her yearnings and promises, her power over him, her deadly contempt for her husband and his honey-haired daughter. What did she look like now? Did her blue eyes, which had always reminded him of the wide ocean of the sky, still glimmer and sparkle when she smiled her smile of lust? And who received that smile now: a teenage quarterback or the man who read the gas meter or one of her husband's cronies? Or had she long since abandoned her quest for fulfillment from small-town studs and returned to Chicago? A woman like Mrs. Davidson, he considered, never loses the need for love, the desire for desire.

The night and the road and the miles piled upon him as he sliced across the silent land.

He was grateful his father had never known of his affair with her. What would Hugh Merritt think of his son flirting with disaster in the arms of a married woman? It shamed him even now.

The voice of time and reason and patience. Hugh Merritt was this and more. His son now remembered: wrapping his small hand around his father's thick forearms, the man's breath a friendly wind around the boy's face; listening to stories of the old days before the war when everybody was poor but worked hard and played harder and knew that bad times wouldn't last forever; riding with his dad down to St. Louis in the summertime to see the Cardinals and Stan Musial and in the wintertime to watch the Hawks and big Bob Petit, the boy's first hero—beside his dad; eating supper, the three of them, Mom, Dad, and the boy, not talking much but just being together, leaving the rest of the world to spin its falsehoods and hatch its plots and fight its battles without them.

One day Dad came home from the hardware store with a secret smile and a wink and told you he had a surprise, and you tugged on his arm and asked him what it was. From the cavernous womb of the old stationwagon he pulled a big fan-shaped piece of plywood painted white with an orange hoop attached at the bottom and you choked back the tears (because boys don't cry) and shouted with joy and ran for the ladder. Dad got his tools from the garage and hefted the backboard onto the roof and labored for an hour with screws and brackets, balancing his bulk above you, finally climbing down. On his orders you ran to the car and retrieved a plastic bag that smelled of newness and Christmas and everything you always wanted and tore it open and clambered up the ladder with the snow-white nylon net and threaded it through the orange eyelets and jumped down to survey your work. He then tossed you a brand-new Wilson basketball and the pebbly grain felt alive in your hands and you heaved a shot at the goal and missed, but he laughed and said, "Try again," and you tried again and again until you made it.

For nearly all of the past twelve years he had banished Williamsburg and Mrs. Davidson and his father from his mind. All else gave way before his fullblown allconsuming pride. He had rarely visited his mother, despite her repeated urgings. He had molted his smalltown heritage with the unconscious ease of a reptile. And yet he could never totally shed the influence of his upbringing; he could never really forget the men and women who had shaped his life from birth through adolescence. Evelyn Merritt periodically sent him articles from the local paper which chronicled his career in the distant city. Williamsburg had not forgotten him either.

As memories thrummed ceaselessly on his heart he steered the car through the dense blackness of the Indiana countryside. Indianapolis, the somnolent capital city, did not stir. The driver pressed on. He veered northwest on I-74, scooping toward Danville. He held the wheel in a taut grip, mastering the meandering stretch of road with tight-jawed determination.

Patty phoned me this morning, nearly hysterical. Mike has disappeared.

It struck me immediately, as her worry-charged voice crackled over the phone, that our young god has fallen from the Olympian heights to which he soared so quickly. She sensed it too. Mo called her, she said, asking for Mike. "Bee, we've got to find him," she begged. "Mo told me he may be involved in a crime. It's serious and I'm scared for him. Where could he be?"

Mike's behavior over the past few weeks had shown me that he was capable of anything, so I could imagine a thousand ports to which he might have sailed. Ever since the debate with Whiting, and after the election itself, he has drifted, the dried and wind-split pieces of him, farther and farther away from us all.

I reassured Patty as best I could. "He may be out on one of his wool-gathering walks," I suggested.

"No," she replied. "He didn't take any luggage or clothes, but I know he's taken off to somewhere."

There was no use denying that I did too. But where? "He left no message? He didn't say anything last night after I left?"

"He must have been up all night. He never came to bed. And this morning when I woke up"—the words tumbled out like the dice of despair and they came up craps—"he was just gone."

The picture of his sober eyes and the bizarre repentant tone of his voice came back to me as Patty asked me to call Mo. Suddenly I was as scared as she was.

Mo was expecting my call. He asked me to come over to his office.

The corridors (or catacombs) of power are dingy indeed. Is it because so much work dirty gets done there that the floors, walls, and sagging ceilings seem always to be coated with soot? Or is it because the dustrags and mops and vacuum cleaners are wielded so lazily and hopelessly under cover of darkness? Whatever the cause, Mo's office is dismal as a dungeon, though the prisoner himself hasn't yielded up his determination to survive his sentence: on the contrary, he thrives on impossible challenges and lost causes.

It's been a long time since I've seen him. Nearly five years. He hasn't lost the radical's ever-wary eye or his seemingly boundless public energy, but time has depleted his reserves of good will and powdered his thinning hair with gray. His paunch is more pronounced, but one gets the impression it's not an outgrowth of idleness or gluttony, rather the evidence, the extension of his particular pursuit of happiness in a very unhappy world.

The impotent late-morning sun filtered through a barred and begrimed window behind his cluttered desk. Mo rose, his hair mussed distractedly, his tie askew, his eyes troubled, and pumped my hand vigorously. "I hear you're working on a novel," he said matter-of-factly but with a hint of genuine curiosity.

"I took a sabbatical to join Mike's campaign, but

now I'm easing my way back into the book. I have a feeling it's going to take a different direction now." I don't like to talk about my writing, but he seemed interested and I was about to let spill a few details. He didn't press me, though.

"We're looking for good things from you," he advised avuncularly. *"Sheila and I,"* he clarified. *"You've got talent and guts. Not much of either in circulation these days."*

What do you say to such great expectations? I mumbled that there is a lot of work yet to do. Then there was a painful, almost poignant few seconds of silence as we had reached the limit of preliminary remarks. He began to speak, almost reluctantly, of the business at hand.

"Everything I'm about to tell you is in the strictest confidence, Bee, but I want you to know what we're up against. Patty doesn't know the full story yet, although I'm sure she has her suspicions. I'll rely on your discretion with her. She'll want to know what we talked about, of course."

Well, after a setup like that, my heart was pounding fiercely and I sat back, prepared for the worst. And I sure as hell got a red-hot earful.

Mo reconstructed the whole story, from Mike's nocturnal mission of mercy to Matt Rafferty's assassination. Without naming names, it became clear from the start that Mike's sponsor Mortimer Wright is implicated too. It was Rafferty, Mo said, who really put the pieces of the puzzle together—with scant evidence but with plenty of intuition and spit. Now Rafferty turns up dead and Mike disappears.

"Our office has enough to go to the judge right now for a warrant on Mike. But I want to hold off on the chance that we can get him to turn himself in." There were no tears in his eyes as he said it, but I could see that the whole thing was ripping him in

half. "Where the hell is he, Bee? Do you have any idea?"

"I had been picking my brains all morning for a clue, without success. But then it dawned on me with the clarity of one of Moses' visions, and I remembered our conversation of three weeks ago. "He's gone back to Williamsburg," I said, and I knew it had to be true.

Mo's big hand fell onto his littered desk. "Goddamn it," he muttered. "Where else?"

As I write, the night has long since descended on the hollow day. And I thought the campaign had been climax and catharsis enough. Those weeks piled so quickly one upon the other in intense succession, each a drama in itself, that it was impossible to see the real tragedy unfolding. But Mike knew: he knew it every hour of every endless day, and he was just waiting for the world to cave in on him. All he had left was his "cause," his last chance to buck the odds, to pay for his sins—but it wasn't enough. Why does it become so obvious only now when it's too late to stanch the onrushing current of time. Where did he go wrong? Even more to the point, perhaps, where did we—his friends and camp followers—go wrong?

For Mo there remained the gathering up of loose threads, first among them Mike Merritt. "I'd like to ask you a favor," he told me. At my nod of agreement, he continued: "You know his mother. I want you to call her. Find out if he is there, or, if he isn't yet, whether she has heard from him. You might have to make up a story, just so she doesn't become alarmed. She's got to be able to handle him—and to get him back to us in one piece."

He volunteered his phone and exited, leaving me with my unwanted task. After jousting with Information for several minutes I came up with the number and dialed. Four strident, faraway rings. Then I heard her plaintive, pious, lonely voice.

She was surprised to hear from me and we chatted a few minutes. "I'm so proud of him," *she said of her son.* "Everyone in town is too. Has he said anything to you about coming home for a visit? I know he must be terribly busy now, but I'd love to see him."

I stepped gingerly toward my purpose. "As a matter of fact, he's on his way to see you right now, I believe. When I spoke to him last night—"

"Wonderful. Is he bringing Patty along? Did he say how long he intended to stay?"

"No, Mrs. Merritt. Patty isn't coming this trip and I'm not sure how long Mike plans to be out there. There are many things which require his attention here."

"He's taken on a big job," she affirmed.

"Yes he has." *How to say it?* "Look, Mrs. Merritt, when Mike arrives would you have him call Patty or me immediately? It's very important."

"Something wrong?"

"Well, no—nothing that can't be taken care of with a quick call."

She was unconvinced. I had betrayed my own anxiety. "Bee, you must tell me what's happening."

I gave her a few innocuous details: there were legal problems; Mike was distraught; we weren't sure how or when he would arrive in Williamsburg; she mustn't worry. But it was enough to shake her pretty badly. I could tell by her halting, sibilant response.

"Yes," she said. "I'll see that he calls immediately. Is there anything else you can tell me?"

As I had earlier with Patty, I attempted to minimize the possibility of real trouble. And I met with equally limited success. The women in his life know him better, I think, than anyone else, including me, a lifetime student of the subject. From them more is required, and to them more is revealed, even in his great silences. They are able to tap his reserves of *love and his sense of duty, both of which run deep in his tormented soul. No, I couldn't fool his mother. I rang off with assurances that it would all work out fine, but now nothing can reassure her until she sees him for herself. Then, perhaps, if there's a miracle to be wrought, she will perform it with the help of her God where the rest of us have failed.*

When he crossed into Illinois on Interstate 74 he was shot through with exhaustion. A salmon sun covered the southern horizon, illumining the bare fields and the roadside ranks of trees, which were already stripped of their colors and saluted the sky with naked limbs. A strong wind, the first fierce breath of winter, blew from the north.

At Champaign he picked up 48. He dropped down to fifty to prolong his last hours of speed, silence, and solitude. Shortly it would all be over. Mom would be the first to hear his tale, down to every unreal detail. She would dissolve into tears, then he would too, and together they would wait for the end. Misfortune had Mom's number. Married to a man weaker than herself she had borne a son yet weaker. She drew strength from loving them both. To comfort him she would plumb the abyssal depths of her beleaguered faith. *God will embrace you and He will forgive. The light of His mercy will conquer the darkness in your soul.* Thoughts to solace him while he hammered numbers on license plates or bundled the prison laundry.

All around him stretched alien land. He had struggled all through his boyhood to escape it. The spaces were too great. Dad too had been intimidated by the land but he couldn't shake himself free. Circumstances had penned him in, like the hogs and the cattle. Mom loved the land. She grew up on a farm her father ran until his death ten years back. As a high-schooler he spent summer weekends there, baling hay and learning to master a tractor. His grandfather was tall, erect as a general, with a long seamed face. His leathery hands were amazingly strong; also his wrists. He could lift a chair with a thumb and two fingers hooked around the base of one spindly leg. He examined his own hands on the wheel; they were callused from shaking hands across New York State. All that was behind him now. It was hard to believe.

Outside of Springfield he picked up 36. At the sign for the Lincoln Home he trembled. It was odd they hadn't caught him yet. Surely the police had alerted the Highway Patrol or the FBI. He had penned his own name at the rental agency to let them know he wasn't fleeing, only withdrawing. Perhaps they presumed he was in Argentina or Colombia or Tangier.

Seven o'clock. Mom would be getting out of bed about now. Did she still wear the green robe—the color of faded grass—and the slippers with fat puffs on the toes? She might now be at the kitchen table, staring over her coffee at the barren yard and her empty garden. In the summer she grew peppers and lettuce and enormous blood-red tomatoes. What a lonely existence she led. He had offered to set her up in New York. She could even hold onto the house if she liked. But she had refused. "This is my house and I wouldn't feel at home anyplace else." And now he, who felt at home nowhere, was running back into her arms.

He spotted the first sign for Williamsburg, pop. 7,904. Five miles ahead would be a second sign, three miles later, a third. At the truckstop a man was pumping fuel into an eighteen-wheeler. The restaurant gave off an orange glow. Highway 36 melted into South Street. Gleaming tractors filled the John Deere lot and brand-new pickups were massed outside the Ford dealership. The little homes on the outskirts of town resembled the abodes of nomads. In front of each was a scraggly patch of lawn covered with a car that seemed solider than the house. Cemetery Hill was haloed in the morning mist.

He turned onto Broad Street, crossing the tracks and the white houses and the Maid-Rite, then cut through the heart of town. All the places of business were closed—Gibson's and First Federal and Thompson's Hardware, where his father had worked.

At the corner of Willoughby Street he spotted his house. A light was on in the living room. He pulled into the driveway behind the new Granada, his most recent birthday present to Mom. He killed the engine and sat for a short spell looking at the weathered backboard and the rusty rim atop the old garage. Then he stepped out and circled the house. He rapped on the kitchen door.

"Mom."

She greeted him with tear-glistened eyes. Then he threw himself in her arms and wept.

Mike has been back a week now, after a 72-hour absence that was nearly impossible to keep from the press hounds. He is charged with half a dozen crimes, the most heinous being conspiracy to murder Jasper Brown. His conviction seems unlikely. Mortimer Wright's suicide three days ago eliminated the only other surviving principal in the sordid drama. Now there is just Mike, a heap of corpses, and no evidence. Wright was a hideous little creature but he did his work well. He fashioned his own demise with a cleanly placed bullet and a minimum of fuss. His detailed account of his own criminal activity named no other parties.

At the first pre-trial hearing the judge was all sternness and moral outrage. The eyes of the nation are upon him and my guess is he intends to milk it for all it's worth. He set bail at $100,000, an excessive figure which he justified by pointing to Mike's "attempted flight from justice." The defendant himself is unperturbed. He is still in a daze and seems genuinely deaf to the thunder of scandal. He spends *all his hours inside my apartment. We talk a bit but mostly he reads and writes things on a long yellow pad.*

Patty came over yesterday. I left her with her husband and retired to my bedroom. An hour later she knocked on my door asking me to walk her to the corner. We ended up on a cement-covered dock watching filthy water slap at the piles.

"You know I'm going away," she said.

"Overseas?"

"Yes, to Europe with my mother."

"That's a good idea."

"Not because of the trial or the scandal or even what he did. He told me what happened and I believe him. But he shut me out of his life. He ran from me."

"You don't have to explain."

"Don't be so understanding," she said. "Tell me I'm rotten."

"But you're not."

"If you disapproved I could think maybe you expected better of me. Mike was understanding too. He apologized so many times I wanted to scream. When I told him about Europe he barely listened. I don't matter to him and I never have. I was another acquisition."

I didn't argue.

"Do you think he'll go to jail?" she asked.

"Mo says it's unlikely. There's no evidence."

"What's going to happen to him?"

"I don't know. The other night he said something about working with the kids in the Center."

"When I come back I'm going to file for divorce."

"I see."

"No, you don't. Nobody does. Even my mother thinks I failed him. But he didn't give me a chance. I wanted to love him more than anything else in the world."

"It couldn't have been easy."

"You know, I find myself thinking about Darlene. What happened to her was so horrible. Mike was willing to die for her. I respect him more for that than for anything else. I'm glad he knew her. She brought out something special in him that I couldn't."

"Don't be so hard on yourself. He loved Darlene because he couldn't have her. She was the only one who said no."

This seemed to cheer her a bit. We were both shivering when we left the dock and headed toward Sheridan Square where I settled her into a taxi.

"He loved me at least for a while, didn't he?" she said.

"Of course. And he still does." Then I closed the door and muttered her address to the impatient cabby.

Events have vanquished my fear of the future. It no longer seems a glutinous web spun idly by disdainful fates. Who are we to proclaim the end of mankind, to prophesy doom as though we welcome it? Across the room Mike is reading St. Augustine and scratching notes. There is always work to do. That is the chief lesson I have learned from him. My work is my novel, that demanding querulous bitch who dares me to write her, a skeleton bereft of flesh and feature and feeling. I geared up last night by flipping through this journal. Maybe it's hubris but I liked what I saw: an accurate record of the man of action in the prime season of his life. Of course the life is as yet half-lived; it wants a resolution which can only come through time. Up until now Mike's history has been one continuous fall—from the heaven of his dreams to the hell they have made for him. And what a fall it has been! It deserves a novel, but in this day and age only a fool would attempt to write it.

THE SEA RUNNERS
By Ralph Hayes

PRICE: $2.50 T51647 CATEGORY: Novel

WILD RACES AND SWEET RISKS!
They were runners with a fast crowd. But Steve Cahill out-distanced them all, running from his past. He loved the wrong women, befriended the wrong men, and risked his life for a single prize. It all happened on a lush island sizzling with life, and shadowed with death!

Other Tower Books By Ralph Hayes:

51577 PROMISED LAND —$2.25
51452 SHERYL —$2.25
51442 EASTERN SHORE —$2.25

THE GLORY TRAP
Dan Sherman & Robin Williamson

PRICE: $2.25   T51646
CATEGORY: Novel

THE NEW YORK TIMES
THE GLORY TRAP

"SOPHISTICATED AND DIVERTING!"
— *The New York Times*

He was a discredited and marked agent. She was a young British woman on the run. Together they fled into the vast European underground, living in shadows under the unrelenting threat of death! Explosive espionage suspense!

"ROUSINGLY GOOD ADVENTURE!"
— *King Features Syndicate*

"DAN SHERMAN IS A FIRST-RATE STORYTELLER!"
— Morris West, author of *Proteus*

SEND TO: TOWER PUBLICATIONS
P.O. BOX 270
NORWALK, CONN. 06852

PLEASE SEND ME THE FOLLOWING TITLES:

Quantity	Book Number	Price

IN THE EVENT THAT WE ARE OUT OF STOCK ON ANY OF YOUR SELECTIONS, PLEASE LIST ALTERNATE TITLES BELOW:

Postage/Handling

I enclose...

FOR U.S. ORDERS, add 50c for the first book and 10c for each additional book to cover cost of postage and handling. Buy five or more copies and we will pay for shipping. Sorry, no C.O.D.'s.

FOR ORDERS SENT OUTSIDE THE U.S.A., add $1.00 for the first book and 25c for each additional book. PAY BY foreign draft or money order drawn on a U.S. bank, payable in U.S. ($) dollars.

☐ **PLEASE SEND ME A FREE CATALOG.**

NAME_____
(Please print)

ADDRESS_____

CITY_____ **STATE**_____ **ZIP**_____

Allow Four Weeks for Delivery